Mob Bride

The O'Rourke Brotherhood

Sabine Barclay

Cover art by Dar Albert at Wicked Smart Designs

Published by Oliver Heber Books

0 9 8 7 6 5 4 3 2 1

"The value of our lives is not determined by what we do for ourselves. The value of our lives is determined by what we do for others."
~ Simon Sink

Find me writing Historical Romance as Celeste Barclay.

Happy reading,
Sabine

Subscribe to Sabine's Newsletter

Subscribe to Sabine's bimonthly newsletter to receive exclusive insider perks.

Have you read *The Syndicate Wars*? This FREE origin story novella is available to all new subscribers to Sabine's monthly newsletter. Subscribe on her website.
www.sabinebarclay.com

The O'Rourke Brotherhood

Mob Boss

Mob Star

Mob Princess

Mob Saint

Mob Bride

Mob Knight

Chapter One

Shane

UNEXPECTED MOVEMENT DETECTED

What now?

I tap on the security feed from one of my construction sites. Which fucking family is it this time? I swear to God, if it's the motherfucking Diazes, Imma torch their entire fucking art gallery. Let's see how that fucking opening goes tomorrow night.

"Ted, change of plans. We need to check out the new mall site. Trespassers."

My bodyguard nods and speaks in his earpiece. I'm with my brothers and their wives at a concert that's about to start. Fucking orchestra pit seats. These cost me enough to keep Finn and Ally's impending bundle of joy in diapers for the next two years. So much for being part of their celebration.

I tap Finn on the shoulder and explain I have to go and that I'm taking three of our guys. With eight of my family out in such a crowded place—including three wives, one of whom is three-and-a-half months pregnant—we have nearly every available guy with us working security.

It's walking distance to the site, so that means no chance of headlights tipping these fuckers off and no driving blind onto the site. The heat-seeking sensors our security system includes for situations just like this shows one person. It doesn't matter that they're alone. All four of us have our guns drawn as we circle whoever the hell is wandering around our property.

Motherfucking son of a goddamn bitch.

"Put 'em down."

"Shane, th–"

"Now. Go."

"Bu–"

"Mikey, do it. All of you go."

I point my gun to the sky and put my other hand up as I wait for my men to leave. When I'm alone with my unwanted visitor, I squat and lower my gun to the ground before pushing it away.

"Put yours down."

"No."

It's not like I expected a different answer, but I'm giving them a chance to lower their gun. I straighten and step forward.

"You can move it from pointing at my chest to my head, but you won't shoot me." That's met with silence. "If you were going to shoot, you would've already. You wouldn't have waited to see who approached. You would be fine with dying because that's what would've happened since there're four of us and one of you. That's what'll happen if you shoot me now. No one who's had the shite beaten out of them like you have and is hiding wants to die. Just the opposite. Put the gun down."

Still nothing. That's not the surprise tonight.

"Do you know who I am?"

"No."

"Do you know who owns this site?"

"Don't care." The defiant tone matches the steadiness of the hands still pointing a Ruger 9mm at me.

"Thought so. If you did, you'd know I'm angrier than you can ever imagine. If I have to take that gun from you, I will hurt you. If I see another bruise on you, I'm going to lose my shite in a way you don't want to imagine."

"Red hair and a temper. What part of that do you think makes me feel safe?"

"The part that said none of it's directed at you. Who the feck touched you? Unless you're in a fecking fight club, you're going to tell me."

I walk toward the woman who looks like she's been through a meat grinder, and it takes every ounce of resolve not to yell at her. I want to know who the fuck laid their hands on her. She should be at the fucking hospital not trying to defend herself again.

"That's none of your business."

"You made it my business by trespassing and hiding here. Put the gun down because I will hurt you when I take it. I told you that already. I also told you I'll lose my shite if I see another bruise on you."

"Walk away. That solves both our problems. Back up, and you don't have to worry I'll put a bullet between your shoulders or through your head." The defiance is still there. Good.

"And I told you I know you don't want to die. I normally don't repeat myself twice, let alone three times."

"And you can see why no one's bullying me a second time tonight."

I don't like to live on the edge or whatever cliche fits, but I'm used to it. I have a healthy fear of dying. That's why I'm still alive at the whopping old age of thirty-two. I keep walking until I'm my arm's reach from her. She's at least eight inches shorter than my six-three.

"You call whatever the feck happened to you tonight being bullied?"

"What else do you call being relentlessly forced into something you don't want to do?"

My eyes skim over her, and she finally understands the rage I feel but am not showing. She shakes her head and finally points the gun at the sky like I did before lowering mine. Except she doesn't put hers down.

"I got beaten up. No one raped me. Calm down."

I cock an eyebrow. "I'd say for someone who's had a gun pointed at them for five minutes, I'm pretty fecking calm."

"And I'd say you're a pretty fucking good liar. Imagine why I'm not feeling so trusting. Besides, you already told me you're angry. Red hair and a temper." She cocks a dark brow at me.

"I did say that. Telling an angry person to calm down usually has the opposite effect."

I reach out, and she immediately shifts to bring the gun down. My touch is gentle as I turn her chin toward the moonlight, so I can see her better. She was in the shadows, but the moon and nearby streetlights allowed me to see more of her than just an outline. She's in worse condition than I thought.

"If I were going to hurt you, I already would have." My tone is softer because my rage is about to boil over. "Boyfriend or girlfriend?"

Her gaze shutters.

"This was personal. This wasn't someone tried to mug you, and you fought back. This wasn't some drug deal gone bad. This wasn't some argument at a bar that escalated. This is someone who knew you and wanted to punish you. This was personal."

"How would you know the difference?"

Because I've beaten enough people to death to recognize the difference.

I can't tell her that. I avoid the question.

"You won't go to the hospital, or you would've already. I know two doctors, both women, I can take you to. Beyond age and any underlying health conditions, they won't ask anything except whether it hurts when you cough. They aren't nosey like me. Do you want a neonatologist or a former navy surgeon?"

She stares at me dumbfounded before she jerks away. Pain shoots through her, and her face shows it. She nearly doubles over. Fear and adrenaline kept her distracted while we were talking, but that one move reminds her she's lucky she isn't dead. I've done far less than she's survived and killed bigger men than her while doing it.

"I'm not going anywhere with you."

"I didn't say you have to. They both make house calls." Not that I want to pull Ally away from her celebratory night out. I'm going to call Meredith, but I want this nameless woman to feel like she has a choice, even though she doesn't.

I know she won't tell me the truth about her name, so I haven't bothered asking. But I can offer mine. "I'm Shane O'Rourke." I observe intently, but the name doesn't register. Unless she's a sociopath, she isn't hiding recognition.

"Jane Doe."

I grin and nod. She says it like we're meeting at some garden party in the Hamptons. I reach out to her again, and she moves to bring her gun down again. She stopped herself when she realized I wasn't hurting her when I touched her face. She's not trusting this time. It's easy to take it from her. I could've done it before, but I didn't want her to feel entirely powerless. But the movement obviously caused her pain, and that concerns me more than the chance she'll finally shoot me. She tries to fight me to keep it, but she's no match for me.

"Enough."

I bark the word, and it spurs her to fight harder. I'm bullying her, and she said she wouldn't let that happen twice tonight. With her gun away from her, I take six steps back.

"I'm reaching for my phone to call the surgeon. She'll come here."

She narrows her eyes at me and continues to glare during my entire conversation with the woman who's been sewing me up since Misha Andreyev cracked a beer bottle over my shoulder in eighth grade and gave me ten stitches. It's one of the few distinguishing marks that tells me apart from my twin. Fully dressed, people outside my family can only tell us apart from the freckle on the left side of Sean's throat.

Yes. Finn, Sean, and Shane O'Rourke. We're that Irish. Toss in our cousins Dillan, Cormac, and Seamus, and it comes as no surprise we are *the* Irish in New York. We run the mob.

"When the doctor gets here, I'm going to get a look that tells me she's displeased I didn't take you to the office trailer to lie down on the couch while we wait. I won't force you, but I guarantee you won't resist her."

"I've resisted you."

"That's because I'm only Irish American. She's British."

"What does that mean?"

"She'll have you doing whatever she wants with one rhetorical question. Just give in before that. It's way easier, and I won't get more than a look."

It's not that Meredith was Atilla the Hun's personal physician, but she could've been. She's saltier than a middle school PE teacher. There's no excuse she hasn't heard, so she buys no one's shite.

"Would you at least sit down before you keel over?"

My frustrating stranger resists agreeing, but the adrenaline is totally gone, and the agony's setting in. She's in so much pain she lets me help her to the floor. I say nothing to her while twenty minutes pass, and we wait for the doctor to arrive.

"Carys?"

The woman's head snaps up as Meredith runs toward us.

"Mom?"

The fuck?

Meredith carries one of those old-fashioned doctor's black bags that sorta folds down at the top when it's opened. She flings it out to me, not caring that it hits my gut hard enough to make the air whoosh from it. She drops to her knees as she opens her arms to the young woman. Carys—that's a beautiful name—why'd I just think that?—falls into her mother's arms. Meredith's far gentler with her daughter than she's ever been with me or the men in my family. She rarely casts us anything but a scowl with her lips pressed flat that clearly tells us we got whatever we deserved for not being quick or attentive enough.

"What happened, lovie?" Meredith croons the question to her daughter, and I can tell the woman's barely holding herself together.

I feel like an intruder as I watch them. I should turn away. I should mind my own business like Carys told me to. I should give them space. But rage has me wanting to hear Carys's explanation. No one I've seen who looks like her hasn't wound up unconscious and in a hospital. How she's awake is beyond me. It makes me wonder if she's on something.

It's too dark to see whether her pupils are dilated. So, when Meredith flaps her hand for me to give back her bag, she pulls a tiny flashlight from it. She waves it across Carys's eyes, and I watch the pupils contract the way they're supposed to. When Carys practically snarls at me, I realize I've stepped closer. Curiosity killed the cat, and she looks like she's ready to leave me dangling from a tree. I remind myself she's in pain; otherwise, she'd seem ungrateful.

"Carys, what happened?"

Meredith speaks as she cups her daughter's jaw and runs the pads of her thumbs over the younger woman's cheeks. Carys can't stop the wince when her mother's thumb presses a particularly sore bruise. She pulls back and shakes her head. She sets her face in a mulish expression I've seen far too many times from Meredith when she's insisted on giving one of us a shot of pain killers that'll knock us out.

"You can trust Shane. I've known him since he was a kid."

"No. It's none of his business."

"Carys, please. If for no other reason than I need to know what injuries to look for and treat."

"I'm fine."

I can't stop the snort that escapes me. I usually show no emotion I don't want others to see, so that surprises even me. There's stubbornness—which my twin has in spades—and there's foolishness. She possesses an unhealthy dose of the latter.

"Shane, give us a minute."

I nod, not that Meredith can see me. I'm sure she hears my footsteps retreat. I turn my back but strain to hear.

Nothing.

They're whispering too low for me to catch anything until Meredith's angry voice reaches me.

"You will tell me now."

"Or you'll ground me? Let go, Mom."

I hear the whimper that has me spinning around to spy Carys standing on wobbly legs. Uninvited back into the conversation, I walk over as I speak.

"She ought to turn you over her knee. Where do you think you're going? You're likely to trip over something and impale your empty head on a stake."

Meredith stands in front of her daughter, and I know I've gone way, way, *way* too far.

"Your parenting skills are lacking, Mr. O'Rourke. Butt out." Carys looks ready to give me an obscene hand gesture from behind her mother.

"Probably because I'm not a parent. But I've been your mother's patient enough times to know you're cutting off your nose to spite your face. Let Meredith help you. She knows what she's doing."

Carys's eyes narrow as she tries to lean around her mother to see the older woman's face.

"And just how is that for a pediatrist, Mom?"

"Pediatrist?" That shocks the shite out of me.

"Do you really think I've told my daughter who I work for?" Meredith more mouths the words than says them. "I'm not a pediatrist. I'm an orthopedic surgeon who specializes in feet and hands. She's being facetious."

I know where she got that from.

"You definitely never told us you're in private practice for someone who acts like he could be a mobster. I'd ask how long, but you said you've known him since he was a kid. So at least thirty years."

"I was a toddler thirty years ago. Twenty years almost to the day." Why am I letting her goad me? Because it's keeping me occupied rather than asking my own questions and demanding answers.

"I'm taking you home, Carys."

"No. That's the last place I'm going. Not yours and not mine. I'm not getting you killed, too."

Chapter Two

Carrie

The man is fucking gorgeous as sin. He's also insufferable as hell.

I know exactly who Shane O'Rourke is. It also means my mom works for the fucking mob. What the ever-loving fuck?

I thought I keep a lot of secrets. How the hell has she hidden this for decades from the sound of it? What the fuck am I supposed to do with this little bombshell? Fucking hell. Who outside the O'Rourkes knows about my mom?

Motherfuckers. Did they set me up? Is this why they gave me the assignment? Does my boss know my mother works for the Irish mob? Are they using me the way I'm supposed to be using fuckface? He's a separate issue, yet he's the reasons I'm fucking in this goddamn Twilight Zone.

I have a jumble of questions rattling around in my head, and I can't ask a damn one of them without giving away everything. Everything I don't want to name because I'm in more pain than I've ever been in.

"Mom, I'm fine. I need ibuprofen, some water, and a good night and day's sleep. I'll get some arnica too."

"Arnica?"

I glower at Shane. "Let me guess. You're the little piggie who made his house out of straw." His brow furrows. "You sound like a pig snuffling truffles when you snort."

His russet eyebrows shoot straight up, and I want to gloat.

"Carys." My mom hisses my name.

He won't whack me in front of her. At least, I don't think so.

"I'm feeling a little testy." I opened my mouth to say I just want to go home, but home isn't my parents' house anymore. Home is supposed to be four hundred miles from here. I'm not supposed to be in the city. "Do you have any ibuprofen in your bag?"

I know she does. Shane's still holding the old satchel my granddad gave Mom when she graduated med school. He hands it to her, and she pulls out an economy size bottle of pills. I look at the giant standing next to her. If the medicine went by weight, he'd need half the bottle. That weight is all lean muscle that flexes every time he moves. Such a shame he's a mobster and an ass.

Granted, I can admit to myself when I'm being a royal bitch. But I don't feel at my best. Everything right down the microscopic strands of hair on my toes hurts. I feel like death would be a vacation.

I accept the pills Mom hands me and pool enough spit in my mouth to get them down after several swallows. I take a fortifying inhale and turn in the direction Mom came from. I'm shaky, but I can make it.

"Put me down! What are you doing?"

Shane's incredibly gentle as he lifts me into his arms. I barely feel the pressure of them, yet I know I won't fall. Maybe I'm in too much pain to register anything more. But I suspect he's that gentle.

"So you can fall over on a construction site and sue me? No thanks."

He looks straight ahead, not even sparing me a glance. Rude.

You're almighty ungrateful. Just because you're in pain doesn't mean you get to be rude to people. Especially people helping you.

That's my mom's voice in my head. I can hear it as clearly as if she were speaking it aloud.

Fine. I am being ungrateful. And I can be more gracious.

"Thank you." I keep my voice low since he did, too. There's no need to speak any louder than a whisper since our faces are practically touching.

Shane does his best not to jostle me, but the ground is uneven, and there are some steps. His hold tightens enough for me to keep feeling safe. It's really like being enveloped by a bear. I'm so fucking tired I stop fighting the temptation to rest my head against his shoulder. Just for a moment.

I spy him glancing down at me as I close my eyes. Not that it takes much since they're nearly swollen shut. They probably will be by morning.

"I have to pull the car around." My mom's voice is a million miles away.

"Joey can drive your car home. I'm taking you in the SUV."

My eyes fly open—they open half an inch. "No." I'm emphatic. "Mom, it would be better if I didn't go to your place."

"Why the bloody hell not? You need a doctor if not just your mum."

"It'll just cause more problems. It's better I'm not there. I'll deal with this when I get to the hotel."

"You can't possibly think you're walking into a hotel looking like you do." Shane's incredulous. Obviously, he won't be on my side.

"The hotel? As in one you're already staying in?" Mom's confused and frankly hurt.

"Yeah. I was going to call you in the morning to see if you were free for brunch. It was supposed to be a surprise."

Forgive me, Father, for I have sinned. Lies upon buckets of lies. I had no intention of telling my mom I was in the city.

"You couldn't surprise me before brunch? Carys, I'm doing my best not to demand some ruddy answers because I know you're in pain. But you are sorely testing me. Why were you staying in a hotel? If you insist it was to surprise me, I'll—" She's at a loss for words since I'll be thirty-one in a month.

"I'll have men follow you, and they'll tell Meredith why." Shane's lips nearly brush my forehead as he whispers, and I know Mom can't hear him.

"Thank you for carrying me. Don't get involved."

I get a disdainful huff this time. "I'm well past 'involved.' I'm in the bloody thick of it."

Shane's men spread out to surround us as we head to what will be a parking lot. He calls out orders before I can stop him. I expect him to put me down, but he doesn't. He isn't the least fazed by carrying me. I shift to give him a hint.

"Stay still."

"Put—"

"Not only will I have men follow you, I'll wait until they tell me you don't look like you've been pulverized, then I'll spank you."

"You will never." He doesn't need to know I like it kinky.

"There are three—four—people in this world who tell me what to do, and I actually listen to them. My cousin Dillan, who I work for, my parents, and your mother. You do not make the short list. Stay still."

My elbow pushes against his chest as I try to get down. I wish I could stay in his arms forever because I've never felt so safe in my adult life as I do with this grizzly bear wrapped around me. But it's too dangerous for all of us if the wrong people see us. Besides, I don't want him dictating what I do.

"My list is shorter. My parents. You don't make my list either. Put me down."

"I don't enjoy repeating myself."

"Simple solution. Put me down. That's the last time I'm saying it, Shane. I'm serious." My gaze darts to my mom before I look up at him again. Then I sweep my gaze over our surroundings.

"There's no one here but us."

"You believe that because your men haven't told you otherwise and because your security system hasn't either. That doesn't mean we're alone. Please."

"After you tell me who did this."

His voice matches the steel in his arms. My mom's gaze bores into me. I let my shoulders droop as I whisper a name I made up a year ago. "Jesse."

Shock registers on Mom's face, but Shane's is unconcealed rage.

"Man or woman?"

I keep my lips sealed. I cringe when my mom answers for me.

"A guy she dated for a few months. They broke up when Carys moved to Pittsburgh." She narrows her eyes at me. "The city I thought she was in today."

"I'm not because I wanted to surprise you." I sigh. "I also came to see Jesse. I arranged to see him *after* I'd already decided to come see you." After being about thirty seconds ago.

"Your ex-boyfriend did this to you? Why?" Shane's demanding tone tells me I'm not getting out of this without some kind of plausible answer. Silence won't work.

"We started talking again three weeks ago, and I thought there was a possibility we'd get back together. Clearly, we are not."

"Clearly, you haven't answered why." Shane's snarling now. Sexy as sin if he didn't direct it at me.

"We had an argument. One I will not discuss with a stranger or my mother." Let them make of that what they will. Hopefully, they think it's about sex.

When Shane's gaze hardens into two emerald slivers, I know that was the wrong thing to imply. He sets me on my feet but keeps his arms around me to support me. He whispers again, and I'm certain my mom wants to know what he's saying. I appreciate the discretion.

"Before, during, or after?"

My gaze locks with his, but I stay quiet. The more I say, the more lies I have to remember later. My mind's already full of them.

"Did you consent, but he didn't like your limits?"

I can only stand, staring and blinking. I swallow after a few seconds. How the hell does he know I might like it kinky or even just rough?

"Carys, answer me. I've reached my breaking point with you being uncooperative. Why?"

If I were someone else, he'd scare the shit out of me. I'm certain he scares the shit out of most men. But he's not the biggest man I've faced before.

"I warned you."

Fucking hell. He's going to have me followed. "It's private, Shane. Don't you think this is humiliating enough without having to reveal stuff that private? My mom's standing right here." I hope he buys my beseeching look.

"He nearly killed you, Carys. He will kill you. No man does this without expecting his victim to die. When he finds out you didn't, he will try again. Can you guarantee you'll be so lucky a second time?"

He's right about all of that. But this is an occupational hazard. I don't want to think about work. At least not directly. I push all thoughts of it to the side.

"That's why a hotel would be best. It keeps me away from my parents. Once I'm in my room, no one is going up without asking for my room number. I'll tell the desk staff absolutely no visitors."

"You'll tell them that how? You can barely stand up, let alone walk up to the counter to tell anyone anything. And how will you explain your mangled face?"

"Thanks." I glare at him, but then I relent. "I'll figure it out. You need to stay out of this, and so does my mom. Thank you for trying to help."

I'm sincere about that one. From the way his expression relaxes, I can tell he knows I mean it.

"I know a place you can go. It's a rental my cousin owns that's vacant right now."

Mob? Empty place? It's a safe house. It's what I need, but Shane more connected to my life is the last thing I need.

"I'll post guards around the block and the four surrounding ones. No one is getting near you. Your mom can check on you or even stay with you. You can rest there for as long as you want. It's furnished, so everything you could need is ready for you."

I want to claim it's against my better judgement to agree, but it's probably the only sound judgement I make tonight. "All right."

I say nothing else until we get to the house. It's in one of the nicer parts of the Bronx. It surprises me it's here. As in, I'm surprised it's the Bronx, and the house is so nice, considering I spotted a deserted train station like two blocks from here.

I hadn't listened to Shane talking to a guy he called Joey as my mom handed over her keys. But I guess his bodyguard arranged things because I spot the cars with men assigned to my detail in them. It's not like black sedans line the street. I just know what to look for, which means I'm searching for anyone watching me, but doesn't work for Shane. I sense they're there, but I see no one. I'm silent while he points out the cars I already spied. I remain silent the entire way to the safe house until Shane helps me back out of the car.

"Let me help you inside, then I'll leave you alone with your mom. Do you need anything?"

"Just sleep. Shane, I'm sorry I dragged you into this. And I'm sorry about the way I've acted." All three statements are genuine.

"You're in pain. I'm certain those ibuprofens didn't even take the edge off. I don't blame you for being testy."

"That's a nice way to call me a bitch." I smile, but his gaze hardens to the piercing shards of emerald they did when I confessed about my fictitious ex.

"Do not call yourself that. No one gets to insult you."

"Then you won't like my self-deprecating sense of humor." As though he'll ever hear it.

He sweeps his gaze over me before he locks his with mine. "One of these days, you'll push too far, and I'll push back."

Shitty metaphor, all things considered. But I get it. I dip my chin before I let him help me inside. I don't move past the front door. Blessedly, he gets the hint. He hands the keys to Mom, gives her a kiss on the cheek, nods to me, and leaves. Just like that. He parted with the last word. For now.

Chapter Three

Shane

What the hell is going through that woman's mind? I could see the cogs turning, but I couldn't hear what she was thinking. She's got a poker face better than anyone I know who isn't in a syndicate. But I knew each time she devised a lie. Her tell was she had no tell. I know her frustration toward me helped mask the pain, so I encouraged it. But she was artfully hiding a ton of shite.

I shouldn't care beyond the fact she's Meredith's daughter, and Meredith is a close family friend. I shouldn't care that I could murder whoever hurt Carys, and no one would know. It would mean that person can never go after her again. I didn't lie when I said whoever beat her took it personally and will be back to finish the job. I don't believe it was some ex. Maybe, but I don't believe it. Something about our push and pull made me wonder if she's into kinky shite like I am. If she is, and her partner got pissed for whatever reason, she would have already been in a vulnerable position.

I have a million more questions like how'd you get away? How'd you get onto my site? Is the piece of shite alive? Where is he?

My parents and aunts and uncles drilled it into my cousins, my brothers, and me you never *ever* turn a blind eye to someone who can't defend themselves. We do enough evil without contributing more by ignoring those we can protect. It doesn't matter if they're not "our people"—mob affiliated.

They're also extremely strict about not swearing in front of women and children. We can get away with shite now that we're all in our thirties, but fuck? Fuck no.

Feck.

That's what we're allowed to say in front of women, nothing in front of kids, and only to each other. If we swear at each other and say fuck, they'll find a bar of Irish Spring and scrub our mouths clean.

My mind's wandering as I sit in the car outside the safe house. I got in after Meredith locked the door—I listened for it—and I've stayed through all the shifts. It's nearly five, and I'm wide awake. I'm not searching the streets, trying to see as many blocks down the road as I can. I did that for the first hour. But I'm attentive, even if my thoughts drift.

Why is she such a good liar? Does Meredith know she was lying and said nothing in front of me? Doesn't Meredith know Carys lied through her teeth?

I'm supposed to be at Dillan's house to work out with the others, but I texted Sean to say I wouldn't make it. They all know what happened. We had a six-way call after the concert. I don't even regret missing it since I helped Meredith. Carys is a burr up my arse, but I'm still glad I was there.

What the hell is Meredith's daughter doing with some shitbag who beat her? What the hell was Meredith's daughter doing anywhere near the site? How the hell is the woman I found Meredith's daughter? The odds aren't ones I'd take to Vegas.

"Tommy, look." I point toward the front door.

Is she fucking sneaking out?

"Is Meredith behind her?" Tommy leans over the steering wheel to get a better look.

"No. She just shut the door." *What is she doing?* "Stay here."

I ease the door open and slip out. She spots me immediately. I didn't think she was looking in my direction. At least her situational awareness is sharp.

"I don't want to argue with you, Shane."

"Good. Go back inside."

She looks at me for a moment before smiling as best she can, considering her left eye swelled shut, and her left cheek has a bruise the exact size of a fist. "Have a good day. It was nice meeting you."

The hell?

"Does your mother know you're going out?" When did I turn eighty?

"Yes. She knows I need to go back to my hotel and grab my stuff before I catch an early train."

"Does Jesse know where you're staying?" I will never forget that name.

"No."

"Are you going to be anywhere near his place?"

"Thank you for worrying about me, even if was just for my mom's sake. I gotta hurry, or I'll miss the train."

"I'll drive you." Let's see how she gets out of this. I don't believe there's a hotel room. At least, not one she already has reserved. The more I thought about it last night, the less I believe she believed she could enter a hotel the way she looks now. She might have seemed stubbornly naïve, but she wasn't. She was stubbornly manipulative.

She glances at her watch. "Okay."

She knows she surprised me. We cross the street, and I open the town car's back door. After I walk around to the other side and get in, I lower the privacy glass. Tommy twists to look at Carys and me. He has no reaction to seeing her face up close. At least no outward reaction. He's one of our most stoic men, but in another life, I think he would have been an empath. Irony's a bitch.

She tells him the name of a place in Washington Heights. That's not what I expected. It's not a dangerous area, but it's not where I'd expect her to stay unless it was to be as far away from something as she could get. I don't think it was about being near a guy because I don't believe Jesse exists. It'll be a drive from the Bronx to the top of Manhattan, so I expect uncomfortable silence. I don't have to worry because she's asleep within three minutes of Tommy pulling away from the curb.

It's not cold in the car, but she shivers. I slip my suit jacket off and spread it over her. I watch her sleep. The only time I do that is when I'm monitoring someone at that abandoned train station. She was bound to have noticed when we approached the safe house. I saw her brow furrow. I watch people in the depths of that train station to know when they're rested enough to go another round with me, and which implement to choose to beat them or torture them with.

She doesn't stir despite some rough potholes Tommy can't avoid. She's out. It's obviously what her body needs, and it's keeping me from peppering her with questions. I don't enjoy having so many unanswered ones rattling around in my head. Nothing good comes from me not knowing everything that's happening in any and all situations. I suppose some would say it gives me anxiety. What it gives me is an increased likelihood of dying. I'd prefer not to. My mom would kill me.

ME

I want Carys's entire life story.

I wait for my brother's response. Our older brother, Finn, is a forensic accountant and has some of the best hacking skills you could imagine. But my little brother—by three minutes—has a master's degree in national security and can find anything under the sun. It may take him five minutes, but if it exists, he'll find it.

SEAN

I started last night when you told us what happened. We all knew Meredith had a family. But she's tightlipped about everything. Carys has active social media but it looks typical. She lives in Pittsburgh so there are pics from there. Most of it is here. I checked her bank accounts and police record. No unusual activity at the bank and nothing since she was sixteen and got a speeding ticket. Lead foot. Fifty in a twenty five.

ME

I remember something about that. Grandda was pissed because he thought Meredith wanted a favor. Mom was the one who asked. Once Grandda found that out the ticket was gone in ten minutes.

SEAN

I remember now God I haven't thought about that since it happened.

ME

Neither have I it just came to me. What else? Employment history?

SEAN

She works for a clothing manufacturer in their HR dept

I glance at Carys. HR? I could definitely see her firing people. Nothing about the prickly porcupine I've met makes me think she'd welcome someone with open arms to a new job.

SEAN

Come by after you drop her off and we'll have breakfast. I'll dig deeper into who she is.

ME

Sounds good. We're pulling up to the hotel now.

I slip my phone back into my pocket before I gently nudge

Carys awake. Her eyes flutter open as best they can, and if it weren't for her battered face, a groggy, sexy kind of look would normally get my cock to twitch. But hers does nothing except make me want to wince. She's a beautiful woman, even with the condition she's in.

That's not what makes me so angry looking at her. I'd feel this kind of rage regardless of how attractive a woman is. It's the idea anything could diminish that spunk I saw yesterday. Considering how much pain she was in and still must be in, I can only imagine what she's like on her best days. She'd match wits with me and likely spin me in circles.

"Carys, we're here. We're at your hotel. Do you need me to carry you in?"

I cock an eyebrow, purposely arrogant. She scowls at me, and even though my face doesn't show it, I'm smiling. It reassures me she can still manage. I follow her into the hotel. I'm hardly impressed by it, but it's not bad enough to make me worry. She bypasses the front desk and goes straight to the elevator.

I don't look to the side, but my peripheral vision tells me the front desk clerk isn't paying enough attention to care what we're doing, which means he didn't notice the condition she's in. It's a blessing in disguise. Normally, it would piss me off to walk into a hotel with someone who needs protection and realize even the staff doesn't care what happens here.

I follow her onto the elevator, and we ride up to the seventh floor. When she lets us into the room, I scan my surroundings. She unpacked, but there's something about the room that feels off. It doesn't feel lived in. I'm certain her story would be that she arrived, put her stuff away, and went straight to see Jesse. But even though I see the empty suitcase, which means she tucked her clothes away somewhere, it doesn't feel as though she spent any time here at all, like a maid unpacked for her and left the room looking untouched. Except this isn't the kind of hotel where they have that kind of maid service.

I give her space as she collects the few items she has in the drawers, but I keep an eye on her. She has very few things, as though it truly was just for a weekend stay. I turn away when she goes for her underwear drawer, but I notice she has three matching sets, so that makes me wonder what she's wearing now.

That slight sense I got that she's into kink roars back to life. If only she were someone else, and if only this were a different place. But she's in no condition to be thinking about getting tied up and spanked. And worse than that, or maybe it's better than that—I don't fucking know—she's Meredith's daughter. I'm not taking advantage of this situation because I don't want Meredith to skin me alive. Considering she's a surgeon, she's just as well equipped to do that as I am.

Once Carys is entirely packed, she comes to stand in front of me with her bag. I reach to take it from her, but she pulls her arm away.

"Shane, you've been really helpful, and I appreciate your kindness, but I'm good from here. The subway is just a couple blocks over. It'll take me to the train station. I'll get on board, and I'll go home, and I'll put all of this behind me."

"Neither you nor I believe that, Carys. Not that you're going to the train station on your own, or that you're going to put this behind you. Let me help just a bit longer."

I reach out for the bag again, and she shakes her head. Her chin sets in that mulish expression, and that spunkiness again reassures me. And if it weren't the result of her trying to protect herself and guard herself, I'd find it sexy as fuck. But I don't right now. I find it frustrating instead.

"Carys, I won't argue with you. I won't go around in circles. Just give me your bag and let me help you. I don't get why you're so opposed to it. We may not know each other, but it's obvious I know your mom. It's obvious she trusts me. It's obvious she wants me to help, or at least is letting me help. So, I'm not some stranger danger. Let me get you to the train station, make sure you have everything you need, and then I'll leave you alone. You never have to see me again. You never have to hear from me again. Let me do that much if for no other reason than you're Meredith's daughter.

She's been good to my family for nearly as long as I can remember."

She stares at me uncertainly. That just gave her a million questions she'd love to ask about who her mom is to my family and how she became involved. It's obvious now she serves as the Irish mob's emergency physician. We stare at each other for what feels like an eternity, but I'm certain it's only a few seconds until she relents. She reaches out and lets me take the bag from her.

We leave the room and the hotel in silence. More silence as we walk to the town car. More silence as we ride to the train station, bypassing the subway. The subway really was only a few blocks away, and we could've walked. But she looks in no condition to do much more than stand up and breathe, so I decided to bring her straight here. I take her inside, and I watch her scan her phone, so she does have a ticket. She's going somewhere.

I watch the screen pop up, and it's a train west to Pittsburgh, so at least that much is true, even if other stuff still doesn't add up. I have her bag, and I walk her to the platform where the train is already waiting. I watch her board. I step back and head toward the end of the platform, but I don't leave until the train is out of sight. I watch it the entire time to make sure she doesn't slip off. But she's gone now, and there's nothing else I can do. At least for now, nothing directly with her. I head back to the car and let Tommy know to take me to Sean's.

On the way, I look up her social media and scroll it a little more, but I'm finding nothing I didn't already see last night when I trolled her. No. Troll implies I'm going to use this information against her and bully her. That's not the goal. The goal is to be informed. Maybe I will wind up bullying her about something else—oh, like taking better care of her health—but I won't use her social media against her.

I text my brother as I pull into the driveway to let him know I'm here. Before most of my generation started getting married, we had an open-door policy at all our homes. We came and went as we pleased, and we never worried about walking in on something intimate because none of us brought women home. Our places are our sanctuary, our reprieves from the outside world, and that includes the women we fuck. But now that Dillan and Finn and Sean and Seamus are all married, we no longer have that policy.

Only Cormac and I are the last bachelors standing, so I make sure my brother knows I'm here. I make sure I don't walk in on anything I shouldn't see. Lord knows I've come close even with a warning when I've arrived. It's that way at all the married couple's homes—my parents included.

"Sean?"

"Yeah, we're in the kitchen."

That means his wife, Nikki, is with him. That's not a bad thing. I really like both of my sisters-in-law, but it means we'll have to wait to discuss business.

"Hey Nikki, how are you this morning?"

I lean forward and give her a kiss on the cheek as she lifts her chin to me. My brothers certainly didn't have a simple time dating the women they fell in love with, but the couples in my family don't marry unless it's to their soulmate, and no one is better suited to my twin than Nicolina.

She grew up with mobs all around her life, connected to the syndicates in Boston and Quebec, but now she leads a much quieter life in New York. Isn't that ironic? I serve myself some of the quiche sitting on the counter. Then I take a seat at the breakfast table.

We chat as though we're the most normal family. We talk about the concert I missed and about how excited everyone in the family is to hear Finn and Ally are expecting their first child. Our family can definitely use some good news these days.

Nikki takes a cue once we're all done eating and leaves the kitchen while Sean and I do the dishes and clean up.

I get straight to the point. "Have you figured out anything else about her?"

I want to know; I don't want to wait. He grins at me because between the two of us, he's the patient one. He's also known as the most stubborn. I don't know about all that. He's an I-can-wait-you-out-until-forever and I'm a better-hang-on-and-keep-up-because-

I'm-ready-to-go kind of guy. But I would say we equal each other in stubbornness. We walk alike, talk alike, sound alike.

We're fucking Patty Duke from that old TV show my mom showed us when we were kids, except if I remember right, Patty Duke and her mirror image were cousins. Sean is my baby brother by just a few minutes. God bless our mother because we went to our due date, and we were both almost eight pounds each. There's nothing little about either of us and never has been.

"Hello. Earth to Shane. You want to know so much, and yet you're not even listening. You don't pay attention. As usual."

I flick water at Sean, but I stop letting my mind wander as we dry our hands and head over to Sean's computer.

"Let me see what I can find, but it may take me a while. I'm going to have to dig a lot deeper than I already have. I found pretty much the same thing you could when you looked through her social media. But like I said before, I got into her bank accounts and her police record, and the other stuff Finn could have done for you."

"That's why I came to you for the stuff Finn can't do. I've got my work to deal with, so I'll leave you alone. You do you, I'll do me, but by the end of this I want a dossier on her as thick as the CIA would hand over."

Sean rolls his eyes, but I open my laptop which I'd left here last night before we all went to the concert. We planned to meet at Dillan's to work out, then I was going to come over here, anyway. I look at invoices from the construction site where I found Carys last night.

I look at the schematics for the mini mall that's going to go on that site, and I look at the Gantt chart to see we're almost a week ahead of schedule on construction in New York. That's about a holy miracle. I never expect things this good to last.

It's been kind of quiet the last couple of months. The Diazes, the Mancinellis, and the Kutsenkos have done nothing to piss us off, and we've been too busy with our own happy blissful moments and marriages to do too much more. Well, it's all relative.

Things took a nasty turn for Seamus's wife, Tiernan, but that was really more about her own family down in Trenton. Another syndicate was involved, but we didn't know until the very end.

"Hey, take a look at this."

Sean turns his computer toward me with the portable tri-screen monitors attached to it. I glance at the computer's clock and see we've been working in silence for forty-five minutes. Damn, that went fast.

It looks like a social media profile, so I shrug to my brother.

"Isn't this what I've already seen?"

"No. I got into posts she deleted. You said she dated this guy a few months back, and there were photos of him. Well, I did a reverse search to see if I could find anything up with these photos. Look at him. Same time and date stamp on the picture with Carys is on this one with a joyous family." He clicks on something else. "And look at this. Another one with him with a woman who looks nothing like Carys, but probably is supposed to be his mother."

I frown. "What the hell? What does this mean?"

"It looks like she doctored the photos. She spliced him out of these and put herself next to him."

"Who is he? I can't tell." I lean in to see better.

"I'm going to keep digging, but it almost looks like these photos are the kind that come in a frame you get in a store or online, like the model photo or whatever."

I watch Sean click around some more and between his main screen and the one on the left. He pulls up photos of Carys and this guy that have the exact matching background and pose as the ones that seem to be stock images.

Holy fuck.

What the fuck is going on? Why did she manufacture a boyfriend and go so far as to put together fake photos? I don't know what to make of this. I feel like I'm constantly saying that to myself ever since I met this woman, and that wasn't even twenty-four hours ago. This makes me even more suspicious.

"What do you think? I'm tempted to call David and see if he

can dig around near whatever neighborhood she supposedly lives in out in Pittsburgh."

"What? You don't believe she actually lives out there? You think she got on a train to go almost four hundred miles for nothing?"

I shake my head. "I don't believe she stayed on that train. The more I see, the more I think she can't help but lie. Who knows? Maybe she's leading some double life.

"What do you think? She's like some bigamist or something, and she's got two families tucked away?"

"I don't think she has any families if she's using stock images of this guy to pose as a boyfriend she supposedly broke up with." If she was leading a double life, she wouldn't have any pics up either family could find.

"I don't blame you for being curious, but what do you think Meredith will say when she finds out you've been digging into her daughter's life?"

"Well, I guess that means Meredith just won't find out. But part of me thinks I might be doing her a favor if something's going on with Carys, and her daughter is in this much danger."

My brother smirks at me. "You really think that's how Meredith will take it? You really think she's going to just say thank you if you arrive with that CIA-level dossier with information her daughter's been keeping from her? I highly doubt that's the reaction Meredith will have.

"She is British. She'll smile on the outside while she fumes on the inside."

Sean smirks. "And you better believe that and remember it the next time she needs to give you stitches."

We both groan. Meredith was far gentler with her daughter last night than she's ever been with any of us. It's not like she's got ham hocks for hands, but she hardly has much sympathy for us and usually looks at us as though we got what we deserved.

I pick up my phone from where I left it on the table and pull up a contact, then tap it. It rings twice.

"Hey, boss."

"Hey, David. How's it going?"

"It's going fine. Weather's hotter than the devil's balls in August, but other than that, it's good."

I chuckle. It's certainly one way to put it. We're having a heat wave, too.

"Hey, I need you to do me a favor. You have time to look somebody up for me?"

"Always. Shane, just let me know who and what you want me to do to them."

"I don't want you to do anything to this person. I just want you to check out where they live and see if they really do. I don't want you poking around. I don't want you going inside. I don't even want you staking out the place more than to tell me whether it's actually lived in."

"I can do that. Who is he?"

I pause for a moment, but I dive right in. "It's Carys Pritchard."

"Pritchard. Isn't that—is she related to Meredith?"

I hear surprise, and it doesn't shock me. I've got to tread carefully on this one because David knows Meredith. He grew up with Uncle Donovan.

"They're related, but something came up, and I just want to make sure she's okay."

"Is there somebody I should pick up and bring to you? You going to come out here for them?"

"No, nothing like that. I just want to make sure she lives in a decent place, and she's safe wherever that is."

"All right, I can do that. You want me to look in some windows, though? See if it's got furniture in there, what kind of furniture it is, that sort of thing?"

"If you can, without getting caught."

He chuckles. "Have I ever gotten caught?"

"Don't tempt fate, David. There's always a first time for everything."

"True, true. I'm not looking to get put away, but I can do the job. I can go after nightfall and see what there is to see. Maybe she'll do me a favor and leave some curtains or blinds open."

"That's fine. But we don't want anyone thinking you're skulking around in the dark, looking in a single woman's windows. You really will get hauled in, and we're too far away to get you out anytime soon."

"I got you, boss. Don't worry. You called me because you know I know what I'm doing."

"Keep me posted on what you find."

I hang up and shoot him a text with Carys's address Sean found while he worked. The lease looks all on the up and up. There's nothing about it to make me suspicious, but I just don't know. It makes no sense to me why this matters so much. I keep telling myself it's because she's Meredith's daughter.

I know that has to be part of it, but it really has something to do with that feisty spirit I saw. The idea anything could extinguish that—that anyone might make her a target—makes a rage boil in me I can't explain. It just feels so wrong.

And in a world where most people would describe everything I do as wrong, that's saying something.

I can't do anything until David gets in touch with me, but I'm certainly not through with Carys Pritchard.

Chapter Four

Carrie

That man is fucking gorgeous as sin, but he's fucking insufferable.

Pretty sure that's the second time I've thought it in as many days. Fucking wouldn't let it go. He's worse than a dog with a fucking bone. Now my happy ass—well—no—not much happy about me right now. My fucking miserable ass—is on a train headed toward Pittsburgh, which is exactly what I didn't want.

But here I am. I'd bought the ticket just in case I needed to prove to my mom I was supposedly headed home. I should have expected Shane to still be outside the door, but clearly I'm not thinking a hundred percent straight because it shocked me to find him getting out of that car and crossing the street.

It annoyed the shit out of me when he insisted on coming to the hotel with me. Nobody is supposed to know where that is. But what choice did I have? I certainly couldn't take him to the alternative. So, I had to use the hotel. It's a good thing I had so little to pack there because that place is no longer safe. Now I have to set something else up as my own safe house.

Finally. Three stops out of the city, I can get off and head back into New York. I doubt he's followed me this far, but if he has, he won't notice me. I can slip past him.

He can take his jolly little ass all the way to Pittsburgh.

Well, no.

Fuck.

If he does, that means he knows where I supposedly live. If he knows where I supposedly live, he's going to come knocking.

Fuck my life.

Why does this have to keep getting more and more complicated?

I exhale a deep sigh as I gather my overnight bag and climb off the train. I head into the station, keeping my head on a swivel as though I'm looking for where I'm going, which I am. But more importantly, I'm watching for whomever might follow me. I don't expect to recognize anyone, which is what makes it all the more nerve-wracking. But I've got a sixth sense about these things, and I've been trained enough to know how to spot a person assigned as your safety detail and someone assigned to track you until they can kill you.

I don't see either type of person—not just man—person. There are plenty of women mercenaries out there. If life takes a different direction at some point, that very well might be me.

Oh, thank God.

There's a train in an hour. That's not so bad. I can wait it out here in the air conditioning.

Home sweet fucking home, if you can call that the case for this apartment I'm in near Greenpoint. It's a pleasant part of Brooklyn, and my supposed boyfriend moved me in a couple months ago. It's better than the small studio I had when I initially started this assignment. I hate the idea someone is paying for me and keeping a roof over my head. That it makes me a kept woman.

But then again, the apartment I have—that I supposedly live in, in Pittsburgh—as well as the safe house hotel room—are all paid by someone else. So, I guess I'm a kept woman in one way or another.

I'm in what used to be a predominantly Polish neighborhood. Gentrification's making it a bit too hipster for my taste. The people around here know who I am, which means it was a good thing I bought that hoodie from the train station. I know I looked ridiculous wearing it in this heat, but I needed it and the sunglasses to disguise the mess I'm in. I lock the door behind me, head straight to my bedroom, and toss my overnight bag on the end of the bed.

I try not to look at the thing when I don't have to. The bed, not the bag. I head into my bathroom and strip off all my clothes. Oh, blessed shower. I took one last night at the safe house, but I had to put the same clothes back on. Blood and dirt and everything. My mom objected, insisted we should go back to my parents' house where I still have a few pieces of clothing. I argued I should go to my hotel where I already had clothes. She tried to tell me Shane could get something for me from one of his sisters-in-law or his mom or someone, but I categorically refused to take anything else from him.

Thank God I didn't. Can you imagine what he would have said or at least his expression if I walked out of the house this morning in clothes he got for me? No fucking thank you. I don't let myself look in the mirror at my bruises until I'm clean and I feel like I can look at the world with fresh eyes.

Motherfucker.

The things I do for work. I lift my arm and try not to howl from the agony. I look at the bruises all along my right ribs. Makes it hard to breathe.

Thank goodness.

My mind might be going a mile a minute, but I haven't really had to talk much since I got into the SUV last night. It hurts too fucking much. My face is a mess. My eyes remain nearly swollen shut. There's a bruise across my left cheek. My lips are split. I'm lucky I still have all my teeth. My mom gave me a shot of powerful shit last night. She gave me some pills this morning. I took a dose before I left and one just before the train stopped in the city. It's the only reason I can keep going.

I twist to look in the mirror. There are livid bruises across my kidneys, or at least where I'm pretty sure they still are. That fucker's boot felt like he kicked all my organs right through my stomach and left them on the floor beside me. I'd probably be in less pain if he had. I'm lucky I could keep my mom from examining me, but now I need to play the part and put these on full display. I'm not letting that fucker get away with this.

⁂

I might have had to grin and bear it while it was happening—really grimace and bear it—but Bartlomiej won't put up with this. That's the only consolation I have. It's knowing my boyfriend will beat the shit out of his brother for beating the shit out of me.

I pull into the driveway, and I recognize the cars parked here. Fucking hell, one of them's Jacek's. I steel myself against seeing him, even though it'll be to my advantage he'll be here when I tell Bartlomiej what happened. I won't lay it on too thick, but I also won't—or can't—avoid telling him the truth. I head to the door, and the guard nods and opens it for me. I step inside and can hear voices, but none are Bartlomiej's. I walk into the living room, and there's a handful of men sitting around watching a soccer game.

Shocker. These guys are the most underemployed henchmen I've ever seen. But I suppose that's a blessing in disguise. I say hi and head toward Bartlomiej's office. The door's open, and I can see Jacek, but no Bartlomiej. The fuck is Jacek doing sitting at his brother's desk? He knows how much Bartlomiej hates it when he does that.

I smile.

He shoots me a grin in return. It's pure evil.

The guy was in the army as an explosive ordnance disposal tech, and I don't know if it unleashed a pyrotechnic in him or if that was already there, but he definitely came back from his four tours not right in the head.

He is the top henchman in the Polish mob here in New York. Bartlomiej trusts his advice, but only as far as he can throw his brother. Considering he's scrawny as fuck and wily as a fucking coyote, that's unfortunately a pretty far distance since Bartlomiej is only a little shorter and a little lighter than Shane.

"Where's your brother?"

"Well, good morning to you too, sunshine."

I don't respond. Jacek grins even wider. It makes my stomach turn over.

"You're too late, little darling. He had to go out of town this morning."

I can't stand him. The day I can put a bullet through his head cannot come soon enough. I turn around and hear him get out of his seat. I'm quick without running. I get back to the living room where I'm confident the guys won't let Jacek touch me.

He tries to get closer, but he knows there're limits to even his power when the other men are around. I stand as close as I can to the sofa and cheer along in Polish for the team I know the men favor. They laugh and joke with me, but they all keep an eye on Jacek. No one says anything about my face, but I'm certain word's already gone around that I can thank Jacek for my new look.

They can all tell he's paying too much attention to me, and it makes them all wary. They know he doesn't like me, and they've become rather protective of me over the last few months. If they weren't all psychopaths who enjoy their jobs—not just because they're paid, but because of their loyalty to Bartlomiej and Jacek's mother—then they might actually be nice men. But I can never take for granted these men make a living torturing and killing other people.

"Hey, I need to take off now. I've got to head back home. I'm not feeling my best today."

That's an understatement of a lifetime. I'm still in so much pain, and the medicine is wearing off. I won't hide it for much longer.

Tymoteusz looks at my face, noting the bruises and split lip, then glances at Jacek. He stands and offers to take me home, and I gladly accept. Jacek tries to block the way, but Tymoteusz pulls out his phone and taps Bartlomiej's contact.

Jacek knows his cousin won't back down, not with his temperament and not because of his position. After Jacek, he's the next highest man in the hierarchy. Tymoteusz escorts me out to a car, and we chat on the way back to the apartment Bartlomiej chose for me. Pays for me.

That reminds me. Once I'm in my apartment again, I grab my phone from my back jeans pocket and pull up Bartlomiej's contact as I kick off the shoes he bought me. They land in the bottom of my closet. I take off the shirt he bought me as the phone rings. The jeans are mine, and the bra and panties are mine—though he's picked those out for me too. As the call goes to voicemail, I slip off the jeans and loosely fold them and the shirt before dropping them on the end of the bed.

"Hey handsome, it's me." I might have thrown up a little in my mouth. "I'm bummed I didn't get to see you. Something came up last night I was hoping to talk to you about. Bartek, I really need you, so I'm looking forward to when you get home. Let me know when you're back in town. I really want to see you. I miss you. Love you. Bye."

I hang up the call and feel like washing my mouth out with soap. Not just for the lies, but the kind of lies. I manipulate Bartlomiej almost as much as he manipulates me. He believes I'm a good Catholic girl who refuses to give up the V-card until I'm married. He thinks I'm playing hard to get. No shit, Sherlock.

But that doesn't mean I haven't felt backed into a corner more than once and wound up doing things more intimate than I'd like. The rules are clear: there's no expectation of sex as part of the job. Other intimate things can happen if refusal results in imminent danger.

Bartlomiej is a fine line between pleasure and pain. He likes both in equal measures, as long as he's doling it out. He certainly has no interest in receiving pain. He's never physically forced me, though I wouldn't put it past him when he drinks. He's backed me against walls and into corners. He's grabbed my arms too roughly. He's threatened me without outright threatening me.

He won't kill me for not sleeping with him, but he expects everything leading up to that. He gets frustrated when I don't meet those expectations because I have boundaries I won't cross. He thinks it's religion. I know it's ethics and my sanity.

That's why I hate looking at my bed. I've spent the night a few times at his place, but he says he likes to get away from there since it's also where he conducts so much business.

He usually shows up here if he's not already with me. Somehow, I have skills better than I thought because I had him latch onto me like a Stage Five Clinger within two weeks of meeting him. He moved me in here within a month, but I made him sign a contract saying I can leave anytime I want—which is utter bullshit because I can't—at least not yet—and I live here regardless of whether we're having sex.

You better believe I had that written in there. That was uncomfortable as hell to have presented before his branch's elders, but I knew it was the only way to guarantee my alleged maidenhead would stay intact. I haven't been a virgin in so long, I almost can't remember.

I'm not looking forward to seeing him since it inevitably means I'm going to have to go to bed with him when he gets back, but he talks in his sleep and not like some shitty eighties song. He really does. I don't know if his men know or not, but when he's with me, he falls into a deep sleep. I suppose that says something if he trusts me enough to relax. Being with him all the time also means I'm privy to a lot more than people realize. So far, I've turned most of that evidence over. But not all of it yet.

I'm not ready to file a full report. If they knew half the things I had to put up with, they'd probably yank me out. It's not that I've been in direct danger, but the places where Bartlomiej has meetings and the men who attend definitely make me think I'm a cat with nine lives. And there are some meetings where I think I'm on my ninth.

These are the men who are the lowest of the low among the

Polish mob, the lowest of the low among the Armenians and the Albanians. He also meets with their leaders. Bartlomiej has more spies than a medieval royal court. He needs them in those syndicates and some of the other lower-level ones because he can't get any into the Four Families.

The O'Rourkes, the Mancinellis, the Diazes, and the Kutsenkos. Those are the four families who rule New York. They all think they have the biggest slice of the pie, and sometimes they do. It goes back and forth. Right now, none of us are really sure who has it, but the Kutsenkos are my target. So that's why I put up with all this bullshit and why I didn't run for the hills and demand to be taken off the case.

Now it's just a waiting game. I take a nap for a few hours, but I can't go anywhere until my meeting at one a.m.

It's quarter to one, and the city is quiet. That's all relative since it's New York. There's still plenty going on. Plenty of lights and noise. But there aren't the crowds on the sidewalks like there would be at one in the afternoon.

I head to the car I keep parked a few blocks away in a garage I pay cash for. Bartlomiej and Jacek don't know I have one. They believe I get around either by subway or rideshare. At least before I knew Bartlomiej, and he started sending drivers for me. I know that's not a courtesy. It's his way of keeping tabs on me.

It surprises me he hasn't called yet, or at least texted. He's somewhere between protective and possessive. It changes by the day. Sometimes I can almost imagine him as a normal man who dates and cares about his girlfriend. But two minutes later, he reminds me of who he really is. A man who has no limits, no boundaries.

I'm one of the few people he appears to respect. I think it's because I played hard to get in the beginning. He saw me as a challenge, but he also respects I'm among the few who don't bow down to him and grovel or nearly piss their pants in his presence.

I pretended not to know who he was or how important he was when I supposedly moved into the neighborhood. That was five months ago, and it only took a month before I became his girlfriend. Or at least that's what everybody believes.

I pull up to the house in Queens and go straight into the garage. I don't turn off the engine until the garage door is two inches from the ground. I don't get out of the car until it stops rattling. I slip into the house and greet the two guys. I go straight to my boss.

"You look like shit, Carys."

"I feel like shit, Johnny. Thanks. In case you hadn't noticed, I got the shit beaten out of me last night."

"Yeah, your future brother-in-law certainly didn't take well to you asking a few too many questions."

"They weren't questions that should've pissed him off as much as they did, unless he has more to hide than any of us thought."

I'd managed to shoot off a text before I got to the construction site, telling my handlers what happened. I sent pictures of my face and my ribs, but I didn't tell them where I was running to hide. I didn't know where I was going to go. I didn't know the construction site I picked belonged to the O'Rourkes.

I never would have imagined my mother would show up. I wouldn't have gone there. I wouldn't have gotten her or the O'Rourkes involved.

But that's what ended up happening.

"So, what's the deal, Carys? Did you see him today?" Johnny's the least patient person I know which makes him a shit handler. But I don't get to pick. At least we get along, and I don't mind him.

"No. He went out of town. He didn't text me to let me know."

"That's pretty unusual, isn't it?"

"Yeah, and it makes me wonder what's going on. I don't know if he really left this morning without knowing what Jacek did last night, or whether he knows and he left, anyway. I have more questions than answers about that. Same thing about Jacek. He's definitely doing more than what his brother ordered. But I can't tell yet if that's a benefit or a mutiny."

"Do you really think he'd go against his brother? Do you think Jacek would go against anybody? Even his mother?"

Zofia Nowakowski. Those two men are boys when they're around their mother. They turn into spineless, sniveling shells of men. I don't blame them. The woman is terrifying. I did my best to make sure I got on her good side from the very beginning. I'm the docile little woman she believes her son deserves. She is straight up former Soviet Union gymnast. Not Olympic level. Pretty damn close. She has the discipline of a Soviet general, and she runs her family just like that.

Bartlomiej may head the Polish mob, but she's definitely the matriarch. She doesn't call the shots in business. But if she had her druthers, she'd already have Bartlomiej married to me and me four months pregnant. That shit's never happening.

"Hard to breathe, hard to talk?"

I'll look over at Steven, the other guy who keeps an eye on me. I only nod. I don't need to let them know my mind's wandering, and it's not because I'm in so much pain. Let them think I'm dazed and confused.

I don't want them to figure out I met Shane last night, and I definitely don't want them to know my mother showed up. But I need to know what they know. I need to know if they've been tracking her all along, and that's why I got this assignment.

Steven nods and turns back to the computer he's sitting in front of at the house's dining room table. He speaks to me over his shoulder.

"We lost your tracker last night. It didn't come back on until this morning. What was up with that?"

I look past him and see he has the record of my movements leading up to two blocks before I got to the construction site. I turned it off before I knew where I wanted to go. I didn't want either of them coming to get me. I'm not ready to pull out of this assignment yet. I put too much into it for one beating to end it all.

I don't think they would intervene. But I didn't want to run the risk.

Now I'm fucking glad I had the gift of second sight and turned it off. I'm sure we track all the syndicate leaders. The last thing I need is for them to put two and two together and know I met with Shane. No. Not met with. Met. I certainly didn't plan on meeting him.

Hot as he may be, I know he's going to be a pain in my ass. There's no way a man like him will give up wanting to know more about a woman who gets beaten up and happens to be his doctor's daughter.

"What do you have for me? Any clues about where Bartlomiej might be? Any hints?"

I redirect the conversation back to what I need to know. I can't let on to Bartlomiej if I find out where he is, but I want to be prepared.

"No, we don't know where he went. That came as news, when you walked in. Wherever he is, it's definitely overseas. Most likely somewhere in the former Eastern Bloc."

That makes me raise my eyebrows.

"Armenia?" I test the waters.

Both men stare at me, then Steven swings back around to his computer and starts typing furiously. I watch as an email account comes up. I walk closer and lean over his shoulder, translating the Polish into English.

I'll land in six hours. We'll meet at the cafe. Be there. Don't make me hunt you down.

It's an email Bartlomiej sent. But the recipient's email is a jumble. There's nothing recognizable about it. It's certainly one nobody wants easily deciphered. There's no salutation. There's no sign off. It's just those few sentences.

"Can you track the IP?"

"No, not yet. It's through a VPN. It's well encrypted."

I'm sure it is.

I can think of at least four men who could hack the shit out of that and already know. One is Shane's twin brother Sean.

Another two are Sergei Andreyev and Anton Kutsenko, the intel gatherers and hackers for the Ivankov bratva.

Joaquin is the one who serves the Diaz Cartel. The man is probably the smartest of all of them. And across all the syndicates, he's the fucking laziest. The man does the bare minimum to meet his uncle's expectations. It's not even like he's off womanizing or gambling or drinking like people might expect the stereotype. The guy likes his fucking Legos.

Legos. A fucking cartel *barón* likes Legos.

Thinking that tempts me to laugh. But I don't need to share my thoughts with anybody. It's Lorenzo and Carmine who are the chief intel gatherers for the Mancinelli Mafia. Lorenzo's a skilled hacker and Carmine's just nosy as fuck. I'm certain those men know exactly where Bartlomiej is right now.

It's a shame I can't go knocking on Shane's door or even Sean's and say, "Hey, what's up? Where's my boyfriend?" I can only imagine how that would go over. That makes my lips twitch.

"You've got nothing for me?"

I turn back to Johnny and cross my arms. Oh God, that hurts. I let them fall to my waist. That hurts even more as it jerks my shoulders.

"Not right now. Keep your tracker on."

"I don't know what the deal was. I didn't think I was anywhere where it wouldn't pick up."

I lie through my teeth. Both men stare at me before they nod. I'm the picture of plausible innocence. They know how well I can lie. But they know how often I tell the truth because I hate lying when I don't have to. I consider this one of those necessary times. They might not agree.

Steven's a little more thoughtful than Johnny, who'd be all business all day if he could. "Do you need anything? Do you have the supplies to deal with those injuries?"

"Yeah, I got an industrial-sized bottle of arnica I'll probably go through in the next two days. I got some ice packs as well. I have a stocked first aid kit."

This is hardly the first time somebody's whaled on me, but it's certainly the worst. It's not an experience I need or intend to repeat. I could have done without it the first go around.

"All right, you can see I'm in one piece, and I know no more than you do. If you've got nothing else for me, I'm headed back to the apartment."

I'm exhausted, and that was a monumental waste of time going around in circles for nothing. I could sleep for a week at this point. Or at least until Bartlomiej comes back in town. Both men agree, so I head to the garage. I back out down the driveway. And look around before I pull onto the street. My headlights are off. I never have the daytime running lights on. I never have them set to auto. I decide who and when someone sees me. And right now, I'd like to stay invisible.

I don't think I have ever slept so much in my life. The only time I woke up to know what was going on was when I was starving, thirsty, had to go to the bathroom, or for my mom. She's called every day for the last three days, and I don't blame her. She thought—blessedly—three days cooped up inside, sleeping most of the time, was the best medicine for my injuries.

I had to be careful about what was in the background when I sent her pictures to prove the swelling was going down. My parents helped me move into the apartment in Pittsburgh, so my mom and dad would both know if the background didn't match where I supposedly live. Bathroom selfies are the best.

I got a message from Bartlomiej this morning telling me he was back in town, and he expects to see me.

I'm too invested.

I remind myself of that while I dress and head out to the subway. My thoughts keep me occupied while I ride the few stops from my apartment to Bartlomiej's house. The guys say hi to me, and I can tell they're all still worried. I look a hell of a lot better than I did the last time I was here.

"*Księżniczka?*" Princess?

I hear Bartlomiej call out to me as I walk past an MMA cage fight on TV. I'm not a fan of his nickname, but whatever.

"Here I am."

I walk around the corner and find him in the kitchen with Jacek and Tymoteusz. Tymoteusz crosses his arms and glowers at Jacek, who smirks at me. Bartlomiej takes in the bruises I'm still sporting. The swelling's gone down around my eyes enough for me to open them, but they're still blackened. My vision's still blurry longer than it should be after I wake up.

"Jacek, you didn't tell me the truth. You said you roughed her up a little because you thought she was lying. You didn't tell me you beat the shit out of the love of my life."

Ugh, that makes my stomach curdle. Tymoteusz pushes away from the counter and walks over to me. He puts his arm around my shoulder, daring to touch me in front of his cousin. He walks me over to the kitchen table and pulls out a chair for me. He stands behind it, my self-appointed guard. When he looks at Bartlomiej, which I can see through the reflection on the window, his expression is clear as day.

"It's as I told you, Bartek."

Bartlomiej nods and comes over to me, approaching slowly, uncertain what I might do. It shocks me how easily I burst into tears. Not because I want his comfort. I'd rather go swimming in the sewers of New York than accept his hug, but I do. It's tears from the pain and frustration. I haven't let myself feel my fear, anger, pain. I was saving them for this moment. I just didn't have to make the tears come.

I sob against his shoulder as Bartlomiej alternates swearing at Jacek and cooing to me, trying to calm me down. It surprises me when he lifts me into his arms. He's gentle. He's done this plenty of times, but it's always been from lust or jest. He carries me out of the kitchen and up to his bedroom, where he carefully places me on the bed. He sits down facing me and cups my hands between his.

"Oh, *księżniczka*, I'm so sorry. Jacek said you two got in an argument, and he slapped you around a bit. I've already dealt with that, or at least I thought I had. Clearly, he wasn't telling the truth, and I didn't believe Tymoteusz. I thought he was exaggerating, since he's in love with you."

I shake my head, and I wince in truth. "Bartek, Tymoteusz doesn't love me. He's loyal to you, which means he's protective of me. He knows what kind of man Jacek is. I wish you could see what all of us do. I know you don't trust Jacek, and you're stuck because he's your brother. But he's way worse than you believe."

I lift my shirt and pull it over my head, wincing again in truth. Bartlomiej swears under his breath as he feathers his fingers over my ribs.

"Did he break any?"

"No. I don't know how he didn't. It certainly felt like it, but I don't think so."

His gaze meets mine. "Did you see a doctor?"

I shake my head. "No, how could I? Any doctor would insist I call the police and file a report. I can't have my name on any records. It'd only point back to you. I couldn't do that to you."

Fuck, I'm laying it on thick, and he eats it up like a bowl full of ice cream.

"My sweet love, if only I could be someone else. If only I could take you far, far away."

"I wish that, too, but it is what it is. It was what it was. It happened. There's nothing either of us can do about it."

"Oh, no, there's plenty I can fucking do about this. I ought to find an accommodating gulag somewhere for him in Siberia."

"Maybe, but you know you need him too much for that."

Weariness crosses his face as he nods. "He still isn't off the hook. Kaja, there's no way I can ignore this. He will find out exactly what it feels like to be you."

My assumed name is Karolina Sobecki, but I go by Kaja.

"No, Bartek, that's not what I want. It will only make things worse. He already resents me for the time you spend with me. He doesn't trust me because he doesn't know me like you do. I don't want him to know me the way you do." I give him a pointed look and offer him a shy smile.

He leans forward and kisses my forehead, avoiding my split lips and bruises. "I don't want anyone to know you the way I do, either."

"Then you can't blame him for being protective of you."

"That may be true, but I can blame him for taking matters into his own hands. He waited until I was gone to do something about his mistrust."

"I appreciate you want to come to my rescue, but you must be exhausted after your trip. You were gone for three days. I had no idea where you were. I was so worried about you."

"Worried I wouldn't come home to deal with Jacek?" He cocks an eyebrow.

I feign hurt and look away. Tears welling in my eyes again. This I have to force. I whisper to him, refusing to look at him when he tries to nudge my chin toward him.

"How can you say something so horrible? If that were true, after this happened, don't you think I would have fled? Do you really think I would have come here the next morning looking for you, terrified of facing Jacek again? Think what would have happened if your men hadn't been here, and I'd found him seated at your desk. He could have trapped me in the house, done anything to me. You wouldn't find my body. There'd be too many pieces if he even left that much."

"Kaja, you exaggerate."

"That's not exaggerating, Bartlomiej. That's exactly what he told me. I know what kind of man he is. Why should I believe anything other than what he tells me?"

Bartlomiej stares at me and nods slowly. He knows I speak the truth. "Stay here, *księżniczka*. Rest. Text me if you need anything."

He moves to stand up, but I squeeze his hand. "You're leaving me already?"

He stares at me once again and shakes his head. He gets up, and I reach for him. He kisses my forehead like he did before and walks around to the other side of the bed. He kicks off his shoes and lies down next to me. Again, he's shockingly gentle as he draws me against him.

He's a handsome man. He's got a good body. He knows what he's doing with his fingers and tongue. If only he weren't who he was. Not just my mark, but a bona fide sociopath.

That makes me think of Shane. He's the same kind of man as Bartlomiej in far too many ways. But I didn't recoil inside when I saw him or when he touched me. Bartlomiej's being just as gentle as Shane was. That was completely different. I have no reason to believe that since they're both mobsters, but it was.

Bartlomiej strokes my hair, and it tempts me to fall asleep since I'm still so tired. I'll allow him to think I'm dozing. I feel him reach into his pocket and pull out his phone. He lets go of me, easing his arm out from under me, checking to make sure I'm still asleep.

Then I know he's texting. I open my eyes just a slit. Not enough for him to tell I can see out from under my lashes. I'm well practiced at this since this is about as much as I could open my eyes for the past three days. I can see his phone screen. It's a burner.

BARTLOMIEJ

It was a success. The shipment's coming in on Tuesday. The handover is Wednesday morning at three. I want all the men there. I don't trust Bogdan.

I keep my breathing even while my pulse races. This is the type of information I need, but I don't know what kind of shipment it is. That just leaves me wondering, who's going to claim it?

Chapter Five

Shane

It's been ten days since I found Carys on my build site. Coincidentally—unfortunately—I needed Meredith to give me six stitches in my right forearm yesterday after a not so fun altercation with Lorenzo Mancinelli. The arsehole sliced me with his knife. In all fairness, that was after I shot so close to his shoulder the bullet singed his suit coat. I missed on purpose. He got me on purpose. There wouldn't have been a problem if he'd stayed in Queens with his wife and baby like he was supposed to instead of going to Brooklyn to collect rent money from a shop owner we're extorting.

Enzo, a dad? Hell hath frozen over. No one even knew his wife, Michelle, was pregnant until she was like seven-and-a-half months. She works from their home a lot, and she and Enzo are the biggest homebodies in their family, which is surprising since he owns restaurants and nightclubs.

The stitches meant I had a reasonable excuse to ask Meredith about Carys. It would have been a dick move not to. I've still heard little from David, which is odd. He shot me a text last night. Three words: working on it.

Meredith chewed my arse because she knows I assigned a protection detail to her. They're discreet, so we all know no one's aware they're there when she's at work. But she spotted them immediately. She claimed I was overreacting, and that I was wasting money paying the men to babysit her.

I told her she wasn't my mother, so I didn't have to listen to her. That resulted in me getting a shot of painkiller in the arse—through my suit pants when she dropped a pack of butterfly stitches on purpose, and I bent to grab it. Hardly sterile, but she knew I'd survive. Needless to say, I remembered what my mom told me when I was twelve, and Meredith sewed me up for the first time. "Listen to her like she's me because you don't want me being the one coming at you with a needle and thread."

I still didn't call off the detail, but I admitted I set it up. I dropped it down to two men while she was at work, and two guys in separate cars at opposite ends of her street at night. I compromised and agreed to end it in two weeks if nothing happened.

Frankly, face-to-face, most syndicate men would back down if they had to stand before Meredith's withering stare. It's one she perfected after twenty years as a British Royal Navy surgeon—she started specializing in orthopedics after she got out. But a bullet is a bullet, as I proved to Enzo's suit coat. Fucker owes me one for the unrepairable rip in my coat's sleeve.

I wove in questions about Carys while we argued, pointing out her daughter would never forgive herself if something happened to Meredith because she'd shown up not knowing it was her daughter who needed help. I asked how Carys would react to her mom declining the detail. I asked if she wouldn't expect me to do the same for Carys if she lived in the city.

When I asked about Jesse—thinking I was sly—she looked me straight in the eye before her gaze darted to the gun still holstered under my arm, then back up to my eyes. I didn't react, but we understood each other. She'd just put a hit on her daughter's ex-boyfriend.

I didn't tell her what Sean and I found with the photos. They were fake pics, and Sean's found nothing about a guy named Jesse.

Meredith had little to offer on her end since she hadn't met the last two guys Carys dated. She suspected Carys had been involved with someone in Pittsburgh, but—typically British—she doesn't discuss her daughter's dating life.

"David?" It's an odd time for him to call, but at least there's no one around to overhear us.

"Hey, boss. Sorry it took so long, but I wanted to be sure."

I'm in my car alone on the way to a meeting I'm not invited to. It's sweltering even this early in the morning, but I have a baseball cap on and long sleeves. The red hair and freckles give me away to anyone with even a smidge of a connection to a syndicate. Three brothers married three sisters, so the only dominant genes were recessive ones. The six of us—Dillan, Seamus, Cormac, Finn, Sean, and I—have close shades of red hair somewhere between our dads' dark strawberry blond and our moms' russet. Our dads have blue eyes, but all of us inherited our moms' green ones. It makes us way too recognizable.

"What'd you find out?"

"No one's been to her place in days. She doesn't get mail delivered there. Not even a flyer. Her designated parking space was always empty. Pittsburgh's got public transportation, but nothing convenient enough between her place and where she supposedly works."

"Supposedly?"

"Yeah. I checked the employee directory on the voicemail."

I should have thought of that.

"Her name's not listed. I slipped in and poked around when the night custodian arrived. Her name isn't anywhere. Not on a desk. Not on a cubicle. Not on an office door. I checked the reception desk, and her name wasn't on the directory there either. I know you told me no peeking in windows. She lives on the fourth floor, so I went to the roof across the street with my binoculars. Blinds were closed the entire time. I can get that to keep out the sun. But lights never went on at night. Boss, it's not just that she doesn't live there. No one lives there. My guess is she doesn't even live out here."

"Thanks, David."

"Anything else? You want me to keep watching in case I'm wrong, and she comes round?"

"No. We're good."

"Do you think she's okay? I don't want to think something's happened to Meredith's daughter. It would devastate her."

"I know. That's why I wanted you to check on her. I think I know where she is. I just wanted to be sure she wasn't out near you before I get nosey somewhere else."

"All right. Let me know if you need anything."

"Will do. Bye."

"Bye."

I tap the end call button on my steering wheel. I don't have a fucking clue where Carys is. But David doesn't need to know that. I trust him, but he had his job, and now it's done. We don't gossip. We don't shoot the shite.

I have to table my thoughts because I'm at the far end of the lumberyard in Yonkers. I pull into the shadows and park. I own several cars, all of which cost more than some people's homes. But not this one. I own the Toyota Corolla I'm in, but all of us use it when we want to blend in. It might be a late model, low end car on the outside, but we've had it customized. The headlights don't flash, and the horn doesn't beep when we lock and unlock it. The dome light won't come on if there's a bomb. The entire frame is reinforced against impact big and small—from bullets to bulldozers—and the windows are shatterproof.

The shirt I'm wearing has the lumberyard company logo on it, so I look like I probably have a reason to be here after hours. I have my excuse ready. I'm here to grab my proof of residency for my daughter's school that I printed on the company machine and shouldn't have. Whoops. I got distracted by a call and forgot I left the electric bill in the machine's tray. I need it to register her, or she'll lose her spot at the magnet school. If that happens, not only will my wife and daughter kill me, I'll lose my son's sibling privilege to get into the school next year.

Yeah. I've used this story a few times before. I have it down pat. I've practiced it with my mom a few dozen times until she said I could pass for a dad—vaguely aware of what's going on and not interested in dealing with his wife saying she knew she should have just taken care of it herself—like everything else in their house. I'll take my mom's compliments any way I can get them. My dad and uncles were—are—totally hands on dads. They knew way more than any of us wanted. My mom was going off her dad; our mob boss until I was in high school. This is not when I want to reflect on that old coot.

I creep along the side wall where I know the security cameras aren't pointing. They're fixed lens and only focus straight in front with a forty-five-degree radius to either side.

ME

I'm in place. I'm calling you

Finn shoots me a thumbs up emoji just before I hit the call button. I drop the phone back in my pocket. If anything happens, Finn'll know right away. I'd wear a wire, but the men know what to look for. If shite goes wrong, Finn can hang up before they take my phone. They won't know anyone was listening. It wouldn't be ideal to end the call, but I might live ten minutes longer than if they found me miked or with a camera.

"What the fuck's taking him so long?"

I recognize Bartlomiej Nowakowski's voice. That piece of shite.

He's sucking the Kutsenkos' balls to keep them happy. After the shite that went down with the Albanians and the Russians, the Polish aren't looking for the same trouble. They're skating on cracking ice with the Italians, too. They don't look in the Colombians' direction, and we barely tolerate them. That's why I want to know about the shipments he's getting from Bogdan, the youngest of the four Kutsenko brothers.

I already looked around as I drove by. I don't see any of Bogdan's cars or any of their decoys. I recognized Bartlomiej's though. He thinks having a mid-shade blue SUV makes him less noticeable. When you're the only fucker without a black one, you stick out.

I ease inside one of the bay doors and duck behind six stacked sawdust barrels. It shields me from sight, but I can see around and between them. Bartlomiej's standing with his hands on his hips, even more pissed than usual. Something's going on because his brother's keeping his distance. Normally, he'd be the one bitching about people wasting his precious time.

Twat.

Something's getting Bartlomiej even more worked up. Five minutes pass, and he's pacing. I'm wholly unprepared for him to draw back his fist and slam it into Jacek's face. He goes for the throat punch next. Jacek stumbles backward but regains his balance. He goes on the defensive and swings at his older brother. Five men rush forward. They might be siblings, but no one gets to touch a mob boss. The guys restrain Jacek as Bartlomiej swears at him.

"You fucking waste of shit. You told me they'd be here. You confirmed it. Instead, we're standing here with our dicks in the wind when I could be home with Kaja."

Kaja? Since when does Bartlomiej have a woman he cares about? I heard he was seeing someone, but he's always seeing someone. The man is a serial dater. He enjoys knowing he always has a pussy waiting for him. I can only imagine the poor girl stuck with him up her arse—and not figuratively.

"You fucked up, Jacek. I won't forgive you for this. I should be home with her. You're the reason for that." He jabs his finger into his brother's chest. "Go near her again, and I don't give a shit about your position in this family. The only thing you'll be to me is dead. Leave my woman alone."

Wow!

Their dad died when Bartlomiej was seventeen, and Jacek was fifteen. They saw it happen, and it was brutal. Bartlomiej became their leader in name, but his mother pulled the strings until he finished college. By then, Jacek was in the army. Bartlomiej's been running his syndicate for real for ten years. Jacek's been beside him except for the four years he served on active duty. They're as close as I am with Finn and Sean.

This is big.

"She got what she deserved." Jacek spews that line as his brother turns away. Bartlomiej freezes before he turns like he's some actor in a drama—slow-mo.

"You had no right to touch her. If you had a problem with my girlfriend, you come to me."

"I bet I touched her more than you have. She's leading you around by the dick. Maybe if you shoved it down her throat more often, she'd know her place. Lord knows you aren't shoving it up her pretty little virginal cunt or ass. Maybe that's what I'll do next time."

Bartlomiej roars as he barrels into his brother. He knocks Jacek and the five men holding him in place onto their arses. More men rush forward and barely pry Bartlomiej off Jacek before he beats his brother's head against the concrete.

So much to unpack. Bartlomiej's dating a virgin? Not on God's green earth. But whoever she is, he's more protective of her than he is loyal to his brother. That's interesting. It must be serious. Could he be on his way to a little white chapel? I wonder where they're registered.

"Bartek! Bartek! Enough. They were here. They saw you."

Fucking hell.

Bartlomiej steps away and shakes off the men restraining him. He runs his hand over his hair as he stomps to the bay door across from me. He doesn't look at Jacek as he bellows at his men.

"Take him out to the car. If I see him before I get home, I'll kill him."

I pull my phone out and open the camera. I zoom in as far as I can go. Four black SUVs drive by. The second one's back passenger window is down. I recognize Bogdan as he rolls past, shaking his head. No one's ready for Niko to drop the front passenger window of the third car and pepper the place with a full magazine from the high-powered rifle he points out the window.

I scramble from my hiding place before any of the Poles turn in my direction to flee. I don't need the Kutsenkos finding me here either if they decide to do more than a drive by. I duck out of the door and am about to turn toward my car and sprint when I notice a flash of dark hair that stands out next to the building's white-washed walls. The person's wearing a hoodie, so I can't tell how long the hair is. Whoever it is, is short but fast.

Did they see me there?

I change course and push myself to catch up to them. When I'm close enough, I wrap my arms around them, throwing my weight forward, knocking us both to the ground. I take an elbow to the nose before I can wrestle them beneath me and push up onto my hands and knees. I'm looking at the barrel of a gun. I'm looking at Carys.

"What the fu—feck are you doing here, Carys?"

I barely catch myself in time not to swear in front of her. The whole no curse words in front of women and children is so ingrained in me that even in moments like this, I still know better than to swear in front of them.

She shoots me a mutinous glare and refuses to answer. Back to this. This is how we met. A gun pointing at me and her refusing to speak. I scramble to my feet and pull her up as I go. Her wrist is in one hand, and my gun is in the other. I glance around, and I'm certain someone is bound to be watching us.

Motherfucking son of a goddamn bitch. There is.

"Carys, we have to go. We can't stay here."

"No shit. I *was* leaving. You're the one keeping me here."

"Yeah, well, Jacek is over there watching us."

Her gaze darts to him, then she spins on her heels. She could be a track star for how she moves. Definitely pushes me to my limits to sprint after her. I know I'm going in the opposite direction of my car, but there's no way in hell I'm leaving her on her own. I'm running, twisting to look behind me half the time. I'm trusting Carys won't let anybody shoot me from the front as I try to protect us from the back.

"This way." Command fills her voice.

It would be a sexy challenge if we weren't trying not to die. I follow her as she takes a sharp left around the corner of the building. We're running toward the SUVs, but the Polish targets occupy all the passengers' attention. Carys pulls a key fob from her pockets and clicks it. I hear a car unlock.

I wait. My eyes scan our surroundings to see if anybody hears the car and shifts their attention toward us. Thank God nobody does, at least not that I can see. At least we're out of Jacek's sight.

"Come on." She's impatient now.

I jog past her to get to the driver's side. There isn't enough time for her to argue with me as I pull the door open and slide in. She changes course and goes to the passenger side. I have the car on and in drive before she even closes the door. My family has always claimed I have a lead foot, and here's why.

I'm the one who usually drives one of the SUVs on missions. Maybe I was born with a lead foot, and that's why I'm a driver. Or maybe it's the other way around, and I got my lead foot from being behind the wheel. Either way, I get us out of there. I'll have to send one of the men for my car later, or I'll have to go back for it.

"Carys, you are going to give me some answers. What are you doing here?"

She again refuses to speak. I accept the silence for now. I take us to another part of Yonkers where I'm certain nobody will follow us. I pull into a parking lot behind a sporting goods store and turn off the engine. She'd dropped the fob into a cupholder, so I put it in my pocket. We're not going anywhere until she answers my question.

All I want is the answer to that one question. What is she doing here? I twist in my seat and reach across her as she moves to unfasten her seat belt. She tries to fight me, slapping my hand out of her way, but I grab both of her wrists and pin them to her lap. If she really tried hard enough, she could break free. I wouldn't do anything to add to her bruises, but she knows the struggle is futile. She'll wear herself out before I'll give in.

"Carys, just answer the one question. What were you doing there?"

"The same thing as you. Watching."

I was hoping for a more specific answer since that states the obvious. "Why were you watching?"

"You said you only had one question, and I answered that.

"Don't be obtuse."

"I'm not being obtuse. I'm being awkward."

The grin she shoots me is mirthless. She knows she's not humorous. She knows she's riling me up. She's goading me, and I don't know why other than she doesn't trust me, which—considering the circumstances—I suppose is a rather understandable reaction. After all, she's just watched Polish mobsters get shot up by Russian bratva while a senior leader of the Irish mob had his gun drawn, also watching them.

"Carys, you can guess why I'm here. I still can't guess why you are. Until you give me an answer to that question and any other ones I have, we're not going anywhere."

She pulls and yanks her hands as hard as she can from me. I release them, worried she's going to end up jabbing her elbow into the door. I'm only letting go because I want to avoid giving her more bruises. She glares at me yet again—or maybe it's still—as she reaches over and reclines the seat. She crosses her arms and closes her eyes.

You've got to be kidding me. Really? This is how she wants to handle it? All right. I recline my seat as well, cross my arms, and close my eyes.

"If I didn't know better, I would think you just snorted. But that couldn't possibly be true since you're ignoring me."

She says nothing in response to that comment, and I don't want to fight her any further. At least not right now. This isn't a battle I'm going to win, and it's going to be a war of attrition, anyway. I can wait her out because if I lose this early battle with too much of an obvious victory for her, then there's no chance I'll even the score.

I keep my eyes open just enough to see what's going on around us. There's no way in hell I would ever close my eyes and keep them shut somewhere so exposed. Especially not when we've just witnessed a shootout and not when Jacek Nowakowski saw us together. It's bad enough he saw me. It's bad enough he saw Carys. The fact we were together will make her a target for a man she doesn't need to meet.

Then again, maybe she has met him. She was there to observe just like me. She had to have known who she went to watch. Does she know him in person? I look at her, and my blood boils as I take in her bruises yet again for the umpteenth time, but something clicks.

"Jacek did that to you, didn't he?"

Her face shows no expression, no reaction. It's completely void of anything. She appears relaxed, and if I didn't know better, she'd look like a corpse.

"Carys, answer me. I am not joking. I'm not playing around anymore. Did Jacek Nowakowski beat the shite out of you? You better answer me because otherwise I will take you to my cousin's house. I will drop you off there. I will have them put you under lock and key, and I will go shoot that fecker."

She finally opens her eyes and turns her head to look at me.

"That would not be a wise choice, Shane. You and I both know that. You won't touch the second-in-command of the Polish mob. They might not have the power and influence you do, but you were there to observe what's going on with the Russians. You need to know what they're up to just as much as I do."

"I need. You want."

Her eyes narrow at me. "So you say."

She has one of the most expressive faces I've ever seen when she allows her emotions to show. When she doesn't, she's as stoic as anybody in my family—as any syndicate member. My grandfather, uncles, and dad trained me to be this way. Considering the shock I witnessed on Meredith's face, I doubt she knew someone trained her daughter to be so emotionless.

There're so many more questions with this woman than there ever are answers. We fall back into silence for the next twenty minutes. Shockingly, there's no tension between us. It's actually companionable silence, which is not something I expected. I finally feel like it's safe for us to go somewhere.

"Carys, tell me where I need to take you."

"Back to your car."

"I am not going back to get that until I know you're somewhere safe."

"The safest place I can be right now, Shane, is away from you. It's you in your car going wherever you need to go, and it's me in my car going where I need to go."

"No, I won't agree to that. I'm taking you to my cousin."

I have both hands resting casually on the steering wheel. My gun is in my lap. I'm unprepared for how fast she draws hers and puts the muzzle to my temple.

"You know I can take that from you if I want to, and all I'm going to end up doing is hurting you. We went through this the other night. I told you the last thing I want is to be the one who adds more bruises to you. This won't end well for you, Carys."

"You are going to unlock the door, Shane. You are going to let me out. You can do whatever the hell you want with my car, but I am not staying with you. It'd be better for both of us if you got out and let me drive away."

"You alone—knowing Jacek saw you—will not convince me of that."

I hear her take the safety off the gun. Now it's my turn to have my face completely neutral, devoid of emotion, but my heart is pounding. I truly believe she'll shoot me, and I have a healthy fear of death. It's what's kept me alive. I rest my hands where she can see them.

"All right, I'm unlocking the door."

My left hand moves to the button and pushes it. We both hear the doors click open.

"Get out, Shane."

My options are leaving her behind where she would have to walk or call a rideshare—there're certainly no taxis around here for her to hail—or I'm the one who walks or gets a rideshare. Obviously, I won't leave her completely defenseless. Her handgun won't do shite against a team of men carrying rifles.

I'm the one who's going to wait for someone to pick me up. My left hand pulls on the handle, and I ease the door open. I keep my hand where she can see it on the handle as my right hand moves to unfasten my seat belt.

"I'm not leaving my gun behind, so I'm going to reach for it."

"I know you are. That's why I already have my gun to your temple. I can pull the trigger faster than you can aim at me."

I'm in no mood to test that theory, so I let the belt go over my left arm and climb out of the car. I leave the door open, and Carys crawls across to the driver's seat.

"Give me the fob."

I hand it to her, and she shuts the door, locks it, then turns on the engine. She gives me one last look. As she pulls out of the spot, then pulls out of the parking lot, I watch her go.

I pull up the rideshare app and reserve a car to take me back to mine. Well, not exactly all the way back to my car. The last thing I need is for an Uber driver asking questions about why there are police at the scene, which I'm sure there inevitably are.

I have them drop me off a couple blocks away, and I walk over there, keeping my head on a swivel as I watch for anybody from the Polish mob or the Bratva lingering, keeping an eye on the scene. In particular, I'm wondering who Jacek left behind to wait for me. I'm certain he knows I didn't arrive with Carys, so I must have a car somewhere. I make it to the Corolla without incident, but my Spidey-senses are tingling. I know people are here. I just can't see them. I hit my cousin's contact on my phone as I pull out of the parking lot.

"Hey, Dillan. It was a total shitshow. The bratva showed up and rather than doing the deal with Bartlomiej, they attacked, shot up the place, took out several Poles and nearly got me."

I don't mention Carys yet. I'm not sure how I want to handle that piece of information. I need to think about it. If I tell Dillan, he's going to insist we tell Meredith. There's some reason Carys is living a double life. She was adamant about keeping her distance from her mom the other night, so she's obviously trying to protect her parents.

"You got out all right? Nothing happened to you?"

"Yeah, I did. Bartlomiej had already gotten pissed at Jacek and sent him out. He was at the car waiting on the other side of the building from where Bogdan and Niko pulled up. He saw me, so he knows I was there."

"How much do you think that's going to cost us with Bartlomiej?" It's a reasonable question. I don't have a solid answer now that Carys is a factor.

"I say beat the living crap out of him. Make him stay quiet about me being there, not the other way around."

"Well, in a perfect world, maybe we would do both, Shane, but you know that's not what's going to happen. You know he's going to tell his brother everything and then Bartlomiej is going to come knocking on the door with Jacek right behind him to back him up."

"I know, but maybe we can delay the inevitable for a little while. Let me deal with Jacek, see what he wants to do. Maybe we can keep it between the two of us."

"I'll let you try. But the moment he gives you any shite, you come to me, and we deal with it as a family."

We all learned a few years ago, anytime anyone in any of the syndicate families tries to do something on their own, it all goes to shite. We're all better off sticking together as a family and working as one unit.

"I will. Just give me a day or two to figure out what's going on."

"All right, two days, but I want to report in the morning, and I want a report tomorrow night."

"I know. I'll let you all know what's going on once I have more info, or I'll let you know I have nothing."

We hang up, and I pull up to the garage where we keep our fleet of SUVs and cars like the Corolla. They're not beater cars, but they're close to it. I hand over the keys to the guy on shift today and get into my car. I want to know where Carys went, so I pull up the app on my phone.

What she doesn't know is I dropped a tracker under her seat while she had her eyes closed. It's already pinging to let me know where she is. She's headed to Greenpoint, which has traditionally been an Eastern European—particularly Polish—neighborhood. Some gentrification has made it more hipster, but that's Bartlomiej's area. If she believes she's not done spying on them, she didn't learn her lesson.

I make my way over there and follow the signal to a parking structure where I see Carys getting out of her car. She must have driven around for a while before coming here, otherwise, she should have arrived at least twenty minutes ago. She's on the phone, but she's looking around. I pull up alongside her and roll down my window. She almost stumbles as she catches sight of me, barely catching herself before she trips.

I don't know who she's talking to. I can't hear what she's saying, but she gets off the phone in a hurry. She looks around and spots the nearby subway station. I'm already turning off the car as she makes a dash for it. I'm out of the car, right on her heels. She's down the escalator and through the turnstile faster than I expected. This woman definitely runs often, runs far, and runs fast. I'm right behind her, but she catches the subway right before it pulls out.

I'm stuck having to wait for the next one if I want to follow her, but the tracker was in her car, not on her, so I don't know where she is now. I don't know where she's going, but she's coming back here at some point. We're near here because this is where she left her car.

I head to a coffee shop that opened a few minutes ago and order a drink and hang out by the window where I can see the subway stop. It's two hours of me scrolling news articles and doing email before I see her reappear. Her dark head of hair is very distinct. There are few people with jet black hair and blue eyes. Once she's on my side of the street, I'm ready to leave and trail her. I know she's looking around, but I'm careful. She won't see me until I want her to.

She heads into a much nicer apartment building than I expected. For this area, it's definitely luxury. I watch her get on the elevator as I slip past the concierge who's busy talking to an older couple. I watch the elevator until it stops.

Now I know what floor she's on. I push the elevator button and wait for it, but it's taking too long. Somebody's going to notice. I glance around and spot the stairs. I take them up to the fourth floor. I'm not winded when I get where I'm going, but I'm definitely breathing a little harder. I run because it's good for me and necessary—as today proved—not because I enjoy it. I already did my cardio this morning, so I'm over this bullshit. I'm walking wherever I'm going next.

I hear a door close, so I make a beeline for it. I put my ear to it and detect some movement. I stand close enough to the peephole she won't see my face as I knock, not wanting her to refuse categorically because it's me. I don't want to be so loud as to draw attention from her neighbors, but I want it loud enough she knows I'm not giving up. I'm certain she knows it's me, but there's a long pause before I hear anything near the door. I wonder if she thinks it's Jacek instead of me.

"Carys, open the door. Let me in." I lean away from the peephole and give her a meaningful scowl.

I hear her unlock the door and open it just wide enough to hiss at me.

"You need to get the fuck out of here before somebody sees us together, which is already bad enough since Jacek did. You trying to get me killed?"

I press my hand against the door, putting some weight against it. I nudge it open. She doesn't have the weight to block me if I decide to open it all the way. She backs up, letting me in, and that's when I see the gun pointed at me for a fourth time.

"If you don't stop pointing that at me, I'm going to take it from you. It's not a toy."

"What about my reaction to you—all four times I've pointed it at you—makes you think I think this is a toy? Go, Shane. It's too dangerous for you to be here, and you're going to get me killed. People talk, and I'm certain somebody's seen you. They know you came up here to me. You've signed my death warrant."

"Why does it matter who sees you here? Who here would know I'm a mobster?"

She stares at my red hair as though I'm an idiot. I have to admit with this still being a Polish mob territory, having an Irish mobster show up is enough to make anybody talk. And with my red hair and green eyes, there are few people in any syndicate-affiliated neighborhood who don't know I'm an O'Rourke. They might not know which O'Rourke I am, but they know I'm one.

"Shane, please, I'm truly begging you. You have got to go. You said Jacek saw us. He's going to tell Bartlomiej he saw us together."

"If he saw us together, then he saw me run after you and tackle you. I didn't give you a choice."

"Yeah. And then he saw us talking, and he saw you following me with a gun drawn."

"Just like you were." I push the door shut behind me since—from the way Carys's gaze keeps darting to it—leaving it open makes her more anxious.

"But I also know you kept checking behind us rather than pointing it at me. You were protecting me, just like I was protecting you."

"Why does it matter what Jacek says about you? How does he even know who you are? Why were you near enough to him for him to attack you?" I can see that she's debating what she wants to tell me.

There's a definite look of dread that settles over her face.

"Wait here a moment. I need to get something. I need to show you why I was there and why you being in my apartment isn't a good idea for either of us."

She heads into her bedroom, leaving the door open so I can see what she's doing. She goes to her closet and uses a biometric pad and punch code to open a gun safe. She checks her weapon before she stores it, but I see her get something else out. My stomach drops to my toes. I don't know which one she's got, but there's no other reason for her to have a black leather badge holder.

She NYPD? FBI? ATF? Interpol? Who the fuck knows? She realizes I've spotted it in her hand, so she says nothing when she hands it over to me.

I flip it open.

DEA.

I saved a woman whose only job is to put somebody like me away for life.

Chapter Six

Carrie

"You're DEA."

Shane hasn't moved; he just stares at me. I doubt that he's ever at a loss for words, but he just continues to stare and blink. I can't tell if it's still shock keeping him quiet, or he's trying to contain his anger. His face is completely expressionless, and it makes it impossible for me to gauge, so I remain silent too. I want to believe he wouldn't explode and do anything to me, but I won't tempt fate by saying the wrong thing.

It takes at least a minute before he opens his mouth and starts demanding answers.

"You will tell me why you never admitted this when you had the chance. I asked you why many times, and you've never told me this."

"Can you blame me? How could you possibly think I would admit this to you? I don't want anybody in your family to know because it puts my mom in the middle of all of this. I had no idea she was your family's doctor. She doesn't know I work undercover. She knows I work for the DEA, but she doesn't know what I do. She thinks I'm in a more administrative position. How she thought she could work for you when her daughter works for a federal agency is something I still need to figure out. Shane, are you going to tell your entire family?"

He stands watching me for a moment before he shakes his head.

"No, I won't say anything. At least not yet. What are you doing involved with the Poles?"

I knew that question was coming. I have to give him enough of an answer to satisfy him. Otherwise, we're never going to move past this.

"As you probably figured out, I'm undercover. I have been for several months. Don't blow this for me, Shane. It's my job, and it could be my life. Even if it's not mine, it could be my mom's. It could be my dad's. You can't tell anybody. If you do, this is going to blow up in all our faces. How am I supposed to explain to my bosses a five-month investigation all went to shit because an Irish mob leader got involved?"

Now, anger registers on Shane's face. He takes four steps forward, forcing me to take four steps backward. I bump into the entryway table. His hand goes out to my waist, pulling me away, pulling me against his body.

God, how amazing that feels. I want to be a cat and rub myself all over him. He moves me around the piece of furniture, dropping my badge onto it, and backs me against a wall. His thigh goes between mine. The temptation to rub my pussy against him is almost all-consuming. He grabs my wrists and pins them over my head. He stares at me, and his gaze is just so fucking piercing. He has to know what it does to me when he doesn't speak. It's as powerful as when he demands answers from me. Hell, it's way more powerful.

His lips land on mine, and his kiss is punishing. He doesn't relent. He keeps my wrists in one hand while the other goes to my hip. He guides me to move along his thigh. He's hardly the first man I've done this with, but I've never been this aroused, this close to coming so fast. My body aches. My pussy burns to get off.

Once he's got me moving, his hand creeps up my ribs to my

breast. He massages it, squeezes it. His hand slips below my shirt and then down my bra. His skin against my skin makes me moan. The kiss continues. I don't know what to do, but I can't stop. I don't want to stop, so I don't. He pinches and twists my nipple, making me yelp, but I arch my back into it. He suspected I'm into kinky shit, but now he's going to know.

His hand glides out from under my shirt up to my throat, his hand wrapping around it. Only his thumb and index finger put any pressure on it. It's not breath play, and I'm not trapped by his hold. I could push away if I wanted to. That's always the way it is with Shane. I know if I really fought to get free, he wouldn't keep me trapped. But he knows I don't want to go when he touches me.

"Carrie, you have way more secrets than you're willing to share. And I know I won't get all of them out of you today, but it's obviously no secret we want each other."

He releases my wrists, but I keep them above my head for a moment. Then I drop my arms, push my hips forward to continue grinding against his thigh, and put my hands behind my back, crossing my wrists. He cocks an eyebrow, and it's about the sexiest thing I've ever seen in my entire life. His free hand slides down and under my shirt again, but now he gives my other breast attention.

"Carrie, you will admit you want me just as much as I want you. You will admit there's something between us that's been here since the very beginning. I might not have realized it, and maybe you did, but now there's no denying it."

That's the second time in a matter of seconds he's called me Carrie. I don't want to spoil it because I like it, so I don't point it out.

"Shane, obviously, I can't deny it. I'd be a liar if I did."

As soon as those words come out of my mouth, we both freeze. It's obvious I'm a liar. It's obvious all I've done is lie up to this point. But as he watches me, his hand on my throat loosens, and his thumb glides along my jaw. It's as though he understands why I've been lying. He probably does. He won't confront me about that. It leaves so many unasked questions, which means there are so many missing answers from both of us.

There's so much I want to ask him, but I know he can never tell me. Not on a regular day, and certainly not now that he knows I'm a federal agent. If I ask, he's going to assume I don't want to know it as Carrie, but as an agent clinging to the hopes that somehow I can fuck him. He'll assume I'm asking to collect information against him to turn over.

I don't expect answers, but I have my own burning questions.

"Why are you so involved in this? So invested in what happens to me? It goes beyond just my mom being an important person to your family. It goes beyond me just being a woman. You keep showing up at the same place and at the same time as me. You followed me to the subway station, then you were there when I came back. You followed me here. Why does it matter so much?"

Rather than answer me with words, his dexterous fingers unfasten my pants. As he pulls them wide, one hand slips down the front, and one slips down the back. His fingers dig into my ass as his other ones slide along my pussy, dipping between the lips. His grin is self-satisfied, but not quite smug.

Now there are flames dancing in his emerald eyes. He's letting me see that yes, this is lust, but somehow there's also something more. He must see the same thing in my eyes, because we're both leaning into the kiss, this time as equals. But it's not long before I submit all over again. I haven't moved my hands from behind my back. My wrists remain crossed, but my hands open and close.

As desire burns through me—even hotter than it did a moment ago—I'm positive I've never wanted a man as much as I do Shane, and he's barely touching me. Yes, his hand is on my ass, and yes, his thick fingers are digging into my cunt. It's not like he's sucking my tits and thrusting his dick into me. It's so much more than that. I'd give him everything in this moment. I'd tell him my deepest, darkest secrets if he offered to fuck me.

Fuck, if we keep going like this, that's exactly what's going to happen.

I shift my hands from behind my back to press against his

chest, but his fingers move faster. He rubs my clit in perfect rhythm to make me come. I can't stop the moan that rises from deep within my chest. I'm watching him just as he watches me when we pull away from the kiss. He doesn't stop working my body as though he's always possessed it.

Maybe he has. Maybe this is the way it was always supposed to be.

That is the most ridiculous bullshit, Carys. Nothing of this is meant to be. Nothing of this can come to anything.

He must know what I'm thinking because he leans in to kiss my neck right behind my ear. Then he whispers into my ear so softly it's a secret the rest of the world won't know. Just a brush of warm air.

"I'm going to make you come, *cailín*. You're going to do it because I'm going to make you. You know as well as I do this is exactly what we both need. Not just want but need. I need to get you off, and you need me to. We need each other right now."

"Shane, no."

Why can't I do anything to stop him beyond those two pathetic words? I feel my orgasm coming.

"Shane, please make me come... May I?... Please."

I'm desperate, and I'm begging. I'm contradicting myself. I don't even care how pathetic that must make me. I can't stop myself. I creep so close to my orgasm, but I try to keep it at bay until he answers.

"Yes, *cailín*. You can come. You can come because I'm making you. Because your pussy is mine."

Those possessive words push me over the edge. I've heard things like that before during dirty talk. Bartlomiej has told me as much before when he's tried to convince me to be more intimate. But never have I felt like letting a man mean it. Never have I considered it true.

I don't understand what's going on at all.

But my mind blanks to just the pleasure as I come all over his fingers. When I finally relax, he pulls his fingers from my pussy and licks them.

He fucking licks them. And not quickly. Not just, I'll clean them off. He relishes it. He taunts me with it.

I'm not to be outdone. I've been able to feel how hard he is since the minute our bodies touched. He was already hard for me. I felt his dick against the outside of my thigh as I rode his. Now I cup it, rubbing it slowly as my other hand reaches for his belt. He grabs my wrist and pushes it away, but he allows the one that's still on his dick to continue rubbing.

"Carrie, this isn't tit for tat. I didn't get you off, so you'll get me off. That was never the goal."

"The goal was to possess me without letting me have any of you."

Anger flares inside me. I feel like an idiot; regret courses through me. This time when his hand goes to my throat, he squeezes. Not enough to leave any marks, but enough that if I fight it, it'll hurt. He's not whispering beside my ear. There's no soft caress this time. No, this is a brutal mobster who's going to tell me exactly what he expects.

I'm here for that. I'm fucked-up—and as twisted as I am—I want his possessiveness. I don't want him to let go. I'm submitting willingly. Not like how I do during kinky sex, where it's submission just for the pleasure of what's going to happen next. Or submission because I like to be rough.

No, this is far deeper than that.

It scares the shit out of me.

"I did *not* do that to get something out of you, Carys, other than an orgasm." He snaps my name, and I don't like it after hearing him call me Carrie so many times in one conversation. "I did that because I want you, and I care about you. God help me, but I do. This is probably the most ridiculous and dangerous choice I've made in my entire life. And that's saying something, all things considered. I did it because I wanted to watch you. I wanted to push you over the edge. Yes, I wanted to know it was because of me. I wanted to own your orgasm. I want to own all the ones you have from now on. But I didn't do it to get you to get me off. And I didn't do it to get information from you. I didn't do it for any other reason other than I cannot get you off my mind. I've wondered what it would feel like to do that almost since the night I met you. Can you guess what a sick bastard I felt like for imagining you like this when I met you so battered and bruised?"

"Well, at least I know it wasn't all about my looks." I try for self-deprecating humor, but it falls flat.

His hand had eased its hold, but it squeezes again. Not enough to constrict my breathing, but enough to show his dominance. Then he lets go, lowering his hand.

"I want answers, and I will get them. But I won't ask for anything else today, beyond your safety. Jacek saw us. You can't be here. He'll have had you followed."

"If that's the case, you thought it was wise to lead him right to my door?"

"That look on his face wasn't just surprise that anybody was there. It wasn't just a mild observer wondering what was happening. He recognized you, Carrie. It wasn't just me. He recognized you, too. Why is that? You don't have to answer that question, but you know I'm thinking it. The only thing I'm going to ask of you now is that you come with me to a safe house. You cannot stay here."

He repeats himself, and in a normal situation, I would agree with him. But how is any of this even remotely close to normal? I believe him when he says it's about me, and it's not just about my mom and not just a courtesy he would offer to any unprotected woman. He's back to calling me by his pet name, and my mind quietens a decibel or two.

"There's no way I can leave here. If I do, my handlers will know. How am I supposed to explain why I'm in some safe house they'll either already know or can easily find out belongs to the Irish mob? I turned my tracker off the other night, but I can't do it again. That's not even remotely a possibility. Shane, I appreciate your offer. I appreciate you care and you want to help. But you know now I'm undercover. Leaving here isn't an option. If I do, it'll blow everything. My handlers will want to know why I'm at another location. Bartlomiej and Jacek will want to know why I'm not here. It opens up way more questions than just the ones you have. And not answering them is much higher stakes than anything you're asking me."

I watch his expression fully shutter, and it feels like a vise just tightened around my heart.

"Please, Shane, we can't do this again. You know I want to. I think you do too. I don't think it's just talk. I think you mean each word you say. But it's just not an option."

He stares at me, but he lets go. He pulls his hands away from where they rested on my hips. His expression is full of regret. I know he's letting me see that. He's not being emotionally detached like he could be. He's letting me in.

"All right, Carrie. For now, I'll back off. Not because I want to, and not because the DEA is now involved. I'll do it because you're asking. But you know it can't be as easy as me walking away. If nothing else, I've got to protect your parents just as much as I want to protect you."

For some reason, that stings. And not the good kind of burn from the ache in my pussy. It stings that he would equate the protection he wants to offer to me with the same he wants to offer my parents. I guess I wanted protecting me to mean more.

That is fucked-up. That is selfish. And it's irrational.

But it's a visceral emotional reaction. He cups my jaw and runs his thumb against it just like he did a few moments ago.

"Carrie, I'll protect your parents regardless of whether I want you, regardless of your job. Knowing who they are now—knowing what they mean to you—I'm doubly invested in making sure they're safe. This isn't just about them being Meredith and Rhys. They're your parents, Meredith and Rhys."

I listen to him, and I wonder if him saying they're my parents before naming them means something significant as opposed to him naming them and tacking on they're my parents.

Your parents, Meredith and Rhys. Not Meredith and Rhys, your parents.

I'm reading far too much into this.

And it's like a blast of icy air when he steps away from me. It's like he sucks every degree of heat out of me and this apartment. His expression still shows he regrets nothing can come of this. I let him see the same in my face. I know I could have an entirely blank expression just like he can. Who knows if it comes to him easily after years of training or whether it's intuitive?

It certainly took me a lot of practice to make my face devoid of emotion. It's a struggle now to only let it look like mild regret when what I'd really like to do is burst into tears and cling to him. But that's not what's going to happen.

He backs away another two steps before he turns around and walks to the door. I should stay right where I am until he closes the door behind him, then lock and bolt it. But I'm tethered to him, and I follow him like a lost little puppy, wishing he would pet me once or twice more.

His hand goes to the doorknob before he twists to look at me.

"*Cailín*, this isn't over by a long shot. Not what's going on around us and not what's going on between us."

He gives me a hard, fast kiss before he opens the door. I have no opportunity to ask what that means. He's called me it more than once. We both wait in silence, both counting to twenty before he leans his head out and counts to twenty again just like I do. Then he walks out and closes the door behind him.

If ever there was something so symbolic as the door shutting in my face. We've said this isn't over yet. Maybe the door will open again. I just don't know what will be on the other side.

It's been two days since the shootout. Two days since I've seen Shane face to face. But I sense him around me. I know he's there.

If I try to look him up, it'll ping on my computer unless I use my secure VPN again. And that's a risk because it takes my computer offline. I have to say I shut it down and restarted it for an update or just because I felt like it got too hot.

My handlers always frown at me. They know I'm bullshitting them when I say that, but they don't press the issue. I could ask my mom, but that would only raise every bit of suspicion she could possibly have. It won't help if she knows I'm here. The rest of his family probably already does. I wonder if he's going to tell my mom or if his brothers or cousins will.

That's been on a loop in my mind, along with a memory of the feel of his touch and the feel of touching him. The torturous bliss of it all.

But I have no choice now. I have to go to Bartlomiej. He texted me the night after the shootout. He was pissed. He wanted to know the answers, but he wanted to hear them in person. He expected me to see him the next morning. But something came up, and he said he would text me again when he was ready. He said I'd have thirty minutes to get to him; otherwise, there would be problems. I didn't get that text until five minutes ago.

I'm walking down the street to the subway station. I can feel the eyes on me. I know Shane is somewhere nearby. It's not paranoia when I also know Bartlomiej has men because I've spotted them. He doesn't trust me anymore. He always had men follow me when we first started dating. Then he eased off and only had men as my bodyguards sometimes. He's back to being suspicious, which tells me what kind of mood he'll be in when I arrive. I've already considered what I'm going to say to handle this. I take a deep breath as I step out of the subway.

It's no surprise Tymoteusz is waiting for me in a car. His expression tells me I'm in for Hurricane Bartek. He says nothing to me as I slide in the car. It's not like the last time I rode with him, and we chatted about everything and anything. When we pull into the garage, he looks over at me.

"Kaja, consider everything you're going to say. Jacek's been in his ear ever since you ran away with Shane. One wrong word, Kaja. One wrong word."

I nod and pull the handle open. I walk with dignity into the house, and I hear him in the living room. I'm sure Jacek is there even though I can't hear his voice. There are a few other men in the kitchen. I'm certain there are men patrolling the backyard, just like there are men out front. Tymoteusz is following behind me at a discreet distance.

"Bartek?"

I make sure my voice wavers. He spins around in anger, and I burst into tears. I run toward him and wrap my arms around his waist, clinging to him, sobbing. He hesitates for a moment, but then wraps his arms around me and coos to me just like he did the last time I cried after Jacek beat me.

"Bartek, I was so scared you'd refuse to see me. I didn't know if I should come anyway or whether it would make things worse. But I've never been so scared in my life as I was there. It was all because I was stupid and jealous and petty. I didn't trust you. I'm so, so sorry I didn't trust you. I'm so sorry."

I keep repeating that over and over again, hoping he'll start buying what I'm selling. He tries to push me back. His hold on my shoulders is gentle. He's not rejecting me. It's as though he wants to see my face, but I shake my head, burrowing into his chest, squeezing his waist even tighter. I whimper, and he goes back to stroking my hair. If it were anybody else—no, if it were Shane—this would be the most soothing thing in the world. If I were listening to Shane's heartbeat, if it was his hands holding me and caressing me, I would never be afraid of another thing in my life. I'm terrified right now.

"*Księżniczka*, I'm here now. It's going to be all right. We'll talk about it."

I rear back and let him see fear in my eyes as I shake my head. I make myself tremble, which isn't easy because I don't want to make it look pretend. I've practiced making my lower lip tremble for times exactly like this. I must be getting it right because surprise registers on Bartlomiej's face. Then there's a flash of anger before he looks at me with the same softness he usually does.

"Oh, Kaja, I would never hurt you. I just want to talk in private." He leans forward to whisper in my ear. "I just want to hold you on my lap and know you're safe. You have no idea how terrified I was."

I nod. He slides his hand into mine. I half expect him to lead us to his bedroom, but he takes me to his office instead. Fear spikes through me again, and I hesitate as he opens the door. He looks back at me and offers me a smile.

"Sweet one, you really believe I'm going to kill you, don't you?"

I swallow, but I don't make a sound. I just keep looking afraid. I'm far more afraid than I want to admit because there is a good likelihood I'm not coming out of here alive. He lets go of my hand. I take a step back, but he slips his arm around me and guides me into his office. When he shuts the door, he presses me against the wall and practically devours me. But it's not like when Shane kissed me. It doesn't get the same natural reaction out of me.

I have to force myself to kiss him back. His kiss is possessive, but I sense something else. His hands run over me as though he's checking to make sure I'm really here. As though he wants to make sure I'm really okay. Maybe I will survive this after all, but only if I play along. If his emotions are this intense, then they could swing in the opposite direction if I don't do what he wants.

He pulls away and scoops me into his arms and carries me to the sofa. He sits down and cradles me against him. He says nothing. He just keeps kissing my temple and stroking my hair. I'm going to let him lead. I'm going to give him some control. I don't want to do anything to change the tone.

"Kaja, what do you mean you were jealous? What were you doing there? Jacek told me you were spying on us."

"I was." I infuse remorse into my tone. "But it's not because of whatever Jacek told you. I thought you were meeting another woman. I thought that's why you were away for so long. That because you were with somebody else, you let what happened with Jacek happen. He believes anybody who isn't in your family is out to get you. He believes somehow I wanted to hurt you. But all I want is to know we're okay. I had this whole thing worked out in my head. You were going to meet some other woman, and you want to be with her. That you are with her, and I'm the one you see on the side. I don't know if that makes sense now, but in the moment, I was so certain of it."

"You thought I was having some illicit rendezvous at a lumberyard?"

"It was so confusing to me. I didn't know what to believe. I was questioning myself. But again, I was so jealous. It's never been like that before. Bartek, I've never felt this way before. That's why I feel so miserable. It makes me look crazy. I am crazy."

I let tears stream down my face again, and he wipes them away with care that surprises even me. It's more tender than he's ever been.

"Kaja, I've told you I love you. When are you going to believe that? When are you going to know there's nothing I wouldn't do for you? I wish you would believe that. What would it take? Do you want to move in? Do you want to travel with me? Do you want us to get married?"

Whoa. This is moving way too fast.

"Bartek, you know I can't move in with you. It's bad enough I spend nights here and you spend some at my place, too. What would our priest think if he found out? All of your men will think I'm an even bigger whore than they already do. Jacek will believe everything he's been accusing me of. He'll really try to kill me."

I sniffle while I watch him. He doesn't deny Jacek wants to kill me. He doesn't deny what other people will think. He would move me in here against everybody else's wishes or thoughts. Does that mean he really believes he loves me that much? Or is he so narcissistic he believes he's untouchable? I don't know. Maybe it's even a combination of both. He doesn't press the issue again about where our relationship stands. Instead, he moves on to the questions I already expected.

"Kaja, why were you carrying a gun?"

"Because I didn't know what I was going to see. I didn't take it to shoot her. That wasn't it. I guess a reasonable part of me knew what I was doing was stupid and dangerous. I knew I should take some way to defend myself. I guess it was a good thing I did. I mean, I didn't have to shoot. But it certainly got a lot more dangerous than I expected."

I sniffle for effect. His hand on my hip tightens, but it's not with anger. It's as though he can protect me right now from the ghosts of that meeting.

"How did you get that gun?"

"I bought it when I moved to the city before I knew you. I knew I was going to live on my own in a neighborhood known for the Polish mob. I didn't know what to expect."

"I take it it's not licensed."

"If the cops had caught me..."

I let that thought trail off. He responds immediately.

"Nothing would have happened to you. I would have known immediately. You wouldn't have even made it to a police station. You would be with me like this. Just where you belong."

I nod, allowing more tears to dribble down my cheeks. He keeps wiping them away. Do they give Oscars to undercover agents? This is a recurring serial show. Maybe it's a daytime Emmy. I wait for the next inevitable question.

"Why did you go with Shane? Jacek said he saw you with him."

"I didn't know who he was until after we stopped running. I guess he thought I was a weird man or something because he chased me first and knocked me to the ground."

Before Bartek gets upset—even more upset—I rush to clarify.

"I'm positive he didn't know who I was when he did it. He kept insisting he had to get me to safety. How could I possibly turn that down? He wasn't shooting at anybody in the lumberyard. Nobody in the lumberyard was shooting at him. I knew whoever he was, he was a man spying on you. But he seemed like my safest bet. I didn't know where Jacek went. I wasn't looking in that direction. I was looking at the lumberyard. I was looking in front of me. All I wanted to do was get away, and that's what I did."

"Yeah, and you got in a car with him. Jacek saw all of that." Bartek's temper is flaring.

"I know." I aim to sound dejected. "And that was probably just as stupid as going there in the first place. But you're you, and I'm me. I don't know if you can truly understand just how terrifying that was, and how all I wanted to do was survive to get to you. I know getting in that car with him meant I had just as great a chance of dying as I did getting to you. But that need to be here was so much stronger. I feel like such a fool. Can you ever forgive me? Forgive me for doubting you. Forgive me for not trusting you. Forgive me for being—"

My face crumples again as more tears come, and I sob. He no longer looks doubtful, but he is a sociopath. I might pretend because it's my job, but he can hide his emotions or make them appear however he wants with no thought. I've seen him do it. He just drops into whatever persona he believes he has to be.

"Nothing is going to happen. It's all forgiven already. I was away from you the last two days because I was sorting out that mess. It wasn't me avoiding you because I was angry. I was avoiding you only to keep you safe. To not have you anywhere near me after what just happened. But you're here now. You're with me, and I don't want you to go anywhere. At least not for today, and I want you to stay with me tonight."

I nod my head and lean against his chest again, but I continue to cry.

"Kaja, I just want to hold you. I won't ask anything else of you. Just be near me. Don't be out of my reach. At least not until morning."

Chapter Seven

Shane

That is not even remotely how I pictured today would go. I certainly never imagined when I went to eavesdrop, I would find the most frustrating woman I have ever met hanging out there, too. I did *not* expect to chase after her. I did *not* expect to kiss her and make her come. The only thing I expected was for an inevitable shitshow at the meeting because those almost never go smoothly. A shootout was the only thing I could have fathomed.

Instead, I wind up spending half the morning following Carrie—I noticed that's how I think of her now—and then going into her apartment and kissing her. What the fuck possessed me to do that? But nothing I said was untrue. I'm definitely attracted to her, and I definitely care what happens to her. But there are just too many secrets and too many lies from her. I understand why she has to tell some of these lies, why she has to keep some of these secrets. I definitely didn't picture her being a DEA agent.

And that complicates the hell out of everything. Not whether I could date her or even have her as a fuck buddy—I'm not interested in dating a woman who picks an argument at every corner. It complicates things because everybody in my family could be on death row if she says the wrong thing to the right people. I don't know if I can trust her with who my family is. The only reason she might be trustworthy is because her mom is in the thick of it. Any investigation into us could lead to Meredith, even though we've all done our best to keep her out of sight and out of mind.

There's no guarantee a little digging for a court case wouldn't bring her name up. It leaves me with more questions than answers, which is a recurring theme with Carrie. It's a thought I have over and over again. Frankly, it's getting frustrating and old to always think that. But regardless of how I feel about her, she's now become a major problem—hindrance—pain in my arse. I don't even know how to describe what she is.

But I know I'd like to fuck her brains out. Fuck. My cock swells every time I think of her, now that I know what she feels like. If only we could get along.

I've got to figure out what to tell my family about all of this. I can't keep it a secret for much longer, if for no other reason than keeping secrets would only make me guilty of the very things that bother me most about Carrie. But I don't want everybody losing their fucking minds over this until I can give them some more concrete explanations. They're going to have all the questions I do, and probably a few dozen more, since there're five of them to account to. What the fuck did I get myself into?

It's been almost a week of following Carrie around. It's obvious she must make it look like she works from home, since she rarely goes out. Her face's healed enough that she could appear at work without too many questions. But she goes next to nowhere. The few times she has, she's tried to give me the slip. I'm positive she knows I'm out there watching her. She just hasn't spotted me yet.

I've been able to keep track of her, though. Right now, I'm pulling into the grocery store parking lot four lanes over from her. She's not shopping in her neighborhood, which makes me wonder who she's trying to avoid. Is it Jacek, Bartlomiej, or somebody else, or a whole slew of people?

You rarely drive this far to this kind of grocery store just for the sake of coupon deals or quality. I give her space as she gathers a shopping cart and starts making her way through the aisles. I've grabbed one, and inevitably, I'll have to buy shite I don't need and don't want. Otherwise, it'll look strange for me to be walking around the grocery store without a single thing in my hands. The key will be to only buy a few things so I can go through the express lane and finish checking out before her. If I don't finish before her, she really will give me the slip.

I watch the things she purchases. They're all in a quantity for one. Nothing makes me think she lives with anybody else or frequently has anybody else over. She's undercover, but that doesn't mean she isn't in a relationship of some sort for the case, whether it's a friendship, a romantic one, or a situationship. She's not having people visit her, at least not for meals.

It's a quiet day in the store. When we get to the cereal aisle, I peek down the ones on either side to make sure there's next to nobody in either. This may be a stupid decision, but I'm going to confront her because this is as neutral a spot as we're probably going to find.

I inch my cart closer to her as she pulls something down from the top shelf. She senses me and looks to her right; her scowl etched so deeply into her face I fear it might stick that way.

"Shane, not here, not now."

"Good morning to you, too."

"I'm serious. I didn't want you in my apartment, and I don't want you here."

"Oh, but I think you did want me in your apartment, and I think you would want me here if you could. Actually, I think you do want me. We just can't."

"Stop. Somebody could hear you."

"I'm not talking that loud. Even if they hear my voice, they wouldn't understand what I'm saying."

"Oh, yes, they would."

"That's why I'm keeping my voice down."

"Shane, please. You have got to stop approaching me. You know what I'm doing. You're going to blow it all for me."

"And that undercover work is exactly the kind that gathers information to put my family away. So, if you think for even a moment I'm going to ignore what I found out and let you go on your merry little way, you are so gravely mistaken you can't even imagine the outcome."

She stiffens, and I hope she hears the threat and the annoyance in my voice because I'm feeling it. We could have a quick conversation and be done with it.

"Are you threatening me?"

"Not at all, *cailín*. It's more a promise, if you will."

"A promise? Is that what you think that is?"

She scoffs at me, turns back to the box of cereal she reached for. She drops it in her cart and turns around, giving me her back. I push my cart out of the way and snag my arm around her waist, pulling her back against me, moving my hand to just rest on her waist.

"Don't walk away from me, *cailín*. We still have a lot more to discuss. Whether it's here or somewhere else, you are going to give me answers. Do people think you work from home?"

She nods. Immediately, her head turns to look behind me.

"Are you staying home so much because of your bruises? Or is that your natural routine?"

"I knew you were following me. Look, anything I could say that involves your family would directly involve my mom. I have no reason to do that. You will stay out of any reports I make. But you're making it fucking difficult. If people keep seeing us together, you're going to make Bartlomiej question me because it's inevitable it'll get back to him.

"Why is that? Why does he take such an interest in what you do or don't do or who you do or don't speak to?"

"Because I'm a woman living in his community. He knows everything about everybody. It's how he remains in control."

"Is he extorting you?"

My voice hardens, not liking the idea that anybody intimidates her. Well, doesn't that make me the perfect hypocrite? I'm the pot calling the kettle black because I know part of what I'm doing is trying to intimidate her. It feels shitty to know it, but if she won't give me an inch, I'm going to push her a mile.

"No, he's not. I was new to the neighborhood when I moved in. Nobody there knew me, and I had no one to vouch for me. He got suspicious."

"Obviously, rightly so. You've come to a grocery store that's well out of his territory. Who do you think will see us and report it to him unless you're being followed by his men, too? And if you are, why?"

"Shane, there are eyes and ears everywhere. There are no boundaries to where people connected to a syndicate live. If it's not Bartlomiej, then it'll be someone else. Someone could see us and report it to the Mexicans, the Italians, the Colombians, the Russians, anybody. This is not wise."

I squeeze her waist and put my lips to her ears. "Then meet me somewhere. Meet me, explain what's going on, and then I'll leave you alone."

She scoffs at that too, giving me a look as though I'm an idiot. Obviously, she doesn't trust I'm telling the truth about leaving her alone. She's not wrong. I probably won't, but at least with some answers, I won't feel so eager to chase her down.

"Carrie, the longer you stall, the more evasive you are, the more determined I will be."

"As though I don't know that, but that's still... I'm not giving in to you. Shane, I told you the night we met I wouldn't be bullied a second time."

My fingers dig into her waist. "You really equate my words to his fist? Are you trying to imply you think I'll beat you for not answering my questions?"

"No, I don't think you'd ever lay a hand on me in violence. I never thought that. You could have more than once. All four times I put a gun to you, you could have. But I think you're just as dangerous to me as Jacek or any other syndicate man. I think you're just as capable and likely to get me killed as any of them. So, back off, Shane."

She keeps looking around as though she expects somebody to see us. Why is that? I just wish I could get answers to even the simplest of questions.

"I get what your job is, but I also know you rarely work alone in situations like this. How often do you see your handlers?"

She tenses again and gives me a mutinous glare over her shoulder. Just as she turns back around, somebody else's cart appears at the end of the aisle. She moves away from me, and I don't stop her. I expect her to turn toward the shelf and continue our conversation of sorts. Anybody could believe we're just a couple grocery shopping together. However, she immediately walks away. She doesn't acknowledge the person she passes beyond a flash of a smile. He looks familiar, but I don't place him right away.

I wait a couple minutes before I continue to follow her. She pretends as though I'm not her shadow. She doesn't acknowledge me again even as we walk out to the parking lot. It's for the best now that we really are in public again.

I've completely made a mess of today. I don't know what I was thinking. This was a shitshow of my own making. I didn't go in there with a proper plan or a task. I just wanted to know the same things as I did before. What the hell is wrong with me? There's no excuse for screwing the pooch on this one.

It dawns on me as I pull out of the parking lot. I know the man who appeared in the same aisle as us. He's one of Bartlomiej's bodyguards. A pretty senior one at that. I doubt there's a coincidence the three of us were at the same grocery store at the same time. It certainly wasn't a coincidence I was there. I doubt it was a coincidence the two of them were there.

Is he her bodyguard? Or is he meant to just follow her? Did exposing his presence serve as a threat to her? Or was it a reassurance because he got impatient waiting for her to leave that aisle? I don't have the answers to these questions that swirl in my mind.

I bought nothing perishable, so I park and watch her building again. I twist and lean to see who else is staking out her place. I've spotted some of Bartlomiej's men before, but they've never been as obvious as the one in the store.

She took a ride share to get back to her place. Why doesn't she just use her car? I know she has one. That makes me more suspicious. Since she's got plenty of grocery bags, she uses one of those metal folding carts like little old women do. She stacks her bags inside it to get up to her apartment. It would be so much easier if she drove her own car. It makes me think she doesn't want anyone who's following her to know she has her own vehicle.

Is she playing poor little girl who can't afford a car? Is she hiding it for a fast getaway? What role does she play in this community?

That's the first thing—or rather the next thing I need to know.

"Shane, what's been going on with you?"

I look over at Finn. I'm sitting in his living room with him, Sean, Seamus, and Cormac. Dillan's not here because he's having dinner with his in-laws in Connecticut.

"Nothing.

"Well, that's a bunch of bullshit." Sean jumps in, taking our brother's side. "You've been off everybody's radar for nearly three weeks. Ever since the incident with Meredith's daughter at the construction site. You assigned her and Meredith a detail, but almost immediately canceled hers, but you still have the one for Meredith."

"What's the deal? Since you told us she didn't go to Pittsburgh, I can only assume you've made yourself her personal detail."

I look over at Finn, trying to decide whether he's asking me as my big brother or as the second-in-command in our family.

Our dad and uncles retired if there is such a thing. The family always intended for Dillan to inherit the role of our boss from our Uncle Donovan, who was our mom and aunts' brother. There were some hiccups along the way between when the bratva killed Uncle Donovan and when Dillan assumed his role.

But now he's in charge, even though our dad and uncles are young enough for one of them to fulfill the mob boss role. They've put in their time, certainly their blood, sweat, and everybody's tears. They still go on missions with us when we need them or when they want to show the world we always stand as a united family. So that's how Finn, who used to be just our accountant, is also second-in-command.

He obviously reads my mind, and there are so many times where it's more like Finn, Sean, and I are triplets rather than Sean and I being twins. I'm just as close to Finn as I am to Sean. However, there are some things—some genetically ingrained things—Sean and I share I guess we can't with Finn.

"Shane, I'm asking first and foremost as your brother. You're not generally secretive. You don't go off and do things on your own without an explanation. You've asked us to trust you, and we do, but I'm worried about you. As for the second, I need to know what one of my men is doing when he's unaccounted for."

"Are you asking this on your own? Or did Dillan put you up to it, and you just so happen to also have your brother involved?"

His face darkens into a thunder cloud, and I've offended him. "There's no just so happens that I care. I always care. That's a dick thing to say. Yeah, Dillan's been asking me—been asking all of us—if we know what you're up to, and none of us has an answer. So, I decided I would bring it up to you. I just decided a moment ago. It's not like we're all sitting here, so I can confront you. It's not a fecking intervention. I want to know what my younger brother is doing, and I want to make sure my man is safe."

"You only wish for my safety as some little worker bee, not as your brother."

I am way too testy about this. There's no reason for me to be so confrontational, but I'm frustrated. It's been another three days of watching Carrie. It seems like things keep happening in sets of three days. What the fuck is that? Does that have meaning, or am I just reading symbolism into nothing?

"Why are you being like this, Shane?" I look over at Sean.

I want to snap at him and tell him to mind his own business. The problem is, this isn't just my business, and I know that. I don't know if the reason I'm so testy is that I don't feel like I have control over the situation. It's not entirely that I want to control Carrie herself, but nothing about it feels right. Not having control usually means something is going to go wrong. I guess I am a control freak in a lot of ways. But I have to give my family something.

"Things with Carys are more complicated than they seem. I don't know everything yet, but—" Oh, God, I have to confess who she is. "—she's a DEA agent."

I let that hang in the air as four sets of eyes stare at me as though I've lost my ever-loving mind. I very well may have. It's Cormac who comes out of his stupor first.

"She's a federal agent? You didn't think we should know about that the moment you found out? What the feck, Shane?" He's practically yelling by the time he stops speaking. I expected it, whether it was from him or somebody else.

"What I'm thinking is discretion is the better part of valor, and that we don't need a whole bunch of people knowing that yet and drawing more attention to her. She's undercover, and I'm slowly unearthing things about her mission. I don't want to bring it to everybody's attention if I don't have enough information to clue us in."

"Or you could feed us each bit you have as it comes along." Seamus shrugs.

"I just don't want anybody to go half-cocked into this and ruin her investigation, then we end up forcing her hand where she has to include us in any reports she files."

"And you think dealing with this single-handedly is going to avoid that? That you're the best person for this?" Finn crosses his arms even though he's sitting on a sofa. He gives me the same mulish look he has my entire life.

"I think too many hands in the cookie jar just wind up crumbling them all." Shitty metaphor, but it'll do.

"I think there's something more personal at stake."

My head whips around to my twin, and I glare at him. He knows exactly what I'm thinking. I can tell the moment he decides to lay off. We don't have to say anything. That's part of the whole twin deal.

My brothers and cousins stare at me. It's not to intimidate me. It's out of frustration, but they know I'm done talking. They've gotten as much out of me as they're going to get, and that irritates them. That's just too bad.

"Look, I know this isn't how we normally do things. And I know when any of us think we can do a job on our own, somehow it goes to shite. I need you to trust me on this. If anyone gets wind of all of us being involved, we're going to risk our lives and Carys's too, and we're going to risk finding out nothing. Do you want to be the reason something happens to Meredith's daughter? Do you want to be the reason the investigation goes to shite, and they bring somebody else in who includes us in it? It's better off if there's only one of us involved. She already knows and trusts me. Mostly."

I know that's a reasonable explanation. That doesn't stop Sean looking at me, knowing there's more. I haven't told him anything. He just understands. But it'll be about a heartbeat before Finn and the others figure it out too: there's a woman involved, and I'm way too attracted to her.

"What else is going on?" I steer the conversation away from me onto anything but me.

"What's the deal with those construction sites?"

Well, shite.

Finn's question doesn't steer it away from me. At least it's not about Carrie anymore.

"We had a slowdown thanks to Pablo interfering as usual. The fucker just can't mind his own business."

Pablo Diaz is second-in-command of the Colombian Cartel. He's in the same position Dillan was as a nephew set to inherit. Enrique has no children. His oldest nephew, Pablo, will take over the reins when the time comes. Enrique's so fucking stubborn and wily, he'll probably outlive us all even if he's the one with the most targets on his back. Nothing comes in or out of the Americas without him knowing because most of our producers are in Latin America.

"What's Pablo done now?" Seamus demands.

There's no love lost between the two of them because of shite that went down most recently with his wife, Tiernan, while they were dating.

"You know him. He just always has to be up everybody's arse about everything. He doesn't like that my mall construction is moving faster than his. He had a bunch of guys call out sick, and he blames me—" I look over at Cormac— "when he should blame you."

"What? I just did what I was told to do."

Seamus and Cormac always stayed out of trouble the longest. They flew under our parents' radar the most. But Dillan's little sister, Colleen, was the ringleader. She got us in and out of trouble. When she couldn't get us out of trouble, our parents doled out punishments to all of us, but Cormac and Seamus always got off with the lightest. With them, she meted out her own type of justice when we were alone. She was the sweetest little dictator you could ever meet. She told you what to do with ponytails and a smile. You couldn't not go along with her even if you knew nothing but trouble lay ahead of you.

"I told you to bribe some of his guys, not his entire work crew. And one guy went to Pablo and squealed. He told Pablo he'd have to pay the douche double to get him back on the site. Needless to say, he's not alive anymore, but it means Pablo knows all about it and doesn't think it's Niko anymore."

Niko no longer handles their construction projects. Christina, his younger brother Bogdan's wife, does, but she's about to give birth to their second kid any day now. Niko's taken over. It's been a while since we've fucked around with Kutsenko Partners' construction projects because Christina scares us more than all of those shitbag men combined. She's got way more connections than we do, so she can sink an entire project with one word to the right person in the city planner's office where she used to work.

We have no issues fucking around with the Cartel's and the Mafia's projects. So that's why we went after Pablo. Partly as retribution and partly to make sure our build finishes first. We can make a point of that when we pitch to other companies for other projects. That's just how it works.

It's tit for tat with everything in our life. When we gain something, we expect it to be taken away. It's just a question of who's doing the taking now. None of us can kill each other because of our senior roles in the families. It would upset the balance. However, there're times where we're in situations where it truly is life or death. When that happens, all rules are gone. You shoot to live because nobody wants to die.

"Well, it's going to cost us more than I wanted to spend."

Finn's our accountant and notoriously tight-fisted. He has a conniption if he can't account for everything down to the last five pennies. Even that much discrepancy puts him in a snit.

"I know what you're thinking." Finn snaps at me, which makes me shrug.

"Huh? Gotta spend money to make money." I grin at him, and he flicks me off. I'm extremely ready to stop being the center of attention. "How's Ally doing?"

Finn immediately relaxes, and a huge smile spreads across his face. From the way everyone's marrying off, you'd never imagine none of us in the syndicates planned to get married, never planned to have kids, never wanted to pass this family business along to the next generation. Slowly, each of us is settling into our version of domestic tranquility and having kids.

Finn couldn't be more ecstatic. "She's doing well. She doesn't always feel so great. Her emotions are kinda supercharged. Days at work that would normally be hard are now really a struggle. But she loves what she does, and she knows how important her work is. By the end of the day—even though she might cry now—she's glad she can help."

My sister-in-law is a neonatologist, so I can imagine how

working with sick babies must be rough for her. She sees the worst of the worst and tries to cure them. Being pregnant and confronted every day with the tragic things that could happen would be difficult on anybody. Seeing it when you're growing your own baby? That's what I can't fathom.

"Any morning sickness?" Sean jumps in and makes me cock an eyebrow as I look at him. It's not like any of us are ignorant to those sorts of things, but something in his tone makes me wonder. He shakes his head at me.

"No, Lina's not pregnant. Just wondering for the sake of wondering."

Finn's still smiling, but it dims a little. "Yeah, some mornings are really rough for her, and there's been several times at work where procedures that normally never bothered her do now. Whether it's the smell or the sight, it just turns her stomach over. Luckily, she's only thrown up a couple times. At least that I know of. She might not tell me everything.

Finn shoots us a rueful expression. We all know if Ally told him the full extent of how bad she might feel, he would flip out. We try to solve it all, but morning sickness, I assume, is one of those things that's generally only solved with time.

We're all a bit of control freaks because that's how we've stayed alive. I know from watching my own parents and aunts and uncles, and now my brothers and cousins, being unable to fully protect and keep the person you love most well is something unbearable to men who are usually in control.

It makes me think of Carrie again. I worry about her. That said, I think a lot of it is still my ego. It's not by any stretch love. She irritates me too much for that.

The rest of the evening progresses with all of us watching a rugby match. That's our thing in our family. We may have all played separate sports, but collectively, rugby is what we most like to watch and what we all play. You won't find anyone more competitive than my mom and aunts. They'll knock you on your arse, run right over you, score the point, then come back and help you up with a smile. It's rather endearing I suppose.

I'm up with the roosters since I know Carrie goes for early morning runs. I've followed her in my car, but this time I intend to meet her on the trail. She's been going the same way every morning, which in and of itself is an issue. It's too predictable. She should know that. I'm sure she does. She's got to be doing it for a reason.

I park at the opposite end of the trail from where she enters and time it so we'll meet in a spot that's secluded. No one will see us when I stop her. She recognizes me before I recognize her. She comes around a corner and immediately spins on her heels and starts running faster. I take off after her. Blessedly, I've got longer legs than she does. Otherwise, I wouldn't be able to keep up. She runs like a fucking gazelle.

"Carrie, stop." I snag her shirt sleeve.

"Shane, how would you feel if I wouldn't leave you the fuck alone after you told me to? It's like *Single White Female*, except you're a guy fucking stalking me."

I wait for her to stop hissing at me, then pull her off the trail and out of sight. This way, anybody going past won't notice us since we're keeping our voices down.

"Carrie, this all ends when you give me some explanations. I saw you going over to Bartlomiej's the last two days. You were there for a few hours before you left. I know you're staking him out, but who is he to you? Or better yet, who are you to him?"

"Shane, I work for him. As far as he knows, I do some stuff for his legal businesses, like social media management. Every once in a while, I go over there. I walk him through some campaigns. Then I leave."

"And it really takes you five or six hours to do that? Because I know that's how long you stayed two days ago."

She scowls at me. I think she'd throat punch me if she could. "You are going to blow everything if they see some car parked close enough for you to watch me. They'll see you're in it."

"Yeah, that would happen except I set up a dash cam and watch the feed from four blocks away."

That makes her pause and consider it. "Well, I can admit that's a good idea. It should be a pretty obvious surveillance tactic, but I've never used it. What kind of camera do you have?"

"I'll answer that after you answer my questions. You're not deflecting, Carrie. I'm more than happy to tell you what equipment I use, but I don't buy for a second you're some social media manager who goes over to her boss's house to train him on Facebook for five hours. Seriously, nothing would make me happier than to walk away. Let you do you and let me do me. Until I can be positive none of this is going to blow back on my family, I'm not giving in. You've got to give me something.

"Or you could try trusting me."

I stifle a laugh that comes out as a throat clearing. "You don't trust me, otherwise, you'd explain things."

"Or, Shane, maybe this isn't about you, and maybe I'd just like to keep my job and my head on my shoulders. Have you thought about that as a possibility?"

"Of course I have. That's why this could all be over. We could go on our merry little way once you tell me the truth."

The way she looks at me—I can guess what she's thinking.

"Carrie, what happened in your apartment didn't happen because I want to coerce information out of you. That was entirely different, and we both know it. I didn't kiss you or touch you to manipulate you. It's obvious we're attracted to one another, even if we don't get along. Even if it's something we shouldn't feel, we do. But that was then. This is now. We both have a job to do."

"How very convenient for you, Shane, to just explain that away as though we're just supposed to pick things up where we left off before that. Well, you're right. I don't trust you, and I don't want you. It was merely physical attraction. I think you believed you could get me on the hook to make me tell you whatever you want to know as though I'm some poor little infatuated middle school girl. I'm not. It felt good, and I enjoyed it, but it doesn't change my mind.

"I didn't expect it to. All I want is to ensure my family is safe. I don't trust Bartlomiej at all, so I don't think you're safe."

"Of course, I'm not safe. What part of being undercover ever is? Shane—"

She doesn't have a chance to finish speaking as men swarm toward us. There're three coming from each direction, and Jacek is leading the charge from the right. She and I both pull guns. I assumed she carried hers under the sweatshirt she ties around her waist when she runs. I rarely leave home without mine.

The Poles are already opening fire on us. She takes on the men coming from the right, and I take on the ones coming from the left. We have the advantage of cover while they're exposed. One by one, we pick them off until Jacek is the last one standing.

I watch Carrie. It's not hesitation that allows Jacek to get closer. She's making sure he's as easy a target as possible. She shoots, and the first bullet goes through his gut. The second goes into his shoulder. It's not enough to kill him on sight, but with none of his men around to call for help, he'll bleed out. However, if he lives, he'll tell Bartlomiej who shot him.

"Carrie, you need to go. I doubt these are the only men here. There're bound to be more to come, but right now there's no one to collect his body, so take advantage of that and go. Run."

"You're going to stay behind to watch what happens?"

"Yes. I'll stay to make sure whoever comes thinks it was me. You don't need that target on you. It'll only blow up your investigation. You don't need to explain to your agency why you murdered him."

Chapter Eight

Carrie

"Murder?"

"Yes, murder. Carrie, look at the scene. I know you waited for him to get closer to get the clear shot. Maybe you even wanted him to see it was you, but what it's going to look like to your investigators and his men is that you murdered him, shooting him in cold blood before his men could get to him.

"What are you doing?"

"Texting our cleaners."

"Cleaners?" My brow furrows, then my eyebrows shoot straight up. The team that'll come in and remove any sign of a crime scene at all. They'll clean up all the bio-waste, all the shell casings. Anything that could lead law enforcement to Shane's family. I guess it shouldn't surprise me he has them on speed dial. He pauses as we both hear sirens and angry voices.

"Carrie, there's no time left. Go. I've got this."

"I am *not* leaving you on your own to deal with this."

"It would be so much better if you did. Which one of the two of us has been in this position before? We both know the answer to that."

It's against my better judgment, but I listen to him and turn in the direction I came from, which is the opposite direction of the sirens and the angry voices. I get far enough down the path to duck out of sight, but still see what's going on. Shane's got his gun raised and pointing again at the oncoming voices.

"Which O'Rourke are you?"

Oh, fuck me in the ass with a pogo stick. It's Tymoteusz. I definitely can't leave Shane now. I don't know if he'll need me, but there's a good chance he will. I don't want to reveal myself, but I don't want him getting killed on my behalf.

"Does it really matter which one I am? You know I'm an O'Rourke. We're all one and the same.

I hear Tymoteusz grunt. "What the fuck happened to my cousin?"

"What does it look like? He attacked me on a run."

"Oh, yeah. You single-handedly took down these men without a scratch." Tymoteusz's disdain rings in the air.

Shane points to where we stood off the trail. "I had a better vantage point. Jacek and his men didn't plan well, and I could shield myself and they weren't. They were easy picking."

"Fuck you, motherfucker."

"What? Did I say anything that isn't obvious? It's not my fault your cousin's batshit bonkers. Or at least he was."

I watch Tymoteusz approach, and Shane hurries to reload his magazine. I don't even carry a spare with me. He just whips it out of his sweatpants' pocket as though he were pulling out a candy bar. It boggles the mind. He reloads and aims and shoots the trail, right between Tymoteusz's feet. It all happens so quickly nobody can anticipate what he's doing. Tymoteusz's men are ready to shoot, but he holds his hand up.

"No. It's bad enough Jacek's hit. We can't take out O'Rourke. He knows that. He's banking on the fact his family will annihilate mine if we touch a pretty little red hair on his head."

Even from this distance, I can see Shane shrug, and I can picture his smirk.

"Tell me what you want to do." Shane calls out as though he's asking what they want for dinner. "Do you want my cleaners to take care of this? They can get here faster than yours. You going to take Jacek's body? You want us to dump it? I know you hate him, so I don't think it would bother you if we disposed of him for you." The cadence of Shane's speech is so casual; it's flippant even. As though he'd be doing Tymoteusz a favor, and a covert one for me.

In some ways he would be, but that's not how I imagined this conversation to go.

"Where's Kaja?"

"Who?" Shane's confusion is genuine.

"Kaja. She goes for a run here. Where is she?"

"I don't know who you're talking about, and I haven't seen anybody else. That's why Jacek picked here to attack me. There's nobody around, and neither of us could have seen anybody because nobody's gone past."

I know he's going to have questions, wondering who Kaja is, and he'll come to me to see if I know. Fucking hell. The sirens get louder as police approach. Somebody must have called it in. There aren't too many homes nearby, but that also means sound carries with little to absorb it.

"Make up your mind soon."

Shane calls out to them as he continues to text one-handed. He still has his gun pointed at Tymoteusz, but his eyes must dart between his phone and the now seven men who all have weapons pointed at him. It'd be a fucking firing squad.

It tempts me to come out of hiding and stand alongside him, but that would only spur Tymoteusz and his men to shoot. They won't wait to see who's coming, and they definitely wouldn't wait to find out why it's me. I just have to bide my time, and it might drive me crazy.

"Come on. We've got a few seconds left. It's your men or my men. What's it gonna be? Decide."

Tymoteusz scowls but concedes. "Yours."

"You want his body?" Shane speaks of Jacek as though he's the last piece of pizza, not a human being.

Then again, that is a stretch, considering he's acted more like a beast than a person. I know I certainly won't miss him. I wonder how Bartlomiej will feel about this. He cares about his brother because they're brothers, but I know he doesn't like Jacek as a person. However, he relies on him as a second-in-command. This will elevate Tymoteusz if Jacek dies—nobody's checked on him, which says something. The assumption is he's already dead.

That makes me focus on the body for a moment. Double fuck me in the ass with a pogo stick. Even from here, I can see blood is still flowing from him. Dead bodies don't pump blood. Blood drains like a vacuum into the body's cavity. It doesn't continue to geyser. That means Jacek is still alive. That means there's a chance they could get him to the hospital.

It still makes me wonder why none of them have checked on him, even if they assume he's dead. They would still check, wouldn't they? Do they want him to bleed out? Did Tymoteusz give the order not to? Or are none of them motivated on their own to do it? That leaves so many questions without answers right now.

"Yeah, we'll take him." Tymoteusz sounds about as thrilled to do that as he would if he were getting a colonoscopy.

"All right, cleaners are on the way. They'll be here, but we have to move the police to somewhere else."

His right shoulder drops ever so slightly and pulls back just a fraction of an inch as though he's giving me a sign to fallback farther. Somehow, he knows I'm still here. I'm certain he didn't see me. He must have a sixth sense about it.

"All right, how do you want to play this? I'm all for me running, you chasing me, guns drawn."

"The hell we are. No suicide by cop today." No surprise Tymoteusz isn't down for that idea.

"Then you have to shoot in a different place. Draw them away and make them think whatever this is moved on. It would mean people are alive to keep shooting at each other. Do you really want my name connected to your name?"

Even from here, I can see how Tymoteusz's scowl darkens. There's simmering rage now close to boiling over. He knows Shane's right and doesn't want his name connected to them. It'll spread, and once people know Jacek is dead, they'll deduce it was an O'Rourke who did it. It'll only build Shane's reputation in the underworld.

It might lead law enforcement to have another charge against him. But knowing he took down the Polish second-in-command would certainly make many people think twice before crossing the O'Rourkes. They could eliminate more than just Jacek as an enemy.

I wonder if Shane'll say thank you. I've been told I have a dry wit. I don't know how funny that was.

Tymoteusz's still pointing his weapon at Shane as he takes a step back, then another. "Don't fucking shoot me in the back."

I suspect Shane is laughing from the way he sounds when he responds. "Obviously, I'd shoot you looking straight at you. That's what I did to Jacek. Why would I shoot you in the back? I don't fear you."

"Fuck off, motherfucker."

"By all means, you go your way. I'll go mine."

Shane takes several steps backward until he can move into the curve of the trail where he's not exposed. We both watch Tymoteusz's men hurry forward and grab Jacek. There's a soft groan. It makes me want to echo it.

Fuck me, he's not dead. That means I am.

I barely made it home before Bartlomiej comes pounding on my door. My hair's wet from my shower, and I'm still naked. I know it's him because he's calling out to me. He's going to wake the entire building. I hurry to grab my robe with my hair wrapped in a towel. I open the door, but I leave the chain latched as I peek around the door to see Bartlomiej and two of his most trusted men standing behind him.

"It's me, Kaja. Let me in, or I'll kick this door down, so move back."

I know he isn't exaggerating right now. "All right, hang on."

I close the door and slide the chain. I wish I could give him an excuse to leave me alone, but there's no way he's going to take it. Obviously, he's already heard about his brother. I open the door, and he barrels forward, cupping my jaw as he kicks the door shut in his men's face.

"Oh, *księżniczka.*" He's kissing me before I stop him.

It's even more demanding than the last time I saw him upset. I pull away from him to catch my breath. All I really want to do is wipe my mouth. I always have that visceral reaction to his kisses, but now it's stronger than ever.

"Bartlomiej, what's the matter? What's wrong?" I hope I sound genuinely confused.

"It's Jacek. They shot him."

"What? Who shot him? Come here."

I take his hand and lead him into the living room. I sit down on the sofa, and he takes a seat beside me. I try to let go of his hand, but he clutches mine. He's distraught.

He's showing me emotions he'd let no one else see. Part of me wants to skip and twirl and say yippee. I have him so convinced of my affections he trusts me enough to be this vulnerable. Part of me just wants to get this conversation over with so I can get dressed and have breakfast.

"It was Shane O'Rourke."

"What? When?"

"An hour ago. I came to make sure you were okay. It was the same place you go running every day. Tymoteusz said he didn't see you on the trail."

That makes my stomach clench. I know he knows where I run every day. I have to tell him at the beginning of the week what my workout plans are, so he has somebody make sure I'm safe at the beginning and the end of my run.

He likes me to use this trail because it's secluded. It's unlikely I'm going to cross paths with many people. It's also a trail his men could drive up if they needed to. I didn't see any of his men this morning when I returned to the bus stop. I count that as a blessing.

"On the same trail I run? Oh, my god! Where?"

"Around the three-mile mark from the way you go in."

"Really? I didn't see or hear anything. I must have already been on my way back."

He looks at the towel on my head and the hair peeking out near my forehead, then at my robe.

"I stopped to get a sports drink because I forgot my water bottle. I only got home a bit ago. But I finished the same time I usually do."

Which would be true if I hadn't been involved in a shootout. I had to book it back to the trail head once I knew Shane was going to follow me. I'm certain he wanted to make sure I left. It wouldn't surprise me if he got to the parking lot just as I got to the bus stop. At least the bus arrived before I could have another confrontation with him.

"How do you know who it was?"

"The man had red hair, so that gave away he was an O'Rourke. The longer he spoke the more Tymoteusz grew certain of who it was."

"They talked?" I tried to sound incredulous, my face looking puzzled. I have to be careful not to overdo it.

"Yeah, he was just standing there alone, apparently. Happy as you please. They pretty much chatted from what I understand."

"Tymoteusz didn't attack him? Didn't shoot him or anything?" I still try to sound disbelieving.

"No, Shane O'Rourke is part of the boss's family. He's untouchable unless there's a shootout happening right there and then. I don't know what happened. I don't know why Jacek was there, but they found Shane with Jacek."

Oh, fuck me. He didn't say with the body or Jacek's body. How is he barely hanging on?

"He's in intensive care." Did he read my mind?

"Oh, I'm so sorry. What can I do? What do you need?" Do I sound like a loving girlfriend?

I know what I need. I need to finish the job. I should have shot him right through the head or right through the heart, but that would have looked like an assassination. The aim would have made people question who it was even more. I went for the belly and the shoulder to let him bleed out, but to not look like an expert marksman. Like a sniper.

"No, I just need to hold you."

"What's going to happen?"

"I don't know. If he survives the night, the doctor said there's a chance he'll survive tomorrow. If he can survive the next week, then there's a good chance he'll recover. He's in a coma."

"A coma? Like a medically induced coma or one that happened on its own?

"Medically. They said, for right now, that's the best way to allow his body to do some initial healing."

"How long do they think he'll have to stay that way?"

I'm trying for stunned and scared, but not scared for myself. Scared for my boyfriend's brother. Whatever I'm doing works because he hasn't looked questioningly at me at all.

"They don't know. It could be a week, a couple weeks, a month. It just all depends on what happens."

"Oh, my goodness. Thank God Tymoteusz was with him."

"Tymoteusz wasn't with him." Immediately, he looks at me suspiciously.

"I don't understand. If he wasn't with Jacek how did he know? That makes little sense. He'd have to be with him. Otherwise, how'd he know to get to Jacek? I don't understand."

I repeat myself to sound too shocked to comprehend. More than once, I've played the slightly less intelligent female than I am. The sometimes easily confused. It always puzzles me when he buys that because there are other times when he asks my opinion on topics I should know nothing about.

"Tymoteusz said Jacek went after you again, and Tymoteusz went to stop him.

"I didn't know any of the other O'Rourkes ran that trail."

Now he looks at me accusingly. I shouldn't have said other, as though Shane's usually there. He knows I met Shane at the shootout at the lumberyard. Does he believe we had some illicit meeting?

"Do you think Shane used me as a lure? Would he do that sort of thing? Would he use a woman to get your men and Jacek as his target? What kind of man does that? I thought women and children were off limits. You said I'd be safe with you."

I infuse panic into my voice, and he strokes my hair before cupping my cheek. He kisses my temple. And again, it's so at odds with the man I know he can be. The suspicion he felt a moment ago is gone. He went from mob boss to boyfriend in the bat of an eye. It's disconcerting now that he's being so loving to me again.

"They are supposed to be off limits, but things have been fucked-up for the last five years, and it's all because of Shane's family. They broke that golden rule. Now women and children—well leaders' women are—sometimes targets."

"Sometimes?!" I jump out of my seat and step away from him, crossing my arms around my waist and shaking my head.

"Bartlomiej, you told me I was safe. You told me I wouldn't be a target. That it would be okay to be with you. Now you're telling me for the past five years women have been targets. You lied to me. You risked my life even more than I realized."

"Kaja, you know I've been with other women before you. None of them have been targets before."

"Oh, is that supposed to make me feel better? I guess I'm the lucky one." Sarcasm drips from my voice, and I don't have to try. "That does nothing to reassure me. You telling me that just scares me even more. Why me? Why do they suddenly want to go after you? What's going on?"

"I don't know yet. After what happened at the lumberyard, the O'Rourkes weren't who I was expecting."

"Expecting?!" I practically scream the word. "Okay, that

makes me think you knew I was a target. That there was a good chance somebody would come after me. You should go. I don't want you here, Bartlomiej. I don't want to die. Not for you, not for anybody. Leave."

"Kaja." He stands and approaches me, but I back myself against a wall. Part of it is to truly protect my back, but part of it is because I know he'll follow. He'll cage me in, and he'll try to calm me with lust and affection. To him, they are usually one and the same. Ever since Jacek attacked me and beat me, they've been different.

"Come back and sit with me, *księżniczka*. Nothing's going to happen to you. I'm making sure you're properly guarded from now on. You're not going anywhere without at least four guards, Kaja. One for each side of you."

"What? That's no way to live. You're going to make me your prisoner. I told you from the very beginning I wouldn't agree to something like that. You told me it wouldn't come to that."

"Well, it has."

I flinch. I know that's part of what he wants. He wants me to submit to his will, so I have to put up enough fight to look reasonable, but then I have to back down.

"Kaja, this is the way it is. You knew who I was when we started dating. Nothing has changed about that. I know you know little about this life, but you are not that naive."

"No, not naive, but I trust you because you are you." I poke my finger into his chest.

He grabs my hand and pushes it aside and kisses me again. His hands try to roam over my body, but now I push him away.

"Bartek, please, this isn't what I want right now."

"I'm going to make you feel better."

"I'm terrified. Making out isn't what's going to make me feel better."

"Oh, I think it will. I think you need a distraction. I think you need to feel me holding you, loving you, and reminding you who I am."

My hand covers his cheek, and I brush my thumb over it.

"Believe me, I know exactly who you are. I know you're trying, but I'm still scared. Put yourself in my shoes. I know you've known no other life, but there must have been times when you were a kid where you got scared because you didn't understand everything going on. Like when your parents tried to shelter you, but this world exposed you to something you weren't supposed to see. I've had a lot more years of being sheltered—I guess—than you have. This isn't normal to me yet."

He seizes that word. "Yet? As in, you could get used to it?"

"I'm going to try, but you have to give me time." Time for me to finish this investigation.

"You ask for time a lot, Kaja."

I jerk my chin back and scowl. "You're going to throw my virginity back at me because I have a deep faith that says I shouldn't sleep around. I should save myself for one person. You're going to do that right now?"

"I'm sorry. That was unkind. You're right. You know I want that with you in the future."

"I thought we were moving toward something more, but now I need to think about this, and making out with you won't allow me to clear my head. Please, don't crowd me right now. You should go."

He studies me before he moves away. "All right, Kaja, this time. For now, I'll give you space, but only today. I want you to move in with me, at least for right now."

"What?" I shake my head. "No, you're asking me to consider too much stuff right now. I can't. Please, let me figure out one thing at a time."

"I can protect you better. I can keep you safe."

I know I must eventually give in because that's exactly what I've been aiming for all along. I just need to finish this mission before it goes further, and I'm sharing a bed with him every night.

"I'm not saying no entirely. I'm just saying no for right this minute. Let me think, okay? I love you. I want to be with you. But this is all I can handle for one day. Okay?"

"All right." He sighs with resignation. "Fine. I'm leaving four men with you, two outside your door, two downstairs in the lobby."

"Thank you, Bartek. That makes me feel better."

"I'll keep you safe, Kaja."

"I love you." *Like someone loves herpes.*

"I love you, too." He gives me a hard, fast kiss, and then he's leaving, and I'm breathing easier.

I've got to slip out and meet with my handlers tonight. They'll have found out what happened by now. They're going to want the details. The burner we use to communicate had one text. It just said:

Tonight.

That's all well and good, but with four guards at my door and in the lobby, I'm kind of stuck. We keep our communication to a minimum, so I can only text back:

I'll try.

I wonder how much they know about what went down and who was involved. I flop onto the sofa after I get changed. I'm trying to pay attention to the reality show I'm watching, but it doesn't keep my attention. I replay today in my head, making sure I know exactly what to say to Johnny and Steve when I see them. I also think about when Bartlomiej was here.

I never want to be intimate with him. I don't enjoy it, but there's something else about today that made it feel even more wrong. I don't want to consider what that is, but my mind keeps nagging. The answer is right there, but if I let myself actually think it, then it becomes too true.

It felt like it would betray Shane.

There. My brain said it.

It makes no sense at all. He kissed me, and that's it. We're not in a relationship of any sort. We're inconvenient acquaintances. We're physically attracted to each other, but that's it.

He's been trying to keep me safe ever since he met me. I don't appreciate the meddling. I definitely don't appreciate his high handedness, but he's doing what he thinks is best for me. I know a lot is also for my mom's sake.

To do more with Bartlomiej feels wrong, but I doubt Shane is worrying about me and what I might think if he's off with someone else. I don't know if he has anybody, whether he's in a relationship or even a situationship. Who knows? It irritates me even more that I'm concerned about it. I don't want to care.

I look at my front door, and I'm trying to figure out a plan again to get out. I really don't want to go anywhere. I'm so tired. I just want to sleep. I'll just text my handlers back in a couple hours and say I can't.

Yesterday might have been the longest day and night of my life. Bartlomiej texted me four times and called me twice to make sure I was okay. He was very insistent I come by today, so here I am. This is going to be another tedious day, and I still need to figure out a way to ditch his men and see my handlers. I don't know how I'm going to do that.

"Bartek, I didn't go for a run this morning. Can I at least go for a walk? I'll go stir crazy if I have to be in this house all day. You don't even want me to go in the backyard. Please. I just need some fresh air. I need to stretch my legs. You know how I get when I don't work out."

"I don't think one day off from a run will kill you."

"I know that. That's why I asked for a walk." I try to infuse light-heartedness into my tone.

Bartlomiej nods to two of his guys. "I'll round up two more. Meet them at the front door."

Blessedly, I set off for my walk a few minutes later. Now, I'm two miles from the house when I spot Shane's car. I wonder if any of the men see it, too. I can't tell about the guy in front or in back of me, but I dart my gaze to the guys beside me. None of them seem to have noticed, but if they do, they don't want me to. Shane ducks down fast, so maybe he's in the clear. If that's the case, it makes me wonder just how situationally aware these guys are if I'm scanning our surroundings and noticed that, but they don't.

I can't point it out to them or Bartlomiej without admitting I saw Shane, and I have no interest in Bartlomiej tightening his security detail around me. I see another familiar face driving toward me. I can't tell if she'll be a friend or an agent for this conversation, but we've positioned her as a friend of mine before.

I point to the oncoming car. "I know her. I'm just going to say hi." I lean over when she stops and winds down her window. "Hi, Stella."

"Hey, what's with the extra guys? Something happen?" She sounds inquisitive like a friend not conspiratorial.

"You know Bartlomiej. He just likes to make sure I'm safe. I'd rather be too overprotected than not protected enough."

"I was planning to call you to see if you could come over tonight. I broke up with Johnny, so I was really hoping we could have a girls' night to take my mind off it."

That must mean they've reassigned him. I wonder if that'll make her my full-time handler along with Steve. It would make more sense. I've said that all along one of them should be a woman, so we could stage situations like this.

"Yeah, that would be great. I'd love that. What time should I come over?"

One of the men clears his throat, but I ignore him. Bartlomiej never said I couldn't go places. He said I had to go with four guards.

"Why don't you come over at like seven? We can order something and just hang out."

"That sounds good to me. It's been forever since I've had a girls' night. I've almost forgotten what they're like."

"Okay, I'll see you then. I'm so glad I ran into you."

"You, too. Have a good day. I'll see you in a bit.

Angela drives away. Just like my name isn't Kaja, her name isn't Stella. I decide I've pushed my luck with these guys, so I tell them I want to head back. The conversation doesn't go over well with Bartlomiej, but he gives in, and he lets me head over to Angela's place.

It was nice to get away from Bartlomiej, but I have to spend more time than I want explaining what happened yesterday to Angela and Steve. I skip a lot of details and make it sound like I wasn't actually at the scene. I waited until she let me know they'd heard Jacek got shot, but there was no evidence found before I admitted to anything more than just I hadn't seen it.

They don't know about the scene at the trail. They only talked about where I guess Tymoteusz and his men went. They scattered before there were any arrests, but at least it drew NYPD away from the actual scene.

It makes me think Shane's cleaners must have done a good job. The only reason any law enforcement knows about Jacek is because his wounds were so severe there was no avoiding going to a hospital. Gunshot wounds and stabbings usually require getting the police involved, bringing in a man practically dead from two gunshot wounds is definitely going to mean an investigation.

It suddenly makes me wonder if the doctor who put Jacek in a medically induced coma did it because that was the best course of treatment or because Bartlomiej told him to do it, so no one could force Jacek to give a statement right away. I don't know, but either seems highly plausible to me now. I can't convince Bartlomiej to let me go back to my apartment for tonight, so I'm already in bed here.

He said he had some paperwork left to do. I'll pretend to be asleep when he comes in. I need to know when that is and what kind of mood he's in. He promised he'd let me sleep and not touch me tonight because he often wakes me up. I made the mistake of trying to reject him the first night he did it. We had a massive argument. He learned I don't enjoy being woken any more than he enjoys being turned down. I thought he was going to dump me. Now he sticks to some heavy petting then spooning me.

I hear voices, and I don't recognize any of them. I creep out of bed, avoiding any of the creaking floorboards. This is an older home. It's nice, but it has definitely settled. The first couple of times I got up to tiptoe around made a floorboard creak. I passed it off as needing to go to the bathroom or get a drink of water since you have to walk toward the bathroom to get to the bedroom door.

I ease it open, having sprayed some WD-40 on it just a few days ago to make sure it doesn't squeak. I count to thirty before I ease the door open enough to look down the whole hallway. I count to thirty again before I step out.

I ease the door shut behind me before I creep along the landing and tuck myself away in a nook I've always thought a man must have designed because it's nothing but wasted space and a perfect spot to collect dust.

I strain to hear what's going on. I can put a face to the voice. Andranik Derian. He's the Armenian boss. What the hell are they doing together if Bartlomiej was supposed to have a deal with the bratva? Is that why it fell through? Because they know about Bartlomiej and the Armenians?

The Polish might get along with the Armenians for now, and they might get along with the Russians, but the Armenians and the Russians aren't on any better terms than the Russians have been with the Albanians for a couple years now. I know tensions in their motherlands aren't as high as they are here in New York.

"You were supposed to get us that shipment from Bogdan. Instead, it's been days. We hear nothing from you. We know you lost that fucking shootout. We know you never got the product. So, what are you gonna do, Bartlomiej? How are you gonna make it up to us?"

That's what they were really there for. Does that mean the Kutsenkos found out Bartlomiej was doing a deal with the Armenians, and that's why they shot at them instead of following through?

"Look, I told you the last three times we talked I'm working on it. It's not like I can make that many kilos appear out of thin air. It's going to take me a while."

"You've had a while. If you don't get it to me by the end of this week, you and I are done."

Bartlomiej takes a step forward, not appreciating the threat. The two guys are matched in size. Bartlomiej puffs out his chest, and Andranik's man steps forward. The guy looks ready to push Bartlomiej away. His hands are at his sides. I know he's restraining himself.

"Back up, Bartek. I'm already pissed off at you. I already know what happened to your brother. Do you want to wind up like him, but in your own home?"

Bartlomiej laughs. "You don't have enough men for that."

"So you think, but it only takes one bullet. Whether you have a lot of men or none—whether I have a lot of men or none—I'll still kill you."

Bartlomiej's men appear like specters out of the night. They surround Andranik and pull him backwards. He can't do shit since Bartlomiej's men would have searched him for guns. He probably has at least one knife with him. He has no way to put a bullet in Bartlomiej, unless he thinks he's going to pound it in with his fist.

"End of the week, Bartek. I'm not joking. That's all you've got. If you don't take care of it, then I'm going to the Mancinellis and getting it from them. I'll make sure they know exactly why I chose them over you."

"You're going to let them know you need them more than you need me? That's how Salvatore's going to see it. He won't look at it as you picked them. He's going to look at you like you came begging because you can't take care of your people's needs anymore. So go ahead. Go to Salvatore. I don't care."

He does because he needs the payment. He definitely wants the money that would come from however many hundreds of kilos of coke he was expecting to sell. I scoot back as I wait for the Armenians to leave, but they don't. Instead, Bartlomiej turns and walks into the living room, nodding for his men to let Andranik follow him.

Just a lot of posturing. Now they're going to get on with negotiations. I wait for the guards to disappear again. This time I know they aren't lurking because I hear doors shut. I ease my way down the stairs and into the kitchen. The blessing of this being an older home is it's not open concept. I can get into the kitchen and get as close to the living room as I can. They switch to Armenian, which I didn't know Bartlomiej spoke. The languages are nothing alike, so I understand nothing. I consider going back to the bedroom, but there's a chance they could switch back to English or even Polish. Then I could follow along. Fourteen months of intensively learning Polish to prepare for infiltrating the Polish mob made me nearly fluent.

Because I don't understand what they're saying, the meeting wraps up sooner than I expected. I hear Bartlomiej say goodbye. Fuck. I'm trapped in the kitchen because the stairs up to the bedroom are by the front door. I rush to open the fridge as I hear Bartlomiej's voice getting closer.

"Kaja?"

I twist to look over my shoulder. "Hi." I look back in the fridge.

"What're you doing down here?"

"The Chinese we had tonight made me so thirsty, so I came down for a drink. I remembered your mom dropped off that cake, so I planned to snag a slice. But it's gone. You didn't leave me any." I aim for playfully petulant.

He walks over and wraps his arms around me, drawing me back against him. I feel him harden, and I want to jerk away. I shift to close the fridge door, which forces him to step away.

"You know you're not to come down here when I have people over."

I exaggerate my wince. "I know. I'm sorry. I didn't hear any voices until I got in here. Then I understood nothing, so I grabbed the drink. That's when I thought of the cake."

Luckily, I had a glass I used earlier for water. It irritated Bartlomiej in the beginning, but I insist people use the same glass throughout the day if they're drinking the same thing. It happened after he implied I should do dishes when I'm here. I told him the only way I'd play maid is if there was nothing for me to wash. I suggested the one glass rule which he rejected. I took so long doing the dishes the next time—drawing out the time, then insisting it was because there were so many glasses and mugs to rinse then load in the dishwasher—he instituted the rule. Little things like that make him think I'm a girlfriend who plans to stick around.

"Do you want anything, sweet one? There's no cake, but I can make you a sandwich. You ate little today."

"I had plenty at Stella's. I was saving room because I knew we'd have snacks along with dinner. The cake just sounded tempting."

"I'll have Mama bring one tomorrow that's just for you."

"No. That's unnecessary. It was a moment's temptation." I pretend to stifle a yawn.

We head up to the bedroom, and I turn my back to him when we get in bed. He sighs, but just spoons me. I let myself doze, but I watch more minutes tick away on the clock than not. I never sleep deeply here. I didn't trust Jacek not to kill me in my sleep. If he survives, I don't trust him not to kill me while I'm awake. I fucked up letting him live.

Chapter Nine

Shane

She's got a whole fuck ton of things to explain to me. Even more than before. It's almost midnight, and she's still at Bartlomiej's house. I saw her go this morning. She was there for hours, then she went for a walk with four guards. I watched a car slow down, and the woman in it spoke to Carrie. I snapped a photo of the car's plates and sent them to Finn.

Sure, we have access to the same database as law enforcement, but we have access to an entirely different one. We got a guy—fuck, that makes me sound like a Guido—who keeps tabs on stolen and fake plates we use, and we come across. He tracks who they belong to and on what vehicle we found them. It definitely wasn't a POV—personally operated vehicle. It was definitely a government car.

It made me wonder if the woman was her new handler. I camped outside the house Carrie went to and spent four hours at. My heat seeking binoculars told me there were two women and a man inside. Carrie, the woman from the car, and a second handler is my guess. It was nice and dark with a tree with plenty of thick foliage, so I attached a camera that points at the safe house's driveway and garage. The average person looking up at the tree won't spot it. It's the camouflaged kind hunters use, but extra small. I'll keep an eye on who comes and goes. In any situation other than this, I'd be labeled a fucking stalker.

I am a fucking stalker.

But I'm not doing it with ill-intent toward Carrie. Maybe Bartlomiej. Definitely Jacek—if the fucker isn't dead. Last I heard, he's in the ICU in a coma. It couldn't happen to a more deserving piece of shite. I'm doing it for Carrie and Meredith's safety, my family's safety, and my apparent infatuation bordering on obsession.

I glance at my watch again. It's twelve-thirty, and I'm exhausted. I'd rather be home, sleeping in my bed. But I'm watching Bartlomiej's house instead. I recognized the sports car and SUV that arrived around eleven. The Armenians—Andranik—have something going on with the Poles. Drugs? Guns? Those are the two most likely. Whichever it was, now I know for certain who Bartlomiej planned to sell the bratva shipment to.

And now I know why Bogdan and Niko shot up the lumberyard. If they'd wanted Bartlomiej or Jacek dead, neither one would have left in anything but a body bag. It was a warning. Apparently, one Bartlomiej won't heed.

There was a light on in the living room, but I couldn't see any others while Andranik was there. The main bedroom light went on about three hours ago, but it turned off within fifteen minutes. Maybe there're lights on in another bedroom at the back of the house, but I doubt it.

It means Carrie is not only spending the night, but she's spending the night in bed with Bartlomiej. This is going above and beyond the call of duty. Agencies and police departments don't expect undercover cops and agents to sleep with their marks. It might get intimate to keep up the story or to avoid harm, but having sex with a suspect isn't the norm.

This means she's pretending to be his girlfriend. That sparks anger in me I don't recognize. Anger I don't want to analyze. I wonder if she knows about the three sidepieces Bartlomiej has.

Actually, he's only been to strip clubs in the last five or six months for meetings. Usually, he sneaks into the back at the ones he owns to fuck one of the three women he rotates through. He knows better than to fuck any of the dancers at any club the Four Families own, especially not bratva ones. The Kutsenkos and Andreyevs will castrate, then murder any man trying to turn their establishments into whorehouses. The rest of us rough the guys up, toss them out, and ban them from coming back.

Maybe he really is that into her. He hasn't been hanging out at his regular haunts. Is she into him? Is it some kind of Stockholm Syndrome? Is she just pretending she doesn't care for him when she's with me?

That stirs an inexplicable rage inside me, and it only continues to grow the more I think about it. It's really none of my business, and I should back off. I don't want to contemplate why I'm so angry she's spending the night with him. It's not merely every minute she spends with him, the greater the danger she's in.

It's more personal than that. It's more intimate than that.

The night passes slower than molasses in January, and the morning isn't much better. She's in there until nearly one o'clock when she finally goes back to her apartment. Then I'm staking out that area, too. She's down to only two guards. I guess Bartlomiej feels more confident than he did yesterday. Or she's convinced him to back off.

Whatever the reason, I watch her eventually slip out again close to eleven p.m. when she heads over to that house she was at last night. She drives this time, and I wonder what she did to get past the guard I'm sure waits outside her door and the one I see at her building's front door.

The road she takes is narrow and winding. She's not headed where I expected. This takes her toward her parents' house. I'm not sure if that's where she intends to go. I follow her three car lengths behind until I see it's another meeting spot. It's the same woman I saw in the car yesterday. I park and walk closer. Fortunately, there are plenty of trees for me to hide among. I'm light-footed as I approach, making sure I don't inadvertently snap any branches. I can hear them speaking before I find a tree with a thick trunk to hide behind.

"I can try to find out. Nothing's new except Bartlomiej has another meeting with Andranik in a couple days. I overheard that as I was walking past his office this morning. I don't think he realized I'd come downstairs."

"How do things stand between you?"

That's exactly the question I want answered, so I'm glad this woman asked.

"We had some rough spots while we were talking the other day, but it seems to be back on course. I gave enough pushback as though I'm scared to be with him for it to be plausible. He seems to believe I'm conflicted about our relationship, and I'm not sure what I want."

"How close did he think you were to breaking up?"

This woman is a mind reader, a fount of knowledge and wisdom about which questions to ask.

"I think he believes we were pretty damn close because when I said I didn't want to be treated like a prisoner last night and I wanted to go home, I convinced him I only need two guards instead of four."

"What's the plan going forward for this week? Anything other than his meeting with Andranik?"

"Not that I know of yet, but he said he wants me to travel with him. He said we'd go on a trip in a couple days, so it makes me wonder where this meeting will be."

That makes my stomach twist as I think about her leaving town with him and not having the protection of her fellow agents to back her up. There's no way in hell that's happening.

"Do you think that's wise? Do you think you can get out of it?" God bless this woman and her curiosity.

"I don't know. Part of me definitely thinks I shouldn't. I don't want to be in some small, enclosed spot with him while we're in a rocky place in this relationship. But the other part of me knows not going would only make it far, far worse. I'm torn between the two, but I think I'm going to have to concede and go."

The fuck she is.

"What about the other syndicates? Are there any major players involved?"

She doesn't hesitate, at least not outwardly, but there's a moment where her left hand flexes in the dark. I don't know if this woman sees, but I can because of the streetlights behind them.

"No, not yet. Only the bratva when they showed up at the lumberyard. Besides that, it's been quiet. I really think Bartlomiej is on everybody's shit list. I'm sure the other syndicates heard about what happened at the lumberyard and are keeping their distance."

"Well, we need him to be in the same place at the same time as the bratva, or we need to get a new wiretap on him. Can you slide that in for us?"

"I can try, but the man brings his phone and practically sleeps with it instead of me."

Practically sleeps with it instead of me? They share a bed. Does that mean they're not having sex? Just the thought of him touching her—and worse, her touching him—makes me want to hurl. But there's nothing I can do right now. There's no point in wasting energy on things I can't change immediately.

I force myself to focus on Carrie describing being in bed with the piece of shite.

"I'll see if I can get to his phone tonight once he falls asleep. He's a pretty deep sleeper. He often lets it fall next to him since he works on it after I pretend to fall asleep. I'll try to change out the SIM card and put the tap on it."

"Alright, we have to move this forward, Carrie. This is taking too long. They're going to pull you out if we don't make some headway."

"I know, but I've been in this too long to give up at this point. I haven't put my life in danger for this many months to just be told, 'Nope, sorry, we're done.'"

"I know that, but you also know that's not how the agency works. You can't have an indefinite amount of time."

"I do, but if we can score this and not only bring down the

Polish but the Russians as well, then it's just steppingstones until we can move on."

Does she really mean that, or is this just playing her partner to buy more time? Would she go after my family next?

"Who do you have your sights set for the next family to target? I think it should be the O'Rourkes."

"No, definitely not them. I don't think they have enough going on right now to make a difference if we bust them." She's quick to reject us as her next target.

"They always have something going on."

"Yeah, I know, but I really think the Diazes or the Mancinellis would be a better use of our resources. You know I'm not able to go in again, so we need somebody who's a fluent Spanish speaker or somebody who's got Italian. Nobody has Gaelic. At least not yet. All these families switch back to their native languages whenever they want to speak in private. That's why I had to learn Polish."

"True, but I still think the O'Rourkes would be our next best target."

"That might be what you believe, Angela, but I'm the one who picked the Poles, and so far it's been a good play. It's only been the last few weeks that things have gotten complicated."

"Yeah, ever since you got beaten up."

It hangs in the air, and it almost sounds like an accusation. But Carrie doesn't flinch. I can see her face now that she's moved to have more of the light from the buildings beyond her shining on her face.

Does she know I'm here? Can she tell I'm listening? Did she do that so I can see her?

I don't think so. I don't think she has any clue I'm listening, but I think she wants to see her handler better to get an easier read on what's happening.

"That was a mild setback, but it's not left me the worse for wear. Bartlomiej has been more attentive to me and more forgiving. He's been glued to me whenever I'm over there. If I can get him even more on the hook, he won't think I'm a threat. I think he'll propose soon. He asked me to move in with him the other day."

What the ever-loving fuck?

There's no way that's happening.

Again, that jealousy that leads to anger boils in me, clawing to rise to the surface. I'm not accustomed to feeling jealousy like this. My entire life there's been five other guys I've shared everything with, and I never hesitated to do it.

My cousins were raised more like brothers to me than relatives from separate sets of parents. My aunts and uncles are second and third parents to me. I know it's how the other guys feel, too. We've always shared without hesitation, and we always will. It's not because we have to. It's because we want to, so I'm unaccustomed to envy or jealousy.

Even though Sean and I are mirror images of each other, and the only way people outside the family can tell us apart is the freckle on the left side of his throat, I've always felt like a separate individual from him. Our parents ensured we wore what we wanted, we got the gifts we wanted, so no one would treat us as interchangeable.

Outside the family, people guess who's who, so even as kids, when people confused us, and someone wanted to hang out with him or asked him and not me to do something, it never made me feel jealous the way I do now.

It's unreasonable.

"Look, I have to get back to my apartment. The longer I'm out, the greater the chance somebody's going to figure out I left. Let me do what I need to do, and I'll keep you posted. If I end up going on the trip, my guess is Boston. Something's going on with the Polish up there."

"Is he working a deal with them and the Armenians?"

"I don't know if it's just a change of location, or he's got something going on with a syndicate up there. Either way, he's tempting fate, and he's going to come out the loser if he takes us up to Boston. You know the shit that's been going on with the Albanians up there over the last few years. If he draws in people from the other syndicates, he's just going to piss off the Colombians, the Italians, and the Irish here. For his sake, I hope he knows what he's doing. Otherwise, he's going to screw all of us over, too."

"Check in with us in a few days."

"I will."

I watch the women head back to their cars, and the handler leaves before Carrie, which is perfect. I pull out and catch up to her. I drive alongside her, putting down my window and gesturing to her. It only takes a moment before she looks over. I point to the exit ramp we're coming up on, and I give her a look that tells her I'm not joking, that she better follow my instructions.

She pulls ahead of me and gets off at the exit before I lead us to a warehouse. I pull around to the back, and we park beside each other, but we say nothing until we're in the building. Once we're inside, I use my phone flashlight to guide us to the interior office where I can turn on the lights. We glare at each other. She speaks first, both of us understanding a staring competition gets us nowhere.

"Shane, this is none of your business."

"Oh, but it is. You didn't argue with me or stop me when I made you come. You wanted me as much as I did you."

"That was just in the heat of the moment." She tries for nonchalant but fails miserably.

"It was very real. You and I both know that."

"It wasn't for me."

"Liar."

She knows she is. A moment later, we're tangled together for a kiss that rocks my world. I graze my teeth up her neck until I nip at her earlobe. I know it makes her shiver. I fist her hair as I lean back to look at her.

"You're mine, Carrie. You have been since the moment we met."

I dive in for another kiss, and she moans as her hands press my arse, wanting my cock closer. I keep one hand in her hair as I unbutton her shirt, nearly ripping off the last one. I yank down her bra and squeeze her right tit until she whimpers. But it's one of frustration, not distress. I'm happy to indulge in my desires, so I suck on her nipple before tugging it with my teeth. I bite, but not so hard as to break the skin. She arches her back, pushing her tits together. I move to the other side as she lifts that one even higher toward my mouth.

She lets go of the one I just finished devouring. With a popping sound, I release her nipple and lift her. She wraps her legs around my waist, and her fingers dig into my shoulders. I carry her to the desk and unfasten her pants. I ease them and her thong down as far as I can until she brings her feet up to the desk and lifts her hips. I reach the promised land as I continue to lean over her, but now I pull her jeans and panties farther down and kiss my way along her belly until I get to her pussy.

She's shaved bare, and I have another moment of insane jealousy as I think about Bartlomiej. She might have sex with him, but I'll make sure it's my name she wants to scream.

She pushes at my shoulders just as I'm about to lick. I stop immediately.

"Isn't this what you want?"

"It is, but this can't happen. What I said the last time doesn't matter."

"Everything you say to me matters. We both want this, *cailín*. You know that as well as I do."

She looks conflicted as she gazes into my eyes. She glances down between us to where my thumb rests on the inside of the juncture of her thigh and hip. My jeans covered cock presses against her bare pussy.

She opens her mouth twice before she speaks. "All you have to do is look in my direction, and I want you. I need you to know—to understand—the things I do with him are for work. No one expects me to have sex with him, and I don't. He believes I'm a good Catholic virgin waiting for marriage. The other things that have happened were to dissuade him from breaking up with me or when I feared he'd finally lose his temper and lash out. But this is not about work. This has always been about us, and that's why it's never been a good idea." The sincerity in her voice makes me pray she's not lying. "When this is done..."

She trails off and doesn't finish her question. I think I can imagine what she's thinking.

"When this is all done, Carrie, you are mine. I'll keep saying that until you understand."

Our kiss is sloppy and fierce. I ease my way back down to her pussy, kissing along her inner thighs and around her pussy lips until she's begging for me to do more. She kicks off her shoes, and I yank her jeans and panties off. I lick her from top to bottom. I breathe warm air on her, making her writhe. Then I breathe cool air, making her shiver. I go back and forth between the two until she's pushing her hips up, again offering herself to me. I circle her clit before my demanding tongue invades her cunt.

I don't relent as she squirms on the desk before me. My hands grip her hips, my fingers digging into her arse, holding her in place exactly where I want her. She's moaning and begging to come.

"Sir, please, I need to come... Let me come... Please... *Please.*"

The sound of her calling me sir makes my cock pulse inside my pants. My jeans and boxer briefs are way too tight. The temptation to thrust into her with my bare cock and spill is more consuming than any desire I've ever had for another woman. The moment I'm truly inside her, no other man will ever have her. And the moment I come inside her, she will never belong with anyone else.

"You can come, Carrie." I give her permission, and she wails as her entire body tightens. I watch her cheeks flush as she tries to catch her breath. She pants so hard I worry she can't breathe properly.

"I'm all right. That just was—that was—unlike anything else. I've never—I've never—I have no words for it."

I want to hear she feels the same thing I do. I think she gets that because she tries to articulate her thoughts.

"It's like I've died and gone to heaven, and you're waiting for me there. Yet you're the devil tempting me with something I should never have. You bring me such pleasure. You're everything I could possibly want, but nothing I can have right now."

"Call it delayed gratification, *cailín*. You will eventually. Then there will be no doubting we belong together."

"But Shane, that's impossible."

Her words come down as though they're torrential rain on a campfire. She's bringing us back to reality, and it's not a place either of us wants to be.

"Shane, even when this assignment is over, it doesn't change who I am. I'm a DEA agent. I work for the federal government. My job is to go after people like you. My job is to provide evidence to the Justice Department to prosecute syndicate men. And that's exactly who you are. Eventually, things will calm with the Polish and Russians, then attention will turn toward you. I won't be able to hide you forever. I won't be able to protect you."

The sadness in her voice and her eyes makes my heart ache. My hand runs through her hair that's spread out beneath her head. I brush the back of my fingers along her temples, and my kiss is gentler than any I've given before. I cup her cheek with my free hand, brushing my thumb over her cheekbone.

"Carrie, you don't have to worry about protecting me. I'm the one who does the protecting. I will make sure none of this blows back on you, and I will make sure Bartlomiej can't come after you when this is done. You're safe with me. That's one thing I can always promise. No matter what, protecting you is more important than anything else."

"You can't say that. We both know that can't be true. I can't be more important than your family and I can't be more important than your men. They have to come first."

"That doesn't mean they're more important to me. Maybe those responsibilities are what I have to face and handle before I come to you, but it doesn't mean they're a higher priority to me than you are. I will protect you above all else, *cailín*. I know who you are, but that doesn't change how we feel. If it did, neither of us would feel what we do. We wouldn't be here right now. I wouldn't be holding you, and you wouldn't be letting me. You know protecting you is more than just about your badge and my gun. You know it goes beyond that. You know when I tell you I want to take care of you I'm not just saying I want to make you come. You know there's far more to it than just that. Everything that comes along with it is what I want to give you."

She looks at me, and there's confusion in her eyes. Maybe she doesn't understand exactly what I mean.

"Carrie, I want to take care of your physical needs and your emotional needs. I want to be the one you turn to and know my shoulders are broad enough to carry the weight of the world for you. This isn't just about sex. I believe you know that. Deep down, no matter what—no matter whether you work for a federal agency, or I work for my family—there's something between us neither of us is going to ignore. And that means you putting your trust in me just like I put my trust in you. That we'll get through this together."

"You make it sound like this will be an actual relationship." She scoffs. "That's not possible. There's no way your family and your men would ever accept you being with a federal agent. And there's no way I could ever keep my job if anybody found out I was with you. We'd never be together. We'd always have to sneak around. And the more we have to sneak around, the greater the chance somebody's going to catch us. The less time we could have with one another. I don't want to be in a relationship with someone I can't see, can't walk down the street with, can't tell anybody about."

"But you're not saying you don't want to be with me."

Our gazes lock once more, and we stare at each other. I kiss her forehead, her temple, and her cheeks before I press my lips to her.

"*Cailín*, you are the one for me."

"What does that mean? I've never gotten the chance to ask."

"Little girl."

Her eyes widen in surprise, and she cups my jaw. She smiles.

"Does that mean you're my daddy?"

We both stop—frozen—surprised by her question. I don't

think she knew she was going to say that. My hand gripping her hip eases down to her pussy. My fingers slide into her wetness. She's so ready for my cock it makes me ache. My thumb is slow as it circles her clit, and my fingers sweep against her g spot.

"That's exactly what it means, *cailín*. I know you're not a Little, and I don't want one. But you are somebody who deserves protecting. You have been ever since the moment I met you, and you know I haven't stopped trying to do that. Why do you think that is? It's not because I think you're incapable, that you really are a little girl. But you are mine to take care of and mine to protect, and that's what daddies do. So yes, that's what I am to you."

"I've never wanted a Daddy Dom. You're right. I'm not a Little. I don't want to be treated like one, but I feel safe with you. When I think that word, it's not my father who comes to mind. It's you, and it's being safe in your arms, and it's being happy with you. That's what I equate that word to, but I still don't believe we can have that. I still don't see how that's possible, Daddy. No matter what we want."

"Then we work it out. We do this together. I will do whatever I have to, to get you the information you need to finish this assignment. Yeah, it would serve me and my family, but I'm scared for you, Carrie. I know you embedded with the Poles months ago, but he is not a sane or stable man. Any time now, you could say the wrong thing, and he'll explode. It shocks me he's been willing to wait and hasn't pressured you into more."

"He says he loves me." That hangs in the air.

I don't want to ask, but I have to know. "Do you tell him you love him?"

"Shane, of course I do. I have to, but there is nothing about me —not even a follicle—that thinks I want him, that I could love him. Nothing. I say what I have to say, but what I show him is the part of me that has to be there, the part that's never off the clock. When I'm with you, it's the only time I can forget my job. It's the only time I can forget my oaths. When I'm with you, I'm just Carrie. When I'm with him, I'm somebody else. I don't even use my real name. Everything about it is pretend. Now that I know you—now that you've touched me—now that I've kissed you—when he touches me, it makes me feel ill. It used to make my skin crawl, but now all I want to do is shove him away and run. I've had that impulse before, but it nearly consumes me now that I know you, now that I want you. I don't know how I'm going to continue this lie, but I have to."

"I know. Let me help you."

"Daddy, I can't do this because I'm betraying you every time I'm near him. I—I..."

We stare at each other, and I help her sit up when she lifts her shoulders off the desk. I pick her up, and she wraps her legs around me again. I'm tall enough to sit on the desk easily with her comfortably in my lap. Neither one of us says anything until we're both reaching for my pants. I unfasten them and push down my boxer briefs.

Then it's heaven. I'm inside her. I'm bare.

"Carrie, I've never had sex without a condom. I've always, always been careful. Practically double-bagged it. But this is how we're supposed to be. I told you my cum would fill you and replace Bartlomiej's, but I've never done this before. I've never come inside a woman. At least not inside her cunt without a condom. Even though now I know you've never had sex with him, I still want my cum in you. I want it to fill your pussy. I want it to drip down your thighs. I want it inside you the next time you see him. I want that to be our secret. That it reminds you, you belong to me, no matter where you are or who you're with. That I can silently say, fuck him, when you're with him because you have a part of me still inside you. Is that what you want too?"

Chapter Ten

Carrie

"There's nothing I want more than this. This isn't in the heat of the moment despite what I've claimed. I've had the time to think about it. For better or for worse, nothing feels righter than being with you."

"Nothing has ever felt righter than this, Carrie."

He stands and lays me on the desk once more. His emerald eyes remind me of photos of Irish grass. They're radiant, and he makes me feel like I'm the only thing in the world that matters to him. That I'm the only thing that exists. Period.

He thrusts into me over and over with our gazes locked. Time stops around us. The entire building could burn down, and I wouldn't care. We could be in the middle of another shootout, and I wouldn't run from this. I push aside thoughts that would ruin our first time together. I don't want to contemplate there not being another chance to share this with him.

The man is endowed. Very endowed. It feels like he's going to split me in two, and I don't want him to stop. It toes the line between pleasure and pain. I've always thought it's a fine line, but not right now. Now it feels like a line thick enough for me to stand in the center and get the best of both. I've never felt this full before, and I try to shift to bring him deeper, but his fingers digging into my hips stop me.

"What do you want, *cailín*?"

"You... Please... More."

I attempt to lift my hips to match his rhythm, but he holds me in place. He obliges, thrusting harder and faster, making the desk squeak. If he keeps pounding into me like this, he's going to push it across the room.

"I need to come, Daddy."

"No." The single word should tell me not to argue, so I don't.

I beg.

"Daddy, please. I'm so close. I don't think I can stop."

"Yes, you will. Or I'll pull out and edge you while I come all over your magnificent tits. I decide."

"Can you decide I can come soon?"

"You can decide whether you want a spanking."

The thought of him spanking me drives me into an alternate universe where I exist chained to his bed for his pleasure. I want to feel his hand across my ass. I want to feel a crop or flogger he wields land on my ass and thighs. These ideas are enough to send me to the brink.

"Shane, please. I'm so close. I need this. I need you."

He studies me for a moment before he slams into me, his pubic bone grinding against my clit.

"This first one, you can have on your own. The next one is mine, just like all the ones after it."

"When you say shit like that, how am I supposed to stop?"

"Come."

"Shane!"

It's heaven. It's bliss unlike anything I've experienced with past partners. I don't know where to put my arms, my hands. I clutch his forearms, my fingers trying to dig into them. But the sinewy muscle is too tight. Knowing his strength and how he tempers it for me doubles my arousal.

"What are you doing to me, *cailín*? You push me to the brink of control. It's close to being gone. I'll hurt you."

I shake my head vehemently.

"You would never lose control completely. You will always know your strength compared to mine. All you've done since the moment you met me is protect me. Your mind wouldn't let you. I trust you."

There's something in his gaze that changes. It doesn't soften; it doesn't harden. It just relaxes. I don't know how to describe it, but saying I trust him—even if it's just during sex—or maybe especially during sex—does something for him—reassures him. That's what it is. I've pushed back against nearly everything he's told me—insisted upon. He doesn't know I've trusted him since the start.

"Daddy, I trust you to take care of me." I hope he knows I mean beyond right now, beyond just fucking me.

I want to get him off. I need to be the one who does it. Part of it is certainly my ego. But a bigger part wants to reciprocate the explosive satisfaction I got from mine. I don't want to look away, but I struggle to keep my eyes open through all the varied sensations. My head tilts back, but I stop myself. I look between us, noticing how I've coated him until his cock glistens. He's watching us too. When our gazes meet, it makes my heart skip a beat.

"I'll do anything for you, Carrie. I'll always take care of you."

The sincerity in his voice tells me he means way more than just my orgasm. But I already knew that.

"I want to make you come, Daddy. I want to feel your cum filling my pussy. I want to feel it drip down my legs. It'll be our secret, but we'll both know the truth."

"The truth is, you belong to me now, Carrie, just like I belong to you. It's all changed. There's no going back. We can't undo having sex. If I come in you, don't doubt I'm marking you. You know the man I am. You know how I solve problems. I'll do whatever I have to, to make you happy and to protect you."

"Kiss."

His words echo in my ears. I want him to know what they do to me. I cup his jaw with my left hand and burrow my right into his hair. I fist the flame-colored locks and tug before I press his head to me. I snag his lower lip between my teeth. I'm the aggressive one now. At least, I am for a moment. He pulls my hands away and lifts my arms over my head. While he holds my wrists with one hand, his other pinches my nipple.

"Daddy, please come. I need you to."

He hears the desperation in my voice. The ache to pleasure him like he did for me makes me restless. He draws my left leg over his shoulder, leaning forward. He's so impossibly deep that I scream.

"Yes!"

I try to lift my hips, but he keeps me positioned how he wants. He decides what I do and what I get. He's dominating me, and I'm submitting, and it's as though we have found our homeostasis. In my battle for control in the outside world, he gives me balance.

"You will come with me, little one."

"Daddy." It's more a moan than a response.

It's an exhalation of relief. The need that threatened to consume me has an outlet as he rubs his pubic bone against my clit, creating this astounding sensation.

And then it's happening.

It's the best orgasm I've ever had. Not just better than the two he gave me at my place. Not just better than the ones he's already given me tonight. It's better than ever. Better than all the ones I've given myself or any other man caused. None of them compare to this. I force my eyes open to watch him during every moment of this. I want him to have the best orgasm of his life.

He drills his cock into me until we're both coming. He rocks his hips rather than thrusts.

"Carrie."

My name is a puff of air, but the tone is reverent. I still feel like I'm the only thing that exists for him. That I have his undivided attention, and I know that's not something easily accomplished for a man whose situational awareness is always in overdrive. This time, when I bury my fingers in his hair, it's with a gentle caress. He leans over me, kissing my neck and shoulder as I run my hands over his shoulders and back. I feel the muscles bunch and relax as his hands slide under my shoulders to hold me closer.

"Daddy."

"I know, *cailín*."

And I believe he does. I believe this was just as monumental an experience for him as it was for me. This wasn't about two bodies belonging to people who love to fuck and fit well together. We hug in silence until his dick softens. He straightens, and when he pulls out, we see his cum mixed with my pussy's cream. I flex my pussy until I feel his cum dribble down to my asshole. Then I clench to keep the rest inside me. He swirls it around my hole and presses against it, but he doesn't enter me.

"This will be mine, too."

"Not will be. It is. I know what you mean, but you don't have to claim it when I offer it."

He helps me sit up, then cups the base of my head, his thumb on my jaw beside my ear. It's arousing in its intimacy.

"We will make this work, Carrie."

It's a sobering comment, and one I would rather forget. But I can't.

"Shane, I want this, but I don't see how it can possibly work. I don't know that we can make it come true."

I'm a DEA agent, and he's a mobster. The only way it could work is if I quit my job. He can't quit his family or the mob. They're one and the same. It wouldn't be safe for him or his family if he struck out on his own. He'd be dead the moment someone found out. His family would never let him go unprotected, so they'd become targets, too. There's no stepping down. Their successors would kill them before risking them returning and taking back control.

"We will find a way, Carrie. If a future with me is what you want—at least want to try—then we'll make it work."

"You are so used to bending everything to your will. But some things snap instead. I don't know that we can."

"Don't you want to try?" Disbelief and hurt flash in his gaze as he backs away from me.

"Of course I do. But I want to prepare myself in case it doesn't work out. I don't want to float through a fantasy only to have it ripped away from me. I want to be prepared for reality, or my heart will break, and I might never get over it."

I didn't mean to admit that. That gives away too much. He steps as close to the desk as he can, my knees bracketing his thighs.

"Why do you think I'll fight for this? Walking away from you would slay me. I've never lived in a fantasy, but I will make our reality what we want."

That means I have to give up being an agent. It's something that's defined me for years. No one in my family or friend circle knows I go undercover, but it's no secret I work for the DEA. This job has been my identity in so many ways for so long. I've worked tirelessly to get where I am. Never mind this particular assignment. I've busted my ass my entire career. As much as I want Shane, as deeply as I feel for him, am I ready to sacrifice my career for him? I don't know.

⁂

All of this is so surreal. Nothing could have been more perfect than last night. But now I'm back at Bartlomiej's house, and I'm changing into a bikini that barely covers anything. It's better than the dental floss he originally picked out but I refused to wear. I told him the only way I would ever get into it was in the shower where nobody could see it. I refused to parade myself around in front of his man with everything hanging out. This one covers all the necessary bibbidi bobs but leaves very little to the imagination.

I toss my suit on, along with my cover up, and head out to the pool. Every step I take, every time I stand or sit, I remember the feel of Shane being inside me. My pussy aches with emptiness after feeling like his cock would split me in half. It's like phantom pains. I can feel him inside me and his hands on me, but they're not really there. It just leaves a burn only he can extinguish.

Bartlomiej's swimming laps right now, so I take advantage of the time when his face is in the water. His phone is on a towel, so I sit on the end of that lounger. I grab his phone and pop off the case. Fortunately, he and I have the same phone with the same case. He insisted upon getting it for me as a present, but I know he put a tracking app on it. It wasn't hard for Steve to find. It also wasn't hard for Steve to hack into it to change my location to make it look like I'm in one place when I'm not.

While Bartlomiej swims away from me, I grab the tiny key from my coverup pocket and put it in the hole to pop the SIM card out. I drop that back in my pocket and pull out the replacement SIM.

Why the hell do these fuckers have to be so tiny?

They're hard enough to handle when your hands aren't shaking. When he approaches and smiles at me, I have to pause and hide that side of the phone. I make it look like I'm scrolling something. He tucks into a flip turn, once again facing away from me. With his face in the water, I finish putting in the SIM card and replacing the case. I barely do it in time before he stops at the edge of the pool, crossing his arms on the edge. If he wasn't who he is—a psychopath—I might find him attractive, but I never have. Now that I'm with Shane—if you can call it that—I can't find anything attractive about him.

When he crooks his finger at me playfully and beckons me over, I know I can't refuse. I toss the phone behind me as though I don't have a care in the world, but I keep my hand back there just long enough to be sure I put his phone in the same place I found it, which is farther away from me. I walk over to the edge and sit down.

"The water is perfect, sweetheart. Come and join me."

I slip my legs into the water, and it would be perfect if it weren't for him. He wraps his hands around my waist and lifts me down, giving me a peck as he pulls me against him. One hand goes to my ass to guide my right leg around his hip. I pull the left around before he can touch me, except this forces my pussy to rub against his hard-on. I try not to grimace instead, shooting him a smile that earns me a pinch on the ass. It's annoying, and it's painful. Not the way I like pain with Shane.

Everything about being this close to Bartlomiej feels exponentially more wrong than it did just a few days ago. Certainly, more after last night. Before we left, Shane said I'm to do my job, and I knew what that meant. But I can't bring myself to stay in this position because—even if Shane says it's okay—he and I both know it's not. It feels even more like a betrayal because he had to concede any kind of intimacy with Bartlomiej is necessary.

I splash water at him and push off his chest, diving while he splutters. I surface farther away from him, giggling. His expression is one that would make a lesser person crumble. But I know he thinks he's being playful with me. He just doesn't have that many expressions in his repertoire.

He swims toward me, and I evade him. I can't do that forever. I have to let him catch me again, eventually. I swim until I'm almost at a wall, angling myself so my elbow is on the side when he gets to me. I don't want him pinning me to the wall, so I twist and let him bring me against him again. This time I don't wrap my legs around him. Instead, I ease back, laying my head in the water, letting my tits pop up. I know I'm flaunting myself at him, but I also know he likes it. For right now, he's enjoying the view and not trying to glue our bodies together.

"Sweetheart, we're traveling tomorrow. I want you ready to depart at eight a.m. You can go back to your place and grab what you need, then spend the night here."

I shake my head.

"What do you mean, 'no'?"

There's a bite to his tone I don't like. I swim farther away from him.

"*Kaja*."

"Don't bellow at me, Bartek."

"Obey me."

"Obey you? We're not married, and I'm not your dog. I don't have to obey you. You've been asking a lot more of me lately, and I still have a lot to think about. If I'm the target, what does traveling with you mean? Does that make me a target in the two cities? Will somebody from here follow us? Or will we be safer leaving town for a little while?"

"We'll be safer leaving town. Don't tell anybody where we're going, Kaja."

His expression gives me no doubt sharing our destination would mess up his secret plans, and it would finally push him around the bend. I'd reach his limit, and he would hurt me.

"You know I know better than that, Bartek. But I'm still not sure about all of this. Why should I go with you when you're just going to leave me in a hotel room somewhere while you do whatever it is you do? How is that going to be pleasant for me? I can sit around at home without the danger."

"Because I said so, Kaja. Because I want you near me where I can see you're safe. I don't want you out of my sight for more than a few hours at a time. That's all I'm willing to concede. You were at your place last night, and I left you there because I had things to do to prepare for this trip. But you *are* spending the night with me tonight, and that's not negotiable."

I pull myself out of the water and head to the lounger. I spread the towel out on the one next to it and sit down.

"Bartek, you're demanding me to do things, and that wasn't part of the deal when we got together. I told you I wouldn't put up with that. That I'm not one of your men or a dog to command. I'm not your wife. And last I checked, obey is no longer in the wedding vows, anyway."

"Are you suggesting we break up, Kaja?"

I shake my head swiftly as though his question scares me.

"No, Bartek, that's not what I'm saying. I'm saying this isn't how I want things. This isn't how we started or what you agreed to. I don't like this change. It doesn't feel right."

"And if I don't do as you demand?"

I stare at him wide-eyed.

"Bartek, I'm not commanding you to do anything. I thought we were having a conversation. I thought I could tell you how I feel about things. Was I wrong to trust you?"

Trust between us has been the main thing to him. He wants me to trust him all the time, so I'll follow his commands. He wants to trust me, so I don't make a fool out of him. I know it is not an equal give and take.

I'll push the issue right now because I need to have some freedom from him. I got a text this morning saying my handlers need to check in with our division office, and the division chief'll expect me to go with them. I think it's too risky, but I'm not in a position to refuse.

"No, Kaja. You aren't wrong to trust me. Of course, you can tell me how you feel. I'm sorry, sweet one. I didn't mean to make you feel that way."

He gets out of the pool and grabs his towel to wipe his face. Then he reaches over and reclines my chair before he gets on, his body hovering over mine. He kisses my neck, then down my chest to my tits. He starts to pull the top apart, but my hands fly to it, looking around.

"Stop."

I hiss the word, and I may have never meant something more than I do that single word right now.

"Your men are around, and they're going to see me. I don't want my tits on display. I can't imagine you'd want that either."

"You're right. I don't. I wasn't thinking. But you are enough to tempt the devil, my love. You make me forget all reason. You're a distraction."

"And all the more reason I shouldn't go. Bartek, I don't want to do anything that could endanger you."

I cup his cheek, once again coming across as the doting girlfriend. I try to picture Shane instead of Bartlomiej, and it makes it easier to offer affection. But he continues to kiss my chest, working his way back up to the other side of my neck. He nips my earlobe, and it doesn't feel the same as when Shane does it. It doesn't make me shiver the same way Shane does.

When Bartlomiej kisses me—or at least tries to—I turn my face from him, forcing him to kiss my jaw. I hear his frustrated growl.

"What now, Kaja? I can't even kiss you? How does this make you any different from some woman off the street if I can't touch you?"

I shoot him an angry glare. "If you want some woman off the street underneath you, then by all means. I thought the fact I'm just about naked with your cock pressing against me made me something different from all the other women. If that's not good enough for you—if you're tired of waiting—then, by all means, you can be the one to walk away."

"Are you giving me an ultimatum?" He rears back.

"No, I'm giving you an out."

"That's not what it sounds like. It sounds like an ultimatum."

"You're hurting my feelings, Bartek. I don't like you when you pressure me, especially not when you're commanding me and bullying me. None of this is the sweet man you were when we met. Where is he? The one who was patient with me when I was scared."

"Are you scared of me?"

"Not exactly, but after what happened with your brother and then with my foolish jealousy, having you argue with me over me not putting out doesn't feel so great."

"We aren't arguing. I'm giving you a chance to express those feelings that are so important to you."

I glare at him, not liking the passive aggressive comment. I think most girlfriends wouldn't. I retreat to an expression where he thinks I'm about to cry. He croons to me just like he did when I was so injured. Not all the bruises are gone yet, but I'm certainly more presentable than I was right after it happened.

"I'm sorry. I don't mean to make you feel this way. I'm just frustrated. I know doing more than what we have doesn't feel right to you, *księżniczka*."

I might have thrown up a little in my mouth. "You know I have my morning routine when I say my regular prayers and my intercessions for those I think are in need. I've been praying a lot for Jacek lately." Not that he needs to know I'm hoping he'll die. "Today's readings felt like someone selected them just for me. I know they weren't, yet the timing feels like God's hand at work. From Corinthians, it says, 'For this is the will of God, your sanctification, that you abstain from sexual immorality.' I can't think of anything more sexually immoral than fornicating before marriage. Some things you've suggested to keep me technically a virgin certainly don't fall in the realm of most people's sense of morality."

"Kaja, first of all, I didn't know you were that judgmental of how people have sex. And second, there's nothing wrong with a man and a woman expressing their feelings for each other when they're in a committed relationship. I'm not with anybody else and neither are you."

It takes all my effort not to flinch now that comment is no longer true.

"Maybe I could have brushed off that reading if it were the only one. But there was more. There was something from the gospel according to Matthew."

I close my eyes to pretend I'm visualizing the Bible in front of me. I've practiced this a bunch of times for moments like this.

"Bartek it says, 'But I say to you that everyone who looks at a woman with lustful intent has already committed adultery with her in his heart.' Sweetheart, I worry about you. I don't want to be the reason you go to hell."

He chuckles and sets his hand on my inner right thigh. "I hardly think you and me having sex is what's going to keep me out of heaven. I think that ship has sailed."

"Maybe not. Bartek, I know you do what you do because you have to, not because you like it."

There's that naivety he loves. His smile softens when I say that.

"There's a difference between your obligations to your people and what you choose to do with me. Because sex is your free will rather than your duty, I don't want to make it worse for you."

"I hardly think, Kaja, that me making love to my girlfriend would make any of it worse. Just the opposite. Pleasing you feels like a divine act."

"You've known since the very beginning how important my faith is to me."

"Yes, but I didn't think I'd be trying to fuck a nun."

My eyes widen, my mouth drops open, and I push against his chest. He knows he's gone too far when I swing my legs over the side of the chair away from him.

"Bartek, I can't believe you just said that."

I force tears to well in my eyes, and I let them tumble down my cheeks. He's tentative when he reaches to wipe them away, and I allow it for a moment, then I pull away.

"Maybe this isn't right for us. You deserve a woman who can reciprocate your feelings, not keep you waiting and frustrated."

I'm toeing a line again, except this one isn't between pain and pleasure. It's a line between success and failure, and life and death. However, I need to dig my hooks into him deeper. He's like a child with a toy. He'll do anything to hold on to his favorite one, including whatever he's told to do. I suspect his mother withheld affection from him to manipulate him. He gets desperate when I hint at the same thing.

If I can convince him he wants me too much to give me up, I can actually get some of my freedom back. It would be good to go on this trip to gather intel, but it leaves me unprotected while we travel. If anything goes wrong, my intel goes to the grave with me.

There's the Boston DEA field office that would be on call, but it's not the same as the people who've been working this case with me. They're focused on their local syndicates. There's always the risk things could go to shit, and having another agent in the mix could ruin any ongoing investigations they have. I won't be their priority. Their assets are.

"Kaja, I don't mean to hurt you like this. It breaks my heart to see you cry. I'm just in a foul mood today. I really hoped spending time with you would improve it, and even though we're disagreeing, it's better being with you than without. So yes, I can wait. I might die with a pair of blue balls, but I can wait."

His forefinger under my chin lifts it as he returns to the man who wooed me. The one who leaves his violence at the door. The one who could charm a woman unaware of all the vile things he does. When his lips meet mine, I conjure an image of Shane. It doesn't make me any more eager to kiss Bartek, but at least it makes it bearable.

"Thank you, Bartek. I still don't agree with it because I don't feel safe. But if you're going to insist it won't put me on yet another syndicate's radar, then I suppose you can make sure I survive."

I stare at my folded hands in my lap, appearing meek. His body twists toward me, before his hands on my arms pull me back against him so that my shoulder presses into his chest and my head rests against his shoulder.

"If it really upsets you that much, Kaja, then you can stay."

"Thank you, Bartek."

I might still end up going with him—a last-minute change of heart as a sign of dedication—but for now he doesn't need to know that.

I scoot back onto the lounger. "You said you're having a bad day. I'm making it worse. What's the matter?"

I position myself to make room for him, allowing him to wrap his arms around me as I nestle against his chest.

"I can't get into it, but lining up this meeting hasn't been as easy as it would have been if the bratva didn't fuck me over."

"I don't understand any of that. Why on earth would they attack unprovoked if they were supposed to get something out of the deal? It still makes me so angry they risked your life, Bartek. I know they're a bigger syndicate, but tell me you made them pay for trying to kill you."

"This blood-thirsty side of you is sexy as fuck, sweet one. It lets me know you care. The bratva believes I made a deal with someone else, and they don't like that someone else."

Andranik.

"They must really dislike this person if they'll give up however much money they were supposed to get."

Bartlomiej chuckles as he hugs me closer. "The bratva really dislike everyone who isn't one of them. The unbalanced power between the Poles and Russians is nothing new. It followed us to America. It means I can't retaliate in the open, but I've punished them in small ways here and there for endangering you."

"You have? Does that mean they know I was there? Am I on their radar?"

"They don't know you're the reason. They just know I'm pissed about more than the deal falling through."

"I know you can't let the attack go unpunished, but if the Russians are so much bigger than us, wouldn't it make more sense to reconcile with them or at least make some peace? Deals with them must be better than deals with anyone else. How many smaller ones do you have to make to equal one with them? I imagine it must be dozens."

"Us? A moment ago, it was you."

"The more we talk, the more defensive I feel about the threat they pose to you, me, and the people who rely on you. I want to stand beside you when you help those people. That makes it 'us.' Or—or do you not want me to think like that?"

"I've waited for you to feel that way. Prayed you would. When we get back, I want to genuinely talk about our future. Not me issuing you orders or you feeling cornered. Us planning our life together. I love you."

I stroke my hand over his chest. "That'd be nice."

From his sigh, it seems like he didn't notice I didn't reciprocate his feelings or his interest in the conversation. I can't say "I love you" anymore—even if it's pretend—when I'm falling for someone else.

Chapter Eleven

Carrie

I've been eavesdropping on Bartlomiej's call all night. He thinks I'm at my apartment, but I'm in my car a block away. I bugged this office while he showered after his swim. I figured with trip details to finalize and me not there, he would have plenty to say. I haven't been wrong. He's been quite the Chatty Cathy last night and well into this morning.

However, it's the call he's on now that has me most worried. Jacek's has been out of the coma for a couple of days. It was unfortunately short-lived, and the fucker didn't have the courtesy to die. I thought I'd wounded him badly enough he would wind up bleeding out.

Little did I know. That'll teach me never to walk away before I'm certain the job is done.

They've been going back and forth on the phone for the last fifty minutes about the upcoming meeting and how Jacek has certain things he wants to ensure happen while Bartlomiej is gone. As the elder one and the leader, it doesn't thrill Bartlomiej to hear all of his baby brother's opinions. It's been one argument after another this entire call. However, now they've moved on to other things that are way more personal to me. Jacek's been bitching about me for the last couple of minutes.

"Bartek, you are a fool to trust her. I'm telling you nothing good is coming from keeping her around. This will be a disaster if you take her along with you. She's going to be privy to way too much. There's a reason I went after her."

"Yeah and look at what beating the shit out of her got you. Nothing. You are none the wiser than you were before you laid hands on her. You're lucky you're my brother, otherwise, I would have killed you for that. Any other man who hurt my woman the way you did would have died a long and painful death to make up for how angry I am and how you made her suffer. Count your blessings, little brother."

"But look at what's happened since then. How is it such a coincidence she was not only at the lumberyard, but Shane was there, too? I saw them together. He was protecting her, and she was protecting him. They weren't just there by coincidence."

"You really think Kaja is some kind of secret agent who's been watching me? No. We're having a rough spot right now, just like any couple would. I understand why she felt jealous and followed me. I've been pushing her too hard, and it's coming back to bite me. I won't be dealing with the Armenians the entire time I'm up there. I can try to make this an enjoyable trip for us."

"Bartek, I've never known you to be such a fool as you are now."

"Watch it, little brother. I may love you and you might be in the hospital, but my patience isn't never-ending."

"But your foolishness is." Jacek is certainly pushing his luck, but this conversation makes my heart race. "Bartek, think about it. The lumberyard and then on the path. She was there when Shane was, too. He was already having a secret meeting with her. There has to be an explanation beyond coincidence."

"And what do you believe that is? That she's a spy for the O'Rourkes?"

"I don't know. But Bartek, she's the one who shot me."

That revelation hangs in the air for a moment before Bartlomiej erupts.

"You lying sack of shit. How dare you accuse my girlfriend of that just because you don't like her? Just because you think I pay too much attention to her. That is a horrible thing to say, and that's a lie I cannot forgive you for."

"And I would understand that, Bartek, if it was a lie, but it's not. She shot me. She looked straight at me and put two bullets in me. I'm lucky I survived. I don't think it was because she's a shit shooter. I think she believed I would bleed out if she just left me there. Little did she know I'm more stubborn than that."

His stubbornness is certainly not a surprise to me. It seems to fit with everything about him.

Bartek snaps at him. "I don't believe you."

"I can't believe you're turning a blind eye to the obvious."

"Nothing about this is obvious, Jacek. You need to give me more proof than two coincidences."

"Okay, so they were coincidences. Why did they happen so close together? In a matter of a couple weeks, she's at two shootouts, and Shane is also at both."

That hangs in the air, just like his original accusation did. But now Bartlomiej doesn't have a sound explanation, and neither do I. It's one thing for me to have seemed suspicious, and Jacek took things into his own hands. But now he's shoving rather than pushing the argument that I have ulterior motives to what I'm doing.

How the fuck am I going to get out of this?

My mind races as fast as my heart as I try to conjure something I can say once I see him. I doubt Bartlomiej will let this matter rest since Jacek is a dog with a bone.

"Bartek, you need to have the bitch followed. Not just guards, but actual people staking out her place. I guarantee she's slipping out at night, and I guarantee you Shane O'Rourke is up to his shit-stained ass in it."

"How's it possible they're connected? What brought them

together? You think she's Irish, and the O'Rourkes sent a woman in to do a man's job?"

"You know as well as I do, Bartek, that women make far greater spies than men. She's a total honeypot. But no, she's not Irish."

I know I'm not. I'm Welsh. My mother and father both served in the British military before they retired and moved to the U.S. I may have been born here in the U.S., but I still consider myself as Welsh as I do American. I even spoke the language as a child.

"There's some way her family's connected to the O'Rourkes, and that's how she wound up in all of this."

That freezes me in my spot. If my heart was racing before, now it's stopped. Jacek's too close to the truth, and it terrifies me one of them will discover my mom's connections to all of this. It may have started out as a coincidence I chose Shane's construction site to hide at, but there's no way they'll believe that if they discover my mom's the O'Rourkes' private physician.

She'll become just as big a target as I am. In fact, she'll be target number one in order to manipulate me and the O'Rourkes. And if they can't get anything out of her, then she'll be our punishment. My mind continues to leapfrog from one plausible lie to another as the conversation continues.

"All right, Jacek, say you're telling the truth. What now? How do we to deal with her?"

Jacek snorts. "Really? You have to ask? It's obvious what we have to do."

"No, I'm not killing her. I'm not killing my girlfriend. And even if she wasn't my girlfriend, I'm not killing a woman."

"You don't have to. I'm more than happy to do the job for you since you can't."

The accusation Bartlomiej is too weak to get the job done is just as damning as Jacek claiming he's a naive fool. Jacek isn't wrong. No one but Bartlomiej's brother—maybe his mother—would get away with such accusations.

"Bring me proof, Jacek. Indisputable, incontrovertible proof she's what you say she is. Then we'll go from there."

"I already have proof she's not who she says she is."

That makes my brow furrow. What could he possibly have on me that would refute any denial I make? Bartlomiej wonders the same thing.

"Spill it. Obviously, you've been keeping these little gems to yourself. What do you have against her?"

"She's been sneaking out of her condo by going out on the balcony and easing in through the window of the vacant unit beside her. It's right next to the emergency stairs. She's timed it for when the guards do a sweep to the elevators and back. She knows their routine."

"How do you know she does this?"

"Because I put a camera near the ceiling right outside that door, and I have a camera at the exit to the street. Did you know she has a car?"

"What? No, she doesn't. I would know that. There's nothing registered under her name. My men have never seen her go to one. She always uses public transportation, or she lets me send a driver."

"That doesn't mean she doesn't have one. She parks it two blocks away. She doesn't want us to know. But that's how she slips away to meet her handlers."

"Handlers? What the hell, Jacek? What are you getting at? That's more than her just working for the O'Rourkes."

Oh, motherfucker. He knows. Tomorrow's gonna be the day of my death, if not tonight.

"Bartek, she's a federal agent."

"What? That's fucking impossible!"

"No, it's not. I have the footage of it all. Two nights ago, she slipped out and met her handler at a wooded area near McCarren Park. You know there're plenty of trees near there. I watched her meet with a woman. They spoke for about ten minutes. What's even more interesting than that is Shane O'Rourke watched that meeting. Then he led her to one of their warehouses. They were inside that building for nearly two hours. He was probably fucking her the entire time because the kiss they shared when they went back to their cars wasn't one you give your brother or your cousin. They practically devoured each other. I'm surprised she didn't get on her knees for him right then and there. I watched her hand run over his junk, and his hand went down her pants. Whatever they did for those two hours in the warehouse, it wasn't enough for them."

It's all true. We left each other just as worked up as when we arrived. The need wasn't sated, even though we had the best sex of my life.

"So, Bartek, what're you going to do? I've already sent the photos to you in your email."

"What? What the fuck were you thinking, sending them through email?"

"I'm thinking the O'Rourkes should know we're onto them. We watch them scramble to see how they try to fix this. If she suddenly disappears, we'll know I'm right. That she's working with them, and that it's not another—coincidence." He pauses for effect.

The snideness in it makes my upper lip curl in disgust. He's always been such a smug motherfucker. He thinks he knows so much. Unfortunately, in this case, he does. I'm on my laptop to listen to the conversation. I open a secure browser on my VPN and pull up the three email accounts Bartek uses and thinks no one but Jacek knows about. I sit back in my seat in shock as I look at the photos attached in an email.

It is all so incriminating. Not just the photos of Shane and me outside the warehouse. There're photos from us getting in the car at the lumberyard. There're photos from us speaking after he confronted me outside the subway. There're photos of him going into my apartment. There're photos of everything. Any time I've been anywhere near Shane.

There're also photos of him staked out in a car. The landmarks make it obvious he's near my place and Bartek's. The one thing I don't see are photos of an empty car that must have the surveillance cameras Shane described. At least that remains a secret for them.

From the way Bartlomiej swears repeatedly, I know he's looking at the same thing I am. He switches back and forth between English and Polish. He utters Polish phrases the typical person wouldn't know because they're that vulgar. Those are exactly what I studied to make sure I understood for moments just like this—or at least close to it. Never did I imagine my cover would be so spectacularly blown.

I've got to let my handlers know I've been made. I need a plan for retreat if I can't convince Bartlomiej that Jacek is making all this up. The one advantage is none of these photos have a time stamp. I could claim these were from before I dated Bartlomiej. Yeah, the ones from the lumberyard and trail are damning, but I'll claim Shane isn't over me, and he's stalking me. I hate throwing him under the bus, and it's not because I'm putting the job ahead of him. It's to buy me time to let Shane know what's happening, so his family can prepare. There's no way I'll hide whatever lies I spew. Shane and his family are better equipped to handle this than I am on my own.

Obviously, I'm going to have to tell a selective truth to my handlers. They can't know why my cover was blown until I can come up with a conceivable excuse for involving the O'Rourkes as well. That excuse is something I'll form with Shane.

"So, Bartlomiej, I ask you again. What are you going to do about this? Now, do you believe me?"

Silence. No more swearing. No muttering. Nothing. Just silence for several minutes. I wonder what Bartlomiej's thinking. I know Jacek triggered the psychopath in my pseudo-boyfriend. The quieter he is, the more men fear him. They know his mind's working overtime as he devises punishments to rival any military regime's dictator. I am going to die.

I didn't sleep at all last night. I can't pack up my apartment in case Bartlomiej and Jacek or men they send come to check. The agency will take care of cleaning up the safe house and here. But I get my personal effects together and put them into the false panel hiding place I created in the back of my closet. There's a tiny latch that's next to impossible to find if you don't know where it is. Even I have to run my fingers over the wall a bit to find it.

I've just showered and put on my makeup. I'm getting ready to face the day. I plan to go to Bartlomiej's on my own terms. I spent the time while I packed the few things I could, coming up with excuses about how I was involved with Shane before I was involved with Bartlomiej. That Jacek has proved yet again he doesn't like me. That he's jealous of the attention Bartlomiej pays me. That he believes any woman makes them weak. That he would hate any woman Bartlomiej dates.

I know Bartlomiej'll claim he's dated other women in the past who didn't bother Jacek, and I'll ask him which of them he's asked to move in with him. I know he's "kept"—air quotes—other women and put them in apartments. I know he's provided them with clothes and cell phones, but I don't think he's ever pushed so hard to have one of them as involved in his life as he has me. I don't know if he loved any of them or told them he loved them, but I know his feelings now are true since he's so impatiently waiting to fuck me. I have to be careful and spin the tail in a way that remains plausible. This might be the most challenging acting role of my life.

I hear my front door open. It's not the middle of the night when I know men used to slip in to check on me to make sure I was really there. It's been months since Bartlomiej did that, but it's obvious he'll start again. I'm always cautious to ensure my nightly escapades get me back in time for any random bed check.

But who the hell is that?

"Hello?"

I'm ready to go for my gun when three men burst into my bedroom. I'm still in my bathrobe with a towel wrapped around my head. He knocked the towel askew with his kiss, so I pull it off.

"Tymoteusz, what the hell are you doing here? Get out!"

I clutch my robe to me since I didn't have the belt fastened. Tymoteusz expression screams he knows everything Bartlomiej and Jacek discussed last night. He's aware I'm an agent, and I'm somehow involved with Shane. He's always been the one to come to my defense. The one who's protected me. Now he looks like he'll be the one to gut me.

"Kaja, get dressed. Bartek wants to see you."

"I know. I am getting ready. We're going on our trip. You didn't have to burst in here to make sure I'd show up. I already promised him I would."

I try to sound as normal as I can, as though nothing out of the ordinary is happening. But I tremble for good measure. I allow my genuine fear to show.

Bartlomiej's put a hit on me.

He's giving his cousin a chance before he makes it an open contract.

"Don't speak. Get dressed. If you don't come out in the next three minutes, I'll drag you out by your hair naked if I have to."

"Tymoteusz, what are you talking about?"

"Don't. I believe nothing you say. I know who you are. I know you're a liar and a spy. Like I said, three minutes to dress, or I'll drag you out of here naked. I don't care who sees you. I'll dump you in front of Bartek naked as the day you were born. It'll make it easier for him to slash your throat if you don't have a shirt in the way."

My eyes widen, and my hands tremble.

"You can cut that shit out, Kaja. You may have fooled me before with your shitty acting, but you don't fool me now. Don't play innocent with me because I know what you are. Give me your phone. You're not calling Shane O'Rourke to beg him to save you."

I stand my ground for a few seconds before I go to my bedside table and throw the phone at him.

"Get out. You're wasting my three minutes."

There's no point in pretending now. It'll only piss him off more. He walks out along with the two men who stood as silent guards, guns pointing at me. They don't close the door behind them. Luckily, I have a walk-in closet. I grab a bra and panties, then step into the closet. I find clothes that'll be comfortable to run in.

If I wear sneakers, it'll make it too obvious I plan to bolt. I won't wear heels since I'll break my fucking neck in them, and ballet flats will come off. Instead, I pick some flat boots that will make it easy for me to go the moment I have the chance. I'm silent as I leave my bedroom. I grab my purse, which I can already tell they've searched. There's nothing incriminating. That's one thing I'm always sure of. I always expect there's the chance I'll be made, so I carry nothing with me besides mace, which makes sense as a single woman living in New York. That's entirely plausible.

I head out to a car parked in the underground garage. The two men who came with Tymoteusz get into the driver's seat and the front passenger seat. Tymoteusz slides into the town car beside me. He has his gun resting on his lap, ready to put it to my head if I even breathe the wrong way. We ride in silence as we head toward Queens. We aren't going to Bartlomiej's since he lives pretty close to me in Brooklyn.

I keep an eye on our surroundings. I appear as though I'm sulking as I gaze out the window. That's just fine, but I'm thinking about each place I could get out and run. They didn't pay attention to me as I climbed in. One guy opened the door, but he focused on his partner, so I ensured the childproof lock was off. When I'm ready to run, I don't want to pull the handle and be stuck.

As we get into Queens, I expect to wind up at one of Bartlomiej's empty properties. We draw close to a neighborhood I recognize. It's where all the Four Families' married couples live. Now, that's a trip and a half.

All the current senior members of the Mafia, the Cartel, and the mob grew up in the two same neighborhoods. Eventually, their parents had empty nests when the guys were single and on their own. A bunch of them lived in Manhattan, but as they got married over the last five years, not only did those couples move back into Queens, they all bought homes in the neighborhoods where their parents live.

When they were growing up, the district borders in the neighborhood meant they went to different elementary and middle schools, but they wound up together in high school. I did a full background check on all the major syndicate members. Obviously, it came back with scant details of their adult lives—plenty on their business and legal issues, just not them personally—but there were photos from different extracurriculars they did while they were in school together. It's no surprise all of them were athletes in high school and college. None of them gained their physiques by sitting around or even by just going to the gym.

I might have recognized Shane the night we met if the lighting hadn't been so poor. It also didn't help that my eyes were nearly swollen shut.

I don't know why we're taking this route, but I pray it's to my advantage. The syndicate community is gated, but there's a car about to turn into it, forcing us to slow down. I unfasten my seat belt, praying it doesn't make too much noise. Fortunately, Tymoteusz just lowered the privacy window to tell the driver to go around and to stop wasting time.

I pull on the door handle just as my belt slips from over my left shoulder. I bolt from the car, slamming the door shut behind me since the windows are bulletproof. It goes both ways. Just like a bullet can't come into the car, a bullet can't leave the car. In the time it takes for the driver to get the window down and the first shot fired toward me, I'm already through the gate. I'm running as fast as I can, even though I hear Tymoteusz and the guard at the gate yelling at me. Then Tymoteusz's bellowing at the guard, demanding the guy let him in.

I look around, trying to get my bearings because I don't know exactly which house is which. I don't know who's a syndicate member and who isn't. But more likely than not, the house I pick'll be one a member of the Four Families owns.

Almost all the houses have their own private gate. I spot a blonde man who's just gotten out of his car. I know who he is.

"*MISHA*!"

I risk screaming and telling Tymoteusz where I am. He spins

around, reaching for his gun. I put my hands in the air as I continue to run toward him. He sees the car pursuing me.

"Misha, please. I'm Shane's girlfriend. Let me in. It's Bartlomiej's men. Please."

I rush to explain as I slow slightly when I'm nearly to the gate. I look over my shoulder, praying he'll let me in, in time to escape. He must recognize Tymoteusz, who's leaning out the window with a gun pointed at me. Misha doesn't hesitate as he draws his weapon.

At the same time, he clicks something in his pocket, and the gate opens. The moment there's enough space for me to slip through, he clicks his fob again, and the gate closes. Despite a leading member of the bratva pointing a gun at them, Tymoteusz and his men continue to draw closer.

Tymoteusz's window remains open with his gun out of it. The moment he's within range, and Misha's certain he has a clear shot, he takes it. The silencer on his gun just makes it sound like a poof of air. The bullet goes right between Tymoteusz's eyes, not dead center in his forehead. The space must look almost microscopic from this distance. It's a testimony to the near paramilitary conditioning the bratva's known for. I lower my hands and sprint to his car.

"Get behind it." He yells to me as he tilts his head toward his car.

Bartlomiej's men—they're no longer Tymoteusz's—drive past. Misha doesn't waste any bullets, certain the car is reinforced, but he doesn't lower his gun until they're out of sight. He doesn't holster it when he turns to me, but at least he points the gun to the ground.

"Shane doesn't have a girlfriend. Who are you?"

"Shane and I are involved. It's complicated, but I mean something to him. Please, I can explain some of it, but I need to get inside somewhere. That won't be the only car following me. They might've been the only ones to get into this neighborhood, but there will be more men after me."

"Who are you?"

"I can't tell you that yet. Not until I speak to Shane. Please, call him or text him. Tell him it's about Carrie. He'll understand what that means."

I'm panting between words, and I feel my heart beating in my ears. I put my hands on my thighs and bend over for a moment.

"How far did you run?"

"I got out of the car at your community gate. I slipped through when another car entered. Actually, that was your car." I didn't realize I must have followed Misha in. I was too busy trying to get onto his property to recognize the car.

"I bolted to the right as soon as I got in because I worried whoever was in the car in front of me would hear or see the commotion. I didn't want them looking in their mirrors and seeing what was happening. I wrapped back around and wound up on your street as I tried to lose Tymoteusz."

"You need to at least tell me how you're connected to the Poles."

I shake my head. "I wish I didn't have to be evasive, Misha, but until I speak to Shane, I have to be."

"You clearly know who I am."

His eyes narrow at me. The accusation and speculation clear. The front door opens, and a striking blonde sticks her head out, calling to her husband. I see the rings on her finger, and I know this is Misha's home, but I don't know her name. She steps out as she spots me.

"Kitty, go back in the house now. Close the door."

"Who is that, Misha? She's clearly winded. Does she need help?" She ignores her husband's instructions, looking around in all directions as she approaches.

"*Kitty*." The warning in Misha's voice is clear, but the look she shoots her husband is placating.

"Misha, you know I'm going to check on her. You either let me, or we wind up in an argument later."

"Of all the times it's been convenient having a wife who's a nurse, this certainly isn't one of them." Misha's grumbling, but there's no bite to his words. This woman, Kitty, comes to stand before me.

"I'm all right. I'm just winded from running."

She sweeps her gaze over me, assessing whether that's true. When she's satisfied I'll survive, she asks the same question her husband did.

"Who are you?"

"I'm involved with Shane. I came into this neighborhood for sanctuary."

I know the Four Families' rule. Sylvia Mancinelli imposed it when she married Don Salvatore. Any syndicate woman can seek shelter with her if it's a matter of life and death. The woman's protected until her family can come to her. It doesn't suspend any hostilities among the men, but it allows the woman a chance to survive. Something about one of Sylvia's sisters being attacked and killed in Palermo and knowing she had nowhere to go.

Since the other syndicate members have gotten married, they've implemented the same rule. I'm banking on that now. Kitty's eyes narrow and her gaze sharpens.

"How do you know about that? You are definitely *not* a wife. You're not a girlfriend. You're not a daughter or a sister."

Her sharp tone takes me aback. It shouldn't surprise me for all I know about the Four Families, that they would know the same about Shane. That he's not involved with anyone right now. At least not formally.

"Please, just text or call Shane. Tell him it's about Carrie. He'll understand. Let him come and get me, then I'll disappear."

Never mind the fact this is the exact family that's my true target. It's through Bartlomiej that I'm trying to gather intel on the bratva. If they protect me, there's no way I can turn them in.

Chapter Twelve

Shane

"Dillan, I'm telling you, I have a bad feeling about this. Bartlomiej is going to figure out what's going on, and if I wait too much longer, I won't be able to pull her out in time."

"Why is this your responsibility? She was an agent long before she met you."

I glower at my cousin and cross my arms as our gazes lock. We're both equally stubborn, and neither of us wants to back down. I understand, as our mob boss, Dillan has to make responsible decisions that will be financially as well as politically advantageous. But I couldn't give a flying shite about that right now. What I care about is the woman I'm falling for.

"Dillan, it's our responsibility because I got her into this, and I know I can't get her out alone. If Bartlomiej figures out she's been with me or that she's a DEA agent, she's as good as dead. I don't want that on my conscience, and I don't want my opportunity for what you and Mair have to disappear. I want what everybody else has found, and I think Carrie's the one I'll have it with. How will I know if she's dead? And even if that weren't the case, she's still

Meredith's daughter. We still have an obligation to them to protect Carrie."

"What do you propose we do?" Finn intercedes as he walks over, the quiet voice of reason. I look at my older brother and shrug my shoulders.

"I don't know yet, but it has to be something. I sense Bartlomiej isn't the one who'll act first. I believe Jacek knows more about what's going on than he's let on. Now that he's out of the coma, he'll tell Bartlomiej Carrie was the one who shot him. Once that happens, it'll just be a slippery slope until he discovers the truth about her. There's no way he'll overlook it, and you know just as well as I do Bartlomiej doesn't have the same boundaries we do. He *will* kill a woman, and he *will* kill Carrie."

My twin puts his hand on my shoulder as he looks at Dillan before turning his gaze on me. "We'll figure it out. We'll get her out just fine. Give us some time to look into this and figure out how to work around her handlers. But are you sure if we do this, she'll come willingly?"

That gives me pause. I know how I want to answer, but I can't guarantee it's the truth, and I can admit that much.

"I believe she will, even if it's just temporarily to get her beyond Bartlomiej's clutches, or even if she goes straight back to being an agent. I don't believe she'll give us up, and I don't believe she'll be a threat to us. I'm willing to take that risk."

Seamus scoffs. "Of course you are. You're half in love with her. But let's think about this reasonably."

I spin on my cousin. "Reasonably? How reasonable was it when you went down to Trenton with just Tiernan? How reasonable was it to stand up against the entire Trenton mob? They might be our bitches, but you were still there alone. Can you blame me for wanting to protect Carrie? At least I'm coming to the rest of you rather than trying to go out on my own to take care of it."

I know my limitations. My temper is sorely tested right now, and I know I'll push my brothers and cousins too hard in the wrong direction if I keep going. I need to rein in my temper if I want to convince them to help me.

"Look, I think Jacek is already informing Bartlomiej. I think if anything's going to happen, it's going to be within the next day or two. Her cover's going to be blown, and I don't know if she can get out of there in time. Bartlomiej will only dig his heels in deeper and hold on tighter if he thinks she's a threat. He'll isolate her from communicating with anybody outside his immediate circle, and he'll tuck her away somewhere nobody can find her until he decides how he wants to kill her. Not *if* he wants to, but *how* he wants to."

My voice grows louder with each word until I'm almost yelling at the end. Cormac comes to stand beside me as the only other bachelor left in the group.

"Look, we get it, Shane. Nobody's saying no. We just need to figure out logistics. We need to buy ourselves some time to read the situation and determine how immediate the need to act is."

I throw my hands up in exasperation. "I'm telling you it's immediate now. Jacek is out of his coma. He'll tell Bartlomiej she shot him. I also suspect Jacek's been watching her more closely than she or I realized. It certainly was no coincidence he wound up on the same trail as us, and I think he's had men tailing me as well as Carrie."

"What makes you think that? Usually, you're pretty good and have a sixth sense about those things." Sean's concern ripples through the air.

"I am. I don't know how to explain it, but I feel like someone's watching me. Every time I turn around, there's a sense eyes or a camera are on me, but I never see it. If they've put together Carrie and I not only know each other, but are involved with each other, then we can count down the hours till Bartlomiej kills her. She needs to come with us, or at least get to her handlers. Either way, she needs to be pulled out."

My phone vibrates in my pocket, so I reach in and mute it. This isn't the time to get distracted.

"Look, are we at least agreed we'll help her?" I direct that question back at Dillan as my phone goes off a second time. Just like before, I mute it.

"Of course we are. We won't let her suffer alone. But how many resources we put into this is not something I've decided."

I inhale a calming breath to keep from losing my shite. My phone vibrates a third time, and I pull it out to check to see who it is. Why the fuck is Misha calling me? I'll deal with it later. I silence it once more and drop it back into my pocket.

"Something more interesting going on?" Finn juts his chin while looking down at my pocket.

"No, it was just Misha. Who knows why he was calling? He can wait."

When my phone goes off again, I check. It's Misha. He must really want something. When I slide down to look at the notifications, I realize all four calls have been from him. I hold up a finger to tell my cousins and brothers to wait a moment. I slide across my screen to answer.

"Misha—"

"I have Carrie here."

"What? What do you mean you have Carrie? Where are you?" I look around at my relatives as my heart rate spikes.

"I'm at my house. She came running through the neighborhood, looking for someone to take her in. Bartlomiej's men were after her. She's here, and she's safe. Kitty's sitting with her in the living room, and they're having tea together. She asked me to call you. She said you would know who she is and why it's important you get to her.

"She's my girlfriend. I'm coming right now."

"That makes no sense because she denied being your girlfriend."

"I highly doubt that, Misha. Even if she weren't, she wouldn't ask you to call me if we aren't involved in a relationship."

"Oh, she said you're involved. She just won't explain how. She said she won't until you get here."

"You're damn right. Just keep her safe. We're on our way."

"We're? Oh, the hell you are. Just you. You are not bringing your rabble-rousing family into my home."

"If you didn't have my girlfriend, and she wasn't at your mercy, I'd tell you to fuck all the way off."

"At my mercy? You insult me. You know I'm not the one who targets women and children."

There's a not-so-subtle dig at my family and our past over the last few years. Thanks to Uncle Donovan and Declan, our reputation for keeping women and children out of syndicate business is ruined. Thank God the other families at least recognize the sanctuary rule that's become an unwritten law among us.

"I'm at Dillan's house, so I'm just around the corner. Give me five minutes, not even. I'll be there. Tell me right now, Misha, what condition is she in?"

"What do you mean? She's fine. Why wouldn't she be?"

I don't answer that question. I just repeat myself.

"I'll be there in five minutes."

I glance over at Sean and Finn. Both nod.

"I'm coming with my brothers. The others will stay here at Dillan's house."

"All right. We'll be expecting you."

I've never bolted out of a door so fast as I do when I run out of Dillan's house. I'm unlocking and starting my car as I cross the driveway. Sean and Finn are on my heels. We jump in my car. The guard at the gate barely gets it open in time for me not to ram through it.

I take the three turns until I get to the street Misha's on. I honk, and the guy at their gate recognizes me. I'm forced to wait until Misha sticks his head out the door and gives his guard a signal. I pull into the driveway and park behind his car. I am already out of the car before the engine's quiet. I dash to where Misha stands with the front door open.

I blow past him without a word until I see Carrie. She hears me come in and turns toward the noise. She's out of her seat just as fast as I was out of Dillan's front door. Then we're rushing to each other. When she's finally in my arms, I know I can breathe again. She wraps them around my neck, and I squeeze her against my body.

I keep my voice low as I talk. "*Cailín*, tell me what happened. Did he hurt you?"

"No, Daddy. He didn't have a chance to touch me. I haven't seen him yet. It was Tymoteusz who came to my place and said Bartlomiej wanted to see me. I was supposed to be going there anyway for the trip. I knew what was coming when Tymoteusz walked into my room."

"He did what?"

"He walked into my room."

"He came into your apartment uninvited and then went into your bedroom?"

"Yes, but—"

"No buts, *cailín*. I'm going to kill that fecker." Even in high stress moments, my parents' lessons are too deeply ingrained to forget not to swear in front of women and children.

"Misha already did."

That stops me in my tracks. I look over my shoulder to where Misha and Kitty stand together. He has his arm wrapped around her shoulders, and her arm is around his waist. They'd be the picture of domestic tranquility if you didn't know who Misha was or that Kitty's family is involved with the Ivankov bratva's rivals in Moscow. You wouldn't guess she spent her entire life around the bratva and has a backbone of steel.

"Why'd you kill him?" I direct my question to Misha, and he smiles.

"Because your woman ran here asking for help, and he was in a car pointing a gun at her. Why else would I shoot him?"

I glance down at Carrie before looking back at Misha. "Thank you." It's the most gracious I can be right now.

What I want more than anything is to be alone with Carrie. I want to truly convince myself she's safe. But I can't do that. It's not like I can take her into one of Misha's bathrooms or bedrooms and fuck her into tomorrow. I settle for a kiss. Once it starts, neither of us wants to finish it. We don't care who's around us or who's watching. My brothers are married and obviously Misha is too. They all love and lust after their wives.

They're no different from how I am with Carrie. When we finally pull apart, our foreheads rest against each other before I lower her to her feet. I slide my hand into hers.

"Come, little one, let's go."

She follows my lead and once again I look at Misha. I dip my chin to him, acknowledging my appreciation. Even though just this morning we were at a meeting that nearly came to blows. Neither of the women needs to know that. My brothers and I nor Misha give away the conflict we barely resolved two hours ago. They wanted something we've kept from them, and we wanted something they're hiding. We couldn't come to a middle ground without going all Rambo on each other, so we kept the things that didn't belong to us and called it even.

I guide Carrie out to the car. I toss the fob to Sean. He knows I want him to drive. Finn goes to the front passenger seat, and I hold the door open for Carrie to slide in. Once Sean's backing out of the drive, I pull Carrie against me as tightly as I can. If I let go, she might disappear, and the thought I wouldn't see her again is absolutely unbearable.

She whispers to me as her hand rests over my heart before she pats it.

"Daddy, I'm all right. Nothing happened to me."

But as she speaks, her hand moves quicker, making me think she's trying to reassure me when all I want is to see and feel she's unharmed. When we return to Dillan's house, I escort her in, but nobody says anything to us. I guide us directly up the stairs to the room that's mine when I spend the night. Sometimes we have missions that run really late, or we have missions that start really early. It makes more sense for people to stay over at one of the married guy's homes. Dillan's house is just as big as Sean's, Finn's, and the one Seamus just bought with his bride. There's space for all of us.

When we get to my room, I lead us in and close the door behind Carrie. Then we're fused together again. I'm pushing her against the door, her hands raised over her head. I can't get enough of her. I kiss her jaw, her throat, her chest, her shoulders, everything. My hands run over her, waiting to see if anything hurts.

"Shane, I'm okay. None of them touched me. Tymoteusz threatened to yank me out to the car by my hair, but he never touched me. He may have planned to do something with me once we got wherever we were going rather than letting Bartlomiej handle it. Until I ran, we rode in silence. When I recognized the neighborhood, I got out. I followed a car in when the community gate opened. Turns out that was Misha. I recognized him as I ran toward his driveway. I knew there was a good chance any house I stopped at would have some kind of syndicate connection, but it was an obvious choice once I recognized him."

"I'm so glad you're alright, *cailín*. Getting that call from Misha might have been the worst call I've ever had. Between knowing you were in his clutches and that you went there to seek sanctuary from Bartlomiej, I've never needed to get to someone faster than I did you. Just let me hold you, *cailín*."

"I'm not going anywhere, Daddy. This is where I belong. This is where I want to be. Can we deal with the shitstorm that's brewing in a few minutes? I don't want to talk about this right now. I know we have to, but right now I just want to know I'm in your arms."

"I want the same thing."

I slide my hands up her shirt, pulling her bra down. I cup her tits and groan. It's the most glorious feeling to have my fingers around these fleshy mounds.

"Take your shirt off."

I give the command, and she responds immediately. She whips her shirt over her head, and I reach behind her to unfasten the clasp to her bra. That falls on the floor next.

Then it's me unlacing her boots and pulling those off with her socks. She shimmies the pants and panties down her hips and legs. My hand immediately goes to her pussy and cups it.

"Never wear panties again, little one. When I want your pussy, I will have it. There's no denying you're mine because you ran to Misha to get to me. I'm telling you exactly what's going to happen since you belong to *me*."

"Yes, Daddy."

Her response is breathy, and it makes my cock twitch. We know there's a mix of truth and exaggeration in the dirty talk. I slide my fingers into her. She's damp, but within seconds, her pussy's flooded and ready for me to thrust into her.

"I'm going to make you come, *cailín*, more than once, but you will beg for each one."

"Yes, Daddy, whatever you want. Just keep touching me, please."

"You were prepared to go on that trip to Boston with him. You were going to share a hotel suite with him. It's bad enough when you stay over at his house."

The anger I feel so often when I think of Carrie and Bartlomiej returns, and jealousy fuels it into a raging fire.

"I'm supposed to accept my woman being with another man, even if it's pretend. Even when I told you it was too dangerous."

"I know, Shane. I want to be your woman, but you don't have to worry about me spending time with Bartlomiej or anyone else in his family. They've made me. Jacek's awake and told Bartlomiej I shot him, but it's worse than that, Shane. There are photos."

The dirty talk is done. My anger yields to fear, my jealousy morphs into possessiveness. I pull my hand from her pussy. Getting her off no longer tops our priority list.

"Daddy, there are photos of us at the lumberyard, outside the subway station, headed into my apartment. Pictures of you watching me speak to my handler and of us going into the warehouse. The most damning of all were the pictures taken of us when we stood outside the warehouse by our cars. All of it proves I'm not who I said I am. Bartlomiej doesn't know which agency I'm with, but Jacek somehow found out I'm an agent. Obviously, they know about us. They think—or at least Jacek thinks—I might be a spy for your family. I don't know what to do now because I have to admit to my handlers my cover's blown. They're going to want to know how and why. And then they're going to want to know who I ran to rather than them."

She runs her hand through her hair. Her fear matches mine, and I see it in her eyes. She called me Daddy when we're intimate, and she's called me that to reassure me. Now she's using it because she needs the reassurance. I slide my arm around her waist and draw her closer.

"I don't have a solid explanation because if I tell them I went to Misha's, it'll be my head on the chopping block since they're my actual target. Shane, I think it's time I tell you everything that's going on."

Exhaustion—the aftermath of her adrenalin surge—sets in as she sags against me. She needs me to take care of her more than she needs to tell me things that've already happened and can't be changed. Whatever might happen can't be stopped right this minute.

"I agree, but it doesn't have to be right this second. We're at Dillan's, which means we're safe. Let's slow down for a moment and catch our breath."

I lead her to the bed, and we perch on the edge. I kick off my shoes before inching back and holding my arms open to her. She climbs on and cuddles against me. I tell myself reality can wait because this is how it should be. This is what I want. But there's a good chance I will never have this again because of whatever she explains to me.

I remember her telling her handler my family isn't the next best target. But that won't be her decision alone. Even without this falling apart, she wouldn't be the next CI since someone could recognize her as Bartlomiej's girlfriend. She won't be on that case, so anything could happen.

I don't want to ask her to quit her job. But that's really the only way we can make this work. We both know that, even if neither one of us wanted to say it the other night. Now that's doubly the case because she ran to one syndicate then another for protection.

We sit together and appreciate the silence for a little while as our mutual fear diminishes. She leans against me with her eyes closed, and I lean my head back against the headboard. I look down at her as I stroke her hair along her back. That's more soothing to me than anything else. Just knowing she's pressed against me and that she wanted my help—wanted me—is everything to me.

Eventually, we both feel calmer, and I know we can't stay up here forever. We can't avoid the conversation either.

"Carrie, I want to be prepared for whatever you tell my brothers and cousins. I'm sure it'll shock me, but I don't want to be blindsided in front of them."

"All right, Shane. I'll start from the beginning. I'll tell you everything I know. Once I do this, there's no going back. My career as an agent will be over. If I don't get fired, then I'm going to have to quit."

"Are you saying you choose me over your work?"

"Partly, but I won't have any other choice. I've fucked over this investigation, and now I'm with you for protection. It will get around. If Jacek could discover our connection, then so will my handlers and the agency."

She inhales so deeply her chest presses against my ribs.

"We've been studying the Poles for the last eighteen months, surveilling them and watching who they do business with. Some of it is with the Armenians, but most of it is with the Russians. They've been on pretty good terms, and the Russians employ a lot of the men from Bartlomiej's community on their construction sites. But recently, the bratva has been branching out and trying to make peace with the Armenians. Bartlomiej discovered this. He tried to circumvent that relationship by swooping in to do the deal on those kilos the bratva was supposed to sell him. From there, he was going to reroute it through his organization, then sell the product at a markup to the Armenians."

She takes another fortifying breath before she continues. This is the part she hates, and I know I'll loathe hearing it.

"I needed a way in to discover all of this. Bartlomiej was always supposed to go down, but ultimately, my target has been the bratva. Since all the guys are married, except Sergei and Anton, there was no plausible way to start a relationship with them. It's bound to be a matter of time before those two guys find women to marry, so there was no point to approaching them if this could have been an investigation that lasted over a year."

That's not the reason there's no point. Just the opposite. A woman wouldn't have been a roadblock.

"I embedded with Bartlomiej because I knew I could pretend to be the type of woman he wanted. Even though he tends to hook up with strippers, he likes the naiver ones. I was the perfect balance of naive good girl with enough backbone to help support his family. I was the type of woman you wife up, not fuck. So even though it took a lot of work to build his trust—enough for him to share things about the family he shouldn't have—I was exactly what he needed. I became the woman he expected me to be. The kind he could take home to mom. It was all an act. It was something I knew I risked my life for. But we were certain he would lead us to the bratva, and he did. I blew my cover too soon for that to do us much good."

"But what about Jacek? What about the night I met you?"

"Jacek has always been suspicious of everyone, especially women. He doesn't trust them. He thinks they all have ulterior motives, and in my case, he wasn't wrong. But I obviously couldn't let anyone know that. I think part of it is he was jealous of Bartlomiej spending time with me he usually spent with Jacek. He certainly didn't approve of Bartlomiej asking my opinions on things. It still amazes me Bartlomiej wanted my opinion and trusted it even when he thought I was so naïve, unworldly, and innocent. It just proved how deeply I'd wormed my way into his life. The night you met me, Jacek attacked me because he thought I was spying for the Armenians. I had no contact with them."

"What made him think that?" The Armenians feel like a stretch despite watching their deal blow up with the Poles.

"I don't know. But he sensed something was going wrong with the bratva, and he couldn't figure out what it was. He assumed it was the Armenians, since that was supposed to be their next deal.

While Bartlomiej was out, his men grabbed me and pinned me to the floor at Bartlomiej's house. There was nothing I could do once they had me on the floor. Each question or accusation earned me a punch or a kick. Each one was about my potential connections to another syndicate family. Obviously, I had nothing to say that would've been true, nor would I have given up anything true, which pissed him off. I had to balance my ability to defend myself with the persona I'd created. It would've ruined everything if I'd fought back too hard. It would've justified his suspicions, so I took most of it. But when he threatened to assault me, that's when I obviously drew the line. I got away and ran."

Tried to assault her? I'm going to cut off his cock and shove it up his own arse.

"I really didn't know where I was going to end up. I didn't plan to hide at a construction site, but they chased me as far as I could get. I kept my head down and hopped on the subway. I only got off in Manhattan because I feared I would pass out if I didn't stop and find somewhere to hide. I wanted to go where he'd least suspect me, but that I could get to easily. I believe he had men on the same train as me, but they never approached me. Once I was outside, I could ditch them because it was so dark out."

"And a construction site seemed like a safe place?"

"It wasn't well lit, and there wouldn't be people there. I didn't think about triggering an alarm system for the entire property. I just saw a place that was dark and obscure, so I went for it. When Bartlomiej came back, he treated me with kid gloves, wanted me closer to him, and that allowed me to hear more details about his deal with the bratva."

"That's why you spent so much time there when you claimed it was for work."

"It was for work, just not the kind I told you. There were things he wouldn't explain that complicated the deal, but I pieced it together. He wanted to expand his network through the Russians to the Armenians. He tried to create friction between those two syndicates, so he could mediate, but we saw how well that went."

"But why the bratva? Why were they your ultimate target?"

That's the most pressing question. The one I want to know the answer to, but she hasn't offered.

"We have intel they've been expanding farther into Eastern Europe, that they are increasing their exports to former Eastern Bloc nations. They've always had a presence there simply because they're Russian, but now they're using that more to their advantage and permeating more cities in more countries. Soon they'll have an entire monopoly on most of the former Soviet Union. Like I said, I knew I couldn't get into the bratva. The Poles were the next best option."

I sit here in silence because I know the truth. It isn't the bratva that's becoming so pervasive. It's my family who's expanding into new markets there, and it's pissing the Kutsenkos off. But even they don't know the full extent of what we're accomplishing. They're stuck twiddling their thumbs.

I'm torn between whether I can tell Carrie the truth about my family. I want to, but she's still an agent and despite how attracted we are to each other, we still don't know each other very well. Until I can talk to my brothers and cousins about this, I'll keep quiet on our involvement. I know silence is as good as an omission, and that can be as much as a lie. It might ruin things with Carrie because I'm not being forthcoming. However, family must always come first. It's not just my life at stake, it's everyone I love. I have to choose wisely, and I can't make that choice alone.

Carrie's hand pauses on my chest, and I know she realizes I'm deep in thought.

"Shane, we have to speak to your family. I have to tell them what I know, and that opens them up to even more risk because of my job, as well as knowing how things stand with the bratva."

"That's not a risk we're unfamiliar with. It's one our shoulders are broad enough to handle. You're in greater danger now that Bartlomiej knows you're a spy and an agent. It'll only piss him off more when he discovers you ran to me. For now, he might think you went to Misha's, and that you were a spy for the bratva all along. Then again, that would almost be a better lie for him to believe than for him to discover you've involved an entirely separate syndicate family."

"I know. I have to tell my handlers they made me, and then they'll have to pull me out and get me to a safe house."

"I don't like that idea at all, *cailín*. They can't protect you there. They don't know what they're up against with Bartlomiej and Jacek. Bartlomiej can be reasonable like you know, but Jacek is crazy. He won't stop until he has you, and that means he will take out your handlers as well as you. You need a place that has protection with people who actually know what they're doing with syndicates. You might have studied the Poles, and the DEA may have come after us enough times, but they don't truly understand the inner workings like a fellow syndicate member."

"I don't know where to go, Shane. My options are limited."

I sit forward and look at her. "Your options aren't limited, and you know exactly where you're going. You know exactly who's going to help you."

"Thank you, Shane. I didn't want to assume anything, and I don't want to cause you or your family to get more attention from the government."

"I know that, Carrie, but I told you I would protect you, and I meant it. If ever there was a time for me to prove it, it's now."

"Daddy, I don't want you to feel like you have anything to prove. I don't want you to feel like that's how our relationship stands. That I'm only with you because of what you can do for me."

Regret fills her voice, and she shifts, so she can lean against me more. Calling me Daddy tells me she needs more sheltering from the world than she realizes.

"I never thought that, Carrie. That never even crossed my mind. I'm with you because I want to be, but I know being with me brings more danger than you're used to. It's an entirely different danger from just going undercover. You went to a smaller syndicate. Their influence doesn't stretch nearly as far as they would like to think. It means I have resources they don't. There are only three other families that truly rival mine, and if the bratva has been your target all along, then you're going to need my family's help."

"I thought they didn't target women and children."

"That's true, but they will use all their resources to shut you down and keep your mission from succeeding. We have to plan for that."

"Do you think I can still feed information to my handlers while I continue to rely on you? I don't know what I'm supposed to do, Daddy."

"I don't know either. It would be best if we speak to my family now and fill them in on what you've told me because they must be part of any decision we make."

"I know. But I don't see how you and I can work. I need to survive this, and I appreciate any help you and your family can give me, but they will never accept me because I'm only bringing all this trouble to your door."

"This trouble exists regardless of you, *cailín*. You might be the one the most recent challenge, but you are not the cause of anything new. And as for accepting you, my family has a far more open mind than anybody realizes. None of the women who've married into this family recently come with uncomplicated pasts. It's a challenge each time, so this won't come as a surprise. They know you're an agent and who you work for."

"But whatever complicated relationship your brothers and cousins may have had, I guarantee none of those women worked for the federal government."

"No, but one of them could bring the feds to our door, even though it wasn't entirely intentional."

Carrie's eyebrows shoot straight up, and I see the shock. Somehow, she must not have heard about Dillan and his wife.

"Carrie, the mob boss married a woman who shared secrets about my family to the entire world. She discovered all of them from infiltrating us. It wasn't intentional that the information went out, but she planned to disclose it all along."

"Oh."

That one word is all she says. It comes out with a puff of air. It proves that revelation stunned her.

She pulls away from me and scoots to the edge of the bed. I follow her. She gets dressed, and we head back downstairs.

"Off to the executioner."

"It won't be that bad, *cailín*."

"My head's bound to be on someone's plate by tonight."

Chapter Thirteen

Shane

Dillan sees us first as we enter his office. I texted him while Carrie put her clothes back on, so anything they discussed that Carrie can't hear ended. All the guys stand as she comes in. Our parents drilled into us anytime a woman enters a room or comes to a table to sit down or leaves, we stand. Immediate family members don't count. But since Carrie isn't one yet, they demonstrate etiquette that's so a part of the core of who we are, we don't even realize we're doing it.

Ironically, the other three families are exactly the same. Their parents drilled etiquette into them just as sternly as our parents did. We are the politest mobsters you'll ever meet.

"Hello, Carys."

Dillan gestures toward the couch I'm already leading her to. I didn't think about it while we walked down the stairs, but I'm holding her hand. It doesn't go unnoticed by any of the guys. She offers him a tight smile when she returns the greeting.

"Hello—everyone."

She hesitates between words, unsure exactly what she should say, if anything. I make the rounds of introductions, and we're soon all seated on the sofas, love seats, and armchairs spread throughout Dillan's office. It's a converted den he expanded through to a guest bedroom, creating a meeting area large enough for all of us.

They just finished the work a couple weeks ago. We wound up in the dining room when we had family meetings that included our dads. They don't come on missions very often, but they still do sometimes.

Carrie gives the quick rundown of what she told me. She hides nothing from them and is open about the knowledge she has. It's not like she confided things in me she was unwilling to tell the others. It pleases me she feels comfortable enough to be that open.

Anything she told me, she knows I would have repeated to my family anyway, so she could have relied on me to do it, but she didn't. When she finishes explaining how she got involved with Bartlomiej and where things stand now, she sits back against the sofa, and I tighten my hold on her shoulders. She starts to lean against me but catches herself.

I know the guys won't think she's weak for it, so I ease her against my side. It only takes a moment before she puts her head on my shoulder. I can tell she's even more exhausted than she was when we got here.

It's worn her out having to run for her life, then sharing secrets that could get her in more trouble than she could imagine. Not just with her work and the Poles, but with us.

Dillan speaks first. "Carys, you have our protection. Not just Shane's, but our entire family. I won't pretend like part of this isn't because of your mother, but most of it is because you clearly mean a great deal to my cousin. We will do everything we can to shield you from the Poles, but that doesn't change who employs you."

She stiffens, so I press my fingers against her shoulder.

"I know, and that's still something I have to figure out because as long as I'm still an agent, I have obligations that could wind me up in jail if I don't fulfill them."

I sweep my gaze around the room, and I know what the others are thinking. If she reports back to her handlers that we offered her shelter, it'll only turn their attention to us. None of us believe she will, but if they figure it out, any additional attention could make them realize we're the ones doing the deal in Eastern Europe. I know it means I'll hide even more from her than I normally would.

I haven't had that conversation with her yet about the lies of omission and the boldface lies I'll have to tell her to protect her, my family, and our men. I don't know if that's something she can accept, considering the position she's already in. I'll cross that bridge when I come to it, but it certainly presents yet another challenge.

"I'm taking Carrie to my place. She'll be safe there, but I want extra guards."

Dillan looks at me askance as though he's insulted I'd mention it. "Of course. That's not even in question. We'll get those men assigned right away. They'll be there by the time you get home."

Uncertain what to say, a simple "thank you" sufficed. We all understand how she feels physically after such an arduous day, and I think we mostly understand how she feels mentally and emotionally. I'm ready to stand and leave with her, even though I know there're other things for us to discuss. However, we can't do that with her here, and Dillan's wife isn't home from work yet, so Carrie would be on her own. Not only would that be rude, but that's not what she needs right now.

My big brother opens his mouth but hesitates. Finn's thinking twice about what he says. He opts for blunt. "What about your work?"

Carrie and I have gone around in circles several times without resolving that. We've stated the obvious more than once, but to what avail?

"I have to see them soon. I've got to ensure they're safe, if nothing else. Jacek emailed a bunch of photos to Bartlomiej. They included ones of me meeting with Angela. He'll have recognized her because we posed her as a friend of mine named Stella. I told Bartlomiej I was going over there for a girls' night, but it was really the safe house for a check in. Since he knows where it is, they need to get out. There's a good chance Jacek's already raided it, assuming I'd eventually go there rather than stay at Misha's. That's the last place any of them know I went. He could toss it to find out more about the set up."

"Carrie, I'm going with you. I'll wait in the car and make sure they're none the wiser I'm there, but I'll be able to protect you if need be."

"Thank you. I can't go back to the apartment I was in, but my gun and badge are in the safe, and I tucked my go bag into a nook I made at the back of my closet. There's a false wall to make it seem shallower than it is. I can't leave that stuff behind. It's inevitable they'll discover it's false paneling in the closet, and they'll crack the safe if they're given enough time. The moment they find my badge, there's no way Bartlomiej won't enforce the hit he put on me.

"I'll get it."

Seamus offers, but his brother shakes his head. Cormac shoots Carrie a quick smile before looking back at Seamus.

"No, you've got stuff going on with Tiernan. I'll do it."

What Cormac didn't say is he's the only completely unattached guy in the family now, so he has less to lose than any of us. I'd offer to do it, but I feel like I need to stay with Carrie more than I need to be away from her to find that stuff.

"I left my purse in Tymoteusz's car. It has nothing in there that can incriminate me, but I don't have the keys to my place anymore."

Cormac grins. "That's never stopped me before."

We all own professional lock picking kits, which are illegal in New York. It was among the first skills we gained when we started our training. We didn't start carrying knives until we turned twelve, but we got our lock picking sets when we were eight and started practicing, so we were experts by the time we started going on missions when we were fourteen or fifteen. Those were petty crimes. Legit missions where there was a good likelihood we'd die didn't start until we were sixteen. Such a fucked-up life we lead.

I can't avoid letting Carrie know those pieces of my history.

They aren't ones I wish to share, and I'm certain realizing how young I started will bother her, but there's no way to undo the past.

"I'll take Carrie to my place. Let me know when you have everything, Cor."

I live in Douglaston, here in Queens. It's an upscale place, and I love living away from the hustle and bustle of the city. All five boroughs—Queens, Manhattan, Brooklyn, the Bronx, and Staten Island—are technically "the city," but that phrase really means Manhattan. I like the residential feel.

Only Finn lived in what most of us would consider Manhattan. He was in SoHo before he got married. The other guys were in East Harlem or Brooklyn. Harlem's on Manhattan Island, but it's not downtown—or rather below the Upper East and Upper West Sides. It has its own feel. Its own vibe, separate from places like SoHo.

Now both my brothers and two of my cousins live here in Forest Hills. Carrie had just as equal a chance of stumbling upon one of my brothers' or cousins' houses or another bratva or any Mafia house as she did Misha's. It was just happenstance she found Misha instead of one of us. When we get to my car, I open the door for her, but she turns to look at me.

"Shane, thank you for everything you're doing for me. I hate putting you in this position."

"It's not your fault, Carrie. Perhaps it's fate that we met when we did. It might not have been the most convenient timing, but it is what it is, and I'm glad we met."

"So am I, but you can understand why I don't love the danger I'm putting you in."

This seems like as good a time as any to explain what it would really be like being with me.

"*Cailín*, get in, and we'll talk on the way to my place."

I close the door behind her and walk around to my side. As I open the door, I take a deep breath, girding my loins.

"Being with me puts you in danger you couldn't imagine, so it's something we must discuss."

I glance over at her as I pull out of Dillan's driveway.

"A few years ago, my uncle led our family, and he made some shite choices that changed the landscape of being in a syndicate in New York. He broke the cardinal rule that women and children are *not* to be involved. He went after a bratva wife, and he died for it. His cousin, Declan, decided he would change the line of inheritance. It was always the plan that Dillan would step into the role as boss whenever Uncle Donovan died. But Dillan was so pissed at how things went down with Uncle Donovan, he took the only vacation he's ever had alone."

Anger and grief war within me, and I'd rather not tell this story. But Carrie needs to understand because she has a choice to make. Accept what I tell her and stay with me or learn the truth and walk away.

"In that time, Declan seized control and made things even worse by retaliating against the bratva for them retaliating against us. He lived the same fate as Uncle Donovan. We just made him an easier target to catch beforehand. We made sure he physically couldn't get away. He was in no condition to defend himself before we handed him over. Normally, we wouldn't turn on our own, and we wouldn't let the bratva think they beat us by being the ones to end Declan's worthless fecking life, but he deserved what he got. He had a thin hold on his position as mob boss, so he wanted to prove he had real control over the family."

My hands tighten around the steering wheel until my knuckles are white. Anger and grief have become allies, and they nearly defeat me.

"He ordered hits on my mom and aunts. Before he could call them off, he died for his sins. That didn't prevent a mercenary from confusing Dillan's little sister, Colleen, for Seamus and Cormac's mom. Dillan was with Colleen when a hired gun shot her straight through the forehead. She was a veterinarian who specialized in rescuing abused animals. She'd just adopted a puppy, and she and Dillan were taking it back to her place."

I swallow the sour bile that rises in my throat. I blink away the tears that always come when I think about this.

"Colleen was the sweetest, funniest, naughtiest kid you could have ever met, and she stayed exactly the same as we grew up. She was the true ringleader in the family. She got us into as much trouble as she could, but she got us out of most of it, too. She had these dimples you couldn't ignore. They made her look so angelic even when she was being a little devil. Cormac and Seamus always escaped getting in trouble. Even though all our parents knew they were involved, they slipped away before anyone noticed. However, Colleen was their judge, jury, and executioner. She made sure they got their fair share of justice."

We pull up to a light, and I close my eyes for a moment to compose myself.

"The bratva believed they were the victims in the shitshow Uncle Don and Declan caused, but they weren't. The two bratva wives who were targets survived Donovan and Declan, but Colleen didn't. It was because of our own family that we lost her. It's not open season on women and children, but they don't enjoy the protections they used to. I can't guarantee you wouldn't be a target at some point. I don't want that to be the case, but it certainly could be."

I glance at Carrie again. She's listening attentively. I see sympathy, not fear, in her eyes.

"There are things I will do—things I've already done—that make me the same monster as Bartlomiej. I can't pretend otherwise. I don't enjoy the things that I do. I don't get the satisfaction out of it Jacek does, but they are my responsibility to do. Sometimes I'll lie to you. I'll look you right in the eye and tell you something so far from the truth you won't be able to guess what's really going on. There are other times when I'll lie by omission. I just won't tell you what's happening. I have to do this in order to protect you, my family, and the men who depend upon us. It's not just those men who depend upon us during missions. It's their families, too. It's the entire community that depends on my family to provide for them."

She rests her hand on my thigh as I speak. The weight's reassuring. It offers me the same silent strength I hope she got from me when I put my arm around her shoulders earlier.

"I'll disappear at times. I'll always do my best to tell you when I'll leave, but I don't always know how long I'll be away. Sometimes I'll still be in New York, other times I could be halfway across the world. I'll always ensure you have extra protection when I'm gone. That means a member of my family."

I know that surprises her because her fingers flex against my leg. But she lets me continue. I think she senses I need to get all of this off my chest in one fell swoop, or I'll clam up.

"Right now, I'll have regular guards outside my place, but if we go anywhere, someone from my family will be with us. If you have to go anywhere without me, at least two of the guys at Dillan's house will be with you. Family means people I share direct DNA with. Three sisters married three brothers, and among them, they had six sons. So, my brothers and Dillan, Seamus, and Cormac. If they're not available, then it could be my dad or my uncles. No one beyond one degree of separation is good enough. I don't trust anyone else to protect you how they can. Nobody else but them will understand what it means to me to keep you safe."

We're at another light. I watch her as I speak. At first, there were varying degrees of shock, fear, and dismay as I told her as much of the truth as I can. Then I saw the sympathy. Now—it feels like resignation rather than relief.

"Carrie, these are things you must accept if there's any chance for us. I know it's hypocritical to expect you to make these changes, while I can make none. It hypocritical I'll expect you to tell me the truth about anything that could pose a threat to you when I'll hide everything. But this is the way it'll have to be. Do you think you can live with that?"

I finally invite her opinion. I've unleashed too much because she remains silent, and that's more unnerving than it would be if she argued with me or even shared her thoughts. I don't press her, and we ride in silence for the twenty minutes it takes us to cross this part of Queens. We're almost to my place before she breaks her silence.

"What happens if you have to be gone for several days, and something goes wrong? How would I get in touch with you if I don't know where you are?"

"It's rare all of us are gone for several days at a time. But if that happens, I'd want you to stay with my mom and dad."

"Stay with your parents? You're just going to have a random woman show up at their door and dump her there?"

"Carrie, you are not some random woman. You know that. You know you mean far more to me than that. I would hope I mean more to you than just being some random guy."

"You do, but it's different between us than it would be with your parents. They can't just have an unwelcome and unplanned houseguest."

"You wouldn't be unwelcomed or unplanned. I'd speak to them and let them know what's going on. My dad would already be privy to whatever's taking me away. They'd want it this way. Carrie, they'd want you to come to them, so they can keep you safe too. You saw the home Dillan lives in. Our parents and aunts and uncles live nearby. They're either in the same neighborhood or the one next to it. Dillan's sits on the corner that adjoins the two the Four Families have basically commandeered. They have an enormous house to accommodate plenty of guests. You wouldn't be any sort of imposition to them. Just the opposite. I'm certain it would mean a great deal to them to know you trust them enough to stay with them when I can't be with you."

"Shane, I don't know about all this. It's a lot to take in when—just this morning—I thought I was still undercover."

"I understand. It certainly makes for a lot of choices, and I'll give you all the time I can to think about that, *cailín*. But at some point, you must decide."

It's definitely resignation in her tone. "I know."

"I won't rush you. You can stay with me for as long as you need. I have more than enough room for you to hang out and not feel like I'm crowding you."

That makes her fall silent again. I don't know what her wishes are as far as any type of intimate relations we could have while she's at my place. I don't want to assume too much. Obviously, I wouldn't turn her down, but I also won't push the issue.

Something else comes to mind, though, as we get closer to my place. "Carrie, how'd the bratva even come to be on your radar? You said they're your ultimate target."

She hesitates before she admits another secret. "We have somebody in the Cartel who told us about it. They heard from Enrique the bratva was making plans."

I'm unsurprised it came from another syndicate and that it was misdirection, but that's something I keep from her. She's on a need-to-know basis, and I'm not sure yet what that includes. Until I have a better idea, it's that hypocrisy making me keep secrets when I expect her to divulge everything.

I know the mole in the Cartel isn't one of ours, so it makes me wonder whether it's bratva or Mafia. My assumption would be not bratva, but with the Kutsenkos, who the fuck knows what they have going on and how they're trying to double-cross someone else. It wouldn't surprise me entirely if they had a mole sending information to the feds to get them to come after them in order to throw somebody else under the bus first.

We're all that conniving. It used to be people only believed Dillan was the logistical and strategic mastermind, but it's become obvious that while he's the best at it, no one in the families lacks intelligence. People who see us think we're all muscle-bound idiots or maybe trust fund babies. Most people don't realize we're all either Ivy League or Top Tier educated.

Most of us have some type of graduate degree, too. There're doctors and lawyers among the families, and within the men, there are several lawyers. Seamus, Cormac, and Dillan are the ones in our family, even though Dillan doesn't get to practice anymore. There's not a dumb dud in the bunch.

I'm going to have to dig further to find out who's the narc.

"Shane, what should I tell my handlers? I have to say something, but what's that going to be?"

"That's a good question. I don't have an answer for that right away, but it's going to have to be something that keeps them pointed toward Bartlomiej, while—"

"Wait, Shane. Misha saved me. I don't know that I can actually turn them in after all."

That gives me pause. Anything that would take down a rival family interests us, and it's certainly something I would be happy to help happen, but I can't deny Misha was important today, and that he kept her safe.

But that's women's business.

Lord. Did I just fall back in time to the eighteen hundreds?

Even though he was her rescuer, everybody knows helping the women in our families doesn't suspend the animosity among the men.

"Carrie, I understand that, and I can see how you don't want to go for them as your target, but it changes nothing about the rivalries among the families. I can't ignore what you've told me.

"So, you're going to use that information against me? Things I told you in confidence, now you want to flip and use?"

"Not necessarily, but I still have to consider all that comes along with this information. It's not as simple as just acting like I didn't hear it."

"Yes, it is."

"Carrie, you know I won't keep these things a secret from my family. I can't."

She looks at me, and I can guess what she's thinking. I'm putting my family ahead of her, but for right now, I still have to. She's not family. She's a woman I'm into, but I'm not in love with her—at least not yet—and we're certainly not married, so I can't make her the priority when my family has so much at stake.

"I just wish there was some way to inform my handlers about Bartlomiej trying to do more deals with the Armenians, and his involvement with the bratva as a middleman while not putting their name out there explicitly."

"I don't know how you're going to do that, Carrie. It's one or the other. Here, there're really no shades of gray. Either you name them, or you don't."

What the fuck is she going to do when she finds out it's not the bratva? Do I lie to her for my family's sake, and let her keep thinking it's them, when it's us, and has been all along?

"Shane, you're keeping something from me."

"Carrie, I'm keeping a lot from you, but that's never going to change."

"No, I mean right now. There's something in this conversation you're not telling me."

"Like I said, there's a lot. There're things that would endanger you if I told you and put my family, and all the people who rely on us at risk. I know you want to understand better what's going on, but I just told you a moment ago I'm going to lie to you. I'm going to look you in the eye and lie, or I'm going to lie by omission, and I hate that's reality. The one thing I won't lie about is how I feel about you and our relationship. But anything else is fair game for me, and I am sorry. I know what a hypocrite that makes me, when I'm demanding so much of you, but it can't be and won't be any other way."

She watches me, and I know she understands, even if she doesn't like it and doesn't want to agree. It's my greatest fear that as I get to know her better, she'll come to resent all those secrets. All the things I must keep from her. It makes me wonder if that'll be what drives us apart. Not the actual danger, not her job, but resentment because I won't give all of myself to her when I want all of her in return.

"Shane, I get it. If the situation were reversed, and this was just about my job, I would be in the same position. There are things I could never tell you about my work, even if you were just a regular guy. I couldn't share so many details of the things I do. I wouldn't be able to tell you where I go when I'm undercover. I'd have to juggle that somehow."

"I know. As much as I want to insist you never go undercover again, I can't. I can't push you that far to give up that much when you're already going to sacrifice to be with me."

She reflects upon what I said, and I know the way I phrased it comes across as though I think she can keep her job, but I don't see how that's possible. I'm picking my family over her, but I'm expecting her to pick me over her job.

This is all such a fucked-up and twisted and broken situation, but it's unavoidable and one most of the syndicate men face when they find the woman they want to be with. Balancing wanting all from the woman we're into while giving so little in return. No one else is with someone in law enforcement, though Aleks Kutsenko's father-in-law is retired NYPD.

I think Carrie's the one, but we won't know if we can't move forward.

"We're still at square one because you can't tell me anything, and I have nothing to pass along. Maybe there's another syndicate involved."

"The Polish get along with the Italians well enough, often better than they do the Russians, even though they usually never work for the Italians. They stick to Russian construction sites and jobs."

Her expression gives nothing away as she leans into what I insinuate. "Why haven't you suggested it could be the Mafia trying to expand?"

"You mean into Eastern Europe? Because the most logical syndicate would be the bratva. The ties between Russia and Poland go back centuries. The Kutsenkos already have a working relationship with the Poles here. It's the only permutation that seems reasonable."

"*Seems* reasonable." She catches that one word. "It doesn't mean it actually is reasonable. I don't know if you're truly using logic, or you're trying to deter me from digging deeper into this."

"I'm telling you my thoughts. That's it."

"What about the facts? You want them from me." She shakes her head. "I get there are certain things you can't tell me. But there have to be a few things safe enough for me to know to make sure I'm pointed in the right direction. I don't want to go after the bratva if it's not them."

"If it's not them for this, then it's them for something else. That's always the case."

"Yeah, but this is what I'm building my investigation on. This is what my boss expects from me. It's to dig into the Kutsenkos."

"Can I ask you what evidence besides the spy in the Cartel leads you to think it's the bratva who's extending into Eastern Europe?"

"Much of the same things as you said. Their existing relationships in history, mostly. But we know there's been more money changing hands over there. We're working on the assumption it's for the drugs."

We pull up to my house, and I drive straight into my garage. When she reaches for the door, I put my hand on her thigh and press.

"No, Carrie, you never get out of a car without either a guard or me waiting for you. If we're pulling into a garage with a driver, you wait until the door is at most an inch from the ground. If you're alone, only then do you turn off the engine and get out. Even if you're with me, you wait until I turn off the car before you open the door."

"Oh, you mean in case you suddenly have to back out in a hurry or in case somebody tries to shoot under the door?"

"Or throw a grenade. There're many things. You don't get out of a car in a boxed-in space until you're sure you're alone."

I watch her swallow as she nods. "I feel like that's something so common-sense they should have taught us at the Academy. I've done that on instinct when I would check in with my handlers at the safe house."

"It is, but we don't want to give away all our secrets."

That was the wrong thing to say. She assesses me, and her gaze bores into my soul.

"Shane, you guys are the ones, aren't you?"

The question dangles in the air, and I'm not quick enough to respond because this is one of those times where I've already told her enough outright lies. Now I'm opting for the lie of omission because she needs to decide what she'll do with that information.

Even if I try to deny it, it's too obvious to her we're the ones responsible for the drugs expanding farther into Europe. Her shoulders hunch as she leans back into the seat. She tilts her head back with her eyes closed. I don't press her for her thoughts, and after a moment, she shakes her head and reaches for the door again.

I let her get out, then lead her into my place. Her gaze sweeps over the entryway and into the living room and beyond to the kitchen. It's a far larger home—a more family-oriented space—than you'd expect for a bachelor, but all of us believe our homes are our sanctuaries. It's where we go to get away from the outside world and away from the men we have to be. I like my place being cozy. It has touches someone might stereotypically expect a woman to have. I like throw cushions and extra blankets, and I like a sofa that screams take a nap on me. She notices that as well as more of the decor.

I have family photos on the walls, which is something only my parents and aunts and uncles do. None of the other guys have put up photos in their bachelor pads. Mostly because of the chance someone could raid us, and that would just connect more and more people to us. I've been very selective about who's in the background and where those photos were taken before I put them up on the wall. But it's reassuring to me when I come home each day.

She walks over to a picture of a stunning redhead I'm standing with my arms around and laughing. She looks at me before turning back to the photo. It would almost look like the woman and I are a couple.

"Shane, have you been married before? Are you with somebody?"

Chapter Fourteen

Carrie

I think I'm going to be sick as I wait for an answer.

"No, *cailín*, that's my cousin. That's Dillan's little sister."

I speak in the present tense as though she's still with us because the idea of using the past tense is too final. It's too real that she's never coming back. I'm not in denial, but I also don't need to rip my heart apart.

"That's Colleen? She was breathtaking, with a slightly darker shade of red hair but the same brilliant emerald eyes."

"Yeah, see those dimples? I remember exactly when that photo was taken. She'd just convinced my parents I was the one who let our family dog run through the house and leave muddy prints all over the carpet, when in actual fact, she did it knowing full well my parents would blame me for it."

"But the hug you're giving her—"

"I know how we look together if you don't notice how similar our faces are. Dillan snapped that photo right before I picked her up, hoisted her over my shoulder, and hauled her out to the pool, where I dumped her in fully clothed."

My mouth opens in a perfect circle of surprise. From the

scorching look Shane gives me, it does things to him. I glance down at the bulge in his pants. It does things to his cock. My guess is he's picturing my lips wrapped around it. This isn't the right time to get even wetter than I already am. I'm a sloppy mess when I'm around Shane.

"Your whole family really is that close, aren't you?"

"Yeah, we are by necessity, but we also are by choice. I genuinely like hanging out with my brothers and cousins. We've all been best friends since—well—as long as any of us can remember. Finn and Dillan have a unique friendship. I guess because they're a few years older than the rest of us, and the two who were always on their own. Sean and I came as a package deal, so there's never been one without the other. Seamus was two months premature, so for most of the year he and Cormac are the same age. They've been inseparable just like Sean and me because of it. That's always meant Finn and Dillan are the ones who don't have a second pea in a pod without each other. But even beyond that, we're still all close."

"That's an interesting family dynamic." I can imagine but not fully understand that since I'm an only child.

"I don't feel any less connected or love Finn any less than I do Sean. It's just different with my twin. We have that intuition science hasn't proven, but so many pairs of twins say they feel. But just because Finn isn't my mirror image, doesn't mean I'm not super close to him too. I am. There's something unique about sharing the exact DNA with another person. I'm intuitively closer to Finn and Sean than I am my cousins. I know Cormac and Seamus feel the same way."

"Doesn't that leave out Dillan? It must be isolating being an only child now *and* the mob boss."

"When Colleen was still alive, she and Dillan were so equally matched you'd have thought they were the twins. If there's such a thing as platonic soulmates, Dillan and Colleen were those. They were so in sync with one another I know there were things Dillan shared with her he probably shouldn't have. But she was the other half of his coin. She was his conscience when he was ready to have none. I know he keenly feels her loss every day. It's something none of us will ever get over. I can't fathom how my aunt and uncle survive it. They wouldn't have if not for Dillan. But now that Dillan's married, he's found a romantic soulmate. He and Mair are so well-matched you couldn't think of a better couple."

Hearing that makes me wonder if Shane might be my soulmate. I've certainly never been attracted to another man the way I am him.

I don't believe he'd bring me into this world if he didn't think there was a possibility I could be. It would be foolhardy on so many levels to bring me closer to him if this weren't for good. But I know it's too soon to be sure of that.

He slides his hand into mine, guiding me into the kitchen.

"Are you hungry, *cailín*?"

"Yeah, actually, I am. I hadn't thought about it earlier, but now that we're in here, I just realized I'm starving."

It doesn't take us long to put something together. We suspend our conversation while we make some lunch. We work well together in the kitchen, and it feels so natural, like a moment of domestic tranquility. This is the sort of thing I want to get used to. The life I want to build with somebody, one like my parents have. Like I assume the couples in his family have.

As I watch Shane, I keep trying to picture us here in five years, ten years. When we're old and gray. It's not as difficult as I thought it would be. I've learned a lot about the man he is because the traits I've seen are so deeply ingrained, they can't change. Family, duty, honor, loyalty, and love are who he is and always will be. They're traits I admire. He's the hottest man I've ever met, but that's not the entire reason I'm attracted to him. That wouldn't make our relationship last. It's who I know he is to his very core. I don't need to spends months or years with him to know those qualities run bone deep. It's why it's been so easy to fall harder and harder for him.

I don't know his entire life's story, and I never ever will. I can accept the lies and secrets because those qualities I admire are the ones driving him to protect the people around him. The man I know him to be already tells me more than hearing childhood stories or hearing about his high school and college glory days.

But reality stomps back in like an elephant after we're done with the dishes. We sit on a love seat together, each of us in a corner, turned to look at the other.

"Is it possible for me to call Steve and Angela to let them know I'm somewhere safe?"

"Do they have a way of tracking you here?"

"Normally they would, but I've turned off the tracker before. I have a bracelet that's a thick silver band. There's a small spot where someone smelted the metal together. That's where the tracker is. The clasp is like a latch. One end of the latch releases the bracelet, the other turns it on and off. I'd just gotten out of the shower when Tymoteusz and his men barged in, so I had to get dressed."

"Barged in? Were you wearing anything?" Rage vibrates from him.

"My bathrobe."

I won't tell him it wasn't closed. He'd Hulk out if he knew. I keep talking before he can linger on that.

"I took off the bracelet just before Tymoteusz dragged me out. I left it behind in my apartment. I can always tell them I took it off to shower, even though it's completely waterproof. It's submergible to like a hundred feet, if not more. I have a way of setting it on my computer to look like I'm somewhere I'm not. Like at I'm at my apartment, when there are times I've been other places."

I cock an eyebrow at him. He knows I mean when I was with him.

"Do you think they'll know by now?"

"Probably. They can't get in touch with me because I don't have the pager or the phone we usually use."

"What will they say to you?"

I grimace. "They'll insist I come to them and stay there. That's why I haven't rushed to contact them."

"What will you do about that?"

"I'll tell them I have a better place outside of the city, where I can regroup and figure out when it's safe for me to come back. They'll tell me I should go straight to the office, then they'll put me in a different safe house."

"That definitely won't protect you, Carrie. Now that Jacek knows, he won't give up. He'll continue to pursue you until he finds you. There's no way he can back down because Bartlomiej will push him to find you. Once Jacek does, Bartlomiej'll let Jacek work you over. He won't do it himself. He's always had his brother do his dirty work for him, and I fully believe Bartlomiej will sanction Jacek going after you. He's already put a hit on you, and time will not calm him and convince him to call it off. Just the opposite. It's just the permission Jacek needs to do it himself. The man was always batshit bonkers, but after his time in the military, he didn't come back quite right. He is the poster child for PTSD. He's every horrible stereotype of a syndicate man and a wounded warrior I know."

"I learned that well before I went in. It's all in his VA file. He didn't pass the psychiatric exam when he got out. It's only gotten worse with time. I saw it that night he attacked me. It was in his eyes. If I believed anyone needed an exorcism, it would be him. Even if I'd hoped Bartlomiej might call off the hit once he calms down, what you said doesn't surprise me."

"Bartlomiej isn't the type to calm down. He only gets himself more and more amped up, and Jacek contributes to that. Feeds off of it. It's their dysfunctional codependency. It won't be over for Bartlomiej until you're dead. That's how it works. The pot bubbles, then boils over spectacularly."

I don't doubt him, but my expression must make him think I do.

"He won't back off, Carrie. I'm not exaggerating. I can't stress that enough."

"I get what you're saying, Shane."

"Do you want to call your handlers now? I have burners you can use. They'll never detect where you are because I have jammers here at the house."

That doesn't surprise me either. "Yeah, I'll take you up on that. Better sooner rather than later."

I glance at the clock he has on the mantel. It's definitely a well-maintained antique. Shane notices where I'm looking.

"It was my nana's before she passed away. Finn inherited the bar she ran, and Sean got much of her jewelry. I got several of her household decorations. Seamus and Cormac inherited stocks, bonds, annuities, while Dillan got all the properties. It might not seem evenly distributed, but each of us got the things we most wanted."

It surprises me he's telling me something so private, but I know he's trying to let me in more. Trying to show me he won't be closed off when he doesn't have to be. I appreciate it.

"It was a hard loss for all of us, but having things like her clock on the mantel to remind me of her makes the loss a little easier. She was gone from us years before she actually died. Dementia stole her from us, but it wasn't long after Colleen's death that she passed as well."

I reach for his hand and slip mine into his and give it a squeeze. I hear sadness warring with fondness in his tone.

It's only been two-and-a-half hours since I bolted from the car. It feels like it should have been much, much longer, but really we've spent most of that time driving from one place to another.

"Could I have a phone now, please?"

He leaves me in the living room as he heads into his study. I hear him on the phone, but I don't know who he's speaking to.

"She's going to contact her handlers. I'm giving her a burner right now. She's not sure what she's going to say. I'll be there for the conversation."

I can't hear whatever the other caller says, so it's silent for a moment.

"I spotted the extra guards already positioned around the neighborhood, so it shouldn't be a problem if they decide to show up."

They? I assume he means Bartlomiej or Jacek.

"Yeah, I know we have ways of blocking their entry, but I don't want that."

Block their entry? Does he mean barricade us in here?

"Even if they figure out where she is, I don't want to make a bigger fuss than need be. I don't know if they'll know the house belongs to me or not, but she doesn't have her tracker on, so that shouldn't be an issue. And if Bartlomiej and Jacek show up or they send men, kill them."

He meant my colleagues at first. There's silence again, and I still don't know who's on the other end.

"Okay, I gotta go. Just wanted to touch base. Keep me posted, Dillan."

I lean back over the sofa, and I can see down the hallway to his office. He slides his phone back into his pocket and opens the bottom desk drawer, then pulls out a phone still in the package. He also grabs a pair of scissors before straightening. I shift, so it doesn't appear like I was spying. He heads back in here, and his expression tells me he knows I listened and watched.

Of course he did.

He hands me the phone and scissors. I'm certain he wants me to see they're still unopened.

"Shane, I trust you. You didn't have to keep it in the package, and you don't have to let me cut into it." I take both items and pull apart the plastic.

"I know, but there's a lot of times when I won't be able to reassure you. Right now, I can. I'll seize these opportunities when they're available."

That fills me with happiness I didn't know I needed. Once the phone's out of the package and I've turned it on and set it up, I sit here staring at it. I'm still incredibly conflicted about what I need to do. There's what I believe is a simple answer, but that doesn't make this any easier. I eventually dial the number and put the phone on speaker.

I hope Shane understands my faith in him since I'm willing to let him hear this call. I could easily step out of the room and go somewhere else or let it be a one-sided conversation. Instead, I'm letting him be privy to it.

"Hello, Kaja."

That voice.

That's not either of my handlers. That's Bartlomiej.

I don't know what to say, so I stare at the phone.

"Cat got your tongue? Or have you let Shane swallow it?"

I turn toward Shane, terrified. He remains quiet but shakes his head. He puts his finger to his lips and points to the phone. His hand rolls in the air as if to tell me to let our silence continue, but also like he wants Bartlomiej to get on with it. Bartlomiej will fill the gap. He can't stand silence, and he loves the sound of his own voice too much.

"You can play the silent game with me, but it won't get you anywhere. We didn't get here in time to catch your handlers, but we know who they are now. We won't stop until we have them. Unless—" He pauses for effect. "—Unless you turn yourself over to me, then we'll leave your handlers alone. They'll be none the wiser."

Bullshit they will.

I know Bartlomiej, and from the expression on Shane's face, he doesn't believe a word Bartlomiej's saying.

"Turn yourself over, and we won't go after the mob, either."

That's laughable. He might be a bur in their backside—might cause a minor problem here and there—but by no means is he in a position to do anything significant to them. The only way he could is if he had the bratva on his side. Considering how the last time went when they saw each other, there's no way the bratva will help them, even if it's something like this.

Shane pulls out his phone and taps the notes app. He types furiously.

They won't stop Bartlomiej and Jacek. They won't help either. That I'm confident of.

Bartlomiej keeps digging.

"Are you with Shane now? Hey, Shane. I'm sure you can hear this. You know, I know exactly where you live, and I bet you took her to your house. You think you're so safe there, but you're not safe anywhere. I can get to you if I want, and that's exactly what I want. If it's not me, then it'll be Jacek. After what he did to her last time, we both know you'd rather I be the one who gets to her. I'll make it nice and quick for you, Kaja. Or should I say, Carys?

That makes both of us go rigid. If he's figured out my real name, then it won't be hard for him to tie me to Mom and Dad. They'll be the next set of targets. Maybe Bartlomiej would take them hostage, but I doubt it. I think he'd truly go for the jugular and take them out to punish me. Shane writes me another note.

I'll tell Dillan to get them somewhere safe right now.

I nod. I watch him switch over to a group text.

SHANE

Bartlomiej's on the phone with Carrie. She called her handlers. He's there and has their phone. He just threatened Meredith and Rhys. We need to get them out.

SEAMUS

I'm closest to their house. I'll go there now. I'll make sure they're safe. I'll take them to the property on Staten Island.

Relief spreads throughout me, but it's short-lived.

"Carys, I can practically hear you breathing. I hear it's labored. Is that because you just finished fucking Shane? Or is it fear? I think it's the latter. I think you know he can't protect you from me."

Shane shakes his head and rolls his eyes to reassure me. The only person who's going to die—the only people who're going to die—are Bartlomiej and Jacek.

"Until later, Carys, my love."

The venom in his voice perverts the comment, and a shiver runs through me.

Chapter Fifteen

Shane

I put my hand on her thigh. The call ends, and I lift Carrie onto my lap. She curls into me, and I know this is where she belongs. It feels so incredibly right to hold her. Like she's always belonged here and always will. She's beautiful, and I love the way she feels when I touch any part of her. But it is so, so much more. She's brave, intelligent, stubborn, irreverent, loyal, confident. My list could keep going. I know she usually does the honorable thing, and she's trying to do it now. She's struggling to balance her duty and loyalty to her job and her feelings for me. I get that.

I don't know all the day-to-day details about her. I don't know her favorite food or the toothpaste she prefers. I know who she is on and elemental level, and that won't change even if her job or allegiance does. The same values that drive me, drive her, too. Love, loyalty, honor, duty, and family. I know I admire her for who she is and always will be. It's why I've fallen for her, and my feelings grow by the minute. The minutia will come with time because the important qualities are there and make me want to stick around for the little things.

I think she feels the same because she relaxes. I glance down, and her eyes are closed as she rests against me.

"Daddy, can we stay like this forever? Do we really have to let the rest of the world find us? Can't we just continue as we are?"

"I want that too, *cailín*. We can stay like this as long as you want. Nobody's getting in here that I don't let in. I have men already stationed around the house, and they're ready the moment they need to act, but I don't believe it'll come to that."

"I hope you're right." Her voice isn't as calm as it was a moment ago. "Shane, I've got to call into the office and find out what happened to Angela and Steve. I can't go without knowing. I'll panic if I don't find out, and it's my duty to make sure our supervisors know something went wrong. Thank God it hasn't been as long as I thought. Nearly three hours isn't too unreasonable. Hell, it's plausible it took me that long to get somewhere safe."

She doesn't get off my lap as she dials another number. I see her finger hover over the speaker button before she taps it. I don't envy the position she's in right now. I wouldn't wish it upon anyone.

"This is Special Agent Carys Pritchard. I need to speak to Supervisory Special Agent Phil Hammond."

"Agent Pritchard, we've been expecting your call. Hang on."

The line goes quiet for a moment, and I can tell we're on speakerphone too.

"Agent Pritchard, where are you? Angela and Steve already reported to us. We know you've been made."

"I'm somewhere safe outside the city. I'll stay here until I'm sure I can get back into Manhattan without anyone finding me."

"Where are you? We'll come to you. You know wherever you are isn't a designated safe house unless you're in Pittsburgh."

"Sir, I'm fine where I am for now. Until I know what's going on and exactly how they made me, I'm better off staying put exactly where I am."

"That's not acceptable, Carys. You will follow this order."

"And if I die in the process, Phil, then what? I haven't given my last report. I'm not doing it over the phone."

"You know this is a secured line."

"Maybe, but not absolutely. I will give my report in person, but not yet. Deal with the Nowakowski brothers and put them in jail, and I'll consider going back."

"What exactly are we supposed to arrest them for?"

This is a second voice. He sounds snide and arrogant.

"Steve, you know as well as I do, there's plenty to arrest them for. You've got probable cause up the yin-yang and back, and if nothing else, you can pin attempted murder on at least Jacek. You have the photos from what he did. There's no way he wasn't trying to kill me when he attacked me. At the very least, you have assault on a federal agent. We have plenty of other evidence already to indict both brothers on drug trafficking. The only reason we haven't brought them in is because we wanted the bratva more."

"About that." This is a woman's voice, but she says nothing else. Carrie mouths "Angela."

I can tell Carrie's frustration is rising with how her handlers press her, but now she can breathe a little easier since they're safe after all.

The woman's voice comes back on the call. "Someone clued them in they're under investigation. I wonder who that could be."

"Are you suggesting I did it?" Carrie's incredulous tone is genuine.

"We know you've been in contact with someone in another syndicate family. Tell us who, and we can make a move."

She meets my gaze. "You know I have CIs all over the place. I'm cultivating a relationship with one right now, but it's too soon to say anything about it."

"Maybe to people outside this agency, but you can tell us."

Angela presses her. I don't like the bitch. It's her tone, too. I rarely say shite like that about women, but I will about her.

"No, I told you I'm not saying anything else over the phone."

"And you need to get your ass in here."

Angela snaps at Carrie, and it makes me want to curl my hands into fists.

"You need to back down, Angela. I'm doing what I can. I'll get to all of you when I can. It's not safe for me to stay on the phone here. I need to go. I checked in to find out whether you and Steve were safe. You are. Now I gotta go."

Her supervisor, Phil Hammond—tucking that name away for later—comes back on the line.

"That is not how it's going to work. You're going to come back into the office, and you are going to debrief us on everything."

"I would happily do that if I thought I'd live long enough to get there, but I don't. So, until I'm confident I'll survive to get there to tell you everything, you'll have to give me some more time. You trusted me to get into the Polish mob's world. Now I need you to trust me to get back out."

"Fine. But I expect daily check-ins from you, since your tracker isn't on."

"I know. I had to leave it behind. I took it off to shower because it was irritating my wrist. I couldn't put it back on without Tymoteusz wondering why I needed a piece of jewelry—at least one that didn't come from Bartlomiej. That would have made him inspect it. There's too great a chance he would have found out it's a tracker. Then I'd be dead."

"The phone you're on doesn't have location services on either."

"Obviously." She snaps the word before taking a calming breath. "If you could track me, then so could they. That would defeat the point of the safe house, wouldn't it? Just give me some time to make my way to you. I'll come as soon as I can."

"And you'll tell us about this new CI you have.

"I have to go. I'll be in touch as soon as I can."

"Agent—"

"I have to go."

Carrie ends the call, looking up at me. She's biting her lower lip, and I can tell she's struggling to keep it together. I know she's in work mode, so she doesn't want to come across as someone who's too emotional. I will disabuse her of that idea.

"It's okay to let me know how you're feeling. It's okay to be scared. I'm terrified."

She looks at me as though I'm lying.

"*Cailín*, just because I don't show my emotions doesn't mean I don't feel them deeply. I've been conditioned not to show them. It took a lot of training over a lot of years to hide what I think and feel so easily."

She's slow to nod, but she does.

"Carrie—"

I stumble over my words. I want to admit a bit more about my life, so I don't come across as so closed off and secretive, but I don't know what I should tell her.

"Carrie, obviously none of us were born with the skills we have. We started with little things when we were eight years old like learning how to pick locks, learning how to pickpocket. By the time we were ten, we were committing minor crimes like that. Not because we needed any of those items we took, but to prove to my grandfather we could. There's a fecked-up family tradition among all four families."

Her brow furrows, and I can only imagine what she going to make of what I tell her next.

"We grew up playing peewee and little league sports together. Our parents were the ones who brought snacks to our games. During the week when our dads were rivals, business was business. But on Saturdays and Sundays, when we had games, it was family time. Wives and children were present, so they put aside their animosities and cheered on whichever team their kids played for. And that often-meant cheering on their rival's children, too. But when we all turned twelve, our birthday gift was a pocketknife. We've all carried one since then."

She can't hide her shock. It only gets worse.

"When we were fourteen, fifteen, we started helping our dads and the other guys prep for missions. Sometimes we went, but we were far from the action where we couldn't get hurt. My grandfather and Uncle Donovan pressed for us to do more when we were younger, but my parents and aunts and uncles wouldn't allow it. Uncle Donovan tried to take us on a mission without our dads one time when we were fifteen. He was my mom's brother. My mom's Breda. Dillan's mom is Siobhan, and Cormac and Seamus's mom is Saoirse. They terrified their brother more than any other danger he could have ever faced."

It makes my lips twitch when I think about my mom and aunts, who're all pretty tall at about five-eight, terrifying Uncle Don, who was like me at six-three-and-a-half.

"They locked themselves in his office one day when they found out what he planned for us. He came out pale as a ghost, clearly shaken. No one ever suggested any of us go on missions where Grandda and Uncle Don expected us to fight like men before we turned sixteen. My mom wanted to prove a point—one I'm not supposed to know about, and neither are my brothers or cousins, but we all do. She put a hit on one of Uncle Don's men just so Uncle Don knew she could. The guy was in the hospital for weeks as a reminder that Uncle Don might've led the mob back then, but his sisters led the family. And family comes ahead of everything."

That's probably one of my proudest family memories. I'm keeping that part to myself. I'm already sharing plenty of fucked-up shite. I don't want Carrie to believe I'm as fucked-up as the things I've done.

She waits patiently for me to continue. In for a penny, in for a pound.

"But by the time I was ready for college, I'd done things I can never describe to you. Things that would make you look at me the same way you must Jacek."

"No, Shane, never that. Jacek does these things because he enjoys them. He's Bartlomiej's chief enforcer because he takes pride in his work, and he enjoys watching people suffer. I don't believe that's you. Maybe you feel vindicated or maybe even—I don't know—satisfied by a job well done."

She offers me a half smile. Neither of us misses the irony of a law enforcement officer understanding my need to murder people.

"But I don't think you do it to get your jollies or to get your rocks off. That's exactly the way Jacek is. Pushed too far, that's the way Bartlomiej is too. You do what you do because it's a job, and I get it now. I understand just how important family is to you and how much people rely on you."

"I'd never do any of the things I have or the things I will do if it weren't necessity. It truly is life or death in most situations."

"I know. I can't fault you for that, so I don't think you're a monster."

"But, Carrie, you need to understand there's nothing I won't do to protect you. You have to be okay with knowing I have no limits. If Bartlomiej or Jacek get too close, then I'll do whatever I have to, to not only make sure they can never touch you again but so all syndicates understand you're off limits."

"I know, Shane, and I don't know what kind of person it makes me because not only can I agree to that, I want that to happen. I want to know I'm safe. But I also want to know if we have any future together—whatever type of relationship it is—it means that much to you. You shouldn't underestimate my willingness to protect you as well. I'm relying on you right now, but I'm not without means or ability."

"I know, Carrie. I saw what you did to Jacek. I know you wanted him to suffer by bleeding out, but have you killed anybody point blank before?"

"Yes."

She says it without hesitation, and the steel in her voice tells me whatever situation she was in, she doesn't regret the decision she made. I want to ask her about it, but for the umpteenth time, that feels like it would be unfair to expect her to reveal something like that when I can't tell her even a fraction of the number of people I've killed.

"Shane, it was in the line of duty each time."

Each time?

What the fuck does that mean?

"I can practically hear your thoughts, Shane. If I had to guess, you'd say, 'what the fuck does that mean?'"

She smiles at me. My expression is completely neutral. I doubt it was that obvious that's what I think. Most of the time people have no idea what's on my mind unless I want them to know.

"Shane, your face betrays no emotions, and that tells me more than if you said anything aloud."

That makes sense.

"They were all in the line of duty, but there were a few times when maybe that wasn't my only recourse. But it was the best one I thought I had. It's not like I'm regularly in shootouts, and it's not like I believe my only course of action is to shoot rather than talk. This isn't some stupid tv show where the law enforcement officers kill a guy when they could maim him and get the information out of them."

"That irritates me so much."

I grin because it's true. If neither of us had context for those sentiments, it wouldn't be so bad. I don't want her to think I'm fucked-up, but then I smile like the fucking Joker. When she laughs, I know we both need to lighten the mood.

"What do you want to do, Carrie? You're safe here, so if you want, we can keep talking about whatever you wish. You could take a nap. We could watch a movie. As long as we stay here at the house, you can go outside as well. But for right now, there're parts of the yard I want you to stay away from. They're too exposed. My men are around the perimeter, and I have a tall wall, but it doesn't make you completely invisible."

"I—I'd like—I—um..."

She stutters over the words, uncertain whether she can reveal whatever it is she's thinking. My hand goes to her arse and squeezes as hard as I dare. Rather than squirm away from the pain, she sinks into it. I run my hand up her ribs until I cup her tit and squeeze just as mercilessly. Then my hand creeps up to her throat. It's not breath play. It's just resting there heavily.

"Little girl, I told you, you're mine, and I will do everything I must to protect you. I'll do everything to take care of you, too, and right now, I think my little girl needs to come to make her relax a little. Is that what you want, *cailín*?"

"Yes, Daddy, please."

"Good."

My hands roam over her body as she sits up enough for me to touch her. Our lips come together in a fiery kiss. Then I'm sliding my hand down her pants. I stop when I feel her panties. I noticed them when we were at Dillan's, but I said nothing. Now I do. I cup her pussy tightly.

"What are you wearing?"

"Uh, panties, Daddy."

"And what did I tell you?

"Not to wear them anymore."

"You knew you were going to come to me, didn't you?"

"Yes, but..."

"But what, little girl?"

"I—I wasn't thinking about that when I got dressed. What if you weren't the one to undress me?"

Now the tears well in her eyes, and I feel like a complete arse for not thinking first before I spoke.

"Shh, *cailín*. It's all right. I'm here now."

"I know, Daddy. I couldn't be sure I could get to you. You're who I wanted and who I was thinking of, but I also feared Jacek would do something to me regardless of his brother's wishes. And after all the times I've turned Bartlomiej down in the months we dated—or whatever it was—mind fucked him—I don't even know how to describe that pseudo relationship—he'd finally get his way. He'd take what he always believed he deserved."

She rests her hand over my heart.

"The only one who deserves any part of me—the only one who can ever take what he wants is you, Shane."

I offer her a dazzling smile to lighten the mood again. She cups my cheeks before giving me a kiss that makes my cock pulse. I want to be inside her, but if I do that, it's going to be over way too soon. I won't even thrust before I come. The idea of her pussy being wrapped around me makes my balls ache something fierce.

"Maybe I'll just keep you naked the entire time you're here. How about that?" Something flares in her eyes; she likes that idea.

"If it means you could touch me anytime anyhow, then I'd be down for that, but only if you're naked, too. Only if I can touch you whenever I want.

"Little girl, you can do that regardless of whether I have any clothes on. If we're in public, maybe don't grab my dick, but you can always hold my hand or wrap your arms around me. Anything. I'll never hide from public displays of affection with you, and in private—well, I hope you cup my dick anytime you want."

"If that's permission, Daddy, then you better believe I'll follow those instructions to the T."

My fingers dip into her moist heat, and I groan from how wet she is for me already.

"Shane, I'm in a perpetual state of arousal—soaked—whenever I think about you, let alone be near you. Even with how scared I was, all I've wanted is to feel you inside me again. You've ruined me for all other men. I can't imagine having somebody else inside me. The way you feel is unlike anything I've ever had before."

"I know, *cailín.* I feel the exact same."

I work her pussy, my thumb rubbing her clit as she raises and lowers her hips in time with my fingers. We continue to kiss; the need growing exponentially by second. I lift her and turn her to straddle me.

"I want to get you off, Carrie. This isn't about me. It's not about reciprocating. It's about taking care of you.

"But that's not what I want. I don't want this to just be about me. I want it to be about equals."

"Later, Carrie. Right now, I think you deserve a bit of spoiling, so Daddy decides."

It might kill me, but I want this for her even more than I want to get off.

"Thank you." Her voice quivers as she gets closer to coming.

"I'm spoiling you, little girl, but you will ask for each orgasm I give you because I can give them, and I can take them away."

"Yes, Daddy."

Her breathlessness tells me that's exactly what she wants. Her pupils dilate, and a flush rises along her neck into her cheeks.

"Daddy, please may I come?... Please?!"

"Yes, *cailín*."

Her moan is one of ecstasy, and I don't think I have felt more manly in my entire life. None of the times I've taken someone out. None of the times I've drunk my brothers and cousins under the table. None of the times I've lifted more than Seamus and Cormac, who're both built like ox. None of those things made me feel like more of a man than right this minute when I look down at Carrie, and I know I've taken her mind off of her problems and given her pleasure—given her relief. That's what makes me happy.

I continue to work her pussy, adding another finger, so now I have three inside her. She's tight, and it reminds me of how good it felt to be inside her. I'll enjoy that later. My fingers stroke her g spot as her feet push down on the sofa cushion, raising her hips as high as she can, chasing my questing fingers.

"Is this how you like it, *cailín*?"

"Yes, Daddy. But rougher. So much rougher."

I pull my fingers from her. She mewls in disagreement, but I scoop her into my arms and carry her up to the guest bedroom. I don't know where she'll want to sleep tonight. I don't want to make it awkward if I take her to my room. Then she decides she wants to sleep somewhere else. But then again, maybe this'll make her think I don't want her in my bed.

Oh, fuck me.

Maybe I should've just kept her on the sofa, but we're here now. I set her down on her feet and go to sit in the armchair in the corner.

"Strip, *cailín*. Slowly. I want to watch every delectable inch of you revealed to me like you're unwrapping a Christmas gift for me."

"But, Daddy, don't you want to unwrap it for yourself?" She practically purrs.

"Tempting, *cailín.* Another time. But for today, I want to watch you do it."

She comes to stand in front of me, unbuttoning her shirt with excruciatingly slow movements.

This is fucking purgatory, and I put myself there.

She peels the shirt down her arms before she pushes down her pants. She leaves just her bra and panties. She kicked off her shoes before she curled up on the love seat with me. She turns around to let me watch her unclasp her bra. She takes it off and flings it over her shoulder at me.

I growl as I catch it. Then she slips her panties down, purposely bending forward as though she needs to push them to the floor rather than letting them drop on their own. It presents the most beautifully erotic scene I have ever laid eyes on. From the way she spreads her feet apart, I have a view of her glorious tits between her thighs and a view of her soaking wet little pink pussy and even her arse. She runs her hands up the side of her thighs, then over the back of them before up to her arse, pulling her cheeks apart. She stands as she does that.

"I told you to strip. I didn't tell you to tease me."

I'm out of the seat. My hand lands across her arse hard enough to make her take a step forward, but I've already slipped my other arm around her waist, holding her right where I want her. My hand rains down spanks, alternating sides, the sound ringing in the air.

"Carrie, you know this isn't a punishment, right?"

"I know, Shane. It's something we both enjoy, and I think this is exactly what I need right now."

"You need to relinquish control. You need to know you're not in this alone, and I need to feel like I have some control when I know everything outside this house is a fecked-up mess I can't fix easily."

"That's right, Daddy. I need to not worry about what's happening for a bit, and I want you to feel like you have control. I know you breathe easier when you do. That bad things happen when you don't. So, if this gives you the same peace it gives me, I'm more than happy to relinquish control to you."

She gets me.

"You need a safe word you can use if it gets to be too much."

"Okay—how about—" She thinks about it for a moment. "*Digon.*"

"What does that mean?"

"Enough in Welsh. Both my parents grew up in Wales, so they had compulsory language education. I spoke quite a bit of it as a kid, but we don't use it that often."

"Would you say you're still proficient in it, even if you're not fluent?"

"Yeah, I would say conversationally proficient. I'm not too bad at reading, but I can't write it well. My grammar isn't that strong. What about your Gaelic?"

"One hundred percent fluent. Reading, writing, listening, and speaking. We use it as much as we do English. You'll notice we often switch back and forth. It's not always because we're speaking about something private. It's just that natural to us. Our parents insist we use it whenever we're with them as though we might somehow forget. My parents learned Gaelic before they learned English. It was the same thing for us. We went to kindergarten already able to read and write some basic things in both languages."

"Wow!"

It makes me silently wonder if we ever had a family, would we automatically raise our kids to be trilingual? I don't know that Welsh would be of much use to them. But if it's part of who they are, then it's a tradition I would want to keep going for Carrie. The way she looks at me over her shoulder makes me wonder if she's thinking the same thing. It's way too soon to even contemplate that, let alone discuss it.

Instead, I focus on where my hand lands with each spank. I get progressively firmer until she's stomping her feet in between. Her arse is the prettiest shade of pink. It almost matches her pussy. The view I have makes me consider all the things I'd like to do to and with her. It's a visceral reaction of longing and excitement when I see her like this. I'm excited for what we're going to do now and all the things we could do in the future.

But it's longing as well, since as much as I want to make something out of this, I'm still not convinced we can. I know she wants it, and so do I, but wanting something and having it aren't always the same, especially when you live in a world like mine.

I help her stand and let go of her waist. Then I spin her around to face me and wrap my arms around her waist. Our kiss is one that builds. It starts out fiery but explodes into a full blaze in just a few seconds. My tongue explores every crease and crevice in her mouth until I feel like there's not a single inch I don't know, a single inch I'm not committing to memory. My hands run down to her back to her pink arse and squeeze. She yelps, but it only pushes her into a heightened state of arousal.

She presses her hips forward, grinding against my cock, which strains against my boxer briefs, irritated I'm so rude as to keep it confined when all it wants is freedom to thrust into her.

"Daddy, I think you're very overdressed for the occasion."

"Is that so, little girl? And if I have plans for you before I decide to get undressed?"

"Plans change, don't they?"

She asks me with a devilish smile that makes me consider changing them. But if I strip, then this will be over far too fast.

"You know, when we were together at the warehouse, it was exhilarating having the threat of being found, but it also meant we knew we had to rush. I don't want that this time. We're in the safety of my house, tucked away in a guest bedroom. There's no reason to rush, since we're going to be here for a while. You're delectably delicious in every way, and I intend to enjoy a mid-afternoon snack."

I lift her, and her legs wrap around my waist. I carry her to the dresser, wanting somewhere slightly unpredictable. I keep nothing on here, since it's a room rarely used. When my brothers or cousins spend the night, they'll come in here, but I keep no personal effects. There are clothes in the closet because we're all an interchangeable size, but they don't really belong to any one person. They were mine when I got them, but they've become community property since then.

She perches on the edge of the dresser, and I tilt her hips in front of me. Her hands go behind her to brace herself before I lean in, her legs now over my shoulders. I lick her cunt, and she squeals and sighs. It's music to my ears, knowing I'm pleasuring her, that I'm the one who will make her come. The idea of Bartlomiej doing this flashes in my head, and it sours the moment.

She must be able to tell. She puts her hand on my shoulder, and I look up at her. I hate she feels she must reassure me.

"Don't think about that. It's not what I'm focused on now. Don't let him ruin the mood for us. He's not a part of this, and I refuse to let him come between us. I'm sorry you even know there was a time when he tried this."

That makes me stand up straight. "Only tried?"

She grimaces. "There were a few times very early on when I let things go further than I wanted, because, at first, I worried about what he would do to me if I said no."

My fingers dig into the back of her thighs. "Did he threaten you? Did he pressure you? Did he force you?"

She cups my cheek and shakes her head. "Pressured me, but never forced me. It was while I was still building his trust, and I needed something to pacify him and get him to buy into me being a girlfriend. He lost his temper one time, and that was the only time I needed to convince me when he was in a certain mood, no wasn't an option. Not because I thought he would force me, but I worried he'd slap me around. Shane, I'm not telling you these things to anger you or make you want retribution even more than you already do. I'm telling you because I don't want to add to all the secrets unnecessarily. So, if there are things I can tell you, I will."

She watches me to gauge my reaction to this. I'm willing to listen, even if it makes me want to wrap my hands around that piece of shite's throat and squeeze until his eyes nearly pop out of his head.

"He believed I was a virgin and very Catholic. I used that to my advantage because not only did it make me come across as sweetly naive and the perfect future wife for a Polish mob boss—untouched and unsoiled by being anybody else's possession—it gave me an out for most things. I claimed, even though it was never penetrative sex, it was still called oral sex, therefore I feared for my immortal soul."

If he bought that bullshite, then she's clearly an excellent actress. It makes me wonder what else she might tell me that's all an act.

Chapter Sixteen

Shane

Carrie reads my mind too well as she brushes her thumb over my cheekbone. "Shane, we started out as adversaries, but we aren't anymore. It took a while for me to come around, but I get it now. This is where I'm supposed to be, and I have no reason to lie about that."

"Are you sure?"

Her chin jerks back. "What's that supposed to mean?"

"Nothing." I shake my head.

"No, it means something. You wouldn't have said it if it didn't. What's that supposed to mean, Shane? Do you think I'm leading you on because I've changed my target to your family? Do you think this is the same act I pulled with Bartlomiej?"

I study her for only a second before I speak with resolve. "No, I don't believe that, and I don't believe you want my help just because you have nowhere else to turn. I believe this is real, but you can't fault me for the questions running through my mind. We're still getting to know each other, and this is a rocky way to begin a relationship. You could just as easily wonder if I'm using you to gain information about the feds' plans for my family. But I think you know I'm not, so I know you're not using me, either. I'm sorry I had even a second of doubt.'"

"It's all right. I admit I've had a moment or two of the same fear, so I can't hold it against you that you do, too. I'd wonder why neither of us doubted this relationship if it didn't happen at least once. I want you to know the few things I did with him weren't exactly under duress, but I knew if I didn't, I risked his temper. I risked blowing the entire mission. I never enjoyed it."

I want to ask her if he made her come, but I might lose my mind if the answer is yes.

"Shane, I don't know if other people read your thoughts, but I'm pretty sure I'm reading them. I faked it every time. I know you and Bartlomiej do similar things, but nothing about your personality reminds me of him. Just the opposite. You couldn't be further apart, and that's why I have feelings for you and never did for him."

She leans in for a kiss, and I give it to her. It's a quick, gentle peck, and then I'm back to the promised land. She scoots even closer to the edge, so it's basically just her tailbone on the dresser, and her hands brace herself once again. I lick her with tantalizingly slow motion. She tries to dig her heels into my back, but I tighten my hold on her thighs, warning her I decide, just like I've said so many times. There will be opportunities for her to lead the way, but this isn't one of them. It's not because I'm a complete control freak. I still want this to be for her. Yeah, I want to get off, but not before she does a few times.

I suck on her clit, flicking it over and over with the tip of my tongue. From her moans, I discover this is something she likes. I'm tucking that away for later and making it part of my arsenal. I ease a finger into her, knowing it won't be nearly enough to satisfy her, but that's not the goal. The goal right now is to torment her, and I can tell it's working. She rocks her hips, and the dresser vibrates, clacking against the wall.

It's a good thing I don't have neighbors with an adjoining wall; otherwise, there'd be no doubt what's going on here.

"Daddy, may I come?"

"Yes, *cailín*. Come on my tongue."

With a long moan, she can't help but press her calves against my back as her thighs squeeze the sides of my head. It's obvious she's a runner from the strength. It's like she puts my head in a vise, but I don't mind. Knowing she's getting off is everything to me.

When she sighs, and I know her orgasm's done, I thrust three fingers into her. When she gasps and clutches my shoulders, she leans forward. It's an involuntary reaction. Her right hand goes to the back of my head, pressing me closer as my lips go back to her clit, but I pull away.

"Hands behind you, no touching."

"Please, just let me touch some part of you."

"Oh, you are, little one. My tongue and my fingers are definitely touching you."

"That's not what I mean, and you know it. Shane, I really need this right now."

I shift my focus and meet her imploring gaze. This is a different type of connection she needs between us. It's not just about receiving physical pleasure, and I get it because this is so much more than just that. I reach my free hand out to her, grasping her wrist and giving it a gentle tug. When she brings it forward, I entwine our fingers together.

I observe her the entire time, and I know this is exactly what she needs. I didn't realize how much I needed it, too. A sense of calm settles over me, and I've never felt more like I have a partner in all of this. I continue to work her pussy, rubbing my thumb over her clit as the three fingers stroke her g spot. I continue to lock gazes with her.

It's intoxicating watching the different expressions flash across her face in a way I never cared about in my past. Before Carrie, it was about getting a woman off and getting myself off. Yeah, I wanted them to enjoy every moment, and BDSM—which is what I always preferred—is about far more than just orgasms. There's a give and take—but in the end—in my situation—it boiled down to domination and submission, not romance or lasting emotional connections. This is exactly what I want with Carrie. I want our connection to last well beyond me finger fucking her.

"Daddy, may I come again?"

"So soon, little one?"

"Yes, Daddy. I can't help it. Too much pent-up lust for you."

She smiles, but I know she's concentrating on not coming until she gets my permission. I wait and count to ten before I agree.

"Come for me, Carrie." She's quick to follow my instructions. She squeezes my fingers, pushing my wrist into an awkward position, but I know she doesn't realize it. Once again, her heels dig into my back as her entire body trembles.

"Yes, Daddy."

The dresser bangs rhythmically, a harmony to her moans. When she's done, her head tilts back, and I watch her chest rise and fall with each inhale. I let her catch that breath before I lift her with her legs still over my shoulders high enough for me to kiss her pussy. Then I guide one leg down to my waist, then the other.

It proves flexibility I didn't realize she had. It conjures images of Kamasutra poses that have always intrigued me, but I've never successfully tried. A bunch of them I've never tried at all. These are things I'll share only with Carrie. It's a novel idea. I'm no man whore, but I'm certainly experienced.

"I have more planned, little one. Catch your breath." I wink.

My brothers, cousins, and I realized all the men of our generation in the Four Families have similar predilections and proclivities. We're all into BDSM. When the guys and I figured that out, we had a moment of fear the other families could exploit it as our weakness. That's the last thing we wanted. So, all of us invested and became silent partners in the best sex clubs in the city.

We don't need our names on the letterheads or anything, but we have the membership lists. We know where all the influential people in New York go to get their rocks off. We know who likes to spank and who likes to be spanked. We've bribed more than one government official or investor with those little nuggets of information. They don't know how we know since our investments are so tangled in the stratosphere nobody can track them back to us.

Finn is an amazing accountant. He works miracles down to the last penny. The guy flips if he can't reconcile an account down to the last five cents.

"I'm guessing I can't ask what's next."

I carry the woman I've fallen for to the bed. I put her down on the side where her clothes still are. It's purposely the side away from the door. She knows I have a gun on me. I haven't hidden it from her because there's no point. Not when she usually carries one herself and not when she knows exactly who and what I am.

But even though I know she can defend herself, and even if she had her gun with her, I'd still take her to the far side of the room where I can guard her against anybody who comes in. She will never sleep closer to the door. I will always make myself the target before her. I will always position myself to shoot without her being in the way.

"You can, but you won't get an answer besides this."

I snag her bra and give her a devilish smile. I put her hands over her head. I use the straps to bind her wrists above her head and around the bar in the headboard. I'd always liked this bed's style. I didn't choose it because I thought about binding a woman to it. That's just a pleasant benefit.

Some guys in my family have taken women back to their places, and some who've had established contracts with subs have gotten apartments for them to meet away from a club and on a neutral ground that wasn't either person's primary residence.

I've been one who goes to women's homes I'm involved with. I've had steady agreements with two women at the club I belong to, but in no way are they dating or even strictly monogamous. If I go to the club, and they're there, terrific. If they want to arrange something in advance, wonderful. But they're free to do as they please, and I'm free to do as I please. Those arrangements ended, but I need to let the women know. Carrie's the only one I want.

I'm past the age of fucking random women, and I always make sure I take every precaution not to get any of them pregnant and keep myself healthy. So, everything I do here with Carrie is a first time for both of us.

She tilts her head back and looks up at what I'm doing. I wonder if she's checking for notches in the headboard.

"Carrie, I've brought no one home."

Surprise registers on her face, and I don't blame her. I'm thirty-two-years-old now, so it must seem odd to her.

"I've dated no one seriously since college. Not more than a handful of dates here and there. You can guess my life isn't conducive to that type of relationship."

"Yeah, I can see why.

"I want this to be something I only share with you."

"Thank you, Daddy."

I brush my lips against hers before I pull her legs apart.

"Spread them as wide as you can. I'm going to have to get some toys for us."

"What?"

"Think about what you'd like."

"Oh, I already have a list in mind. I've had plenty of time for my fantasies, Shane."

"You'll have to tell me each and every one, little girl.

"I'll show you mine if you'll share yours."

"Of course. I plan to act out each and every one of them."

"Promise, Daddy?"

"Promise, *cailín*. It's going to take us a long, long time just to get through mine."

She assesses me for a moment before she nods. Does she understand what I'm implying? That I still believe we have a chance, or at least I want to see if we do.

"Shane, do you really think we can? I want to know before we go any further that if I leave the agency, we're in this for good. If I give up everything I've worked for, for a future with you, do you see the same thing I do?"

"Yes, and I haven't wanted to suggest that, but you know it's the only way. You understand why I can't be the one to leave."

"I do, and that's why I'm willing to walk away, even if I didn't want to at the start. The moment it comes out I've had any involvement with you, I'll lose my job. I'd rather it be on my terms than theirs. We can discuss the details later, Shane, but that's what I'm leaning toward."

I sweep my gaze over the beauty in my bed, and I know I would sacrifice anything I could for her without hesitation. There's something elemental drawing us together. The ideas I had a moment ago seep away. Instead, I no longer want to torment her and make her beg. I think I might be the one begging soon. I tap her pussy before I back up and strip.

My balls and cock thank me. I stroke myself three times before I step closer to the bed. I'm about to climb on when she opens her mouth wide in the only invitation there is.

"You want to suck me off, *cailín*?"

"Yes, Daddy. So much."

"And you think I want it to be over, and that I want to come down your throat?"

"You could."

"Yes, I could, but I'm not going to. I know how wet you already are. I don't need you to get my cock wet.

"But you might want me to." Her smile tells me she knows full well what she's doing with her seductive words and smile.

The look in her eyes is enough to drive any man wild. She's close enough to the edge that when she turns her head farther toward me, I slide my cock into her mouth. Her tongue runs the length of it before flicking the tip. She pulls back enough that my cock is still between her lips, but not down her throat. She licks all sides of it, curling her tongue around it in a way that practically makes it look like her tongue's a bed my cock was always meant to lay on. Then she's working me for real.

Holy fucking shite.

Nothing has felt like this.

It's a recurring phrase when I'm with Carrie. Not only do we fit together and are sexually compatible, but the emotions...

At least the ones I feel are so new to me that nothing else compares. I have no frame of reference for anything similar to it. I can only tell how different it is from everything else. I want this feeling to never end. I want this between us.

She sucks me, and my mind goes blank over and over again. She draws me in, and all I concentrate on is the fight not to come. I don't want it over this soon. Maybe next time I'll come down her throat, but not this time.

"Carrie, let go."

She shakes her head and sucks me practically down her throat. I feel her gag reflex, but she doesn't make a sound. She tries to relax and take me farther. But she can't before I pull out, and she shoots me a dirty look. She clearly doesn't agree that I shouldn't come down her throat.

Instead, I ease her onto her back and climb over her. She spreads her legs again, not having noticed she'd closed them. Her knees bracket my hips as she arches her back, offering me her glorious tits. I gladly suck each one, tugging her nipples between my lips. I give them a quick bite each, making her gasp before my tongue soothes them each time. Then I push up onto my hands and knees, guiding my cock into her. I thrust hard as she lifts her hips higher for me.

I lower myself onto my forearms as I kiss her. We both marvel at the feel as we adjust to each other.

"Shane, that moment when you enter me—it's nearly enough to make me come."

I get it, but she looks like she regrets sharing her thoughts. I brush hair away from her temple with my left thumb.

"You can always tell me anything." I know I can't say the same for me, but I want her to know I'll always listen to her.

"It's always—well, almost always—feels good that moment when it starts. But with you, it's different. Everything about being with you is different. Everything's so much—more."

"I know, little one. I feel the same way, and I have since the start."

"Me too."

With a quick kiss, we're back to moving together. We're so in sync she's soon begging to come, but I'm not ready for this first one just yet. I want to keep her working for it.

"You will wait until I tell you, you may come. If you don't, it will be your last one for today."

She mewls and shakes her head. "You're taunting me, and I don't know if I can last. I'll try, but my body is *not* listening to my mind."

"Then we'll just have to wait and see what happens." I smile mischievously at her.

"I think I know exactly what you must have looked like when you were a little boy getting in trouble."

"Yeah, apparently I haven't changed." I waggle my eyebrows.

I thrust into her over and over until I'm on the brink.

"Come, *cailín*, right now."

She strains against the bra still around her wrists as her heels press into the bed, lifting her hips to meet each of my thrusts. I surge into her as hard as I dare.

"I'm coming, Daddy. I'm coming."

I steel myself against blowing my load. I want her to get off at least once more before I do. I keep thrusting even after her hips settle back against the mattress. She looks at me with a fathomless expression.

It makes me want to be the perfect man for her, whatever that means and whatever that takes. I slide my arms beneath her shoulders, my hands hooking over them as I thrust faster.

"Yeah, just like this, Shane. Rough. *Really, really* rough. Please, I need it."

"So do I. You're mine."

"Are you mine too, Shane?"

"Absolutely. There's no other way about it."

Again and again, we move. I know my weight pins her to the bed, but she does her best to move along with me. It's intoxicating knowing I can make her come repeatedly.

"Daddy, please, may I come again?"

"Yes, whenever you can."

I thrust in one last time, grinding my pubic bone against her clit. She explodes, her hands fisting and un-fisting. I pull out, and she screams. I don't even stroke myself before my cum squirts across her tits, giving her a pearl necklace. Before I'm done, I surge into her again, spilling the rest of my cum inside her. I've marked her as thoroughly as I can. But one of these days, I'll fuck her in the arse too, and she'll truly know she's mine.

"Carrie, that was remarkable. I can't describe the experience because my mind is blank. You wiped every coherent thought from it."

We pant as we gaze at one another. As rough as that was a moment ago, now there's tenderness. I never imagined I had a tender bone in my body. Maybe I'm a changed man.

Chapter Seventeen

Carrie

Shane releases my hands from the bra, and I run my fingertips up and down his back as he rolls us onto our sides. Then he moves, so I'm draped across his chest. My hand and head rest beside his heart. I hear how it pounds just like mine does. I don't know what to say to all of this, and I guess he doesn't either because we remain silent, just enjoying the moment.

Eventually, our bodies cool, and we shiver. It makes us laugh at the same time as we get up and sit on the edge of the bed together. It's another moment before we get dressed. I don't know why we both do this, when I suppose we could pull the covers down and snuggle beneath the sheets and comforter.

Is it a force of habit that we both leave when we're done with sex? I don't think so. Is it too intimate to remain here? Maybe, but it's with silent agreement we head back downstairs.

We're holding hands, so I don't feel like he's grown distant or anything. Just the opposite. It feels like a normal couple where sex is enjoyable and a part of the relationship, but it's such the norm we continue with our day.

We head to the living room, and he grabs the remotes and turns on the TV to a streaming platform.

"Are there any movies you've been wanting to watch? Anything that interests you?"

I name a recent one I saw listed the last time I watched TV.

"Are you hungry? Do you want snacks? I have popcorn."

"No, not hungry yet. Maybe later, but for now, I'm good. Though, actually, I could go for a glass of water, please."

He heads into the kitchen, and I hear him moving around. The phone I left on the table earlier buzzes. I look at the number and realize it's my office. I ignore it, but I also see there're four other missed calls from them. It makes me question whether I can keep avoiding their calls. It's only going to make them more suspicious if I do. When Shane comes back with bottled water, I show him my phone.

"I've got to do something since they've called this many times."

"I know. Call them back, but put them on speaker, so I can hear their tone of voice, not just their words."

"All right." I hit the missed call number and put it on speaker. It doesn't even ring.

"Carys, where the hell are you?"

"I told you already, Angela. I found somewhere safe."

"Yeah, well, not safe enough because someone else is after Bartlomiej."

"What do you mean by that?" I glance at Shane, wondering if he's done something or at least ordered it. He shakes his head.

"He went on that trip to Boston and was attacked."

"Bratva?"

My eyes widen as I keep watching Shane. He shrugs his shoulders. This is news to him, too.

"We don't know yet. It could be, but it could be several other syndicates, too. According to you, he's been pissing a lot of them off."

"He has, but I don't know which ones would make a move on him. It could be a Boston syndicate, not one from New York."

"They left a calling card."

"What? They never do that."

"Whoever attacked did it while Bartlomiej was in his SUV on the way from the airport to his hotel. The attackers left a red apple at the scene."

My brow furrows as I lift my shoulders to Shane. This call is extra stressful, so they stay up by my ears as I hunch forward to lean my elbows on my thighs.

New York's nickname is the Big Apple, but that is so bizarre. I don't automatically believe it means a New York syndicate. Why would they try to lead anybody back to them? I don't know if an apple is significant to any family anywhere.

Shane shrugs again. He would know better than just about anybody if a red apple was a calling card.

"Angela, I don't know what to make of that, but I wouldn't put it past a syndicate from Boston or any other city to put that apple there to draw attention away from them to pin it on a family from New York."

I'm careful again not to say here in New York. I don't want her to know I'm still in the state, let alone the city. I pick my words carefully.

"Until we learn otherwise, that's what it would seem. If you'd been on that trip, they could've caught you in the middle."

I know she's not wrong, and it curdles my stomach. Shane can tell—or maybe he feels the same way—because he pulls me onto his lap just like he did the last time I was on the phone. I curl into him as the line goes quiet. Angela's waiting for me to say something else, and I'm waiting for her to speak.

I won't give anything away until I know what the point of this call is because it's definitely more than just informing me of the attack.

"Carys, you're going to lose your job if you don't get back to the office soon. Phil suspects there's something more going on you're not telling us. He thinks you fled to one of the big families in New York. That you might have a CI among them you haven't disclosed, or you have some other connection to them. He wants answers now."

"Does he think my sympathies switched? Is that what you're saying?"

"I don't know. That's what he hinted at. But you do realize if you're aiding and abetting, they'll arrest you, right? And Phil being Phil, he'll find a way for them to prosecute you to the max."

"I know, but you guys need to give me a bit more time. Now that someone's attacked Bartlomiej, I feel even less inclined to reveal myself than before. I don't feel like it decreased the threat. What happened to him, anyway? You didn't say."

"He survived. His driver got him away from the scene, but the men in his other vehicle weren't so lucky."

"What happened during the attack? Was it people shooting again?"

"They tried to reroute him and funnel him into some type of trap."

"You guys know nothing more than that?"

"No. There was nothing at the scene."

"What about the apple? How do you know about that?"

Things suddenly make a whole lot less sense than they did a moment ago. When she pauses, even though it's less than ten seconds, I know she's scrambling for a lie.

"We have someone in the Boston Poles now. We activated him when we heard Bartlomiej planned to go to Boston."

I look at Shane and shake my head. That's bullshit. If that were the case, I would've known because the plan was for me to accompany him before all of this went to shit. There definitely wasn't an apple. She's merely baiting me to see what I'll confess or let slip.

"Angela, just like I said before, you might think this is a secure line, but I don't believe it is. I gotta go before anyone tracks me. I've been on the phone too long already. I'll be in touch when I'm on my way back."

"Oh—"

"Bye, Angela." I hang up before she can say anything else.

The conversation frustrates me. I don't feel like it's any safer for me to return than it was a few hours ago.

"What do you think of all of that?" I want Shane's opinion because he looked skeptical from the get-go.

"I'm not sure yet. I didn't know there was an attack on Bartlomiej, and I definitely don't know who did it because the list of candidates is pretty fecking long. However, the bit about the apple makes no sense whatsoever, and it definitely felt like you caught her in a lie at the end. I don't know who put her up to that, or if she came up with it on her own, but she definitely wanted to trip you up or get you to come running to whichever syndicate member she thinks you're with." He flashes me a bright smile.

"What do we do about that?"

His smile drops as he thinks about my question. "I need to talk to the others and see if they've heard anything, but I know it wasn't us, Carrie."

"Are you waiting your turn?"

He says nothing. He simply stares at me.

That's as good as saying yes. I don't know how I feel about that. I'm conflicted since part of me is still a law enforcement officer, and the other part of me is—I don't know what the fuck I am to Shane.

Maybe a girlfriend? I don't know.

My mind isn't quite sure how to fill in that blank, but whatever I am, it's more than just an acquaintance. It makes me think he'd retaliate on my behalf. If not for me alone, then because Bartlomiej went after something that's his.

The machismo in syndicates is real. They have to constantly one-up each other, and if Bartlomiej threatened Shane, he has to react. It makes me wonder if another syndicate already feels that way about Bartlomiej and just acted on it.

Not necessarily about a woman, but because he wronged them. If it's the bratva, it must go beyond just fucking up the deal between him and the Russians, then between him and the Armenians. It's all so fucking complicated. You practically need a map to draw out the spider webs of how the syndicates connect. Like, for a long time, the Italians and the Irish got along, but for just as much time, they've been rivals. Right now, I'm uncertain how things stand.

"Do you need to call them now or go over there?"

"It would be best if I called. I'm not leaving you here, and I don't want to take you out into the open, especially not after what we just learned. I need to confirm the attack happened before I believe what Angela said. I have a sneaking suspicion something went wrong, but it was nothing like what she described. Let me figure out what's happening, and then we can go from there. If somebody saw you with Bartlomiej or figured out you were involved with him, *and* you weren't with him during the attack, then you're not only still Bartlomiej's target, but you're also possibly somebody else's too."

That does nothing to set my mind at ease, but I know Shane's right. I sit and stare at the phone in my hand, and I wonder what I should do next.

"Shane, do you think I should dump this burner and start using a different one to keep them from being able to call me?"

"No, I don't think that's necessary yet. It doesn't have GPS on, so between that and the jammers here at the house, they can't trace you. You're safe from that point of view. Nobody's getting in here unless I say they can, so I'm not worried about that either. But the moment we leave the house, it opens us up to an attack. We don't need to make ourselves vulnerable for no reason."

"All right, do you still want to watch a movie?" I offer him a tentative smile as I suggest we try to make things as normal as possible.

"We can, but let me call my family first. I need to take this in my office. I don't know what else might come up. Okay?"

"Yeah, I understand."

He walks away, and I'm left looking at the TV screen. I don't know how long all of this will take, so I pull up a TV show I've seen every episode of. It doesn't matter how many times I watch *Wings*, I still love it. It's a classic to me. I've gone through all the seasons several times, so it's a mindless way to keep me company right now.

I can hear murmurs from Shane's office, but I can't understand what he's saying. There's more than just his voice, so he must have it on speakerphone. Is he doing something else while he's on the phone, so he doesn't want to cradle it against his ear?

The temptation to find out what he's saying is overwhelming. I feel compelled to know because I don't enjoy feeling so helpless right now. Even though I trust Shane, and I want to believe he'd tell me at least some of what is going on, I don't enjoy feeling this out of control. Knowing he's helping should be enough. It was a while ago, but Angela's call shook me more than I realized.

I let temptation get the better of me. I know I shouldn't do this, but I go ahead and creep toward Shane's office. The door's closed. Clearly a sign I'm not invited. I don't quite put my ear to the door. I'm not that bad. But then, I don't have to. I can hear the voices from inside. They're muffled, but I can still make out what the men are saying.

If Shane wanted me to hear this conversation, then I'd be part of it.

My conscience screams this is wrong. Amazing how I've recently learned to ignore it so easily. I don't know who's who on the call besides Shane.

It's Shane who's speaking now, so his words are easy to catch. "I don't give a rat's flying fecking arse what happened to them in Boston. I want them at the station now. I'll go tonight once I'm sure Carrie's safe here and settled in. When I show up, they better be stripped to their pasty arse skin and hanging by a hook ready for me. Rough them up a little if that's what it takes to get them there, but leave them alive enough for me to work them over and get my pound of flesh."

I think it's Dillan who speaks next. "And if they're already pretty fecked-up from whatever happened?"

"Feed them and water them and get them back to being conscious because I want them to be awake when I walk in. I want them to know there are consequences for touching my woman."

"Your woman?" This is an unfamiliar voice.

"Yes, Finn, my woman. And don't act like you've never called your wife that before."

"Yeah, but I thought Carrie could—"

"Carys." He interrupts his brother and is adamant about correcting him.

It's nice to know he wants that nickname to remain private just between the two of us. It makes me wish his name was long enough to shorten. Maybe I should find out what his middle name is.

"All right, calm your arse down. I thought Carys didn't like you."

"We've come a long way now, haven't we?" Shane's tone has a bite to it.

Now, it's a third guy. "We're just trying to understand. That's all. The last time we heard anything about this, you wanted to intervene. Before that, it was to investigate a little more. Then you're chasing after her and disappearing into a bedroom with her. Now, you've got her at your place, and you're speaking as though you're in a relationship together."

Lord, there's a lot of them. If only I knew which voice belonged to which.

"You know she wouldn't be at my house if she and I weren't. You saw how I reacted to Misha's call. You saw us holding hands and how I sat with my arm around her in Dillan's office. There's something between us, and I think it's the same as each one of you has with your wife."

That makes my eyebrows shoot straight up. I'm not sure how I feel about this. Wife? Is that where he thinks this is going? Marriage? Two-point-five kids and a picket fence? I glance toward his front door. There's no picket fence out there.

Instead, there's a tall brick wall with wrought-iron gates and spikes on the top all the way around. But this house certainly could accommodate us and be a yuppie dream house. I glance toward the stairs.

Could I picture having a family with him? Could I picture

kids running up and down the stairs? It's actually shockingly easy for me to do just that. I force myself out of my daydream and back to the conversation.

"What can you tell me about the attack? Have you heard anything, Dillan?"

"No."

"What about you, Sean?"

"I've got feelers out all over the place, but nothing's happening. I've checked the taps we have on Bartlomiej and Jacek. We're not getting anything more than usual out of them. I checked all the emails. I included the secure ones, but there's still nothing there. Nobody's claiming any of this."

"Are you positive it happened?" Shane's skepticism matches mine.

"As positive as I can be, since the news came from one of Carys's handlers, and you no longer trust her."

"Hold on, I've got something coming in. Let me read this text really fast."

I don't know whose voice that is, so, hopefully, Shane says their name.

"What's going on, Cor?" That means it's Cormac.

I wish I knew these voices better by now, but then again, it wouldn't be an issue if I weren't eavesdropping.

"I'm getting a text from Marek."

Marek Nowakowski? He's Bartlomiej and Jacek's cousin. He was Tymoteusz's brother. What the fuck?

"He just said there wasn't an actual attack, per se, but whoever did it, boxed Bartlomiej in, pulled him from his SUV, and stole the cars from him and his men. Nobody roughed him up, but they left him stranded on the side of the road with some old arse jalopy and dangled the keys in front of Bartlomiej before slashing all four tires. They truly left him stranded with a giant 'fuck you' to go along with it."

"Who was it?" That was Shane, so at least I can follow some of the conversation now.

"Looks like Bartlomiej was doing some deal with the Boston

Cosa Nostra and didn't get Salvatore's permission. Carmine and Gabe went up there to take care of it. I expected it to be Maks or Aleks, but my informant tells me it was *Cosa Nostra*."

I lean my shoulder against the wall and tilt my head against it as I try to sort through what I'm hearing. A fraction of what Angela said is true. Something happened, and the Poles were the target, but the facts are nothing like what she said. I can't believe the intel was that wrong that she would fuck up that many details. She was testing me to see if I would contradict her or whether I would find out the truth and bring it back to her.

This line of work is about manipulation all the time, but you don't expect it from within your own team. The people who keep you safe when your life is on the line. I'm going to have to dig more to figure out what the deal is with work. And the only way to do that is to ask Shane for help because I no longer have those resources I can trust. Even then, I would have always been skeptical about digging into colleagues. I've never trusted anybody not in the field with me. They don't have the same vested interest in the investigation or my safety. Now it's a kick in the goddamn balls—if I had them—to find out the people who were supposed to have a vested interest in me living don't, or they're trying to fuck me over.

And I realize my duplicity is somewhat at fault. However, I don't think there's any proof of it. It's all speculation at this point. They're testing me, which also would be fine and understandable if it weren't my life at risk. That's the kicker for me.

Don't trust me. Test me. Question me. Whatever.

But don't do it in a way that endangers me.

I pull myself out of my own thoughts and back to the conversation when Shane's voice permeates my fog of war.

"Who was Bartlomiej doing the deal with? Which one of the *Cosa Nostra* thought to strike out on their own without Salvatore finding out?"

"Vicenzo Girgenti."

I recognize this voice as Dillan's. He responds to Shane, and the disgust is evident with every word.

"He's trying to one-up Salvatore and prove Boston's still a contender for East Coast power among any of the syndicates, but especially the *Cosa Nostra*."

"And he's a fucking fool." That quip comes from Finn.

Cormac speaks up with news that's useful. "I've got more texts coming in right now. It looks like Bartlomiej's headed back to his plane without completing the deal. He's still out whatever product he was going to buy from the bratva, which means he's still out the product he was going to sell the Armenians. Now whatever deal he had going with the *Cosa Nostra* just went to shite. He's certainly not having a pleasant month. It's a good thing you got Carys out while you could. I can only imagine his temper right now, and he's going to unleash Jacek on the world, so he doesn't have to get his hands dirty."

There's a lull for a moment. Then Shane speaks up again.

"I still want him at the station. The moment he returns, have some guys at the airport scoop him up. I don't want Salvatore or Maks getting a chance at him before I do."

I recognize Sean's voice when he asks his twin a question. "Do we let Salvatore and Maks know why you get priority? They're going to find out about Carys eventually, if they haven't already. They'd understand and give him to you if we did."

"No, I'm not ready to put Carys in the center of anybody's radar until we know what they know about her already. It's not worth bringing attention to her yet."

What the fuck does that mean? It's not worth bringing attention to me. As in, he doesn't see me sticking around that long?

He obviously thinks I'm worth some protection, or I wouldn't be here. But he wants to keep me a secret because I'm not worth the effort? I know I could interpret that a couple other ways, but it still stings if that's the case. I thought I already meant more to him than that.

If I don't, then why am I risking my job?

You're being overly sensitive, Carys.

I'm certain he means it's not worth endangering me by having the bratva or *Cosa Nostra* examine me too closely. That's the reasonable explanation. That's what I'm going with.

"If he's headed back, then it'll only be a couple hours before he gets here, assuming his plane's refueled and ready to go quickly, and he's not sticking around for anything else."

That voice sounded a lot like Cormac, but not exactly. Maybe it's Seamus. He's been quiet the entire time. I wonder what his mountainous cousin thinks about all this.

If I were part of the conversation, I'd be able to ask, but I'm not, so I can't. There's another lull while I think everybody contemplates what's going on.

"I'll send Joey to round him up with some other guys."

"Thanks, Finn, but I'd rather it not be Joey. I don't want to put him in the line of fire right now because Bartlomiej's already going to be more pissed off than a shaken hive. I'd rather it be someone we know can get the job done but isn't as valuable as Joey."

Holy fuck. Shane means someone who's expendable. I really just listened to him say he doesn't care if somebody dies. Not true. He cares if Joey does, but it means they have men they don't care about. That's something to work my mind around, even though I've felt similarly as far as CIs are concerned. I've just never been so blasé about it. It's always made me think twice before putting them in danger. Shane says it as though he's ordering orange juice with breakfast.

This is part of the man I know he doesn't want me to see. This is all the more reason he took this call inside his office, where he wanted to keep me away from it. I don't know what to do because a tiny part of my conscience is still niggling at that, but he's also doing all of this—or at least partly—for my sake. I can't ignore he's putting my life ahead of somebody else's, so he can't be entirely detached from me.

I guess he really wants to protect me by not putting me on the other syndicate's radar.

"Sean, any hits on the Colombians? Are they blissfully ignorant, or are they watching from the sidelines?"

Shane turns his questions toward his brother, and it's the same thing I just wondered. I hadn't thought about the Cartel at first, but now I wonder why I haven't heard their names in this at all yet.

"Enrique seems preoccupied with some stuff right now, but I haven't figured out what yet. He's been laying low lately, and I don't think Pablo's interested. He has the shite with the Ecuadorians and Brazilians down there to deal with. Some issues with supply chain management."

I hear laughter at that comment. I'm not sure what the insider part of that is, but clearly the Colombians aren't getting all the ingredients they need for their drug production. That ought to pique my interest, but I can't say that it does. I'm actually surprisingly indifferent to it right now.

It's hardly my priority to figure out the next syndicate to stake out. Normally, this would be something I'd tell my bosses right away. However, I'm not feeling very forthcoming with them right now. I'm tucking that little nugget away for a rainy day. It might be my ticket to freedom from the agency at some point, so I won't give it up yet.

"I just texted Sully and told him to get three guys together to pick up Bartlomiej and Jacek for you."

"Thanks, Dill. Sully's a good one to use. He's smart enough to keep his head on his shoulders, but the only men he can get are ones we won't miss."

"That's why I picked him. Shane, we'll deal with all of this. We'll make sure Bartlomiej's not a part of your woman's life ever again."

"I could get used to the sound of all of that. Carrie not being in danger, and Carrie being my woman."

I hear another round of chuckles as some good-natured teasing happens. But because of that, I don't notice the voices getting a little closer until Shane opens the door and finds me standing right there.

"I gotta go."

"But—"

"Gotta go."

Shane snaps at his family before I see him tap his phone screen. He stares at me. Shock and anger clearly radiate from him.

I've really fucked it up now because I don't know how I'm going to back myself out of this. I remain quiet because anything I say will be a lie, and he'll know. That'll only make it worse.

"How long have you been standing there, Carys?"

That's like a knife through my heart. Hearing him use my full name feels so distant. It puts me in my place, and it reminds me I'm with a mobster who can switch on a dime. I'm not scared of Shane physically. But now I'm scared I've ruined everything. I don't think he'd pull my protection. However, I'm on my own now, and that makes me feel defensive rather than ashamed."

"I was listening. You know that. I heard pretty much everything."

"Why?"

I'm not convinced he genuinely wants the answer to that. It's just a natural question to ask next.

"Because all of this involves my life, Shane. I have a right to know everything that's going on."

"No, you don't. You didn't know where that conversation was headed. There's so much more you could've heard you never should have that would put you in more danger than you could possibly fathom. It's bad enough you just heard what you did. None of that was for your ears."

"You're worried I'm going to turn state's evidence for hearing you commission a murder."

I should have kept that to myself. His expression entirely shuts off, and it's like looking at a marble statue chiseled by one of the master Renaissance sculptors. Absolute perfection, but with no emotion. Instead of leaving well enough alone, I catapult us back to that adversarial dynamic we started with.

"I never said I would do that. Does it mean I'm going to swim with the fishes now?"

That still gets no reaction from him. That's scarier than anything else. I have an inkling of what men about to die feel when Shane is like this. I still don't fear for my safety, but I certainly am not picturing a long and happy lifetime together anymore.

"Carys—"

"Don't call me that. You never called me that."

"Oh, you're lucky your full name is all I'm calling you right now. I trusted you to stay in the living room, or even make yourself another snack, or go up to the bedroom, or any number of things. You've shown me the moment you're out of my sight, I can't trust you."

"And I'm supposed to trust you would've told me what that conversation was about."

"The part's pertinent to you, I would have."

"You were going to tell me you'd have men round up Bartlomiej to take him to wherever this station place is? You were going to share that with me? I don't believe that for a second."

"I was going to tell you I had a way to make sure he could never be a threat to you again. You would have understood what that meant without me giving details. Now you know information someone could force from you. Information they could compel you to testify."

I know that's all the truth. It lurked in the back of my mind.

"Shane, it will never come to that. I would never give you or your family up, and that's why you should have trusted me."

"Maybe. But I should still be entitled to private conversations without worrying you're eavesdropping or believing you deserve to know every nook and cranny of the truth. You should trust me better, Carrie."

"We're not there yet."

"And it's obvious we won't get there."

"What's that supposed to mean?"

"It means you have a very large resort, and you're the only guest. Make yourself at home, *Carrie.* Since you don't have your purse or any of your belongings, I don't have to worry about you using a lock picking set to get into my office. Otherwise, you have the run of the house. I'll make sure there's plenty of food delivered to you. Whatever you want."

"Wait, what? You make it sound as though you won't be here."

"I won't. Obviously, you know what I'm up to. As you know, I have other plans. I might be away for a while. I'll see you when I see you."

"What the hell does that mean, Shane? You're just leaving me here alone in this house?"

"Why not? I'm usually here alone. It's peaceful with nobody else here."

That stings, and he knows it. He said it to hurt me, and I deserve it.

"Are you leaving right this minute?"

"No, I don't need to. But like I said, you have the run of the house. You can do as you please. There's a pool in the backyard. I won't disturb you."

"Shane, this conversation isn't over."

"Oh, yes, it is because there's not a single thing more I can say to you that won't be hurtful in some way or another. And that's not my goal."

His words say nothing more, but his expression makes up for it. He clearly believes what I did was intentionally hurtful. It wasn't, but it's certainly the fallout. He turns around and goes back into his office.

It would be easier if he slammed the door in my face. But it closes with barely a sound until I hear him turn the lock. I'm left standing in the hallway with no one to blame but myself.

Chapter Eighteen

Shane

I need the time alone in my office to calm down. I'm so frustrated, disappointed, angry... A whole hodgepodge of feelings right now. I wanted to believe Carrie would remain in the living room where I asked her—or I guess I told her—to stay. I didn't want to think she'd spy on me, so I trusted her. I now feel like an idiot for doing it. Not so much that I believe she's going to run and tell her supervisors what she heard.

Just the opposite. I'm more worried about what they'll try to get out of her. Not like I expect them to stick bamboo shoots under her fingernails or put the screws to her. However, they could compel her to testify. Then she'd have no choice but to get on the stand and share everything she just heard, which includes the commissioning of murder that could put me and my entire family behind bars. We have enough shite we're guilty of on our own without my girlfriend being the reason we wind up on death row. Well, maybe not death row because the State of New York doesn't have that, but life in prison.

I feel betrayed even though I think I understand her motives.

She's used to a great deal of control just like I am because her life depends on it just like mine does. However, her need for control right now just created a massive weakness for all of us, and I'm trying to cut her some slack because this is all new to her.

She's really only existed on the periphery of the syndicate world. Yeah, she might have been with Bartlomiej for several months and been privy to things going on with the Poles, but that's not the same as living it day to day. Now she's staying in my house with me and is potentially—I guess—my girlfriend. I don't even know now.

It's way different being with an Irish mobster. The Poles are certainly not a syndicate to underestimate, but they don't have even a microscopic amount of the pull my family and I do. She's with one of the senior-most members of the Irish mob. Not for nothing, but I'm kinda a big deal, and that's what scares me for her.

I don't think she understands the true ramifications of all of this, and I'm angry at myself because her not understanding falls on my shoulders. I could have—should have—explained all of this better. I made an unfair—even if I think completely understandable—assumption. Instead of wondering about what she's going to tell her bosses about Bartlomiej, I should have thought more about what to tell her to clue her in beyond what she thinks she knows.

There's just so fucking much more than what she thinks she knows. I need to consider my next steps, so I walk to my desk and sit. It's one of the comfiest chairs in my house. It's an ergonomic, everything cushiony everywhere, top-of-the-line desk chair because I spend too many hours here. Not only do I head up most of our construction projects, but I'm also in charge of our PR. Between the two, it means I make the ugly go away.

I spin the tales in the news that make us the victim when I need us to be and the heroes even when we're not. It also means I decide what other syndicates hear about us, what false information or what truth we feed to them. While I can't deal with what Carrie just did now because I'm too upset, I can think about the messaging we're going to put out about her being with me.

I have to consider this on several layers because I don't know where we stand. Maybe she's just a houseguest or maybe she's the future I hoped she'd be. Either way, she's now linked to me. I wake my computer and check my email and the ones belonging to various other syndicate members.

We all have multiple accounts for the ones we don't mind people hacking. Those are often my primary source of miscommunication. Then there're the extra secure ones for deals we want to do with nobody knowing, but it wouldn't be the end of the world if they leaked. Then there's the highest level of security my twin set up to make sure nobody under the sun can crack it. The perks of having a brother with a graduate degree in national security. We always say if he can find a country's nuclear secrets and keep them to himself, then he can keep our family secrets intact.

I don't notice the time go by until it's been nearly two hours since I locked myself in here. I really need to check on Carrie. That's assuming she didn't just walk out. I know my men would've told me if she tried, but I wouldn't fault her since I abandoned her. Even though I'm still unsure how I feel, it wasn't right for me to walk away from her in a strange house when she's here basically under duress. I close up shop in my office and put my laptop back in the safe where I keep it.

I head out to the living room and find Carrie asleep on the sofa. I glance at my watch again. It's too early to call it a night, but it doesn't surprise me she's taking a nap. Maybe she'll sleep through the night. I scoop her into my arms and wish everything was so simple as this. I make my way up to the guest bedroom and carefully pull down the covers as best I can while juggling holding her.

I ease her onto the mattress and tuck her in. Then I move to the closet to pull out and examine the clothes hanging there. I choose one of my button-down shirts and then go to the very dresser I finger-fucked her on only hours ago and pull out a t-shirt and a pair of basketball shorts. Since she has nothing here, she might be more comfortable sleeping in something else. I head into the ensuite to ensure there're towels, shampoo, soap, and anything else she could need along with a fresh toothbrush and toothpaste.

I leave everything on the counter, so she doesn't have to search. No, it's not because I don't trust her not to snoop. I simply want to make it easier for her. I can be at least a little thoughtful considering her predicament. I'm about to leave when I hear her groggy voice.

"Daddy?"

I freeze.

Does she realize the pet name she used? I look over my shoulder, and she's more beautiful than I've ever seen before. Her hair's a little tousled from her turning over while I moved around, and she's a bit bleary-eyed as she comes around. It makes me wonder how long she slept for.

Her expression tells me she didn't notice what she called me. She pushes up onto one elbow and watches me watch her. I don't step away from the door, and it makes the silence grow awkward. I cock an eyebrow to ask what she wants, but I know there's an element of challenge there. She reads the tone, and I can see her retreat.

"Never mind, Shane." Her jaw clenches for a second. "Sorry. Thank you for bringing me up here."

She spots the clothes at the foot of the bed before her gaze darts to me. Then she looks toward the bathroom.

"I appreciate it. I'll figure something out. Can I order some clothes online? Would that be possible?"

"It is, but you can't use any of your cards, and you can't use your account. We'll put it under mine."

"No, Shane. That's too much. You're already giving me a place to stay. I don't need you to buy me a wardrobe of clothes."

"But you do. Carrie, somebody in my family or I has to buy everything because you can't use anything that'll trace back to your banking info, where things are being delivered, or when you purchase them. If you want, one of my sisters can order it under her account. I can always pick it up, or we can have guys bring it over. But someone has to help you out right now."

I see the war going on in her mind. She knows what I'm suggesting is reasonable, but she's worried about taking a handout from me after our argument earlier. I open the door wider and step into the hallway before I turn toward her.

"Let me know what you think. If you're hungry, come downstairs whenever you want. I'm going to heat up some shepherd's pie I made the other day. There's that and leek soup and several other things in the fridge. Help yourself to whatever you want."

"Shane, is that really it? That's all you're going to say?"

"What do you want, Carrie? Do you want me to forgive you for spying on me, for hearing things that could put me away for life, that endanger my family, that endanger you, that violated my trust? No, I'm not ready to forgive you for that. Are you ready to fully trust me and believe I have your best interests at heart and that maybe you're in over your head and all I'm trying to do is protect you like I promised, to take care of you the best way I know how?"

It all comes out in a jumble in one breath. She glances at her lap, clearly chagrined. Yet, when she looks up at me, there's strength radiating from her, even if I can tell she feels remorse.

"I want to believe you, Shane, but I've dug myself into such a deep hole, I don't know that anybody can pull me out. I'm so used to relying on myself when I'm in situations that're unpredictable. Yes, I've always had handlers when I go undercover, but they're never there right alongside me. This feels much the same way, except the stakes are exponentially higher now because of Bartlomiej and Jacek, along with how I feel about you and what I've just done to sabotage any chance I had with you."

As I listen to her, it makes me genuinely consider how I feel about a future with her. Pushing aside the anger and the hurt, I make myself truly see things through her eyes rather than merely saying I can.

I let the anger slip away because, despite how I feel now in the moment, it doesn't change what I want in the long run for us. I walk back into the bedroom and perch on the edge of the mattress.

"Carrie, if you want a future with me, then there can be one because I still want that, too. We have a long way to go to get through all of this and to see whether we're suited for a future together. We have to get to a point where we can trust one another and know we have each other's best interests at heart."

"Shane, I know that. That was never a question for me. My problem was not knowing what other people might be doing. I fear for your safety as much as I do mine. Part of the reason I listened was because I'm scared for you. I know the power your family wields, and I know how close all of you are. But a bullet is a bullet, and it doesn't matter who your family is. It can still kill you. I want to know what's going on in case it's life or death for you because there's nothing I won't do to protect you. It's not a one-way street between us."

"I know, and I understand this is challenging for you. I don't doubt you have your own skills and things you can bring to this. Can you live with me promising to ask your opinion if it comes to matters I believe are safe for you to know, then trust me when there're things I don't believe are?"

"That's fair. What if you and I disagree on what's safe for me?"

That gives me pause as I think about how I want to phrase my answer, so I don't speak rashly.

"Carrie, that isn't for you to decide. I hate saying that because I understand the unfairness of it. I don't want you to think I'll be heavy-handed in every part of a relationship with you. That's not what I want, but that's how things stand now. I need you to understand there'll be consequences if you don't listen to my advice about this. I'm not threatening an ultimatum of me walking away from you if you don't do as you're told, but I will punish you, little one. I will spank you until your arse is so raw you fear you'll never sit again because I need you to accept, in this, I'll always lead. This isn't your choice."

Her expression when she opens her mouth screams she disagrees. I plow on.

"I know if feels excessive to you, but that's how things stand. If you can't live with that, then there's no moving forward."

"You want domestic discipline is what you're saying."

"No, not in everything. I want you to do as you please or disagree and have a say in how this relationship works. However, with mob stuff and your involvement in it and your safety, it's completely non-negotiable. I have only ever lived this life. It's all I know. You come from a different world. Even though you now know your mom's connected to us, it's not remotely the same. You're not equipped to decide like I am. I don't make these decisions arbitrarily, even if I make them quickly. Part of what you can't do—at least not for a very long time—is make those split-second decisions I do. I must always consider the immediate situation along with the long-term outcomes. Every decision I make is about more than just me and what I need. They're *always* about an entire family and an entire organization. You don't know all the inner workings to make those educated decisions, and you're not used to making such massive ones in the matter of heartbeats."

I'm not sure how she'll receive this mandate, but it's one I suddenly feel adamant about. I never imagined being in a committed relationship, let alone considering any form of domestic discipline. But I told the truth. I don't want to stifle her in any way, except for putting herself in danger.

"Can you live with this, Carrie?"

Her response is faster than I expect. "Yes, Daddy."

She leans forward and takes my hand and gives it a squeeze.

"I think I've already earned my first disciplinary spanking."

"Do you feel you need that to clear your conscience or because you fear without it, I won't forgive you?"

"Mostly the former, but a bit of the latter."

"Carrie, my forgiveness will never be contingent upon a punishment. Once we've worked out the situation, it's done. The punishment stands so you accept the severity of the situation you're entering with me."

"I understand that, Daddy. I'd still feel better right now if I got my punishment."

"You accept a spanking?"

"Yes, Daddy."

"All right. Stand up. Drop your pants. No panties."

I remember she put those back on earlier. I let it go. However, when she takes them off, I stick my hand out for them, and she gives them to me. I shove them into my pocket.

"These are mine now. You don't have any others to put on, and there's no point in ordering any when you get some clothes. I expect to find your pussy available when I want it. Obviously, you have to wear clothes—unfortunately—but no panties anymore."

"I like that idea."

"You like knowing you belong to me, and I decide how and when I use your pussy?"

"Very much. Part of the reason I need the punishment is to assure me that's still the case. I get you forgive me, but I need this reassurance after fucking up so badly."

"You understand this goes both ways? I belong to you as much as you belong to me."

"Yeah, I get that."

"There will be no one else for either of us." I give her a pointed stare, and she nods.

"I doubt I have a job left. Even if I did, I don't see how I can keep it. And if—by some divine miracle—I kept it, then there would be no more undercover work like what I did. I won't put myself in a position to betray your trust. Not in that way or any other."

"All right. Come here, little one."

She stretches out across my lap, and I hook my left leg around hers to hold her in position. I'll always be aware of my strength, but I intend this to be painful. It will hurt, but not be harmful.

"Carrie, you remember your safe word?"

"Yes. *Digon.*"

"All right. If this gets to be too much for you, say your safe word. The last thing I want to do is harm you."

"I know you'd never forgive yourself if you did."

"That's right, and I definitely wouldn't trust myself to do anything like this again. You know I'm not spanking you out of anger, right?"

"Yes, I know, and I don't believe you ever would. I believe you are too methodical in what you do."

That makes my legs tense around her. She twists her head to look up to me, her mouth wide open.

"Shane, that's not—I'm sorry, that—" She finishes with a frustrated exhale. "That wasn't what I meant, Shane. I didn't mean to compare this to your work. I don't see it that way. I only meant you do things with care, and you're thoughtful about them."

I relax. I believe she simply misspoke. To somebody else, it wouldn't matter so much. It's just the umpteenth reminder our situation is so different from a normal couple's.

"I'm going to give you ten spanks on each side. You're going to count them."

"Yes, Daddy."

I squeeze her arse and shake it within my palm.

"Such a fine little arse for my hand, and such a pretty little pussy for my fingers."

I slide them between her pussy lips and dip my middle and ring finger into her. She's already wet.

"This isn't for your enjoyment, *cailín*."

"I know, but this happens anytime I'm around you. I can't help it."

I slide my fingers back between her arse cheeks and tap the rosebud.

"This is mine, too."

"I know, and I want that. Can I have that today?"

"You think you're going to receive pleasure after your punishment? I might edge you, but you won't come."

"I get that. It's not for my sake that I want to have it."

My hand lets go of her arse and runs up and down her back between her shoulder blades to the small of her back. Then I squeeze each shoulder, my thumb rubbing knots against her neck.

"I never want you to feel you have to make restitution after a punishment. This isn't a true D/s relationship. This isn't about you making amends to me, so I can prove I'm in control of you or to prove you're willing to submit to me. This is purely about you understanding I won't accept you putting yourself in danger."

"I understand, but I also want you to recognize the level of trust I have for you and my commitment to us."

"Thank you, *cailín*. Put your hands on the floor or grab my ankle if you don't think you can keep from reaching back. If I catch your hands, I will hurt you. That's the last thing I want. I will find an entirely different way to punish you if you do."

"Yes, Daddy."

I love how she calls me that when she's being playful, and I love when she calls me that when she's being affectionate. But it tugs at my heart when it's said in fear and she needs reassurance, or when it's said in contrition. I hate having any emotional distance between us when things are so fragile. I don't know where my emotions lie on the spectrum of feelings, but I know despite the difficulties we're having right now, I respect her strength and her courage. I respect her loyalty and dedication, and I'm beyond physically attracted to her.

I lift my hand and bring it down on her left arse cheek. The sound fills the room.

"One."

I spank her on her other arse cheek.

"Two."

I rain down two in quick succession, so it feels like one.

"Three, four." Her voice wavers.

I spank the underside of her left arse cheek.

"Five."

I spank it again.

"Six."

I move back to the other side.

"Seven."

I keep going until she gets to twenty, making sure it's ten on each side. She's stomping her feet and crying. I allow her to continue even though I offer her soothing sounds and rub my hand over her arse. I let her cry out everything she's bottled up for so long. I know it goes beyond what we're dealing with right now for her punishment. This is about everything she has no control over. All the fear and frustration she's had that life's forced her to bottle up to remain professional. Eventually, her tears slow, and it's an occasional whimper rather than sob.

I help her roll over and hold her in my arms, her arse resting between my knees.

"It's all right now, *cailín*. It's all over. Everything's back to normal. Everything's okay between us."

"Are you really sure, Daddy? You promise everything's okay?"

"Of course, I wouldn't tell you that if it weren't. If things weren't okay between us, then you'd know."

"I believe that after earlier."

She offers me a watery smile, and I kiss her temple. She curls into me, and nothing feels better than holding her. I gaze at her as she closes her eyes. She nestles closer to me, and all the tension eases from her body.

I wonder how long this sense of peace can last. My experience is peace is but a fleeting reprieve from the unrelenting deluge that's syndicate life. I refuse to ruin this by being maudlin, but it's impossible to overlook a lifetime of experience. Maybe I can manifest it or something.

"How long did you sleep?"

"I think I fell asleep about a half-an-hour after you went back in your office." Shame sweeps over her face, and she looks away.

"I told you we reconciled everything."

"Until you think about it again later."

"Carrie, we've never been on a date, and suddenly, we're living together. It's going to take some time to get used to each other. Today's been worse than most. Tomorrow will be better."

What am I? Little Orphan Annie? The sun'll come out tomorrow. My gut says fat fucking chance. But I won't share that when Carrie's feeling so vulnerable.

"Come, sweet one."

She nearly tumbles out of my lap as she struggles to get up, then backs away. "Don't call me that, please. I hate it."

"Little one?"

"No. You said sweet one. That's what he called me. I hate it."

"They're practically the same thing, and little one doesn't bother you?"

She vehemently shakes her head. I watch her retreat into herself as her breathing suddenly becomes more labored.

"Carrie." I pull her into my arms. "Shh. He's not here. I am. You're with me. I shouldn't have called you sweet since you're my prickly little porcupine, not a gumdrop."

She chokes a laugh as her arms curl between us.

"Shane, are you really going to make him go away?"

"Yes."

I am, but I won't tell her more than that. She doesn't need a hint of what I've envisioned since I met her. Jacek's death will be even worse.

"You can make sure Jacek doesn't get me, right?"

If I'd known one word would affect her so much, I wouldn't have even thought it, let alone said it.

"I have shirts in my closet from high school. Do you know why?"

"You're a hoarder?"

I chuckle. "No. Because I take care of what's mine."

"Does that mean you're going to hang me up in your closet?"

No. But I'm going to hang both of those shitbirds up by meat hooks.

"No. But I enjoy wearing your cunt around my cock."

She laughs, but when I loosen my hold, prepared to step back, she fists my shirt. I hate how she feels right now. I hate how I can't fix this immediately. That I haven't fixed it yet. With my arm still around her waist, I walk backwards to the bed. My free hand reaches between us and unfastens my pants.

"Shane?"

"Come here. We both need this."

I push my pants and boxer briefs down enough to free my cock before I sit on the bed. I lift her and bring her legs around my hips before she eases down my cock. I tuck her head against my shoulder, and we sit in silence. My need to control this situation—the one right now in this room with Carrie and the bigger one playing out in the real world—burns in my chest. I can only satisfy one part, so I focus on the woman on my lap.

I can bring her pleasure, and I will later. Right now, I need to know she's safe physically and emotionally. I need to reassure her she is. Being inside her makes us one body. Holding her while we're joined makes us one soul. I feel that to my core.

I slip my right hand between us and rest it over her heart. She does the same thing to me. I glance at the bedside table clock a few times, and we sit like this for ten minutes. Her cunt squeezes me from time to time, keeping me hard as a fucking brick. But we're not trying to get off. This isn't exactly sex. It's not even really cock warming. It's that reprieve—that peace—I now understand I'll only find with Carrie.

"Daddy?"

"Yes, *cailín*."

"I need this."

"So do I."

"Do you feel you're in control because you could give me or deny me an orgasm?"

"There's that."

"Do you feel in control because you could come inside me if you want?"

"There's that, too."

"Do you feel in control because it's just the two of us in a bubble right now?"

"Yes. I feel in control because you're accepting my help while you're upset. I don't feel out of control when you trust me."

"My mind is finally calm because you have that control. I'm safe with you in every way. I feel taken care of and protected in a way no one else has ever given me. For right now, can I..."

She's holding her breath, and I don't know why. The peace is shattering because I don't know what's wrong. I'm back to not knowing how to make things right.

"Carrie, you can ask me anything. I'll always do my best to give you what you want, and I'll always find a way to give you what you need."

She nods against my shoulder.

"Can I submit beyond just sex for right now?"

"Do you mean you want me to decide everything?"

"Yeah. I know I call you Daddy, and you call me *cailín*. But we both know you're not a Daddy Dom, and I'm not a Little. I'm not even a Middle. I don't want a Dom per se because that would feel domineering and suffocating with the weight of everything else. I just don't want to decide things right now. I don't mind what we do. Just please don't ask me to choose. I can't."

"I know, little one. It's too much."

She nods. I wrap my hand around her throat and let it rest heavily there. I don't need to squeeze.

"We're going to sit here for a bit longer. Then I'm going to fill your tight little cunt with my cum. You're going to fall asleep full of it, and the first thing you feel when you wake up is part of me still in you."

"You say things like that... Shane, I need more."

She shifts restlessly. She yelps when I stand—her body still wrapped around me—and walk to the closet. There're three suits hanging in here and ten ties. I grab three. Each step moves her up and down my dick. I don't stifle the groan, but I battle the urge to press her against the wall and fuck her until she screams her safe word. Later.

Once I'm on the bed again, I use the ties to bind her wrists like I did with her bra straps, except she's on top and not connected to the headboard. I use the other two to blindfold and gag her.

"Show me you can still snap."

She does with both hands.

I fist her hair and yank downward. I'm careful not to snap her neck back, but she no longer controls how it moves. I pull her away from my body before I slap her tits. She screams behind the gag, but her hips move on their own. She's riding me like I'm her prize stallion. I pinch and twist her nipples, alternating between that and spanking them.

"Don't come, little girl. If you do, you won't come again until tomorrow night. I'll just edge you."

Her muffled moan goes straight to my cock. I lift her to change positions, so I'm fucking her and not the other way around. I need to pull out for a moment to regain that vaunted control that's at the heart of this—interlude. That sounds far more romantic than fucking like rabbits on Easter.

My Catholic grandmothers just said a rosary for me in their caskets.

But being with Carrie is divine.

I position her on her belly and climb over her. I trap her legs between mine as I thrust into her. Her shoulders come off the mattress. I watch her face, catching every furrow of her brow, every wince, every wide-mouthed muffled scream. The pain's bringing her pleasure, and that's what I want. I never want to go too far.

I lean forward, my abs skimming over her bound wrists. I kiss her neck from her shoulder up to her ear as I lift the blindfold off. Then I bring my lips to the shell of her ear to whisper.

"You're so brave, little one. You're strong and fierce. Resilient and intelligent. Can you feel how that turns me on?"

"Ymff, dddeee."

I suppose that's something akin to yes, Daddy.

"You're beautiful, Carrie. And I want to devour every inch of you. But it's your personality that draws me like a moth to a flame. Will you scorch me?"

She twists so she can see me when she turns her head. She shakes it. I realize my poor choice of words. She thinks I'm asking if she'll betray me. Fuck. That wasn't what I meant.

"*Cailín*, I meant will you keep me and not let go?"

She nods, and I feel her body relax as her shoulders settle back against the mattress. That was a shitty metaphor that nearly ruined everything. I draw back onto my knees, lifting her hips. My fingers will leave marks from the way I grip them. I'll know she's mine whenever I see them, and she won't doubt it. I can leave my cum in her pussy or jizz on her tits, but that washes away. The marks will last for a couple days. When they fade, I'll give her another set. I don't want deep bruises like if I caned her. Just red marks that'll fade quickly.

"Shane! Shane!"

You've gotta be fucking kidding me.

Chapter Nineteen

Shane

"Don't come up, Cormac!"

What the fuck is my cousin doing here?

"Shane!"

I hear the voice growing closer. I pull out and roll off the bed. I get to the door just as Cormac reaches the top of the stairs. I stick my head out, and I know he understands what he interrupted the moment he sees half of my bare chest sticking out between the mostly closed door and the doorjamb.

"Shite!"

"Yeah. Thanks for—"

"No. You need to hurry and get Carys dressed. Agents are on the way. They have a warrant for her and your place. Someone tipped them off."

I glance back at Carrie, who's sitting up and struggling to nudge the gag from her mouth.

"Hang on."

I slam the door as I run to her side. I pull the gag out, then take off the blindfold, before releasing her wrists. I grab the button down from the end of the bed and shove it at her. It's the first piece of clothing I could reach. I grab my boxer briefs and yank them on, followed by my trousers.

"Stay out of sight."

She nods as she fumbles with the buttons. She abandons it and grabs the t-shirt and shorts. I step into the hallway before she finishes putting them on.

"What kind of agents?"

"DEA. Sean figured out Carys's handlers names and hacked their email. He sent Paul over to the new safe house they set up. He got inside and dropped a bug. We don't know who told them Carys is here, but they have a laundry list of accusations."

"Like what?" Carys steps beside me in the hallway.

"The mildest are failure to follow supervisory instructions. It gets worse from there. Failure to secure or process evidence. Intentional, reckless, or negligent violation of rules governing searches and seizures. Improper association with convicted felon, confidential source, and/or persons connected with criminal activity. Intentional and improper discharge of a firearm. Lack of Candor, and falsification, misrepresentation, or concealment of information or facts in connection with an official government document or in any other official statement, oral or written."

Carrie stares at Cormac, who stares at me.

"Carrie, Cor's an attorney. He specializes in corporate law, but he went to John Jay College of Criminal Justice. While our situation is unique, you're not the first federal agent with ties to us. We're all well-versed on the various codes of professional conduct for federal agencies."

"You've memorized the DEA one?"

"No. They just plagiarize each other, so it makes it easy to remember."

Most women drool when he shoots them the grin he's giving Carrie. I know he's not flirting with her. He can't help his charm, but it has no effect on Carrie. She's looking up at me, waiting for me to tell her what to do.

"How long do we have, Cor?"

He glances at his watch. "Ten minutes tops."

"Get the diluted bleach and go over the TV remotes, the kitchen counters, the doorknobs up here, and run the dishwasher. I'm taking Carrie downstairs. *Cailín*, grab your clothes. I have a safe room in the basement. They won't find you."

I don't realize what I called her aloud until Cormac clears his throat. I glance at him before looking at Carrie. Too late now. I can't take it back, and frankly, I don't give a shite my family knows what I call her. If Cormac knows, then it's the same as everyone else knowing. We gossip worse than old women. If they hadn't already figured out what she means to me, they will now.

I open the bedroom door and sweep my gaze over everything.

"Wipe down the top of the dresser, too." I glare at Cormac when his lips twitch, ready to grin again. Instead, he nods.

He heads into the bathroom, knowing there's bleach under the sink. Sometimes we need a disinfectant stronger than the ones that claim to eliminate odor and kill ninety-nine percent of germs. I cringe when I think about any bleach touching the top of the dresser. Not just because it's an expensive piece of wood furniture, but it has sentimental value now. I plan for all my furniture to have sentimental value soon.

I don't worry about any DNA left behind. All of us know how to wipe that clean. I take Carrie's clothes and drape them over one arm while my free hand grabs hers. I practically drag her down the stairs.

"My shoes."

They're still in the living room where she kicked them off. She dashes to grab them before I lead her to the basement. I'm slower on these since they're steeper. I steer her to the water heater. I know she's confused, but I place my hand on the wall where the polystyrene insulation panels end, and there's a soft puff of air. I push the panel, and the hidden door opens. I like the heat efficiency, but the ends of the two neighboring panel pieces hide the outline of the door.

"The only people with access are my immediate family. My parents, brothers, cousins, aunts, and uncles. No one else. You stay in here until either Cormac or I get you. Don't open the door for anyone else, regardless of who they say they are. If they're my family, they can open the door on their own. They'll know I brought you down here."

"You have a panic room?"

I stare at her in the dim light I flicked on as we headed down the stairs. A single fingerprint pad turns on the lights within the panic room. It illuminates a two-room space. To the unknowing eye, there's an inviting living room and bedroom. Since someone hiding might need to be here for a while, it's comfortable. A battery powers the lights, so there're no electrical wires to track. Unfortunately, it means there's no bathroom to avoid tracing the plumbing, but there is a camp toilet. Rustic but functional.

I withdraw my cell phone from my pocket and hand it to her.

"I've already programmed any number worth answering in here. You'll have reception despite all the insulation down here. Only answer it if it's a member of my family. Nobody in my family has the same name as any of our men, except for Sean. And he's in my phone as Twin. You'll know if it's him. If something goes wrong and they take me, Cormac will call you or come to get you. Either way, you may be here for a little while. It won't be very interesting since there's no TV or computer down here. However, I have a few books that might keep you occupied. *Cailín*, I'm sorry, but you should be okay."

"Shane, that's the least of my worries. I doubt I can concentrate on anything I read right now. Just be careful. None of this would be happening if it weren't for me."

"That's not true, and you know it. I could just as easily be their target. They could just as easily raid me, regardless of my relationship with you."

"Maybe so, but it's happening right now because of me. I'm so sorry.

"Do *not* blame yourself for any of this, Carys. You didn't ask for any of this to happen."

My tone is adamant, and I see her withdrawal when I use her full name. I didn't realize I had. I just wanted to make her understand how serious I am that I don't blame her for any of this.

"Carrie." I cup her cheek and give her a soft, lingering kiss. "Nothing changes just because of this minor inconvenience."

She nods.

"In the grand scheme of things in this world, having your house searched is hardly more than a brief blip on the radar. None of us keep incriminating things at our homes. We lock away the few things that could cause a snafu in places no one will find."

I gesture around the room.

"I'm not overly concerned. They'll be the ones who leave frustrated not me. There're bound to be some reporters who show up, and they'll see the agents leaving empty-handed. It'll make the news sympathetic to us. Dillan's wife will make sure of it."

When her brow creases, I glance toward the door.

"One of these days, I'll fill you in on all the women in this family. But Dillan's wife is an investigative reporter for the major newspaper here in the city. She often works with me on our PR."

I shoot her a pointed look again, and we leave it at that. Another kiss that threatens to delay me heats between us. But I'm pulling away all too soon, then explaining the code to lock the door.

After that, I'm bolting up the stairs to the kitchen where Cormac's running the water. He's just turning on the dishwasher as I walk in.

"I didn't strip the guest bed, but I made it. I wasn't sure if she'd been in your bedroom, so I took care of the surfaces in there, too."

I shake my head. "No, she's been in the living room, the kitchen, and that bedroom. But thanks. I appreciate you covering everything. Did you do the banister?"

"Yeah. I figured from how you pulled her down the hallway, she probably held on for dear life. I'll do the basement banister right now."

"Okay."

"I'll flush the paper towels."

"Perfect."

Normally, we prefer burning things than any other disposal. However, a pile of ash right now on my stove or in a trash bin would look rather suspicious.

Suspicious.

That's laughable. It's certainly an understatement.

Cormac hurries out of the kitchen, not bothering to dry his hands. He's back just as I check my office for anything I might not have thought could be incriminating. My laptop remains in the safe, which is in another little nook in my home.

You'd never guess where to look if you didn't know. I'm certain they'll search for a safe, but they won't find it. The half-bath toilet just went quiet as there's a bang on the door, a garbled voice, and it bursts open. Neither Cormac nor I hurry to stand from where we ran to sit on the sofa in front of the TV that's still on from before Carrie fell asleep.

"Shane O'Rourke, we have a warrant to search your premises."

Now Cormac and I stand. We turn toward the swarm of agents in their khaki pants, polo shirts, and windbreakers. They're interchangeable.

If people thought it's difficult to discern one O'Rourke from another, we've got nothing on these suits. Well, they're not in suits, but that's how we think of feds. It's one of the nicer names we have for them.

Cormac and I hold our hands out to our sides just a few inches from our hips to show we're not reaching for any weapons. He had a weapon when he came in, but he doesn't now. I spotted it in my safe along with several others I had scattered around the house. He rounded all of those up, too. I'll thank him for his efficiency later, but these are skills drilled into us from a young age.

Once our parents believed we were old enough to handle firearms safely, they showed us where they hid all of them in our various family homes, and they showed us how to open the safes. I only remember two raids at my house, three at my grandfather's, and four at Uncle Donovan's. There were ones before I was born, but Finn was too young to remember anything. Clearly, nothing ever came of them since no one's in prison.

"I'd like to see that warrant." I'm commanding without sounding like a dick.

A second agent walks around the one in front who announced their arrival. He holds up the warrant. There's not a chance in hell I'm approaching them. I'm not getting within arm's reach of two dozen federal agents. I stick out my hand and wait. I know he'll eventually come to me. He will figure he's safe with just two of us. I count to three in my head before he takes the first step toward us.

Foolish man. None of them are safe with only two of us. Not having our own guns on us isn't an impediment. We'll take some of theirs. We might not get all of them before we go down in a blaze of glory, but we'd take some. I accept the papers he hands me. I skim them before handing them to Cormac.

"Mr. O'Rourke, you need to come with us." That's the smug arse first agent. Cormac speaks up, and so it really begins.

"Why should I go anywhere with you?"

The lead agent shoots Cormac an expression that tells both of us he's not amused. Cormac cocks an eyebrow. I don't need to look at my cousin to know that's his reaction because it's the same one I have. I see the disconcerted look on several people's faces.

While Cormac and I aren't identical, the familial relationship is clear. His hair is lighter than mine, and he and Seamus have the baby faces in the family. He's also got twenty pounds on me. It's lean muscle that hasn't stopped me knocking him on his arse plenty of times.

However, our mannerisms are so similar it's uncanny to most people. Even though Finn and the other guys aren't my twin—only Sean is—we are such mirror images in absolutely everything, people merely stare. Unfortunately, these agents recover faster from the obvious similarities between Cormac and me.

"Shane O'Rourke, you will come with us."

The agent tries again. Once more, Cormac speaks.

"And who are you?"

It's clear this guy doesn't appreciate Cormac meddling.

"I'm a DEA agent."

"Then let us see your badge. Just because you have a nice jacket on doesn't mean you're who you claim."

The chatty agent looks at the one still standing near us. Smart guy. He doesn't want to get any closer. He nods to numbnuts, who's now even closer than just arm's reach. The guy's slow but removes his badge and flips it open for us to see.

"Okay, that's one of you. But how about the rest of you?"

Cormac and I watch as many of them reach into their pockets. Whichever pocket they withdraw the badge from tells me they don't have a second weapon there. If we have to, that's the side we strike on. One of many tips of the trade our family trained us to notice.

I see various badges flash before us. None open them long enough for us to tell any details.

"Mr. O'Rourke, I would not continue to waste our time."

He gestures for the agents to move forward, many coming in with bankers boxes. They want to make a show of it by leaving with them filled to the brim with evidence they confiscate. Unless they want to take the few tchotchkes I have, they won't find much of interest. When one of them goes for the family portraits on my wall, I stop him.

"Don't touch without gloves on. I'll lift them off the wall. You can see what's behind them. You can see inside the frames. But I don't want your sticky fingerprints all over my family photos."

The guy looks like he intends to ignore me, but I clear my throat. That's enough to make another agent whisper to him. He drops his arms and reaches into the pocket that didn't have his badge and pulls out a pair of rubber gloves. That tells me it's unlikely he's carrying a second weapon in there since he wouldn't want to fumble around the gloves to grab it.

It's not that I expect federal agents to carry knives, but you never know. We always work on the assumption it's possible. They won't fit a second gun in their trouser pockets. However, we expect most of them have a second weapon strapped to their ankle. So far, they haven't drawn them, but we're as prepared as we can be.

I watch the agent lift off the picture frame, look behind it, and shake it. The glass rattles a little, but nothing alarming. He does the same thing for each of them, satisfied there's nothing hidden behind them.

The agent who started all of this withdraws handcuffs and approaches Cormac and me.

"Mr. O'Rourke, you have the right to remain silent."

Cormac steps in front of me.

"You still haven't told us on what grounds you're here. My client isn't leaving this house without you showing a warrant for his arrest. The one you handed my client only states you have authority to search the premises. It says nothing about arresting my client."

Cormac was mistaken, or they didn't show us, but neither he nor I saw anything about arresting Carrie.

"Your client?"

I want to knock the patronizing expression off this fuckwad's face.

"Yes, my client. I'm certain you're aware I'm admitted to the state bars of New York, New Jersey, Florida, California, and Nevada, among others."

Cormac, Dillan, and Seamus are all attorneys. They're all licensed to practice in the states where we do the most business. Dillan didn't get to practice for very long because he stepped into his role as mob boss about five years ago. He has other responsibilities to manage.

While Cormac handles our corporate ventures, Seamus handles our criminal. Depending on what they try to charge me with, Cormac will either continue to represent me, or he'll hand me off to Seamus.

"You cannot be Mr. O'Rourke's attorney. You have a conflict of interest."

"Yes, I can. There's nothing that prevents me from representing him in a situation like this where you have no warrant to arrest him. I'm free to give legal counsel to him as an attorney admitted to the state bar."

Cormac crosses his arms, and his suit coat strains across his back and over his biceps. I swear the man has them tailored extra tight just for moments like this. I know most of us do. It's an impressive sight for sure, especially when I join him and do the same thing. Granted, I don't have my suit coat on right now.

I took that and my tie off and left it in my office when I made the call. It would look odd if I wore it now since I'm sure they staked out the house, at least for a little while before they came in. They know I've been here, so why would I wear my suit coat in my home if I've been here for several hours?

"So?" The agent's face flushes with frustration.

Cormac cocks an eyebrow again. He won't give an inch. "So what?"

"Who are you?"

"Cormac O'Rourke, Esquire."

He tacks that on, matching the patronizing tone the agent's had since he entered my home. Attorneys might have Esq. at the end of their name when it's something formal, but they never introduce themselves with that title.

I smirk, and I don't care who sees it. It's distracting them from looking for Carrie. None of them have headed to the basement, even though several went upstairs. A female agent comes back and speaks to the first guy.

"Steve, we need him to unlock his office. It's biometric."

"Get the enforcer."

I don't agree with Steve's call to use a battering ram on my office door. I shake my head.

"You're going to repair the damages you do to my home."

All they're going to accomplish with that is scuffing up the door. No matter how strong the agent is, my office has a reinforced door just like the one to the panic room. They are not getting through with an enforcer. They could have a medieval battering ram, and they still wouldn't get through.

I know I must comply, otherwise it'll justify grounds for arrest.

So, I walk over with the female officer. I recognized her voice from Carrie's earlier phone calls.

This is Angela.

Her two handlers are leading this. I certainly know where their loyalties lie. It makes me wonder if they're actually the leak. Do they have something going on with another syndicate that's making them toss Carrie under the bus first? I'm a suspicious man by nature, and this is a suspicious situation.

I unlock the office door and push it open, stepping aside to let the agents enter first. This way nobody can claim I tried to hide anything. Cormac has his phone out. I know he's been recording the audio since they came in. Now, he holds it up to video them searching my office.

"Mr. O'Rourke put that away."

"No, I have the right to record what's going on in my cousin's private property. If you conduct the search properly, then there's no reason for you to worry about me recording what happens."

"That's not how it's going to work, Mr. O'Rourke. You have known ties to organized crime. I won't have my agents' faces recorded for you to pass along to your enforcers."

"Enforcers? I'm not sure what you mean by that. What on earth could I enforce? I'm not a cop or a fed."

Cormac's tone sounds genuinely perplexed to anyone who doesn't know him and who he is. He's one of our two head enforcers. Seamus is the other one, partly because of their size, but also because as they grew bigger, they knew pretending like they had the shortest fuse kept other kids from teasing them about being bigger than their classmates.

Despite Seamus being two months premature, he's built like a mountain, just like Cormac. Steve—now I know the lead agent's name—looks unimpressed with Cormac's act. Again, none of this matters as long as it distracts them from looking harder for Carrie.

My ears are peeled to hear whether anybody opens the basement door. So far, no one has, but inevitably, someone will. I make myself as accommodating as I can while they turn everything over. They don't find the safe—which doesn't surprise me—because they don't know what to look for. If they did, they would have found it. But I counted on them not having a clue I hid it in the fireplace.

Eventually, the agents who were upstairs make their way back down. Their boxes remain clearly empty. One of them shakes her head. Now I hear the basement door. My stomach knots, but I show no outward reaction when footsteps on the wooden stairs reach me.

"You're still under arrest, Mr. O'Rourke."

Cormac turns with his camera still on and faces Steve again. "And you still haven't told my client what the charges are. Are you going to arrest him without probable cause? There's no evidence here that justifies an arrest, and you haven't provided a warrant for him. So, what are your grounds for this, other than to intimidate my client?"

"Intimidate?"

Steve scoffs, but then he remembers why Cormac's holding up his phone. There's nothing he can say, short of trying to distract us as much as Cormac and I have been trying to distract them.

"We'd like Mr. O'Rourke to come in for some questioning."

Cormac doesn't drop a beat. "My cousin can give you the link to his calendar, and you can book an appointment."

"Book an appointment?"

Steve's voice rises with each syllable until he's practically yelling the last one. Perfect. Let him get upset. Let him show his arse even more.

"Yes, you have no grounds to detain my client, so you're not arresting him. You said you'd like to ask him some questions. I don't believe my cousin would like to answer any. Therefore, you can schedule an appointment, just like anybody else who'd like to have a meeting with him."

"You are unreal."

"Am I though? Because right now, I sound very much alive with my freedom of speech intact, recording all of this."

Cormac's tone remains innocent, like he and Seamus did when we were kids, and somehow always stayed out of trouble when our parents busted the rest of us. He makes his point loud and clear.

"If you have nothing else to do here now that you've searched the entire premises, and—I heard the agents come in and out from the backyard and the garage—you can leave."

Cormac and I wait, and it takes a moment before Steve orders his agents out of the house. Cormac lowers his camera, but I know he still has it angled toward the door.

"Mr. O'Rourke, this isn't nearly over. You will do what we want, and we will get what we want."

Cormac holds his phone up again.

"That's a very interesting thought to share. I'll be sure that's included when we file a harassment and wrongful detention suit. Thank you for letting us know your plans."

Now Cormac grins, since he'll easily spin that last comment into a perceived threat against us and an admission to premeditated evidence tampering.

Steve snaps his mouth shut and cuts in front of two other agents to leave my house. Angela's the last one out. I gesture for Cormac to put his phone away. I know he's not turning off the recording, but he puts his phone out of sight.

"You're doing her no favors. We will find her."

"Who is her?"

I play ignorant, since nobody has mentioned her name yet. With no warrant, they'd hoped to find her hiding, and that would be probable cause to them.

"Mr. O'Rourke, you know exactly who I'm talking about."

"But I don't. There are billions of people in this world whose pronoun is her. You'll have to be more specific."

"Carys Pritchard."

"Oh, okay. I'm not sure how I can help. But I'm certain whatever you're looking for is very serious. Well, good luck with that."

"You might get away with patronizing Steve, but you won't with me. I'm trying to help, so calm down."

"You don't think I'm calm, agent?" I sound just as innocent as Cormac.

"I know you have her somewhere. You aren't doing her any favors by hiding her. If you're keeping her against her will, then there'll be no coming back from kidnapping a federal agent."

"I'll bear that in mind. Good day."

She heads out and closes the door behind her. I turn around and sigh. My house is a disaster. Everything's pulled apart. They pulled the cushions off the sofa and yanked the stuffing out of them. There's fireplace soot on the living room floor.

I want to run straight to Carrie, but I can't. There's too strong a possibility they might come back and pretend like they thought of something at the last minute, when they're trying to catch us with anything we might have hidden. Instead, Cormac and I put my living room back to rights.

"At least they were polite and unzipped the cushions rather than cutting through them." I hold the cover while Cormac shoves the stuffing back in.

"That's what I expected. We'll see whether they did that to the mattresses upstairs."

"Do you think they really believe I hide anything under them? That's a bit cliché, even for us."

"Who knows what they'd think if they had the chutzpah to come and search your place?"

"You know Judge Hartman loves to dole out search warrants for our families with only the shakiest of reasons."

One of these days—maybe—he'll get lucky. But so far, every warrant he's signed for the Four Families has come up with nothing. He's been on the bench longer than Cormac and I have been alive.

"True."

Judge Herman Hartman has a hard-on for busting the Four Families. But the limp dick needs the little blue pill to keep it up. He wants to make his career by tearing us apart. He merely looks foolish every time he tries.

"I'm going to call Sean and see what else he may have discovered. Then I'm going to take Carrie over there since Nikki's out of town."

My sister-in-law is Canadian, and she went back to Montreal to visit her mother and grandparents. Her grandfather, who heads up the Montreal mob, broke his leg in a fight two weeks ago. I will give the old codger credit. He's still pretty scrappy, but those bones are more brittle than they used to be. Since Cormac and I are the only ones who aren't married, and the feds saw Cormac here, Sean's the right person to go to since his wife won't be there. I won't bring this shite to anyone's door when their wives might be home. I certainly won't do it to my other brother since his wife's pregnant.

Cormac gives me his phone since Carrie has mine, but before I can pull up my twin's contact, I see his name flash on the screen with an incoming call.

"Hey."

"Hey, were you just about to call me?" That twin thing; he just knew.

"Yeah."

"I figured but didn't think you'd use your own phone. How'd it go? I sent Cor as soon as I found out."

"As to be expected. My place's a mess, but they found nothing."

"Good. You should bring Carys to my place."

"I just told Cor that's what I'm going to do, but I'm going to wait a bit to make sure they don't barge in again with some excuse."

"Good idea. Have you gotten Carys out of the panic room yet?"

"No, for the same reason I'm not ready for us to leave here."

"Good, because I want to let you know something happened, and you can decide how to tell her."

"What the feck happened?"

"NYPD tried to arrest Meredith and Rhys for harboring Carys."

"Harboring? They make it sound like she's a convicted felon or something."

"I know. Her parents came over here after they called Dillan."

"All right. What condition are they in?"

"They're fine. Shaken up, but nothing worse than that. They didn't arrest them or anything, but NYPD definitely tried to intimidate them."

"I'll be over in a couple of hours."

"A couple hours? I don't think they can wait that long to see their daughter."

"I understand, but I don't feel it's safe to take Carrie anywhere any sooner than that. As much as I don't want to cause Meredith and Rhys any extra worries, safety is more important to me. With our jammers, I'll have her call your number, and they can talk. She can reassure them she's still fine and safe here, then we'll come over later."

"That's fair."

"Anything else I need to know?"

"Nothing for sure, but there's been more chatter at the safe house. They have some other people there who're still keeping an eye on Bartlomiej. It's going to be impossible for us to snag him and get him to the station for you."

"Fine. That annoys me, but it doesn't surprise me. I couldn't get there anytime soon, anyway. But when you can grab him, do. I don't care how long he has to wait for me."

"We know. Shane, the feds'll push this issue for as long as they can. You know you both can't hide forever. The moment you leave your house during the day, they'll see you, and they'll pick you up. It'll make Carys a virtual prisoner in your home because I know you won't agree to her staying anywhere else."

"She can stay somewhere else, but only if I'm with her."

"Same difference. You need to give this some thought."

I know what he means. He's talking about this relationship and whether it's worth protecting. I believe it is, but I don't know how she feels about me. Hell, I'm uncertain how I feel about her. Obviously, I care a great deal, and I want to see a future with her, but there's still so much we don't know about each other. It's too soon to be sure, so I'm not declaring feelings I may not have. Regardless, I'll keep her safe.

"I'll talk to Carrie about all of this."

"I know. Just tossing it out there."

"I appreciate it, little brother."

I'm three minutes older. I'm certain he grabbed hold of my ankle and tried to get past me. Supposedly, he's the patient one. But he always likes to get places first.

"You're welcome. I'll talk to you later."

"*Is breá liom tú.*" I love you.

We speak at the same time. All three sets of parents insist we say that to each other any time we hang up the phone or leave each other in person. We don't do it every single time, but we try to do it at least once a day for all of us. Nothing says fragility of life like being a mobster.

Cormac and I spend the next twenty minutes straightening up the living room and the kitchen. I want the place to look as normal as possible when Carrie comes upstairs. She'll already be freaked out. I don't want her to see the disaster the moment she comes upstairs.

"I'm going to go down and get her."

"Okay. I'll stay up here in the kitchen. I'll make us all a cup of tea.

"Be sure to add a strong tipple of whiskey to them."

We're that Irish. A cup of tea can solve everything. And our whiskey is *uisce beatha*. Water of life.

I head to the safe room and open the door.

"Carrie." I'm met with the leg of a chair raised over her shoulder like a bat. "What the feck did you do to my chair?"

It's not so much an accusation as the thought tumbling out of my mouth in surprise. I glance over at the armchair and notice the screwdriver on the floor next to it.

"You didn't think I would stay down here without some kind of weapon, did you? I believe this place is impenetrable, and I know no one could coerce anyone in your family into revealing me. But I still needed to feel like I was prepared for the worst-case scenario. This was the best I could do. If I could disable the person long enough to shut myself back in, I would."

"You wouldn't have tried to run?

"To what? More agents upstairs? No. That wouldn't have done me any good. I just wanted to incapacitate them long enough to shut myself back in here."

"That's a good idea. Even though I rather liked that chair."

"Not enough to have it somewhere you could sit on it every day."

"True. At least you used a screwdriver to take it off."

"Did you think I was going to go all Conan the Barbarian and just rip it off?"

We're bantering a bit because I can tell she's still terrified but is trying to keep it together. If this helps keep her calm, then I'll crack jokes all damn day.

"I always thought She-Hulk was kind of hot."

"Is green your favorite color?"

"It would be if it was on you."

"What is your favorite color?"

"Sky blue. You?"

"Same actually."

I step closer, and she drops the chair leg to the floor. I wrap her in my arms, and we simply hold each other. She rests her head against my chest, and I can breathe easier now. She's where she belongs.

"Daddy, I know you look calm because you had to, but I hear your heart racing. I hate knowing I'm the reason for that, but—"

"Carrie, I told you, you're not to blame. This wasn't your fault."

"Maybe the situation isn't, but the raid happened today because they were looking for me, and that's what's making your heart race. Even though I know that, it's still reassuring to have my ear to your chest and hear it. It's so steady, even if it's faster than normal. It's soothing to me."

"Then you can keep your head there as long as you like. Whatever makes you feel safe, little one."

"That's simply being with you. I admit I'm surprised you're

the one who opened the door. I expected it to be Cormac, and I didn't think it would be so soon after I heard it go quiet."

"It's been nearly an hour since they left."

"I know, but I was certain you'd wait in case they tried to trip you up and come back again."

"Yeah, Cormac and I straightened up the place while we waited. It wasn't as bad as it could've been. They know my place isn't a stash house, so they were a little gentler while being so thorough."

Her eyebrows shoot up.

"They didn't rip anything apart—" I pointedly look at the chair leg and playfully frown— "Though they got into everything. They hoped to fill the bankers boxes they brought with them, but they left entirely empty-handed. Nothing was in those boxes. They were so arrogant they didn't bring lids in with them. They thought there'd be enough stuff to fill them to overflowing. I'm certain they intended to take photos and release them. It wouldn't surprise me if there was at least one reporter waiting out there.

"And if there was, they only got photos of those empty boxes which'll paint you as the persecuted victim in all of this."

"Exactly. Blessing in disguise actually, and it'll chap the other families' arses if I'm made to look innocent of anything."

She only nods to that. "Are we staying here?"

"No, we'll go to Sean's in just a little. Cormac pulled into my garage, knowing we'd have to use his car to leave later. I'm afraid you'll have to hide in the back of his SUV to make sure you stay out of sight. He brought that car on purpose. Nobody's going to force you into a trunk."

"Maybe not in your family."

The expression I shoot her now tells her I know that wasn't part of our banter. I don't like the idea of Jacek getting to her, and I know that's exactly who she was thinking of.

"Why are we going to Sean's rather than somebody else's?"

"A couple of reasons. Sean's wife is out of the country right now, so his place is the safest to take you to. Also, since they saw Cormac here with me today, his place is out of the question since there's a strong chance they'll try to search there next, assuming he'll hide stuff for me. The other reason is your parents are there. The police tried to question them."

"What?"

"Shh. Carrie, calm down."

"Calm down? You know that is not the right thing to say right now."

"I know. I'm sorry, but let me explain. They're totally fine. The police tried to intimidate them, but I've met your mom. I know her well enough to know the only people who left that conversation intimidated were those police officers. I know of your dad, so I'm certain they didn't look to him for reassurance."

"That's true."

"You get your spunk from your mom."

"I may have heard that once or twice before."

"When we go over there, you're going to have to explain everything to them."

"I know. I thought about it while I was down here. I hate it, but I can't keep this from them any longer."

"We also need to think about what this means for us."

She goes rigid.

"Carrie, I'm not saying we're breaking up or anything like that. I'm not sure how you see me, but this won't drive us apart."

"I don't know what to call what's going on between us, either. We've never been on a date, but you definitely don't feel like a fuck buddy."

"I will never be your fuck buddy. That implies we walk away after we're done. That won't happen."

"Good. Otherwise, I might have to chain you to my bed."

"You can try, but you'd have to be quicker than me. I intend to keep you naked and in my bed for a month once we get this straightened out."

"Promise, Daddy."

"Bet your bottom dollar, little girl."

I squeeze her arse while we grin at one another, then give each other a quick smacking kiss. It only takes me a moment to fix the chair and wipe down the surfaces she points to. Can't be too careful. We head back upstairs, and Cormac greets her. I can tell he's relieved she isn't upset. It's not like he runs from crying females, but he and Seamus are the two shy ones in the family.

I know he would feel badly if he saw her upset. He'd feel like he invaded her privacy more than he did barging in on us earlier. Thank God, we all have ears like dogs, and I heard him coming up the stairs. Granted, he certainly was loud enough to wake the dead. That reminds me.

"Cor, tell the others no more coming in anymore without a text or a call."

"We already knew that. You didn't answer your phone. I figured you might not have had it near you. It's the only reason I let myself in."

Carrie's face goes beet red, and I shrug. I don't know if she's embarrassed because of what Cormac interrupted today or the implication the open-door policy at my place ended because the guys might walk in on something in the future. Before we all started to pair off, we came and went from each other's homes without knocking.

Now that there're so many couples, we make sure we call or text before we even get to the driveway. Then we let them know when we're coming in the door. Sean and I had an unfortunate incident walking in on Finn and his wife. Neither he nor I saw anything happening, but Ally was less covered up than they would have wanted. I don't want Carrie in another compromising situation like when Cormac arrived.

The three of us finish cleaning up my house. Carrie'd changed while she was in the panic room. I tossed the stuff she borrowed into the washing machine and started a load with just those items. My mom wouldn't approve of wasting water and electricity for two items. I know she'd understand, but I still have a guilty conscience. Before we leave, I take Carrie into the living room, so I can explain what's going to happen.

"Cormac and I will help you hide behind some storage bins we'll stack in his trunk. As soon as we're far enough away to convince me no one's going to pull him over and search his vehicle, you can climb into the backseat, so you're not squashed anymore. We won't stop until we get to Sean's house. I don't doubt somebody'll follow us, but it's highly unlikely they'll pull us over somewhere they know they don't control the scene. A swarm of agents on the side of the road would draw too much attention, and they know sending only a couple wouldn't be good for those agents' health."

Chapter Twenty

Carrie

Hearing someone'll follow us after my colleagues just ransacked my boyfriend's—my lover's—my fuck buddy's—no, he was adamant we're not that—but I still don't know what to consider him—house is hardly reassuring.

"We'll be fine, Carrie. We'll pull straight into Sean's garage. All of us have multiple garage door openers just for this reason. That and none of us enjoy being wet and cold in winter. It's how Cormac pulled straight into mine. He has a garage door opener for here."

His family is ever practical, if nothing else.

"When we go in the garage, we can't say a single thing while we're out there. We're working on the assumption they didn't plant any cameras in the garage. We can't be sure, so I'm praying they won't see us hiding you. It's possible they don't have cameras, but they could have microphones."

"Shane, I know. I've planted plenty of them."

His grim expression tells me he didn't care for the reminder.

"I keep an under-vehicle search mirror in a cut out behind some storage shelves."

That shouldn't surprise me, but it does.

"I have places to hide shite all over my property, Carrie. Cormac's doing a sweep now to ensure they placed nothing underneath his car or mine. There are a few small nooks and crannies where they could place a bug or a tracker, but I don't think most agents are well versed enough in cars to know exactly where, and none of them looked like they had hands dirty from being underneath one of our cars."

"Maybe an auto body class should be required at the academy."

"We are always wary, but neither of us is overly concerned right now. Once you're hidden, we'll go back to the door. I'll open it from inside, and we'll wait until the garage door is halfway open to ensure the agents see us before I step down into the garage. Cormac'll come out of the house behind me. It'll look like we're leaving together, but only the two of us. If we open the door while we're already near the car, it'll make the agents even more suspicious that we've already hidden something in the car or in the garage. We want to make it look as though we have no cares in the world as we leave. Life continues despite the minor disturbance."

I nod since all of that makes sense. I don't know if he just thought of this or if it's standard operating procedure for this family. I suspect the latter. Someone trained them, and now it comes naturally.

"Cor'll get in the driver's seat, and I'll get in on the passenger side. You know it's not a long drive to Sean's house. In case there are any trucks or vans parked in the neighborhood outside my jammers' radius, we'll stay quiet until we know whether they're following us. We'll talk about going to the movies this weekend and our security shifts at the bars Finn owns. I'm not scheduled for anything, but Cormac is a bouncer at McGinty's this weekend. It's the bar our nana owned before she passed away. Finn inherited it. If the car's bugged and we stay quiet the entire time, it'll seem suspicious. We'll chat, so it'll sound like we believe everything's back to normal."

I know how sensitive those things can be. I pray they don't hear me breathing.

"I'll text Sean now to let him know we're headed out. If I have to communicate with anyone once we're beyond my house's jammers and not close enough to his, I'll text rather than call."

"What should I expect when we get to Sean's?"

His expression softens as he lifts me onto his lap on the sofa where we sat down for this conversation.

"I suspect your parents are going to engulf you and not let go."

That makes my heart hurt. "I can't blame them if they do."

"*Cailín*, my parents were exactly the same way the first few times I went on missions alone. My mom wasn't any better before that when my brothers and I went on missions with our dad. She's not quite as bad now as she was in the beginning, but neither of my parents take for granted the blessing it is when their sons come home alive. We don't always come back without some nicks and cuts, sometimes even some stab wounds and bullet holes, but we all live to tell the tale."

I gulp. I'm nauseous at the thought Shane might come home like that, and I'd have to see it.

"Little one, that hasn't happened in a long time. And we have the best doctor in the city to stitch us up."

He grins, but it does little to console me. I snuggle closer. We sit together in silence until Cormac returns from the garage and gives us the all-clear. Just like Shane described, they help me into the back of Cormac's Range Rover. It's seriously cramped even with me curled into as tight a ball as I can make my body. Cormac and Shane suspect we're being followed but aren't sure, so I stay in the back. I don't know what's in the tubs, but they sound heavy. If we get pulled over, they might deter anyone from searching too far into the back. It's stuffy, so I wipe sweat from my forehead when Shane finally lets me out in Sean's garage.

The moment I'm through the door and into Sean's house, my mom's barreling toward me, and my dad's on her heels. My parents swoop me up for a hug that threatens to smother me.

"Carys, thank God. Are you okay?"

Tears choke my mom's voice. She's still hugging me, but she's eased her hold a little. She's wrapped around me from the front, and my dad envelops both of us from the back. He's a tall man, so his arms are long enough to reach around us. They make a Carys sandwich. I loved when they called it that when I was a kid. I just realized I think of myself as Carrie now after hearing Shane call me that so many times.

"I'm all right. Nothing happened to me."

I know my dad's tone. Fuck my life.

"I'd hardly say nothing. You owe us an explanation."

My shoulders droop even though my arms stay wrapped around my mom. When she pulls away enough for me to turn around, I hug my dad.

"I will, but it's going to take a while to explain everything."

"We figured as much."

From the way Shane, Sean, and Cormac wince, they recognize Mom's tone. I bet it's the same as when she deals with any of their injuries. It's not entirely sympathetic, but it is filled with concern.

We head to the living room. My parents sit on a sofa while Cormac heads to a rocker recliner. I hang back, and Shane comes to my side. We choose the loveseat. I know my parents wanted me to sit between them. Shane even nudges me toward them. But right now, I need his silent strength to get me through what I'm about to divulge. He knows what I need because he presses his right thigh against my leg, reassuring he's here and on my side.

"You guys remember how I went to that party my freshman year of high school, and that massive fight that broke out?"

"Yeah, you went with Mary Elizabeth Coniglio."

When I notice Shane and Sean glance at one another, I suspect they know that last name. Shane slides his hand into mine, encouraging me to continue.

Dad's brow furrows as he remembers back fifteen years. "Didn't the police get called to that party?"

"Yeah, Mary Elizabeth and I weren't even there ten minutes before the police came. It was just long enough for my boyfriend to take a few puffs of some pot. Mary Elizabeth and I left with our boyfriends the moment people started yelling. I found out later, she wasn't supposed to be there. Once we left, we planned to find another party because that one turned into a melee from what I heard. I don't know many of the details from that evening because I didn't go to school with Mary Elizabeth. She went to school with a bunch of guys who were arguing over some girl or something."

"That's one way to put it. Carrie, all of us were at that party that night. That fight was over Maria Mancinelli. Three guys from the Colombian Cartel we call *Tres J's* insulted her when she stuck up for a friend of hers who had a crush on one of those psychopaths. A couple Kutsenkos overheard them and stuck up for Maria, which only made the Mancinellis get involved too once they knew Maria was at the center of it. My family gave the Mancinellis a hard time about needing the Kutsenkos to protect their women."

Sean grimaces before he picks up the story from Shane.

"We wound up getting drawn into it because neither the Mancinellis nor the Kutsenkos appreciated our taunting. It turned into a massive melee that got plenty of us injured and nearly killed. The leaders of the Four Families were so livid most of us in all four families wished we hadn't left that party alive."

"Was that when you were both fourteen?"

Mom looks back and forth between Shane and Sean, then at Cormac. I'd noticed he hadn't joined us at first, but I didn't realize he'd gone to the kitchen. He just came out with a tray of cookies and petit fours along with the tea pot.

Shane explains when he notices my confusion. "He and Seamus have always had the best manners. They always ensure our guests have something to nibble on if they want."

He settles into the other armchair before Shane's hand squeezes mine, and he continues speaking.

"Yes, that's the one. It was the first time I got shot. Bogdan Kutsenko didn't appreciate being called a little bitch even if he is one." Shane glowers at his brother. "He shot me, even though I'm not the one who called him that. I guess it was too dark to see

Sean's freckle to tell us apart since we were standing next to each other while we taunted them."

"I didn't exactly come out unscathed. Pablo left me with a scar across my left shoulder blade from where he knifed me."

Cormac frowns and shrugs. "Besides the massive fight that happened there, it was a pretty good party before that."

I tense because that wasn't how I remember that night at all.

"Someone laced those drugs my boyfriend took. He died in the car on the way to the next party. When I realized something was wrong, we went to the hospital. It all happened so fast there was nothing we could do to save him.

Bile burns the back of my throat as I tell that story. The painful memory has layers. I notice Shane glance at Cormac and then at Sean. All have muted expressions, but I can read them now that I'm learning to read Shane's. I sense remorse, like they want to admit something. I hear Shane's inhale before he speaks.

"Carrie, that happened because of my family."

It feels like slow motion as I turn toward him. Shocked is the only word that explains my reaction. I wait for sadness or anger, but there is none. It's just speechlessness. I know he can tell if he doesn't confess this now, and I found out later, I'd struggle to forgive him because this affected me personally. I know it's the kind of secret he'd normally keep to himself.

"Uncle Donovan sent Dillan and Finn to sell what we all believed was just regular pot. None of us—" He points to his brother and cousin, and I assume he also means Seamus, Dillan, and Finn. "—knew it was laced with fentanyl. Uncle Don got the product from his best friend, Colin, who mixed it but f—messed up the proportions. Uncle Don wanted it potent enough to get kids to come back to us for more."

He lets go of my hand and runs his hands over his face as he leans forward with his elbows on his knees. He twists to look back at me.

"It terrified us when we found out. But it didn't stop Uncle Don from forcing us to keep dealing. There was another party about nine years ago. Finn took a date—it was the last one he went on until he met his wife—and she died from OD'ing on fentanyl my family sold the hosts before the party started. It was as clean as it could be, but she took too much while Finn went to get her another drink. He didn't know until Maria Mancinelli tried to revive her that she'd bought the pills he and Dillan sold the hosts. Maria was in med school at the time and did everything she could to help her, but it was too late. I didn't know anything happened to someone after the melee only that someone died at another party."

I continue to stare at Shane. I can tell it's unnerving him. It's got to be at least two minutes before I shift my gaze to Sean, then to Cormac, then my parents, and finally back to Shane. I think Shane's waiting for me to withdraw completely or explode. Instead, I tug on his arm to lean back and slip my hand into his before I continue my story.

"That party made me decide to become a DEA agent. I was so upset by what I witnessed and knowing it was entirely preventable. I committed to doing some good because we all knew there were drugs at that party, and it wasn't the first time Xavier'd taken stuff. We'd actually already dated." I turn to my parents. "I never told you we broke up over his drug use. I knew he'd used drugs recreationally, only at parties and things like that, but I hadn't approved. He told me he was clean, and I believed him because none of the signs from before were there. He'd gotten better at hiding it. Even if we weren't dating, he would've gone to that party, anyway. There's a good chance he'd have done even more drugs than just taking those pills if I hadn't been there."

I nudge Shane with my shoulder because he appears beside himself.

"I don't blame any of you for the choices he made, and I'm already fully aware of your family's enterprises. It hasn't stopped me from being with you."

I turn back to my parents because I'm about to tell them things that'll shock them.

"Once I finished college, a few federal agencies recruited me. You knew all of that. What you don't know is how well I did at the academy. I have a knack for languages, and the agency noticed. I'm also an excellent shot and have always been physically fit since I've run marathons before."

Shane's gaze meets mine. "That explains how easily you kept up with me when we ran and why you went for those runs every morning."

I shoot him a glare, warning him not to say more. The last thing I need is my parents discovering I ran those trails to keep my endurance up for situations like the lumberyard.

"Since I took French and Spanish in school, I learned Italian on my own fairly easily. With blue eyes and fair skin that tans, I can pass for northern Italian. The agency sent me undercover in Chicago."

My mom's incredulous. "I remember when you said you were going to Italy for a few weeks with friends about a year-and-a-half after you got the job."

"I didn't exactly go to Italy, the country, but Little Italy, Chicago. I was undercover for those two weeks and helped do a big bust."

"Was that with the Grassos?"

"Yeah. How'd you—" I don't bother finishing. I just nod instead. All the guys must have done the math and worked backwards until they realized who I meant.

"Mostly, it was one small thing after another around here. A lot of times, I wore a hat and sunglasses or a hoodie or something else to keep my appearance from being obvious. I did a major undercover job three years ago when I went to Boston."

I sense Shane's anger. I nearly died at the bust because a warehouse exploded. He knows about that, but he won't say anything for my parents' sake.

"Mom, Dad, when I told you I went to LA for some training two years ago, it was to infiltrate the Italians out there."

I'm getting to the part of the story Shane already knows, and I sense some of his anxiousness recedes because he knows what's coming.

"Once that sting was over, the bratva down here popped onto

our radar even more than any of you guys usually do. We knew we needed somebody in with the leading family, but it was impossible. Since all the men in the Kutsenko and Andreyev family are already married and would never let their eyes wander, we realized infiltrating them directly was impossible. Trying to become friends with the wives would've been futile. They're all too intelligent and wary not to figure it out."

Shane's steely tone is the one I heard so many times when we first got to know each other, and he objected to just about everything about me. I guess he isn't as at ease as I thought.

"Because Bartlomiej and Jacek have been doing more deals with the bratva lately to make up for something that happened, you figured they would be an organization you could plausibly enter without too many questions and still get closer to the bratva."

I wish my parents knew as much as Shane and his family, so I wouldn't have to explain all my lies. Hell, I wouldn't have lied at all.

"Yes. I took time and went to the Department of Defense's Language Institute in Monterey and was in an immersive program there to learn Polish. That was when I told you they sent me back to the L.A. office for nearly eight months to put me on special assignment for some analysis work. After that lie, I lied and said the agency transferred me to Pittsburgh. I've been undercover with the Nowakowskis almost the entire time I was supposed to be there."

I lean into Shane as I watch my parents' expressions. He wraps his arm around my shoulders and offers me some comfort without looking possessive or overprotective. I want him to be exactly that, but I don't want my parents to misunderstand and think he'll keep me from them. I lean my head against his shoulder. I sense Shane looking down at me. I close my eyes for a moment before I open them filled with tears.

"I've lied to you both so many times because of this job, and I regret it. Not just because of what's going on now, but also because that's not the way you raised me. You didn't raise me to be such an easy liar."

Mom smiles, but there's obvious sadness in her gaze. "Carys, we've kept my connections to the O'Rourkes from you your entire life. I never even hinted I knew anything about their family, let alone about the mob or being a doctor to mobsters. If I'd realized just how involved your job was with organized crime, I wouldn't have stayed on as their physician. I endangered you and your career by allowing you to go undercover when I'm so connected to the O'Rourkes."

"You didn't let me go undercover. You didn't know."

Mom nods. "I still regret I never told you once we knew your interest in the DEA."

I ask what I've wanted to know since the night I met Shane and discovered my mom's connection to the mob. "How did you wind up as their doctor?"

She looks at Shane, and I shift my focus to see his face as he nods.

"I met the boys' grandfather when most of them were still in middle school. Dillan and Finn had just started high school. When Liam O'Rourke collapsed outside the hospital from a gunshot wound, I was just coming in to work and recognized him from a newspaper article. I knew right away whatever got him shot wasn't going away. Maybe whoever put the bullet in him died, but the reason for it hadn't. I didn't want to be the one who called the police because that's what happens with GSWs. However, someone had to. I didn't lie because I didn't know enough to have anything to hide. But I made sure nobody called until after he came out of surgery."

Gunshot wounds aren't something most orthopedic surgeons face. I don't know how she kept it from the police for so long since she doesn't work in the ER, and removing a bullet isn't a surgery she'd perform—at least, not at her regular job—since becoming a civilian. I don't ask because I don't think I want to know. I listen instead.

"I met Donovan, Colin, and Declan when they came to see

him. They wanted to discharge him the same day. I found out from the surgeon when I went to see Liam. I advised against that course of action because he was still too unstable to move. I told him about my experiences as a doctor with the British Royal Navy and how I'd seen too many people die from a GSW even after they removed the bullet. Once he heard that, it intrigued him, and he asked more questions about my work and my experience. I knew why he was asking and what he was getting at."

Her lips flatten before they turn down just like they did when I was a kid, and I did something she didn't approve of.

"I had no interest in working for the O'Rourkes. However, if it got out I was the doctor who delayed calling the police over his wounds—that I'd basically shielded him—it wouldn't be safe for me. Liam felt indebted to me for me protecting him, so he assigned me bodyguards. I got to know the guys. Eventually, it didn't seem so bad to work for him as a private physician, so I joined the payroll."

She offers Shane, Sean, and Cormac a fond smile that's far warmer than earlier.

"It didn't take long for Liam to realize I have a way with you guys that his other doctor didn't. As you all went on more missions and the teams grew, there were more wounds to tend. I became the primary private doctor for your family. I continued my regular job but cut down on my hours. I never told you that, Carys, and we never really discussed how we paid for your college. We just told you we saved. What we never told you was we saved the money the O'Rourkes paid me. That's how we put you through college. It's also funding our retirement when we scale back for real."

We all sit in silence as each of us absorbs the things confessed here over the last twenty minutes. It's a lot to take in for anybody, and I know my parents and I are struggling to come to terms with the massive family secrets we've withheld from each other. Even though I know we understand what we did, it's hurtful that they didn't trust me to know about Mom's work with the O'Rourkes.

I'm certain it's equally hurtful for my parents to know I didn't trust them enough to tell them what my job actually entails. I know from my parents' expressions they feel guilty they allowed me to go into a job where I could have become a target for investigation if anyone discovered Mom's ties to the O'Rourkes. But there's nothing any of us can do to change the past, so it's a matter of acceptance right now. This could drive a wedge between us. However, it's obvious it'll only bring us closer together.

Sean's phone rings on the coffee table beside his chair. He takes a glance and answers it.

"Hey, Dill. They're over here right now."

He goes silent for a moment before he hangs up.

"The others are coming. They're about to pull through the gate."

Shane explains to my parents when they both glance toward the door. "Even though Nikki isn't in town, we've all gotten used to calling ahead now. Nothing's changed, even if it's impossible for any of us to disturb them."

His meaning is clear without him spelling it out. No one wants to walk in on Sean and Nikki having sex. If it sounded like a swarm of DEA agents at Shane's house, then it's a horde descending upon this house when his family arrives.

An older couple arrives with a younger man beside him. The two men look enough like Shane and Sean for me to realize the couple are the twins' parents, and Finn's the man on his own. I wonder if his aunts and uncles will join us. I'm not sure why Shane's parents came, but I guess I should get meeting them out of the way. I suspect that's why they're here.

My parents greet Shane's warmly.

He leans in to whisper to me, and I don't like how he knows something about my parents I don't. "Nobody would guess, but they frequently go on double dates together. It's really very cute."

Then his parents come to say hello to me, and Shane introduces them.

"Mom, Da, this is Carys. Carrie, these are my parents, Breda and Ronan."

His mom's tentative but warm when she greets me. She's

giving me some space until she realizes I'm not too nervous around them. When we embrace, I see the relief on Shane's face since he's standing to the side and watching us. When they go to say hi to Sean, Shane fills me in on more family history.

"My dad and uncles have been in since they were the same age I was when I joined. Their side of the family has been in for three generations and four on my mom's side. Three sisters married three brothers, and my mom and aunts have been daughters to a mob boss, a sister to a mob boss, and now one is the mom and two are aunts to a mob boss. If anybody understands the dangers of this life and the threat the feds pose to our family, it's them."

"That's why it surprises me they're treating me so warmly. Is it because my parents are here?"

I need to know what the dynamics will truly be if Shane and I consider a future together.

"No. My family's more open-minded than you'd expect. From watching my brothers and cousins get married, it's obvious they never expected us to marry women from mob families. They know my brothers' and cousins' wives never planned to fall in love with mobsters. Nothing's been easy for my brothers or cousins and their wives, so my parents get it."

"'Nothing's been easy' is a far sight different from you breaking a cardinal syndicate rule."

His brow furrows. "Which rule?"

"Never support the government or law enforcement."

His grin would be sexy as sin if I weren't growing more nervous the longer I think about how the rest of Shane's family will react when they meet me.

"You're with me, and we're hiding at my brother's house to keep you away from law enforcement. I'd hardly say we're supporting them. Just the opposite. If nothing else, it's a massive feck you to them."

I like how he won't swear in front of me unless he's using fuck to refer to sex. It's sweet. But I still don't feel reassured.

"I know I'm asking a lot of you and your trust, but please believe me, Carrie. They don't object. I'd know if they did."

I look over to where my parents and his are chatting as though nothing's going on that could wind up with their son and me in prison.

Despite my initial fears, I relax because I realize there are a ton of people in Shane's family, and this isn't even all of them. They're pretty easygoing and shockingly normal, apparently. According to what Shane whispers to me as we all sit down for dinner together in a massive dining room, it's baffled each woman who's married into this family. Apparently, Dillan's wife even claims she stepped into the Twilight Zone when she married into the O'Rourkes. It boggles the mind to watch and listen to them tease each other and be so openly affectionate with one another.

But it's Shane's mom who gets down to brass tacks. Shane chuckles and tells me she's full of old-fashioned phrases. She scowls playfully before she gets serious again.

"What're you going to do next? What's your plan?"

Shane and I look at each other, and there's not much more we can do than shrug. Breda looks at Shane.

"The best thing you two can do is go out of town for a while. I'd highly recommend somewhere in the Caribbean or the Med. It's a pleasant time of year for sailing."

"I agree. We ought to get you away from here, Carrie."

I shift my gaze to Mom and Dad to see what they think. Maybe they want to go out of town with me rather than Shane taking me. We haven't even had a first date, and I was going to stay —am going to stay—who the hell knows at this point—with Shane indefinitely. Now we're talking about traveling together. I'm trying not to overanalyze the situation because there's no good explanation for what's going on here besides necessity.

It makes me wonder whether we really have a foundation for a relationship or if it just comes from all the danger. We resolve nothing over the next few hours, but Shane and I discuss places we might like to visit. When everyone's ready to leave, we consider whether to go back to Shane's place.

His parents and brother said they saw no one watching Sean's house, and no one followed them. Sean checks with his security team who patrols his property and the guards at his house's gate. They've seen no one drive by they don't recognize. There are no unfamiliar cars parked on the street. It seems like it'll be safe to return to Shane's place.

We're headed to the garage when I squeeze Shane's hand. "I have a bad feeling about this. Something just tells me this isn't a good idea."

When our gazes lock, he understands how serious I am.

"Do you want to spend the night here instead? Would you feel better not going out?"

"I don't want to impose upon your brother."

"It's not an imposition, Carrie, and you know that. He's more than equipped for houseguests." He gestures toward the stairs. "This isn't the biggest home in our family, but it can accommodate plenty of people. It has six bedrooms. It's not like Sean and Nikki intend to be a stereotypical Catholic couple with that many children, but there's a bedroom for each of us. There are nights we spend at each other's homes to make it easier when we're coming or going for missions. We can stay here. We can go to somebody else's house here in the neighborhood. We can go to a hotel. It's up to you, *cailín*. What do you want to do?"

I consider his offer and nod.

"Could you take me to a hotel instead? Somewhere, maybe neutral?"

Shane's expression reveals nothing as he considers my questions, but I know.

"I can read your thoughts, Daddy. You're not sure what to make of me asking you to take me to a hotel. Shane, I want you—" I keep my voice low. "—there with me, but the more time we're together right now, the greater likelihood they'll take us both in. I don't want them to get you as well if they find me.

"They're far more likely to find you if I'm not with you."

We both know what we've said is the truth.

"Carrie, I have the resources to take care of myself if I'm

arrested, but I don't want you away from me in case they get you. I want to see with my own eyes how they treat you."

"All right. I still believe my going to a hotel would protect you, but I feel like this'll be the night they strike if we go somewhere. Staying here eases some of my fears."

"We stay here tonight, and we'll decide what to do next in the morning."

Shane turns to Sean, and I know he wasn't listening to our conversation. I can't explain it, but he understands Shane when he turns his attention to his twin. Sean nods, and we say goodbye to everybody else while Sean heads up to his room.

It's gotten way later than any of us realized. I know I'm exhausted, and so is Shane. He shows me to the room he usually uses when he stays here. I discover Sean's wife is extremely slender, so even though I'm average-sized, none of Nikki's clothes would fit me. He pulls out a set of t-shirt and basketball shorts he keeps here, but I don't put them on after I strip and neither does he.

"We all have a couple sets of interchangeable clothes at each other's homes. That's why I have the suits hanging in the guest bedroom. I have three spare rooms, and they each have some clothes in there. I already have a toothbrush here, but I'll find a new one for you."

It feels so normal to share the bathroom with Shane, each of us brushing our teeth and then climbing into bed together.

"What do you need, *cailín*?"

I know he doesn't mean toiletries or different pjs.

"I wish we'd had a chance to get some toys."

"Me too. I'm definitely not asking my brother to borrow anything other than these clothes."

I glance toward the door, then at Shane, too surprised to say anything.

"Little one, we're hardly the only couple who likes it kinky."

"You want to have sex here? With your brother down the hall?"

"Try not to scream my name too loudly." His smile is pure sex and sin.

"I—I—don't know." I don't. I'm too surprised.

He guides me out of the bathroom but stops at the closet.

"Stand at the foot of the bed facing it."

His command isn't one to disobey. It excites me, but a shiver of apprehension courses through me when I realize he has a handful of ties as he approaches. Without a word, he grasps my right wrist and raises it over my head as he positions me in front of one of the tall bedposts. He wraps a tie around it before lifting my left one next to my right. I don't know if it's some fancy boy scout knot or what, but I can't budge. He bends and fastens my ankles to the post just like he did my wrists.

"This isn't punishment. Just the opposite. You've been so brave, *cailín*. You impress me over and over. I was so terrified they'd take me from you. That I wouldn't protect you. Your calm's kept me from losing my shite. I want to show you how much I appreciate that."

"Thank you, Daddy. I want whatever's coming."

"If you change your mind, safe word, Carrie."

"I know."

I close my eyes, unsure what to expect. It's the tip of the tie that runs down the length of my back, barely skimming over me. It draws all my attention, so I'm unprepared for the first spank. I jerk forward, and my clit rubs the bedpost as my back arches. I turn to look over my shoulder. I can guess nothing from his expression. He glides the tie up my right ribs, and it tickles. I try to shy away, but the next spank lands on my horizontal crack, pushing my ass up. It rubs my clit against the wood again.

The way he's stretched me, my tits are on each side of the post. He shifts and pinches my left nipple. He tugs, increasing the pressure as the next two spanks send me onto my toes. I'm unprepared for all of this, but especially when he lets go of my stinging nipple and immediately slaps it. It's painful, and my pussy aches for him to slip inside me.

"Daddy."

It's more a moan than a word.

"Yes, little girl?"

"I—" I don't know what to say.

"Do you want to ask me to finger you?"

I nod.

"Do you want to ask me to suck on your clit?

I nod again.

"Do you want to ask me to fuck your arse?"

"Good God, yes."

His chuckle makes me squeeze my thighs. If a sound could be decadent, it would be Shane's voice.

"I don't think you're ready for any of those things."

"I am."

"I'm certain *you* think so. But last I checked, your cunt belongs to me now. I decide."

"Could you decide to fuck me?"

I swallow my scream as his next three spanks are harder than the earlier ones.

"I could, but I won't. Your body belongs to me, *cailín*. You won't convince me to do anything sooner than *I* want. You're mine to pleasure, and this won't be quick. And before you suggest I want to get off, so we should fuck, you should know the view from where I'm standing is magnificent. I'm going to take my time and appreciate it."

His hand runs up the length of my back before I feel his chest press against it. He nips my earlobe before kissing right behind it.

"I own your orgasms, little girl. I give them, and I keep them. You'll get plenty tonight, but not yet. Do you know why?"

His hand grabs my ass and squeezes until it's nearly too much. He pulls the other cheek wide and presses his cock against my hole. I know he won't enter me, but he's reminding me he could

"Because you're Daddy."

"Whose daddy?"

"Mine."

"Am I anyone else's?"

"No. You belong to only me."

"That's right."

He backs away, and it's suddenly freezing without the radiator pressed against me. The man exudes heat. I wait, but nothing happens. I twist as best I can to see him. He's watching me with his right ankle crossed over his left, his arms folded. He's really just staring. His eyes tell me he likes what he sees.

The uncertainty of what's coming next makes me squirm. I know he's enjoying that, but it's driving me nuts. I squeeze my eyes shut, trying to block out how much my pussy aches—burns—for him to be inside me.

"Ugh!"

I don't hear him approach, so I'm unprepared for the spank. I don't scream, but I'm louder than I intend. He kisses my shoulder, then rakes his teeth over it. He kneels and unfastens my ankles. He loosens my wrists enough to turn me around. He presses a hard, fast, and hungry kiss to my lips. Just as I'm ready to sink into it and enjoy it drawing out, he pulls away. He nudges my feet apart and cups my pussy.

"You're so wet for me, Carrie."

"I know. You look pretty hard, Daddy."

"I am."

He strokes himself, and I hate it. I want to do that, and he knows it. He slides three fingers into me, spreading them inside my cunt. He pulls them out halfway but adds his fourth when he drives them into me. He strokes my g spot. My hips jerk forward, then my ass slams back into the posts as my pussy tries to chase his fingers, drawing them deeper. His thumb works my clit, and I close my eyes, resting my forehead against my left bicep.

I need to come.

He knows it and pulls out. He slaps my pussy four times. I both want to retreat and offer him more. He pinches my clit as he leans in to whisper to me.

"Beg."

I don't think twice. "Daddy, please. I need to come so badly it hurts. I need you."

"I know."

He slaps my pussy again.

"Beg."

"I'll do whatever you want. Just, please, let me come."

He pinches my clit yet again.

"No."

He leans in and latches onto my left nipple. He toys with it, using his tongue and teeth before he sucks. I want my hands free to offer him both, but when I tug, I'm reminded I don't get to decide any of this. That thought excites me even more.

"You enjoy being at my mercy, don't you?"

He lifts his head enough to look up at me, so our gazes meet.

"Very much."

He sucks on my other nipple until it's a tight dart. Then he pulls away. I'm unprepared for him to release me from the bed post. But I should have known he wasn't done yet. He moves me to the center between both posts. He has my arms and legs stretched wide and fastened to the posts before I realize what's happening. I'm facing away from the bed, so it's easy for him to wrap a tie around my tits, pushing them together, and making them stand out. He slaps them five times, his broad palm landing against them at the same time.

He drops to his knees and dives in. He feasts on my pussy, his fingers biting into my ass as he holds me in place. His tongue delves into me before flicking and toying with my already sensitive clit. He goes around and around, edging me until I'm in a cold sweat and trembling. He kisses along the inside of my thigh, making my kneecap quiver. He releases my ankles before he stands. When he unbinds my arms, he rubs them and moves them to ensure they aren't stiff.

I don't expect him to wrap the tie around both wrists behind my back. He grasps a handful of my hair in his right hand as his left presses on my shoulder until I sink to my knees.

"Do you want my cock, little girl?"

"Yes, Daddy."

"I bet you want it in your pussy. I bet you don't want to suck me off."

I don't, but I want to play this game.

"I want what you want." Which isn't untrue.

"Open wide, *cailín*."

He guides his dick into my mouth, and I hum as I suck. I love the groan that elicits. He pushes my head forward as his hips flex, but he's careful. He doesn't make me gag. He just controls where my head is. His movements are shallow and slow. I watch him as his eyes slide shut. His free hand cups my jaw, and for the umpteenth time, I'm reminded how gentle he is when he wants to be. His thumb brushes over my cheekbone before he pulls out.

I huff.

He chuckles.

He helps me to my feet and takes the ties off my wrists and tits. He kisses my nipples and across my chest and up my neck over and over. His hands once again grip my ass, squeezing. I push my hips back as though I can burrow my ass into his palms even more.

"Daddy, mark me."

He pauses and looks up at me. His grip grows so tight I whimper, but he doesn't let go. He knows I'll safe word if I can't take it. His mouth travels to the outsides of my tits then the insides, leaving hickies all over them. He trails his love bites down my belly, smattering them across there. I watch, loving all of this. When he stands again, he cups my jaw.

"Tell me how you want me inside you. Use my cock to get off, little girl. Let me see what you want."

It's a command wrapped in the pretty bow of an offer.

"I want missionary. I want to see all your muscles flexing in your shoulders, pecs, and abs. I love watching it. You have the best body, and it turns me on to see how strong you are, yet you hold back to make sure you never hurt me."

"Get on the bed, *mo stór*."

"What does that mean?"

"My darling."

I obey as my heart feels like it's too big for my chest. I don't know why that endearment means so much right now, but it's everything to me. I open my arms and legs, wrapping them around him as he settles between my thighs. Then he's inside me. The gentleness is gone. He controls my body again.

"Harder, Daddy. As hard as you can."

"Never, Carrie. Only as hard as I dare."

I could love this man. I want to. I'm definitely almost there. We're about as unconventional as you can get, considering our dates have involved running from or hiding from a rival syndicate and law enforcement. Fucking Bonnie and Clyde.

He lifts my right leg over his shoulder and pounds into me.

"Come, Carrie. Now."

I tilt my hips up, and he rubs my clit just right.

"Fuck, Daddy. Yes."

I force my eyes to remain open because I don't want to miss a moment of this. His body is magnificent. Watching his muscles flex is the hottest thing I've ever seen. It drives me wilder.

"Fuck, Carrie. I can't last like I thought I could."

"Come, Daddy. Please. I need to know I made you come."

My need to make that happen replaces my need to come as my second orgasm hits me. He slams into me, grinding his pubic bone against my clit as he pants. He rocks his hips, rubbing against me. I know he's coming. I did that. I made him come.

He lowers my leg, and I hook it over his hip. His kiss is soft and languid, and I don't want it to end. We're both panting and sweating as we watch each other when we draw apart. There's nothing to say. We understand each other without words.

He rolls us, so I'm straddling him. We work together to pull the covers over us. We remain like this until his cock refuses to stay hard. I shift to snuggle into the crook of his arm. We're both out like a light in an instant.

Our peaceful sleep shatters when hands yank me from the bed where I'm still snuggled close to Shane. I scream as I'm practically dropped on the floor naked. Shane's scrambling to reach for the bedside table before he realizes—just like I do—this isn't exactly an enemy attack.

"Carys Pritchard, you're under arrest."

Shane can't draw a weapon on federal agents. Instead, he swings and nails one in the face before he rips the comforter from the bed and tosses it toward me. He has no issue crawling across the bed naked as he wraps the blanket around me.

"Get the fuck out, so my girlfriend can get dressed."

"This time around, Mr. O'Rourke, you don't issue the orders."

I gawk at Steve, completely stunned he's the one who came in here and put his hands on me. The moment they realized I was undressed—which should have been instantly, since I always sleep with my top arm above the covers—they should have only sent in a female agent to get me out of bed. Shane would have stayed covered up if that were the case, but four agents in this bedroom—three of whom are male—means there's no way Shane would react calmly to this. It's clear he doesn't care who sees him naked, but he very much cares I'm exposed and vulnerable.

"Get. The. Fuck. Out. Of. Here."

Each word's punctuated with venom as he glowers at Steve. When I sweep my gaze over the other agents standing in the room, it registers they all have their guns drawn.

"Shane!" That's Sean's voice yelling from down the hall.

"Yeah?"

"They got you, too?"

"Yeah, they don't want to let Carys get dressed."

"That's some bullshit. We'll have all of their names and badges."

The brothers go back and forth down the hall, forcing the agents to turn their attention toward the voice coming from a bedroom they can't see. It gives me the chance to grab the t-shirt from the end of the bed. We woke up a couple hours ago, clawing at each other, needing to feel our bodies joined again, so we never wound up putting clothes on. Once I'm covered with the t-shirt, I stand and reach for the shorts, but Steve grabs my wrist.

"What do you think you're doing? Keep your hands where we can see them."

I look incredulously at him. The t-shirt covers my ass, but not much more than that. I put my hands up and glance over at Angela.

"Hand me my shorts, please. You can search them before you give them to me."

She grabs them and pats them down before she flings them at me. I'm being treated like a suspect, not a colleague. Then again, they arrived, declaring they're arresting me.

Once I have my shorts on, Shane pays attention to his own nakedness and grabs the clothes he laid on the bed when he got me the shorts and shirt. Neither of us speaks, exerting our right to remain silent. They try to ask us questions and demand answers, but we both clam up. As they cuff us, his gaze locks with mine, and I'm certain I understand what he's thinking. I should remain silent, and his family will get us out of this somehow.

We meet Sean on the landing, and he's handcuffed as well. It wouldn't surprise me if they're going to charge him as an accomplice to my alleged crimes. Or they'll say he harbored a fugitive, or he's aiding and abetting my evasion from law enforcement.

The twins dressed identically. They're even wearing the same basketball shorts. There's a slight difference in pattern to their t-shirts, but they have the same brand and design to them. It truly is uncanny, since I'm certain they each have other clothes here in their closets but picked matching outfits. I wonder if they've always done that. Or are these their getting-arrested clothes? It wouldn't surprise me if this family had an entire wardrobe designed just for encountering law enforcement. I know that's ridiculous, but it still feels like a possibility.

They separate all of us when we get downstairs. There're cars waiting for us. Among them are three sedans with metal grates to separate the arrested party from the law enforcement. I recognize the agents who take Shane and Sean. Angela and Steve climb into the car with me.

Immediately, the game begins. It's not good cop, bad cop. It's good cop, good cop. They try to sweeten me up by reassuring me everything'll be fine, and that they'll help me, and that it's all been an act to convince our colleagues they're taking my arrest seriously. Steve's voice makes me want to drive my fist up his nose.

"Carys, we know you got caught up in all of this, and I'm sure it began as a way to protect yourself against Bartlomiej, but you've got to come into the office without resisting.

He falls silent for a moment. I assume he thinks I'll agree with him, but I keep my lips sealed. Angela glances over at him. I see her head move through the cutout pattern of the metal grate. She gives it a try.

"Come on, Carys. We know you wouldn't have done any of this if you weren't under duress. Shane O'Rourke's obviously forcing you."

That's laughable considering how they found us asleep, curled up together. I never once went anywhere near Bartlomiej when I slept in the same bed with him. Anytime he tried to make us cuddle, I'd claim I was too hot and roll away. I've never been more comfortable than sleeping beside Shane.

I nearly forget Angela's speaking.

"We know how men like him are. So do you. You were just embedded with a syndicate, and you dated their leader."

She knows how much I loathe it when anyone outside of the Poles refers to the assignment as me dating Bartlomiej. She's trying to wind me up, but I won't let her know it affects me. I'm positive she knows Shane is nothing like Bartlomiej.

We're all familiar with the various crime family members' dossiers. I might not have known Shane before meeting him, but I was aware of him. I'm certain he does the same things Bartlomiej does, but in no way does Shane come across anything like Bartlomiej.

I'm not the first agent embedded in a syndicate. Many undercover agents wind up quitting the assignment early on out of fear. Some stay even longer than I did and find it's far healthier for them to report very little. There're plenty of people throughout the agency's history who haven't fallen prey to the syndicates and have provided information that's brought families down.

But the Four Families who run New York now are far more subtle and far wiser than their predecessors. Consequently, it's been a long ass time since any of the federal agencies have scraped together enough evidence to make an arrest, let alone any convictions.

I listen to Angela and Steve continue to grasp at straws, but I don't engage. I look out the window as we head to the DEA building on 10th Ave in Manhattan. At least they haven't taken me to Central Booking to hand me over to the police to be locked up for the rest of the night.

I noticed Shane sleeps with his watch on, and as he wrapped the comforter around me, he pressed a button on the side. My guess is that's a tracker. I noticed Sean has a matching one he wore. They're identical right down to their taste in accessories. The only thing different between them was Sean had on his wedding ring. I'm certain it won't go over well if anybody tries to take that from him.

If both watches have trackers, then Shane and Sean both activated them. Their family will know what's going on, and they'll grasp the severity of the situation when both trackers ping them traveling to the same place.

When we arrive at the DEA building, Steve pulls into the underground garage. That's not always how we—they—do things. I'm not one of them anymore. *They* only pull into this garage when *they're* transporting suspects or convicted criminals *they* want nobody to see. I suppose I fall under the category of suspect for right now. If things go to trial, there's a good chance I'll soon be labeled a felon.

Chapter Twenty-One

Shane

I've been arrested before.

I doubt Carrie has, and that makes me more anxious than anything these fuck faces can do to me. I pray having been on the other side of this, Carrie remembers all the things that annoyed her as a law enforcement officer with recalcitrant suspects or witnesses and employs every one of them now. I don't doubt she intends to remain silent, but I know they trained her to wheedle info out of people. I don't want her to fall victim to the same tactics.

The two up front keep droning on about how my cooperation will make things go faster. That it'll be better for Carrie and my family if I answer their questions. Not a flying fucking chance on the hottest day in hell.

My family's trained me for these situations since I was five. Never talk to strangers. Never talk to anyone who shows me something shiny. Never talk to anyone who asks about my parents, grandfather, or aunts and uncles. Now Grandda isn't an issue, but my brothers and cousins are a concern. The rules remain the same.

The car I'm in pulls abreast of Carrie's. They're making sure we see each other. They want guilt to push either or both of us to confess. From Carrie's expression, I know it's done the opposite. It strengthens her resolve. Her lips don't move even when I see Angela twist to look back at her. Carrie just looks ahead.

"You're going to bring down an agent who was well on her way to a supervisory position. You're ruining her career."

It's the driver who states the obvious. Where was he weeks ago when all of this started? Not that it would've changed anything, but he wouldn't be spelling it out like I'm an idiot. There's no going back from this. Whether Carrie and I are together is moot. Her career is done.

It means she'll need protection for the rest of her life, regardless of her relationship with me. If the feds have come after her once, they'll keep coming back. I could never see her again, and they'd still believe there's information she could share. If nothing else, they'll want to keep punishing her.

Cormac, Seamus, and Dillan are waiting for us when we pull into the underground parking structure. The agents aren't gentle with Sean and me, but Angela's more careful with Carrie. That's until Cormac goes to her side, Dillan comes to mine, and Seamus goes to Sean.

"All of you, move out of the way." The guy who drove the car I was in tries to muscle past Dillan.

"We're not in the way." Dillan goads them by opening the door and holding it until everyone walks through.

"You can't intimidate us." Steve doesn't sound as confident as he wants.

My cousins merely smile. It's disconcerting as fuck if you aren't used to it. When the agents look at Sean and me, it really throws them for a loop. We cock opposite eyebrows—a trick we trained ourselves to do when we were eight. I raise my right one when he raises his left. When we stand in front of each other and do it, we're mirror images. When we stand side-by-side, like we are now, it makes our faces blend even more.

I "accidentally" step on the guy's foot who rode in the

passenger seat of my car. I move myself as though I try to make more space on the elevator for everyone else. Instead, I position myself, so I'm standing behind Carrie. As people shuffle on, she steps back. Her shoulders bump against my chest.

We're not in handcuffs, so we brush our hands against each other's. I link our pinkies, and she curls hers around mine. I sweep my gaze around the elevator, looking where the walls meet the ceiling, then across the ceiling.

"*An gceapann tú go bhfuil sé glan?*" Do you think it's clean?

I want to know if the others spotted any cameras in here. Seamus responds first.

"*Ní fheicim tada. Aon duine eile?*" I don't see anything. Anyone else?

"Enough conspiring."

It's an agent who manhandled Sean. I stare at him, and he senses me because he shifts to look at me. I memorize his face. I see the moment he realizes just how greatly he erred. It won't be today. It won't be tomorrow. It won't even be in a month. It'll be when he grows complacent. When he thinks I've forgotten about him. That's when I'll strike. No one touches my baby brother.

"*Má thagann sé chuici, fanann sibh go léir léi.*" If it comes to it, all of you stay with her.

Sean looks at me, and we smile. It unnerves all the agents, especially when he sounds exactly like I just did.

"*Beidh mo chúpla agus mé go breá. Cosain mo dheirfiúr.*" My twin and I'll be fine. Protect my sister.

No one but my family sees my relief. They accept Carrie because she's important to me. But I just got their blessing. They'd never stand in our way if we get more serious, and they'd want us to be happy. This is different. They consider her one of us already. When they protect her, it's not out of duty because she's a woman or out of obligation to me. It's because she's family.

"Speak English." It's the driver from my car.

I squeeze Carrie's pinky again, as the men in my family and I laugh.

"*Is dóigh liom go bhfuil muid ag cur brú orthu.*" I think we're pissing them off.

Cormac's dry tone only adds to the agents' annoyance since none of them understand us. This is precisely the reason my family speaks Gaelic and will continue to speak it for as long as we're in the mob. That means every generation until the Rapture.

We all speak Spanish, which isn't questionable in NYC. Everyone here speaks at least a little Spanish and a healthy dose of Yiddish. But we went way beyond that. All of us speak additional languages. We're all close to fluent in Italian and Russian. We've added Hebrew, Chinese, Arabic, Polish, Albanian, Japanese, and German to our family repertoire. All the places we either do business or give us trouble.

Sean learned French because of a girl he liked. She dumped his arse for being evasive, uncommunicative, and unemotional. Shocking. He still enjoys those shitty arthouse films, though. Nikki claims she likes them. I think he tortures her with them since she's a native French speaker.

Sean beats me to it with his next question. "*An bhfuil a fhios ag ár dtuismitheoirí?*" Do our parents know?

Seamus grins, and now all the agents are certain we're conspiring or criminally insane. "*Bhí mé le Mam agus Da nuair a fuair muid an foláireamh. Bhí Da ar an bhfón le do cheann. Fuair sé an foláireamh freisin. D'iompaigh sé amach. Tá ár n-aithreacha ag glaoch i bhfabhar. Tá ár uncail eile ag dul chuig a tuismitheoirí.*" I was with Mom and Da when we got the alert. Da was on the phone with yours. He got the alert, too. He flipped out. Our dads are calling in favors. Our other uncle's going to her parents.

The non-Gaelic speakers probably picked up Mam and Da—we usually use Mom, but in Irish, it translates to Mam—and figured out we're talking about our parents, or at least Seamus and Cormac's. "Our other uncle" means Dillan's dad, Uncle Tate.

Calling in favors means these wankers are going to be riding their desks or unemployed by morning. I'd feel sorry for them if they hadn't touched my woman and my brother.

Carrie leans harder against me. I know not understanding

bothers her. Probably frightens her more than anything, but it's the only way my cousins, Sean, and I can communicate right now.

"*Is dócha go bhfaighidh muid saor í roimh ceachtar agaibh. Cad ba mhaith leat dúinn a dhéanamh?*" We'll probably get her free before either of you. What do you want us to do?

Dillan has a point. Even though they claim they're after her, once they have two mobsters in for questioning, they won't let us go. They'll hold us for the full forty-eight hours. They might do the same to Carrie, but I don't think so. I believe they'll want to see where she goes next. Somehow, they knew she was with me at my place. My guess is they followed Meredith and Rhys or tracked their cars. When they went to Sean's, they figured she was there too. When everyone else left, but they didn't see me, it probably confirmed she and I were staying at Sean's.

"*Rwyf am i chi fynd at fy rhieni.*" I want you to go to my parents.

My accent is atrocious, but from the way Carrie tenses, then relaxes against me, I know she understood. I told no one I started learning a little Welsh when I met her. I needed something to occupy my time while I watched her. When she said she spoke it as a kid, I doubled my efforts.

"*Nid yw hynny'n ddiogel iddynt.*" That's not safe for them.

She speaks slowly, ensuring I can follow what she says.

"*Maen nhw'n gwybod mai dyna sydd fwyaf diogel i mi.*" They know that's safest for me.

I won't lose my shite if I know she's with them.

I'm confident with my grammar, but I don't know if she can understand my shite accent. I thought about investing in a decent language program, but I'm nearly as frugal as Finn. If this doesn't work out, then I'd rather use YouTube videos to teach me a language I won't need.

Because little brothers are a pain in the arse, Sean snickers at me. "*Tú asal saor. Fuaimeann tú cosúil le cac. Íocfaidh mé as do chlár ríomhaire dúr don Nollaig.*" You cheap arse. You sound like shite. I'll pay for your stupid computer program for Christmas.

"*Conas a bheadh a fhios agat?*" How would you know?

I sound more contentious than I mean.

"*Toisc go bhfuil cluasa agam.*" Because I have ears.

We're teasing each other, but Sean sounds as argumentative as I do. It's a simple ruse. Let them think we don't agree about whatever they assume we were plotting. They'll try to leverage that between Sean and me. They'll try to drill a hole in our family armor, which means they won't focus on Carrie. They'll think they can go after something bigger. When they do that, my brother and cousins know I won't risk telling lies that don't match Carrie's.

Dillan chimes in just like he always has, especially when Sean and I really disagree. "*Tá sé ag iarraidh dul i bhfeidhm uirthi. Is léir go gcaithfidh sé cúiteamh a dhéanamh as rud éigin má tá sé ag déanamh iarrachta chomh dian sin.*" He's trying to impress her. Clearly, he needs to make up for something if he's trying that hard.

"*B'fhéidir gurb é an t-aon rud atá deacair?*" Could it be the only thing that's hard?

Cormac isn't one to be left out, and since Seamus isn't either, I know he'll have something to say next.

"*Insíonn tú dúinn, a Sheáin. Tá tú mar an gcéanna leis. Rudaí beagán flapach?*" You tell us, Sean. You're made the same as him. Things a little floppy?

"*Éist do bhéal fecker.*" Shut up, fecker.

Sean and I speak, and to anyone who doesn't know us, it's virtually impossible to tell whose voice is whose. Even in Gaelic and even in jest, our parents would skelp us alive if we swore at one another. That's the Golden Rule in our family.

Thou shalt not curse at one another.

Life's too short to take back harsh words when you might not speak or hear any again. Sean and I aren't angry at Seamus, but we'll both remember that for later. Joking or not, no guy wants to be asked if he has a floppy dick.

But it feeds the act we're putting on. It's working because Carrie's wound up tighter than a bow string since she doesn't understand what's happening yet. She will with time—assuming we'll have some. My free hand taps her arse before giving it a quick squeeze.

They must be taking us up to the eleventh floor, which is the top of the building. The elevator's stopped three times, and everyone's taken one look at five red heads and stepped away from the open doors. If that sort of power didn't come with the looming threat of death every time we wake, it could be intoxicating. But none of us revel in it. None of us enjoy it. We have that power because it's the only way to stay alive.

I glance down at the top of Carrie's head. My chest tightens to where I want to rub it.

What have you done? You've sucked her into this world. You're endangering her life every single moment she's connected to you. She'll never be free of her association with you. You've ruined her life.

That last thought runs on a loop.

I sense Sean's eyes on me. I shift my focus to him. He sends me the same look he has since we were children: I know what you're thinking and don't.

It's usually before I got us both in trouble. I've given him the same look enough times I understand it without being twins.

It's the twin thing that made him guess what's on my mind. Science can't explain it. *Yet.* One day, they'll understand twin intuition. I think it's because we've shared so many of the same experiences and have been virtually inseparable by choice our entire lives. We're so attuned to one another we know however we'd feel in a situation is likely how the other does, or we understand when the other would feel the opposite.

I swallow and dip my chin. I can tell Sean's still worried, but he relaxes. No one outside our family knows our tells. Grandda and Uncle Don knocked any emotional response out of us, as in knocked us to the ground, knocked us out—that was Uncle Don's best friend Colin. Fucking ham hocks for hands before he got what he deserved. Death.

When the elevator finally chimes, and we reach the top floor, everyone files out. Sean and I are in t-shirts and basketball shorts, but our cousins are in their regular tailored suits. We spend a fortune on clothes since we wind up burning so many of them. When we leave the station, we leave anything with DNA evidence behind. That means burning everything and dropping it in the Long Island Sound. Because of our builds, off the rack doesn't work for us. We'd split the seams across our backs if we got jackets that match pants we need. Our pants would slide off our arses if we got them to match the jackets.

Even without our suits, Sean and I, along with our cousins, are an imposing sight. It might be worse with Sean and me in athletic clothes. It proves what everyone suspects. There's as much muscle under our designer clothes as people suspect.

"Mr. O'Rourke, this way."

The agent whose foot I stepped on tries to usher me in one direction while Steve takes Carrie in the other. I ignore him. They didn't arrest either of us—despite what Steve said when he burst into the bedroom—so I'm not leaving her side unless they physically restrain me.

"Mr. O'Rourke." The guy's tone is more demanding this time.

"My client isn't under arrest. He's here against his will, but he'll cooperate if he can stay with Ms. Pritchard. He won't interrupt. Since she isn't in cuffs, and I doubt you've Mirandaed either of them, they're merely here to answer your questions."

Dillan's spewing shite, and everyone knows it. They can separate us if they want, and I'm certain they do. They could arrest all of us if they wanted. It's merely a question of whether any of them dare.

Cormac's still beside Carrie, keeping her between him and me. "Right now, my client is here as a favor to you since it's clear she's not a suspect since you haven't arrested her. She can't be a witness since she's seen nothing. The same is true for both Mr. O'Rourkes. Perhaps we can sort all of this out if we sit down together and get on the same page."

Cormac's hardly conciliatory. It's hardly a suggestion. He makes the agents look like Chihuahua pups when he's a Rottweiler. His imposing size gives every word he utters more intensity. When Seamus steps beside him, the agents relent. For now.

We file into a conference room, and the agents guide Sean, Carrie, and me to chairs apart from each other. My cousins sit on one side of each of us while an agent sits on the other. Then there's silence. Do they think we're going to open the flood gates suddenly and tell them everything? If they couldn't intimidate us enough to force us to go where they wanted, silence won't intimidate us either. My gaze locks with Carrie's.

"Ms. Pritchard, you abandoned your assignment." I recognize the voice belonging to the man who just entered the room. His name was Phil, and I heard him on the call Carrie made to report in after she arrived at my place.

She's still looking at me. I dip my chin. She'll have to feed them something, or they will arrest her.

"I fled Tymoteusz Nowakowski and his men when they planned to kill me."

"But did they try?"

"Yes."

That surprises Philly. I can see him now that he's standing across the table from Carrie. He thinks his height, since she's seated, will intimidate her if his seniority and position as her supervisor don't. Mental and physical manipulation. Oh, how I know it well.

Carrie volunteers nothing more. It obviously irritates Phil.

"How did they try to kill you?"

"When I ran, they shot at me."

"Where did this take place?"

"Queens."

"Where in Queens, Carys?" He softens his tone, and I watch Carrie struggle not to smirk.

"A neighborhood. I don't know what it's called."

She probably doesn't. It's not like the gates leading into Beverly Hills with huge gold lettering. It's far more subtle. Even before most of the Four Families moved in there, it's such a wealthy neighborhood no residents want to draw attention to it.

It's why the community has a gate, and so do most of the individual properties.

"What happened in the neighborhood? How did you get there?"

"I told you I ran. They followed me and shot at me."

"You're in one piece."

"Thank God." Carrie's tone has a twinge of sarcasm, but I think she genuinely feels that way. I know I do.

"How did you get away from them?"

"I hid."

"Where?"

"A house. A gate was open, so I ran through it. I hid on someone's property until I was certain they couldn't shoot me."

"Then what?"

"I left."

"And went where?"

"Somewhere safe. I told you this over the phone yesterday, Phil."

"How did you get to Mr. O'Rourke's home?"

"By car."

"Who drove it?"

Her brow furrows, and she appears confused. "I don't remember."

I believe her. I don't think she took in much of what happened then except I was there, and she felt safe.

Phil turns to me. "Mr. O'Rourke, did you pick up Ms. Pritchard?"

Four voices respond. "No." I remain quiet.

"Your antics might have worked in the elevator, but they won't work here with me."

I wonder if someone called him and let him hear the conversation or if there is a camera in the elevator. Maybe he's assuming something happened since we clearly annoyed his agents.

"Mr. Shane O'Rourke, did you pick her up from wherever she sheltered?"

"Yes."

"Why?"

"She was in danger."

"From whom?"

"She already told you."

"Did you know that's who she ran from?"

"I found out."

"How?"

"I heard it."

"From whom?"

"Someone."

Phil's rapid firing the questions, and I'm just as fast to answer. It's easy to predict what'll come next, so it's easy to have a response ready.

"My agents found Ms. Pritchard naked and in bed with you. You were naked, too."

I watch Carrie, who shows no outward reaction, even though I'm certain she's mortified. There's no question posed, so I remain silent. I won't offer anything, and I'll only give the most evasive answers.

"Ms. Pritchard, were you there by your own free will, or did Mr. O'Rourke force you?"

"I chose where I slept."

"And that was with Mr. O'Rourke."

"You said 'there,' as in a location. I told you where I slept. Your question didn't ask with whom."

"Don't be pedantic, Carys."

"Don't co-opt my responses."

"Did you sleep with Mr. O'Rourke?"

"Your agents found me in bed with Mr. O'Rourke, who was also asleep."

"Are you having sex with Mr. O'Rourke?"

"No. I'm sitting in a chair."

"Are you sexually involved with Mr. O'Rourke?" Phil's patience is about to snap.

Carrie doesn't answer. Even if they'd arrested her, they cannot compel her to respond.

"Carys, will you go to jail for him?"

"Mr.?" Cormac's dismissive tone irritates Phil even further, but it distracts him from Carrie for a moment.

She shifts her gaze to me. I know she wants to know how she should answer that. But I don't know. I look at Seamus, sitting across from me. His expression says no as loudly as if he were screaming. When I return my attention to Carrie, I think she understands because her expression goes entirely blank.

"Supervisory Agent in Charge Phil Hammond."

"Agent Hammond, I'm advising my client to decline answering any further questions of this nature. You may limit your questions to her investigation of the Polish mob. But further inquiry into my client's private life is inappropriate."

"Further inquiry? She's sleeping with a—"

"A what, Agent Hammond?" Cormac presses, and he's about to sink his teeth in.

"A man with known ties to organized crime."

"Known ties?"

"Yes, your family is the New York mob."

"Says who?"

Cormac knows none of the agents will reveal sources, and there aren't any active or old cases against any of us linking us to organized crime. The NYPD's arrested all of us at some point. Mostly when we were teens and still learning how to steal shite without getting caught. A few times were to distract the police from the people actually committing crimes. Nothing's stuck.

When Phil remains quiet, Cormac leans forward. "Who, Agent Hammond?"

"I don't have to answer your questions. We're here to ask Ms. Pritchard and your cousins questions."

"You've just made a serious accusation with no grounds. It sounds like you're toeing the line of defamation by making such claims with no evidence."

"No grounds? Everyone knows who you are."

"Who are we, Agent Hammond?"

"You're damn mob."

"Says who?" Cormac will take them around in circles until Phil's dizzy, and my cousin walks away the same way he does after ten shots of Irish whiskey—sober as the day he was born. Though, ask him about Halloween two years ago, and he'll say the eleventh is a doozy.

"I won't go around in circles with you, Mr. O'Rourke. Carys, look at what you've gotten yourself involved with. You abandoned your assignment. You're sleeping with a man suspected of countless crimes. You've destroyed your career. But if you cooperate, we won't charge you with any misconduct or crimes. Tell them you'll speak to us alone."

"I have a right to remain silent. I have a right to an attorney. I have the right to stop answering questions. I'm not under arrest, but those rights still apply. I have nothing more to say."

"If you won't cooperate, we'll arrest you, Carys."

I want to climb out of my skin. It was always going to come to this. Why they didn't formally arrest her at my house is a question I don't know the answer to. But we've bought my dad and uncles more time to pull strings. That's been the goal.

Phil looks at Angela, who stands and pulls out her handcuffs. I watch the woman put them around Carrie's wrists as she officially Mirandizes my girlfriend. Carrie doesn't look anywhere but straight ahead. Cormac insists upon remaining with her, but it leaves Sean, Seamus, Dillan, and me in a room full of federal agents I want to butcher.

Phil looks at me and gloats. It doesn't last when four sets of emerald eyes silently warn him it's bad for his health to antagonize us.

"Agent Hammond?" A young man who looks like he should still be in middle school sticks his head in.

"Yeah."

"Um, Sir. Director Spenser'd like to speak to you."

Philly Boy's day just went to shite. The four of us lean back in our chairs, leaning on our left elbows on the armrests as we spin our chairs in unison to better see Phil. Like synchronized swimmers, we rest our jaws on our left hands as though we're bored.

"Transfer him to my office."

"Uh, Sir, he said you should take it in here on speaker."

I think that color is called puce. It's the one Phil's face turns when he reaches across the table to the phone in the center.

"Director Spenser, this is Spec—"

"I know who you are. If you aren't charging the O'Rourkes with anything, let them go."

"But—"

"Hammond." Spenser sounds like he's reprimanding a naughty schoolboy.

"Yes, Sir."

"Where is Agent Pritchard?"

"She's on her way to Central Booking."

"Good. Keep her there for the full forty-eight hours."

You could hear a pin drop.

Everything's in suspended animation as I turn to look at Dillan, who turns to look at me. We both turn to look at Sean and Seamus. Dillan spins his chair, so he can pin me in place if he has to. The temptation to go over the table and strangle Phil is nearly palpable. I want to find out where Director Spenser is right now and bash his brains in. I want to do a lot of things, but all I can do is sit there.

Dillan's whispered comment only makes me angrier. "*Fuair Mérgrég tríd. Beidh sí mar sin.*"

Telling me his wife got through it, and so will Carrie does nothing to calm me.

It was the ATF who tried to use Mair against Dillan. He was practically a rampaging bull while trying to get her out of there. Fortunately for us—not so fortunate for them—we had three women connected to our family in lock up that night. They protected Mair, but I don't know that Carrie'll be so lucky.

"*Cuirfear croitheadh uirthi nuair a fhaigheann aon duine amach gur gníomhaire feidearálach í.*" She'll get shanked the moment anyone finds out she's a federal agent.

She might not be a police officer, but she's still law enforcement. She'll be a target the moment she walks through the door. Spenser knows that.

"What do you want?" I'll sell just about anything I have to get Carrie out. Anybody need a kidney?

"Mr. O'Rourke, make a full confession of all your crimes, and Agent Pritchard won't step foot in Central Booking."

Dillan's leg nudges mine. He knows I'll spew every lie I can come up with—I'll confess to murdering JFK and dumping Jimmy Hoffa's body—if it'll get Carrie out. But no one in my family thinks I'll sell them out. They know I'll lie, and that worries them even more.

"I'll make that confession when I see Ms. Pritchard leave this building with her attorney and get into his car. I'll make that confession when you bring me a notarized agreement that this arrangement is binding."

"Tick tock, Mr. O'Rourke. By the time I send something down that's notarized, she'll be in an orange jumpsuit."

"I suggest you don't drag your feet then."

My tone's so menacing the remaining agents in the room shift and reach for their weapons. I shoot them scathing glances.

"You don't issue orders, Mr. O'Rourke. It's the confession, or Ms. Pritchard spends the next two days in jail. I'm certain she'll feel chatty before then."

He thinks Carrie will roll on me. I don't. I think she'll die before that happens. And that's what terrifies me.

"Agent Hammond!"

We all turn to a woman who rushes into the conference room. She glances around before she keeps her voice down. It's not enough to keep me from hearing.

"The Nowakowski brothers are dead. Their plane crashed just before they were to reach Newark. It's ash and debris in the ocean."

Who the fuck stole my right to punish them?

I stare at Dillan, but he shrugs. Seamus and Sean frown. None of us know who it was because it wasn't any of us. I figured they'd returned yesterday, but it must have just happened if it's news.

"Anyone claiming it?" Director Spenser must have heard her because he asks the sixty-four-thousand-dollar question.

"No. We're uncertain, but we think it's the Diazes."

What the ever-loving fuck does Enrique have to do with this?

"The Cartel? Why?"

Spenser's demanding, but not in the way one would sound if the news surprised them. It's more like wanting to know why something got fucked up. What's his connection to the Colombians?

"We don't know for sure. Apparently, Bartlomiej Nowakowski had a lot of enemies."

I doubt the woman realizes the extent of that understatement.

"But we don't know for certain it was them?"

There's something different to Spenser's tone now. Like he wants to check before he claims something entirely different. Like he's double-checking.

"No, Sir."

"Arrest all the O'Rourkes in that room for murder."

"We've been here. How could we murder anyone? When did this happen?" Dillan's the oldest in the family. Even before we knew the roles we'd eventually step into, he was always protective of us. Mostly, he was protective of Colleen, but because all of us were always together, he felt responsible for everyone. Shite is about to rain in heaven.

"Uh—um—ten minutes ago." The woman doesn't know where to look, but Dillan's tone has compelled stronger men to bend to his will.

"Then you have no probable cause since we've all been here."

"Obviously, you planted a bomb." Phil's on board with his boss and is ready to run with this.

"I bet that confession's sounding pretty good right now, Mr. O'Rourke. Admit to this, and there won't be any need to hold Ms. Pritchard or your relatives."

"Bring me that notarized agreement. I'm certain you can draw something up and get it up here in a few minutes, Director Spenser. You'd hate to have me forget everything."

I will burn this motherfucking building to the ground before I help this piece of shite. But I'll go to prison for life to get Carrie and my family out of this.

"Very well, Mr. O'Rourke. Agent Hammond, bring Agent Pritchard back in. She's our star witness now. She can explain everyone's role in this little love triangle she's found herself in between Bartlomiej Nowakowski and Shane O'Rourke. Who knew she'd bring the mighty to their knees?"

I narrow my eyes. That fucker doesn't mean that as a metaphor. He's implying—fuck him.

Dillan nudges me. He holds out his phone.

CORMAC

This is Carys. Show Shane your phone.

DILLAN

Ok.

There's a pause, then the next text comes in.

CARRIE

Shane will you marry me?

Chapter Twenty-Two

Carrie

I stare at Cormac's phone, unsure what possessed me to send that text. But I don't regret it, and I won't retract the offer.

"Carys?"

I glance up at Cormac, who's utterly stunned.

"You told me they'd force us to testify against each other. That they'll make it impossible for us to avoid either incriminating ourselves or each other. If either of us pleads the fifth, we're just turning the attention to the other. I won't do that, and I know Shane won't accept anything happening to me. This is the only way."

I'm whispering furtively to him now that we're in an interrogation room alone. I've been in here enough times to know they have the entire place bugged. Even when it appears like the camera in the far-left corner of the room is off, we're—they're—still recording shit. They don't believe Cormac's my attorney, so they'll claim there's no attorney-client privileged information. But they're scared enough they haven't kept Cormac from remaining with me.

I maneuvered us, so we're facing the two-way mirror. Let them know we're talking. As long as they can't see his phone screen and can't hear us, I couldn't give two shits that they can see our mouths moving. Let them wonder what we're discussing.

"He won't agree while you're under duress."

SHANE

It's me Carrie but D's typing. I won't trap you. Now's not the time to decide.

"See."

Cormac may as well scream, "I told you so." But I'm not interested in hearing it. I type out another text instead.

ME

It'll protect both of us. They can't compel us to testify against each other. There's a two-day wait after getting a license in NY and NJ but none in CT. From here to Greenwich takes 45 mins to an hr. We can get married as soon as the courthouse opens.

I check the clock on Cormac's phone. It's nearly five a.m. The courthouse opens in three hours. I know we can fill out the marriage application online because I had a friend in college who eloped with her high school boyfriend while he was on leave from the Merchant Marine. The marriage lasted about as long as his leave—three days. But they didn't divorce for another three years.

I never planned to get divorced, but I will if it means marrying Shane now keeps him safe.

SHANE

There has to be another way. I'm not marrying you to keep me out of prison.

ME

Then marry me to keep me out of prison. I don't care who keeps who out as long as neither of us goes in.

My palms grow clammy as I wait for his response. Is he discussing this with his family? Does he wish Cormac was part of the conversation? His displeasure echoes in the room even though he's said nothing since the ominous "see."

SHANE

What about your parents? What if they can't be there?

ME

They'll understand. Yours?

SHANE

They'd understand too. But

But what?

I wait.

I tap the screen to see the clock again because it's been long enough for it to dim.

ME

Shane?

DILLAN

Carys it's Dillan. They're taking him to be fingerprinted

ME

Then what? Are they taking him to central booking?

DILLAN

We don't know yet maybe

ME

You can't let that happen.

DILLAN

We'll take care of him. Let Cor take care of you. Listen to him so Shane doesn't worry.

I look at Cormac, who's reading along with me as the texts come in.

ME

Tell Shane I'm serious. We can be in CT from here in an hour. Once we're both cut loose, we go.

DILLAN

I'll see what he says

I hand the phone back to Cormac, who rests it screen down on his thigh. I noticed he doesn't have a wedding ring when we were at Shane's yesterday. I saw Sean's, Finn's, and Dillan's then and Seamus's today. I'm certain they don't have marriages of convenience to keep their wives out of jail. I'm certain they didn't do it to keep themselves out.

It'll devastate my parents to miss my wedding and to learn I married Shane for any reason but love. My guess is his parents'll feel the same. But I don't give a shit if it protects him. We can divorce or even get it annulled if he wants.

He wants. Not if I want.

I don't know what the fuck I want short of getting away from here. Am I so eager to escape I'm willing to commit to marrying someone I don't love?

You're practically in love with him.

Practically doesn't mean I am.

But you could be.

Maybe one day. We can't wait around to see if we fall in love. We need to buy ourselves enough time to see if we don't fall in love.

"Cormac, what will happen to him if they book him and take him to jail? Will there be people there who want to hurt him?"

"Yes."

.Fuck.

"Are you always so blunt?"

"No. I just watched a woman text my cousin a marriage proposal, so she can stay out of prison and hopefully keep him out too. That cousin's getting fingerprinted, so the feds can put him in jail for at least two days. If they game the system, they can keep him there indefinitely. I'm trying to work out how to get you out if your boss sends you there, after all. I'm a bit short on words to spare right now."

He's frustrated, but he's not mean.

"Cormac, you know I didn't propose just to keep myself out of prison, right? I'm terrified some rival will be there and shank him within five minutes of them tossing him into gen pop."

"And he's terrified of the same thing for you. The difference is he knows what to look for and will fight dirty. You might fight dirty, but it'll be too late. I have to keep you out of jail, or Shane's likely to die suicide by cop because he won't stop until they kill him, or he gets to you."

"Don't say that." With each word I rasp, I feel like Cormac knocks the air out of me.

"You're not naïve, Carys. You know Shane well enough to consider spending your life with him."

"We can always get a divorce if he doesn't want to stay married to me."

Cormac assesses me, and I feel like I've failed whatever silent test he gave me.

"No one in the O'Rourke family—not on either side—has gotten divorced. And it's not because of the bullshit you've seen our faces, now you have to die. Couples with arranged marriages stayed together because of duty. But my parents and aunts and uncles married because they can't fathom a day without their partner. Dillan, Finn, Sean, and Seamus married their wives for the same reason. Shane deserves that, too. He deserves a marriage meant to last with his soulmate. Not some quickie that can be undone in Reno in less time than it takes to get married."

"And how's he supposed to have that when someone knifes him in the back in prison? He wants you to protect me. He trusts you to. I need you to trust I'll do whatever it takes to protect him. I don't give a shit whether you or anyone else approves. You can judge me after we keep him out of Sing Sing."

That prison's super-max and not somewhere most inmates ever leave alive. If they prosecute me, and I wind up convicted, I'll be headed to Bedford Hills. It's the maximum-security prison for women in New York State. I'm not eager for a life sentence, but I stand a better chance for survival than Shane does in Sing Sing.

Cormac watches me until he nods. Something about what I said or how I said it pacifies him.

"If he says yes, it won't be—"

He doesn't finish because the door swings open. My old handler, Johnny, walks in. It shocks me to see him with a shit-eating grin. We didn't always agree, but I thought we got along better than I got along with Steve. Steve was always nice to my face, but I knew he was an asshole behind my back. I thought what I saw was what I got with Johnny.

"I smell fresh fish." He sniffs dramatically, and I want to punch him. I'm not some new inmate.

"Who're you?" Cormac's hackles are up, and it makes Johnny miss a step.

"Mr. O'Rourke, I'm Special Agent Johnny Ramirez."

Cormac grins, and it chills me to the bone. "Well, I'll be a monkey's uncle. How's your dear old dad these days? Still making little rocks out of big rocks?"

My eyes widen. I didn't know Johnny's dad was in prison. I glance between the two, and Cormac smirks.

"Didn't tell your agent your daddy's in the pen for selling narcotics and insider trading? I should have recognized you the minute you walked in. You look like your dad."

"What?" I don't understand what's happening.

"Oh, yeah. Johnny's dad turned state's witness against the Diazes about seven years ago. Maybe you can answer a question my family's had since then. Who've you been sucking off to keep your job? After all the shite they found on your dad, your knees must have callouses to have kept your job."

"Johnny, you told me your dad died. You went to his funeral."

"He went to his sentencing. His dad narced on the Diazes. He's only alive because he's a little bitch and reports everything to the warden. The warden protects him, but he hasn't always done such a good job, has he, Johnny? It's been at least a year since he was last stabbed. That's a long time to go without a reminder you don't turn on your own."

Cormac unlocks his phone and hits his contacts. He puts the call on speaker.

Oh, hell.

"*Enrique, que pasa, amigo?*" Enrique, what's happening, friend?

"What the fuck do you want, Cor? I'm busy."

"Yeah, I heard. Should I be saying *felicidadas* soon?"

"I don't need nor want your congratulations. What do you want?"

"Guess who I'm sitting in front of." He holds the phone out to Johnny. "Speak."

"Enrique."

"*Hijo de puta. ¿Qué coño haces con Cormac O'Rourke? Me cago en—*" Motherfucker. What the fuck are you doing with Cormac O'Rourke? I'll fucking—

"Enrique, you're on speaker. I'm at the DEA office. Imagine my surprise when Johnny Ramirez just walked in."

"What're you doing there? They finally catch you and your miscreant relatives?"

"Someone's after Shane's girlfriend."

"The DEA agent? What the fuck does she see in him, anyway?"

The *jefe de jefes* knows who I am? I might be sick.

I know what Shane's family does. I obviously know what the bratva does since they were my marks. But Enrique Diaz controls any and everything coming in and out of Latin America that the O'Rourkes, Kutsenkos, and Mancinellis don't. And those three families only have a sliver of the pie compared to Enrique. The mob, bratva, and Mafia have their producers and distributors in Latin America. They sell their shit in America and wherever else in the world they want. But for every one pot farm or coke lab they have, Enrique easily has four.

"She sees a nice Catholic boy who loves his mom."

"The feds need a better vision plan then."

The man grew up in Colombia but was educated in America. He has the best of both worlds. He's better educated than just about anyone in organized crime who isn't a member of the mob, bratva, or Mafia ruling families. I doubt there's ever been a time when so many Ivy League and Top Tier educated men have run New York City's underworld. Enrique's one of them, but he also knows the fucking Amazon like it's his backyard.

"Anyway, imagine my surprise to find Ramirez here. He was one of Shane's girlfriend's handlers. From the way he walked in here, I'd say he sold her out to someone. And that someone got her boxed in."

"Are you suggesting that *pedazo de mierda* came running to me, hoping turning on a woman would dredge up some forgiveness from me?" Piece of shit.

Enrique and his five nephews have set up labs all over the place, so deep into the jungle, no one can find them without one of them taking them there. It also means no one leaves without one of those six men helping them. Apparently, Enrique pays them, feeds them, and houses them well. He protects all their families and makes sure their money makes it home to wives, parents, and kids. But they aren't free to come and go.

They're not slaves. More like indentured servants. They're people who wronged Enrique or his family, and Enrique's sentenced them to hard labor until he—or Alejandro—the nephew who's his representative down there most of the time—says they can go free. I've heard you could fill every seat in Yankee Stadium with the bodies they have buried down there. I doubt that. It would mean they left evidence behind. Enrique Diaz is many things, but sloppy isn't one of them.

"Maybe he wants you to forgive his *papí*, so he handed Shane's girlfriend over to you."

"Hardly. He knows he could give me all of Midas's gold, and it wouldn't be enough. This is news to me, Cormac."

"Hmm."

Doesn't Cormac believe him? If I weren't watching Cormac

watching Johnny, I might believe Enrique. He sounds convincing. But Cormac obviously knows the man well.

"I don't give a shit, Cor."

I don't get what just happened. What did one syllable mean?

"About those congratulations. Put our table near the chocolate fountain."

"*Come mierda.*" Eat shit.

"Is that what you're putting in the fountain? No thanks. Put the Mancinellis there instead."

What the fuck are they talking about? A *quince*? As far as I know, there aren't any girls turning fifteen in the Diaz family, so a *quinceañera* seems unlikely. The only reason I've heard about that gets them all together is wedding receptions.

"*Adiós, gilipollas.*" Bye, asshole.

"*Vaya con dios, cucho.*" Go with God, old man.

You'd almost think they were friends with how chummy their voices are. I know Cormac doesn't mean *cucho* literally—hunchback. In slang, it means old man. It can be a term of endearment, but I don't get the sense Cormac sees Enrique as family. I mean, I wouldn't call the *jefe de jefes* that.

I observed Johnny the entire time Cormac was on the phone. The man is a shade of white I've only seen on corpses.

"You don't look so great, Johnny."

He forces his gaze away from Cormac to me when I speak. He comes out of his stupor as he stares at me.

"Carys, you're so deep in the shit you're going to come out the other side of the world."

"Your concern warms my heart." *Jackass.*

He got over his fear because now he's being a smug asshole. Cormac clears his throat to remind Johnny the rope upon which he wobbles is fraying with each word. Cormac's clearly not here to make friends.

"What do you want, Ramirez?"

"I came to check on Carys."

"Liar. What do you want with my client?"

"Client? Carys, is this for real? Steve and Angela said you

have an O'Rourke pretending to be your lawyer. He sounds serious."

"Does Mr. O'Rourke look like he has a sense of humor?" Cormac looks like he eats puny federal agents for breakfast.

He crosses his arms, and his suit jacket strains across his shoulders and around his biceps. His baby face—and Seamus's—bely how strong they are until you see moments like this when he looks like he's about to Hulk out of his suit. Johnny sees it too. He's sticking close to the door and doesn't have the swagger he had when he entered.

I hear Cormac's phone buzz. I glance toward him. I'm about to turn back to Johnny when he shows me the screen.

DILLAN

It's Shane. I'll marry you.

Chapter Twenty-Three

Shane

This is about as good an idea as a Green Card marriage, except those can end when the person gets their Permanent Resident status. The things the feds would charge Carrie and me with have no statute of limitation, and even though it would protect us from having to testify against each other, there're other people who'd testify. They'd see us locked up, then throw a party. But this is one of the few things I can do to help protect Carrie, so I will.

It should make her untouchable, but my family history's proven we tend to fuck that up and ruin Christmas for the whole family. Things are getting better, though, since we've shown the other syndicates we're reformed. Now that Uncle Don is gone, and that shitbag Declan didn't get more than a blink of the eye in charge, we've reestablished some sense of homeostasis. Or at least created a new one that works for most of us.

It's not the way it was back in the day when women and children were one-hundred percent off-limits, but we're getting there. I'd say they're ninety-six percent off-limits, which is better than the zero percent they were during Dillan's predecessors.

If I marry Carrie and the other syndicates understand there's no limit to what I'll do to protect her—and that goes the same for the rest of the members of my family—then maybe there'll be a scant number of people willing to testify against us. And those who do, know there's a target on them. Just like those fuckers who manhandled Sean will die—just not today or tomorrow—so will anybody who dares testify against us. We'll wait long enough for it to not be an obvious connection, and then they'll be gone. It'll look like natural causes. We've gotten very good at that.

It's not ideal to start a marriage this way. But if I hadn't truly believed this is where we're heading, I never would have pursued her. I've known that all along, but I haven't said it because I haven't wanted to get my hopes up she'd feel the same way and want the same things I do. I know she suggested this out of necessity, not love. But who knows?

Maybe we'll make it work and have a happily ever after. That or we'll be the first couple in my family's history to get a divorce. Not exactly the first I want to be known for. But that's neither here nor there. We'll make the most out of it and do what we can. That's why I agreed to this.

I'm waiting for Dillan to get back. Then they should release me. I've got a new set of fingerprints on file. Not that it's changed since I was fifteen. That was the last time I got booked for anything. It's not like some movie where I've scraped off my fingerprints to leave nothing there, or somehow implanted a new set to confuse them. It's just good ole me. What you see is what you get, at least with my fingerprints.

"Okay. Paperwork's taken care of."

"Am I released on my own recognizance? Do they expect me to hand over my passport?" I ask this in all seriousness, since it's a good likelihood that's the temporary outcome until an arraignment or a trial.

"No, they have no real probable cause, so I forced their hand. They have to cut you loose."

"I can live with that. Where's Carrie now?"

I sent my reply to her proposal, then Dillan took his phone when he stepped out. I don't know what may have happened while he was dealing with my paperwork. No one's said anything about her actually going to Central Booking.

"I texted Cormac."

"Do you know what they've been asking her?"

They'll try harder with Carrie. While they attempt to wait it out with Sean, they'll keep her in there and try to scare her.

"I haven't heard from him yet. All I know is they took her in a separate interrogation room like they did you and Sean. As best I know, Cormac's still with her, even though they tried to separate Seamus and Sean."

"I bet that didn't go over so well."

"No, I'd say it didn't. Seamus started writing names and making phone calls."

"Speaking of phone calls, where are our dads?"

"I don't know. I left a message for mine, but I haven't heard from him yet."

That inspires no relief in me when they're supposed to be pulling strings for us. I wonder if they're getting to Judge Hartman finally, since he's the one who signed that warrant to search my house.

He's the one who's always behind all of this. I'm curious to know what Phil or Hunt—I learned that's Spencer's first name—fed him to convince him to sign the warrant. It doesn't take much, but even he knows he has to have some solid ground to stand on, or else he'll lose the bench.

He's been sitting comfortably for the past twenty years. He definitely doesn't want to lose that position because the moment he does, he becomes a target to every syndicate. He knows we can't do much to him now. He's banking on if he dies or disappears, it'll all point back to us, since we're the ones he goes after most frequently. It means we put up with him and thumb our noses at him every time he reaches a little too far.

Dillan and I watch Angela come into the room they took me to, so they could separate me from Sean and Carrie. We never left the DEA office, so Central Booking won't be my hotel tonight.

That's certainly not somewhere I'd like to accumulate points because there's no trading them in for an upgrade.

"Mr. O'Rourke, you're free to go. We apologize for the inconvenience."

"Inconvenience, my Great-Aunt Fanny."

"Be that as it may, Mr. O'Rourke, we apologize for interrupting your day."

I'll take it, since it's better than nothing. "What about Carys?"

"What about her? For someone who's not involved with her, you seem awfully concerned about her."

"Why wouldn't I be? She's done nothing but her job, and almost died for it several times. Now all of you turn on her. What's being done to call off whatever Bartlomiej ordered?"

"He's dead. Anything he put in place is gone."

Dillan and I snort, but I won't argue with her, since this room is likely bugged. I'm pretty certain it is, even though the red light in the corner went off when Dillan said he wanted to speak to his client privately, as opposed to his cousin. For people like us, the ears never go away. Admitting the hit will stick until Carrie's dead or someone changes their next leader's mind will only confirm we know more about the inner workings of syndicates than we'll acknowledge. It only opens up more questions none of us wish to answer.

"What are you going to do to protect Carys until you're certain the Poles won't retaliate?"

"I'd think that would be your problem now."

Problem?

"I thought you and Carys were friends."

"We were, but I'm not friends with people who sleep with mobsters. She's done that at least twice."

I shoot her a disbelieving look. She laughs at me.

"You really believe she never fucked Bartlomiej in all that time? You really think her virgin act lasted? I never took you for a naive man, but apparently she has you just as pussy-whipped as she got Bartlomiej. There's no way she did that without putting out."

If I didn't know Carrie as well as I feel I do, Angela's words would create the doubt she's trying to stir, but I don't believe her. I don't believe Carrie lied to me about this. I choose to believe she didn't. More fool am I if I'm wrong, but I don't believe so.

I think she would have admitted that long ago. I'll tell her what Angela said, and I'll read her reaction. My family trained me to sniff out a liar, any and everywhere. She's been evasive. She's bent the truth, but she hasn't truly lied to me yet. I don't believe she'd start now.

I wanted her to explain her comment, but now my expression is impassive. I won't let her think she's rattled me since she hasn't. Let's see what she goes back and reports to Stevie and Philly. Angie ranks about as high on my list of trustworthy people as they do. I get she has a job to do, but she doesn't have to be so gleeful while selling Carrie out. She's playing the game we all do when we interrogate someone, but her game isn't as good as mine.

"Thank you for letting me know, Agent. I'll be sure to remember you so graciously educated me on this."

She can take my thanks however she wants. I said nothing verifiably threatening, so she's shite out of luck trying to prove that. She nods and puts papers on the table in front of me and hands me a pen. You better believe I go through it with a fine-tooth comb, then hand it to Dillan, who takes twice as long as I do. Not because he needs to, but to make sure they understand we aren't taking this matter lightly.

It would be wonderful if you could easily sue the government for wrongful detention and harassment. It's pathetically cliché how they've given themselves immunity from breaking their own laws. Yet, they think we're the reprobates. We have our own system of laws we adhere to, and when we don't, justice is much swifter. We've all seen that.

In my fucking case, the Cartel was swifter than us, and they stole my right to get back at Bartlomiej and Jacek. But that doesn't mean we won't still strike the Poles. This isn't over by any stretch now I'm involved. Whoever steps into their boss's role needs to come in understanding what's waiting for them, and exactly the shitstorm their predecessors left them in. This will carry on for months, and depending on how they respond to their first warning, it may take years before I'm satisfied.

"My client will sign this. I want my copies in triplicate."

"Triplicate? Mr. O'Rourke, do you think you're going to get a carbon copy?"

"No, I think I want to send a copy to Judge Hartman to make sure he realizes he no longer has the power to persecute Ms. Pritchard according to this agreement. I'd like to keep one for my records and have one to send to whomever when I need it most. A bird in the hand, and all that."

The agreement doesn't force me to confess in order to keep Carrie off their radar. It's an agreement that sets both of us free. It states there're no charges formally filed against us, while reserving the right to pursue legal prosecution in the future. It also states Carrie's release isn't dependent upon her confession to any of my alleged crimes either. Since they didn't charge us with anything, and they aren't holding us as witnesses, they can't detain us.

They could hold her for professional misconduct, but they must not have the evidence they need to take it past an accusation she could flip into a case for harassment. They can't even claim she was consorting with a known convict because no one's been arrested as an adult. My record as a juvenile was expunged.

Grandda made certain of that right before he died. One of the few things he generously did for the other guys and me. He could have let the few charges of petty theft for pickpocketing and a couple for grand larceny since I jacked cars stick as a lesson to us. However, he didn't. He saw down the road that having a record wouldn't serve us when we stepped into leadership. We try to stay off of the government's radar. Even more importantly, having a record is bad for business. It makes people wary to do deals with you when they believe you're going to get caught.

I'm eager to see Carrie, but I maintain my calm appearance as I wait in the hallway for her. It's a relief when I spot Sean coming out of the room next door to mine. The only reason they can tell us apart is because Seamus and Dillan had to officially put their names on the documents as our legal counsel. Otherwise, it would tempt us to let them take Sean and let me go, only for them to find out later they swooped up the wrong one of us.

Law enforcement's questioned us before, and we've done the same thing, which complicates police procedurals. It forces them to admit they went after an O'Rourke—any O'Rourke—when they get the wrong one of us. They loathe explaining their mistakes to their superiors when the fingerprints don't match. They're one of the few things that aren't one-hundred percent identical between the two of us. They always have to let the wrongfully detained brother off.

It royally pisses them off when we're courteous and cooperative. They'd love to pin us with resisting, evading, or striking one of them. It definitely chaps the FBI's arses when that happens because they're the ones gunning for us the most. The Attorney General's office would love nothing more than to convict any of us in the syndicate families, and there's little we love more than fucking them over.

The weight of the world lifts from my shoulders when Carrie steps out of the interrogation room. I want to open my arms to her and hug her, but that hardly works if we're trying to refute the claim we're romantically involved. At least I can offer her a smile when we get to the underground parking lot, still escorted by agents.

The cars are still waiting for us, except one of them is now a limo. I'll never get too old to have a wave of relief sweep me away when I see my dad. My mom always makes me feel emotionally safe, but my dad makes me feel physically safe, too.

Though I will say, my mom is much more apt to wage a vendetta than any of us men. My aunts are the same, so that sense of physical safety is immediate with my dad, but when I think long term, it's my mom and aunts. They'll make sure no one touches a hair on our heads ever again if we come back anything less than their perfect weans—children—they birthed.

When I look at Carrie as my dad walks toward us, I sense she'll be just as protective if we last and have kids. I never imagined I'd say yes to a proposal without having said or heard I love you first.

I don't let go of Carrie's hand as Da hugs me. I know he feels my sigh because he squeezes tighter. Sean does the same thing, and I know my dad squeezed him, too. It's harder for our mom to wrap her arms around both of us than it is for my dad, but they both manage. There's never a first and second with this sort of reunion, and neither of us ever wants to make them wait because neither of us can.

When Carrie tries to give us some space so I can wrap my arm around my dad instead of just Sean's back, I don't want to let go because I have an irrational fear she'll disappear if I do. But she shakes her hand loose. Sean has an arm around Da and an arm around me. Now I do the same. She was right. This feels way better, but I turn my head to watch her.

"Sean, Nikki's already home. I called and let her know. She's ready to fire up her computer and bring the entire American government to its knees."

My sister-in-law has the same national security grad degree my brother does, and it's come in handy more than once. I know Sean feels guilty she cut her trip short by a day, but I'm certain he's relieved to know she's still okay. She flew on our family jet, so there weren't any gate agents blocking her way. She didn't go through customs like other people would. Let's just say we have a fast-track pass for things like that.

"Thanks, Da. I'll call her when I get in the car."

They took our phones, but they had to give them back upon our release. Since Carrie isn't carrying one, I'm not worried they found anything on hers. Sean made sure all of ours are so encrypted, it looks like the only thing we do with them is play Candy Crush. I don't even understand that game.

I watch as everybody heads to all the cars but one. They're saving a town car for Carrie and me. Thank God because I can't last another minute. The moment the door closes, we're on each other. Clothes go flying everywhere within the limited space. The privacy glass is always automatically up in any town car or limo. It doesn't come down unless the passenger makes it.

The drivers can signal us, and then we can drop it. By now, anybody who drives for our family—and my guess is anybody who drives for any of the other syndicates—knows better than to drop the glass unexpectedly on a couple in the backseat. It wouldn't surprise me if half my generation was conceived in a town car.

I smile when I see she still doesn't have any panties on. She had none to put back on, but it makes me happy, nonetheless.

"Daddy, this pussy is yours."

"You're right. It is mine. And I'll do whatever the fuck I feel like doing to it. And right now, I'm starving. I never had breakfast."

"Daddy, I'm just as hungry."

I examine the surrounding space. The seat's too short for me to lie on my back easily and let her climb over me, facing the opposite direction.

"That marvelous idea may have to wait until we're home, *cailín*."

"I know, Daddy. It doesn't mean that's not what I want."

Instead, I press her backwards on the seat. I start with her forehead and kiss my way down the entire length of her body. All the way down her arms to each fingertip. Down her legs to the top of her foot which she twitches.

I realize she's ticklish. I run my thumbnail up the arch of each foot, and she squirms.

"I will tuck that little nugget away from later, *cailín*."

"I'm sure you will, Daddy. Another divine way to torture me."

"Maybe." I waggle my eyebrows at her, and she laughs.

Oh, how I love the sound of it. I haven't heard it nearly often enough, but it's smoother than the finest bourbon, richer than the finest wine.

It goes straight to my balls and makes them ache, but I'm not ready to fuck her yet. Otherwise, this will be over way too soon. I'd embarrass myself because I'd barely be inside her before I came. I need time to calm my dick down, so I feast on her. I lick her from stem to stern. I press my tongue into her pussy, flicking it back and forth until she's writhing on the seat, trying to press my head closer to her. I pull away and shoot her a warning glare. She immediately puts her hands over her head and tucks them to hold on to the edge of the seat.

"Good girl."

The happiness I see when I say that makes me want to find a reason to say it every day for the rest of our lives.

I go back to what I was doing, and she squirms again. Not because she's ticklish. This is for a different reason. It's because she's fighting not to come without my permission. I sense she's nearing frustration rather than enjoying the edging.

"Daddy, may I come? I really need to."

There's a tremble to her voice. I shift up to rest my elbows just above her shoulders. Her legs open even wider to accommodate my hips between them. Then I'm inside her.

Thank God.

We laugh when we sigh at the same time. An instant later, we're kissing. She draws back at first, not liking the taste of herself, but it doesn't stop her. There's nothing to say with words right now. We say it all with our bodies.

We're saying what we should have before she proposed. What we should say before "I do." But neither of us is ready for that. Are either of us ready for marriage?

Chapter Twenty-Four

Carrie

I'm breathless as I stare up at Shane. I sweep my gaze down the length of his body to where his joins with mine. I release the seat and tentatively run my hands up his ribs to his pecs. He balances on his left forearm as his right hand captures mine over his heart. We watch each other, neither knowing what to say.

When the car stops, and we feel it shift into park, we sit up. I peer through the window and realize two things. We've been in the car longer than I thought. We're outside the Greenwich courthouse. Shane notices at the same time I do because we're soon scrambling to get our clothes back on. I see everyone gathering on the steps, and my parents are there too.

Holy fuck.

We just pulled up to our wedding.

I glance down at my clothes. I'm in Shane's—Sean's—shorts and t shirt. The same ones I wore while my colleagues mocked me and sneered.

How shortsighted. How narcissistic.

If they believe I'm involved with Shane, then they should've thought twice about how they treated me. Even if he does nothing to any of them, they should have a healthier fear of his family. I worried about him while we were apart. My reasonable mind knew they'd never do anything to him in that building. At least not with Dillan in the room with him and Cormac and Seamus in the ones next door. But that didn't stop my worry.

It made me think about how far I'd go to defend him. I realized with what I've learned about the people in that building as well as how the agency works and how criminals get caught, I know how to get away with a shit ton of shit. As we get out of the car and join our families, I sweep my gaze over them, too. I'm already aware I'm protective of Mom and Dad because they're my parents, but I've felt a new sense of defensiveness since hearing the NYPD approached them.

I recognize Breda and Ronan, but there are two women who look like mirrors of my future mother-in-law, and two men who mirror my future father-in-law.

"Your family genetics are unbelievable. Like, you should be in science textbooks." I keep my voice down, but Shane laughs hard enough that I swat at his ribs.

"Easy, *cailín*. I laugh because the other women have said things similar to that."

I don't know who the women not related to Shane's mom and aunts are, but there are four closer to my age. I assume they're my soon-to-be sisters-in-law and cousins-in-law. I feel out of place at my own wedding. I know my clothes shouldn't matter, but they do. I look down at my rumpled outfit and try not to wince.

"Carys?" It's Saoirse—Cormac and Seamus's mom—who steps forward.

"Hi."

"Cormac and Seamus both texted me to say you and I are the closest in size. I hope you don't mind, but I brought some things you might like. The girls helped me decide."

I look at the garment bag now draped over her arm and realize she's referring to the women my age. Shane takes the bag with a kiss on his aunt's cheek. He starts to open it, but the woman introduced as Márgrég—Mair—snatches it from him.

"Absolutely not. You are not seeing your bride's outfit until she steps before that judge. Go fill out the paperwork. Her parents'll tell you her Social."

I don't expect Shane to know my Social Security Number yet, but he doesn't even know my birthday. I don't know his. Then again, he probably does since he dug into my life. I should have done the same. I don't know his favorite food. I don't know if he has any allergies. I don't know—"

"*Cailín*, we don't have to do this if you're not okay with it."

Shane's leaning over to whisper in my ear. I feel like I'm in a haze as I shift my focus from Mair to him. When our gazes lock, everything clicks. Cliché as that is, it does.

"My birthdate is April twenty-third. My favorite food is spaghetti, and I don't have any allergies."

He blinks twice before he smiles at me. He leans so close, his lips brush my ear. "My birthdate is February ninth. I don't have any allergies. And my favorite meal is you. But if I can't have that, I like cake with way too much frosting. I plan to celebrate by licking some off you tonight."

He chuckles when he sees how I flush. Not blush. Flush. Heat radiates from my cheeks. I know no one heard him. It's my erotic thoughts that match. I'm having them with his parents and mine right there. Standing, watching, knowing. Fuck my life. I'd say fuck me, but he might take me up on the offer right here, right now.

"Come on."

Mair grabs my hand as she hands off the bag to the beautiful woman with the long braids down her back and the clearest complexion I've ever seen. I know her name's Ally, and she's Finn's wife. He's almost too gorgeous to take in, and she's breathtaking. They're equally matched in beauty. It makes us mere mortals wonder if we're walking on the same planet. It makes me even dowdier.

"Do you wear makeup?" This comes from my other future sister-in-law as we walk into the restroom inside.

Nikki could have stepped off a runway in Paris. She's willowy, and I bet there's not a single piece of clothing she's ever tried on that doesn't fit her perfectly. A quiet woman passes me the makeup bag Nikki pulls from her purse.

"Thanks."

Tiernan's Seamus's wife, and something about her puts me at ease when she speaks softly.

"We're a lot. I'm the newest to join the family, and I'm still getting used to it. I think I know what you're thinking. As pretty as all of them are, their hearts are far more beautiful. Don't be embarrassed you aren't getting the heavy white dress and uncomfortable shoes with the tiara that pokes your scalp. We'll help you get ready. But honestly, Shane looks at you the same way all the husbands look at their wives. You could show up in a burlap sack —though I bet he's wishing you'd show up naked—and he'd still think you're the most beautiful woman in the world. That's how they see us. I know from the other girls—I know from myself—we don't see ourselves the way they do. For what it's worth, your dark hair, blue eyes, and fair skin that obviously tans well make you look like one of those classic porcelain dolls. The kind so special your parents say you can look but don't touch."

She grins at me, and I feel better. I never thought I looked like a doll, but I think I know what she's talking about. I have the stereotypical Welsh coloring. Dark hair, blue eyes, the dark side of fair skin, and high cheekbones. That's like saying all Scots and Irish have red hair—my new family excluded.

I obviously pass for more than just Welsh, but that's because I think most people don't know what a Welsh person's "supposed" to look like. Pasty with rotten teeth is what someone once told me. I reminded them I'm not English. Their Liverpudlian ass didn't appreciate that.

"Thank you. That means a lot. I'm feeling a little overwhelmed suddenly."

"One thing you'll realize quickly is there are few pretenses among us all. Who you are is who we want to know. Who you are is who Shane l—cares about."

She stops herself. I follow her gaze and catch Mair turning her head away. Do they know we don't love each other? Did Shane tell Dillan, and he told Mair? Can they all tell? Maybe not if Tiernan was about to say love and caught herself.

"Let's see what Mom brought you." Nikki grins as she pulls out the dresses Mair hung over the outside of the stall wall.

They vary in style from casual summer dress to cocktail. I don't know what to pick since Shane's in basketball shorts and a t-shirt like me. There's one I like, but it would be way over the top in comparison. It's way over the top for a JOP. Then again, I don't know if people wear proper wedding dresses to have a Justice of the Peace marry them.

Wait. Mom?

It's Tiernan who explains again. "We don't say anything in-law. We're just brothers, sisters, cousins, moms, dads, aunts, and uncles. I don't know how your parents will feel, but I know Aunt Breda and Uncle Ronan would love it if you called them Mom and Da. If you're not comfortable with that, then Breda and Ronan will make them happy, too."

"I've never thought about calling anyone else Mom and Dad."

My face heats again as I think about calling Shane Daddy. I definitely never imagined I'd call a man who isn't my father that. The women snicker, and I don't understand what I said that's so funny.

Ally takes mercy on me. "We don't talk about it because it's private between husband and wife, but it's not a well-kept secret. All the couples find themselves in the same dynamic. I bet you call Shane Daddy."

I stand there with my mouth hanging open for a moment before I snap it shut. I try again, but I just look like a trout catching flies.

Nikki's cool hands grasp my forearms and give them a squeeze before she speaks.

"Carys, we all call our husbands that. We've all said it louder than we intended or let it slip when we think no one's around. I promise you when you hear our husbands call us *cailín*, it's not something any of them throw around easily. It's not something any of them called a woman before meeting the one they married. If it's what Shane calls you, know he's called no one else that. But the moment he did, whether or not he realized it, he decided he'd marry you."

I try to remember when that was. I think the night we met. The night I was half-dead. The night I never wanted to leave his arms, even if I sounded ungrateful. The night I felt safe for the first time since I became an agent who goes—went—undercover.

"Thank you for explaining." I offer a weak smile, but it brightens when Mair teases me.

"Don't you dare tell Shane where you got these from. Better yet, don't tell Dillan because he'll plotz." She opens her purse and pulls out a pair of fuzzy pink handcuffs. "My guess is you both like it kinky too. I might have slipped over to a sex shop and gotten these and a few other things in a bag in my car before I went to pick up Nikki, Ally, and Tiernan."

"And we might have stopped at another store to get a few more things before helping Mom pick out these dresses." Nikki opens her purse and pulls out a paddle.

Ally and Tiernan giggle and dig in their purses. No wonder they're all carrying such big ones. Ally waves a dildo before dropping it back in her purse, and Tiernan has a set of nipple and clit clamps.

"I didn't think my bachelorette party would be in a courthouse restroom, but thank you. I—I—" I'm choking back tears. "I feel welcome."

"You are." Four voices chirp the same response.

"We need to hurry before Shane's dressed and bursting in here." I watch Mair, and it's the most serious she's been since I met her fifteen minutes ago.

"He's getting dressed?"

"You think our mom and aunts would let him show up to his wedding in shorts and a t-shirt?" Ally tsks. "Hardly."

"She talked Ronan out of insisting all the guys wear their tuxes. It is an impressive sight, which would not be low profile." Tiernan grins. "But wait until you see them all dressed up. It's—

it's—well, it's about the hottest fucking thing you've ever seen. You've seen them. They're all nearly as good looking as Seamus, so it's—"

"Ahem!" Ally hip checks Tiernan. "I'm married to the pretty one according to the other families."

Tiernan shrugs unrepentantly. "Pretty is nice. Seamus is gorgeous."

Mair snorts. "Have you seen Dillan when he's brooding? It does things to a girl."

"When isn't your husband brooding?" Nikki teases her, but she looks at me and winks. "If one is good, two is better. Our husbands are the hot ones in the family."

I glance at the door as I suck my lips in to keep from laughing. "How dressy will he be?"

"Their usual." Four voices respond once more. It's fucking uncanny.

"Tailored suit. Okay." I turn back to the dresses.

"Mmm. Suit with a vest." Nikki waggles her eyebrows at me. "If Sean looks good enough to—Well, I figured you might think something similar about Shane."

I assess the dresses again and pick one. I slip into the stall and soon shed clothes I'd gladly never look at again and step into the dress. I come out, and the smiles on the girls'—I guess I already think of them like that, too—faces make me feel confident. Someone produces a pair of shoes that are the perfect size. I didn't get to put my boots on until Angela tossed them at me once I was in the back of the DEA car. I'm glad to have something nice to match the dress. I stand in front of the mirror as Nikki and Ally do my makeup and hair. I don't resemble the bedraggled woman who walked in here.

"Thank you." I give each of them a quick hug.

"I'll check how things are going." Nikki heads out while we put the dresses back in the bag, and Ally and Mair put away the makeup.

"Fuck. I don't have a ring for Shane."

"Don't worry about that. Da took care of it." Ally looks like she knows way more than she's saying.

"They're ready."

The girls surround me, so I can't see much as we walk into the courtroom. It's like some kind of choreographed show because suddenly, my dad's next to me, and the girls are walking ahead of me. I can't see Shane, but I see the other men lined up. From right to left, it's Dillan, Cormac, Seamus, Finn, Sean, and then—

Holeee mother.

The most gorgeous man I've ever seen is standing, smiling at me. His hair looks a little damp, like he ran a wet comb through it. He's in a suit that proves he and his twin are identical because it fits him to a tee. I glance around, and I notice their dads and mine are in the same Kelly-green tie the guys are wearing. I hadn't noticed before, but Dillan, Seamus, and Cormac were in coal gray suits. Now Shane and Sean are too. Ronan, Tate, and Kieran are all in a slightly lighter, more steel gray color. The nine of them with their varying shades of red hair are enough to stop traffic. I look at Breda, Saoirse, and Siobhan. Their red hair is darker than their husbands' closer to strawberry blond. My mom's black hair is the perfect contrast to their russet.

"I trust him, pumpkin."

I look at my dad and nod. "So do I. For better or for worse in all of this, Shane is the only right choice."

"If that changes, come home. You know I never talk about it, but don't forget I met your mom when she patched me up after I nearly died during the mortar attack. I'm not a British Royal Marine anymore, but I have a long memory. Shane's not the only one who's skilled and protective."

"I know, Dad. Thank you for understanding all of this. You and Mom."

"We want you happy and safe. We see you can have both with Shane."

"We'll see."

My dad lets go of my arm and stands next to my mom as the judge begins. My parents speak when it's their turn to say they're giving me away. They're holding hands, and it makes me wonder if Shane and I will get to where they're at. I look at his parents and the other older couples. They're all the same.

My gaze meets Shane as I listen to him recite his vows. Then it's my turn. We both pledge to love, and it saddens me. I know I'm there. But I don't think he is. Yeah, he's fond of me. We definitely enjoy fucking. That doesn't change the reason we're here. He's marrying me to protect me, not because we love each other.

I can't believe the ring he slips on my finger. It's gorgeous. It's an antique style, but the diamond must be at least three carets.

"It was my nana's."

How can I accept something so special?

Nikki taps my shoulder and hands me a man's yellow gold band.

"That was my grandda's on my da's side."

Shouldn't a different couple have these? The couples who meant their pledges of devotion. It feels like we're stealing these from them, even though Cormac's the only guy left.

"You may kiss the bride."

Shane slides his arms around my waist, and I glide my hands up his biceps until I encircle his neck with mine.

"No one has ever looked more beautiful than you, *cailín*. I'm the luckiest man alive because I get to be your husband."

Before I can respond, he lowers his lips to mine. The rest of the world disappears. It's the two of us. This kiss is unlike any I've had before. Not just with Shane, but ever. I'm completely lost to it. It's perfect.

Neither of us moves to pull apart. It just keeps going until we're breathless. He cups my jaw and kisses me again once we've taken a breath. I wrap my arms around his waist. I feel the gun I should have expected. I'm certain all the men have theirs. I don't want to know how they got theirs past the metal detectors we all went through. It's a stark push back toward reality, but he doesn't let me tumble into it. He keeps kissing me.

No one rushes us, but I sense people walking away. He

brushes his thumbs over my cheeks when we finally pull apart and look at each other.

"Husband."

"Yes, Wife?"

"Just trying it out. I like it."

"So do I. I think it suits me when you're the one saying it."

"Will you call me Wife again?"

"Wife, get used to hearing it. I like it as much as *cailín*."

We gaze at each other, and something passes between us.

"Shane—"

I'm interrupted by Cormac hurrying toward us, saying my husband's name at the same time as me.

"We have to get out of here. Joey spotted some of Jacek's men in the parking lot."

"What?" I jerk backwards as I turn panicked eyes up to Shane.

"Come on, little one. We have to get you and the other women out of here."

"But I haven't signed anything. It's not legal if I don't sign."

I spin and search for the court clerk. I rush to her and snatch a pen from the desk.

"Where do I sign?"

"Congratulations. I wish you the best."

"Thanks."

It's far too curt, but I'm tapping my toes and forcing myself not to tap the desk with the pen as she puts the papers in front of me. I could sign away my first born for all I know. I don't read any of it closely. I just skim enough to know it's the marriage license then the register.

"Thanks." I mean it more this time.

Shane wraps his suit coat around me. I notice all the men have done the same with their wives. They're herding us to the back of the building where there's a larger parking lot. As we each step out, our husbands pull their guns with their right hands while using their left hands to shield their wives with the suit coats pulled up to hide us.

We're almost to the cars when I recognize the popping sound.

We run.

No one slows until we make it to the vehicles. I try to look around, but the men have formed a circle around the women, and I can't see past them. I'm disoriented as I hear a series of more shots, and none of the surrounding men fired them.

"Tate!"

I watch Siobhan push forward as her husband lurches to the side. His shirt's blossoming red along his right side. She knocks him to the ground and tears the gun from his hand. Ally and my mom wiggle their way to Tate and roll him over as the men try to get Siobhan back into the circle. I watch her lift the gun; her left hand holds it with her right cupped around the bottom of her other hand. I watch her squeeze the trigger before my gaze follows her line of fire. I spot a man I recognize stagger backward. Then he disappears as he falls to the ground. Even from this distance, I can see the wound. She shot him dead center of his heart. She shifts to her right, and she fires again. This one lands through a man's left cheekbone.

"Do you have a spare?" I whisper to Shane as he leans over me, but his upper body's twisted away from me as he searches for other shooters.

"Left ankle."

I shift, trying to reach his leg, but Mair and Dillan are in the way.

"Dillan give her mine." Shane barks the command, then Dillan's handing me a pistol butt to me.

"You do *not* expose yourself unless there's no one left to shield you, Carrie. I'm serious."

"And I'm seriously not letting one of them shoot my husband."

He drops his voice as he glances down at me, but I'm pretty certain other people hear him. "Unless you want to start married life with an arse you can't sit on for a week, stay put."

"You can't spank me if you're dead."

He stares at me for a long moment, our wills at battle once again. One day, I need to explain to Shane my resistance to telling him about my mission wasn't to protect it or even to protect me. It was always about protecting him. That's why we butt heads. It's when we want to protect each other. But neither of us wants to accept that means our partner's putting themselves in danger.

He cups my jaw in a punishing hold, not allowing me to look away. Our gazes lock while it's quiet. No one's shooting right now, but the urgency in the air doesn't ease. We stare at each other as I shift the gun in my hand to have a better grip.

He brings his lips to mine. "Feck, I love you, Carrie."

Then his kiss devours me. I fist his tie and yank down as I pull away.

"You have a nasty habit of kissing me before I can speak. I love you, too."

Hardly the romantic moment I might have wished for, but then again, I proposed via text, and we got married in a courthouse.

"We have to get Tate out of here. He's losing a lot of blood." My mom barely finishes speaking when Siobhan's string of curses would put a sailor to shame.

"Tatum, I'll kill you if you die on me. You fecking promised me a trip to the Maldives. I want that fecking little pod room in the water with the hammock. You promised."

"I know, *cailín*. Finish killing them, then we go home. I'll make it up to you while I book the trip."

I glance at Shane before looking at Dillan. Their faces are fuchsia, and I don't think it's from running. I look at the other guys my age, and they're all blushing. Ronan and Kieran don't seem to notice, and neither do Breda and Saoirse. It's only now I notice they have guns, too. Their purses are open beside them with half the contents of both on the ground.

I'm unprepared for Breda to spin on her toes and drop her weight on top of Shane, who virtually crushes me as I land on my back.

"Mom!"

Shane tries to twist, but I see a well-manicured hand on his head push it down. Then I hear a gun fire right above us and a casing falls next to my right shoulder. Another three land beside it.

"Stay down, Shane. Do as your mother says." Ronan is brooking no argument from his thirty-two-year-old son.

"Mom, I'm squashing Carrie."

The weight lightens, but only enough for me to take a deep breath. I can't move.

"Pumpkin?"

"Yes, Dad. I'm all right. You? Mom?"

I try to turn my head to see them because they're now behind me.

"Fine." It's my mom. Thank God.

I hear her speaking quietly to Ally. They're talking about keeping pressure on Tate's wound while Ally packs it with her sweater.

"Ronan, Kieran, get your brother out of here. Take Meredith and Ally."

"Siobhan—" Tate's voice sounds reedy.

"Exactly. Can you just do as you're told for once, *mo fhíorghrá*?"

Shane whispers to me and explains. "My true love."

The way he translates it. It makes me think...

"Ronan, do it. My sisters and I are fine. We'll take care of the weans. Siobhan won't stop yelling at him if you don't." Breda hasn't moved from blocking Shane and me.

I sense the hesitation before Kiernan and Ronan crawl to their brother's side because none of them want to leave their wives and children. Everyone knows the younger men won't leave their wives, even though I'm certain Dillan wants to help his dad. I'm the only one trained to stand a chance defending us in this. Tate can't move on his own, so he needs men strong enough to lift him. That means his brothers.

"Mair, take my spare."

It surprises me how strong Tate's voice suddenly sounds and that he's telling his daughter-in-law to take his gun.

"Sean, we need to get the rifles."

"Lina, stay down and let me cover you until we get there."

Everyone shifts to fill the gaps as Kieran and Ronan pull, then lift Tate. My mom and Ally follow, and my dad goes with them. It shocks me to see he has a gun, too. What kind of fucked-up world have I entered?

Shane moves off me, and I sit up. Mair, Tiernan, and I are still inside the circle. Breda, Saoirse, and Siobhan are the ones most exposed. They're shielding the rest of us. I watch Dillan take an elbow to his gut from Breda. All three of them will die before they let their children, nieces, and nephews be targets before them.

I roll onto my knees with Shane now facing away from me. I peer past him, scouting for movement. It's quiet, but none of us believe it's over.

"Seamus."

Tiernan barks her husband's name as I watch her raise her gun over Seamus's shoulder before she pulls the trigger, letting off four shots in a row. Glass shatters, then a horn blares. I shift to look around Seamus, who's easing his wife's arms down.

"Let Lina in."

Sean's voice is a harsh whisper. Nikki—I thought that was her name—maybe Lina's a Sean only thing like Carrie is only Shane's—commando crawls between Seamus and Shane. She has a rifle set on a tripod. She tilts her head, bringing her cheek close to the weapon, so she can use the sights.

I watch her inhale before her finger squeezes the trigger with the practiced hand of someone who knows it doesn't take as much force as people assume to fire a weapon. I watch my sister-in-law—the sniper—pick off men at a distance that practically defies the gun's capabilities. She's better than anyone I've ever seen. She spots men I couldn't until I watch them fall.

"Come on, Carrie. We move now before we get pinned down and can't get out."

Shane helps me to my feet, and we're all running again. I notice an SUV is gone. I spied it earlier among town cars, two limos, and another SUV. My parents, Ally, Ronan, Keiran, and Tate must have taken it.

Men run toward us, their guns drawn, but no one in my new family aims at them. One of them runs to Dillan, wrapping his arm around Mair as Dillan does the same.

"They circled us. We have a way out now, but that's why we couldn't come to you."

"We know, Joey. Get Greta in the car with my mom. Take them home."

"Dill—"

"No, Greta."

Greta? Is that like Nikki's Lina, and I'm Carrie?

"Dill—"

"No. You're pregnant. You aren't staying here."

Mair squeaks. "Dillan." She hisses his name.

"Woops. Now get in the fecking car." He sounds utterly unrepentant. I guess that wasn't something they were sharing yet.

"Mair, let's go." Siobhan pushes her daughter-in-law toward a town car.

"Only because you need to get to Tate, and it's not about me anymore. Dillan, I swear."

"I know. You aren't raising our baby alone. I love you, *cailín*."

I can't keep up with what's happening as I'm bundled into a limo with Breda, Nikki, Saoirse, and Tiernan. None of the men get into this one or any other.

"Shane!" I try to get out.

"Go, Carrie."

"Shane!"

"Go to her." Seamus calls out as he and Cormac step in front of Dillan.

My God. They're not his cousins anymore—or maybe they're not just his cousins anymore. They're guarding their mob boss. I don't doubt any of them would take a bullet for each other, but they're purposely making themselves the target. I glance at Tiernan, who's buried her face in her hands and won't watch.

"Carrie, I need you to go with them. I need to know you're safe. I can't do this if I don't."

"I feel the same. Please, don't make me go."

"This won't end here, Carrie. You can't go where I likely will. I love you."

He leans into the car and kisses me.

"I love you, too. What kind of frosting do you like?"

He grins. "Cream cheese, little one."

Then he's running after the rest of the guys.

Tiernan's dry eyed when she looks at me. She studies me for a moment.

"I know the man my husband is. I saw him. I needed that, but I wouldn't wish it on anyone else. Those memories will never leave me. He didn't want me to see what he did, and Shane doesn't want you to see that sort of thing either. Figure out a way to be okay with this because it doesn't matter who you were before today. You're a mob wife now."

Chapter Twenty-Five

Shane

I'll kill the motherfucker who ordered this. The fucker who ruined my wife's wedding day. This was already less than ideal, and now she'll forever remember this day as the first time she realized what it means to be in a mob family.

"*Ar dheis.*" To the right.

Seamus spots them first and pivots, shooting as he drops to his left knee beside a car. The rest of us fan out and do the same. We regroup.

"*Chonaic mé beirt ag rith go dtí an taobh thuaidh.*" I saw two running to the northside.

Cormac and Seamus break off and head where Cormac saw guys I didn't. I turn to my older brother. He's been quieter than usual.

"Finn? Finn! Feck!"

"What?"

Sean and Dillan call out together.

"It's just a nick. I'm fine."

"The feck it is. Let me see."

I dash to Finn's side. I spotted the blood on his shirt when his suit coat shifted as he moved to peek around a car hood.

"Stop looking at how pretty I am, little brother. Your wife'll kill me if you die because you're chasing after your big brother. *Again.*"

"Arse. Let me see." I push his hand away as I pull his shirt up.

"Is it bad?"

Sean shoots as he asks. He can't look over at us, but he's backing toward us.

"No. He told the truth for once. It's just a nick."

He played his last senior football game with a cracked clavicle he got the day before during a fight with Luca Mancinelli over Luca calling Sean and me pussies. He gave Luca a concussion that kept him out of the game, but he didn't tell anyone about his collarbone because he didn't want to be benched. No one knew until Mom spotted him taking off his padding and noticed the bruising and swelling.

Lord, I'm glad I wasn't him. I've seen Mom pissed as a kicked cobra, but that was whole other level that day. She grounded him from his car for a month, took away his phone for the three days Meredith insisted he stay in bed, and she made him clean up dog shite in the yard for the rest of the school year. But when she wasn't chewing him a new one, she was telling him stories and jokes no mom should know and singing the same lullabies she did when we were little. Anytime the pain meds wore off, she sang to him until they kicked back in.

"Stop fussing and pay attention. I'm more scared of your wife than you. You'd shoot *at* me to make a point. She'd just shoot me. She wouldn't miss."

I grin.

"*Próistí!*" Cops!

Dillan calls out as Cormac and Seamus race toward us. We book it back to the SUV left for us. I dive into the driver's seat, and Sean gets in beside me. It's a tight fit, but Cormac, Seamus, and Dillan wedge themselves into the second row until I'm peeling out of the parking lot. Finn got in through the rear door and is checking the rifles we always keep in the SUVs. Dillan goes over the back of the seat into the third row once I'm on the road. Finn joins him and hands rifles to everyone but me. Seamus props mine between the side of my seat and the center console. I have my handgun resting on my thigh as I hold it with my right hand and steer with my left.

"What the feck just happened?" I ask what we're all thinking.

"I don't know. There were too many to have followed us with no one noticing. Someone tipped them off." Sean twists in his seat to look back at the others.

"But who? None of our drivers knew where to go until they were on the road. I texted Mom once Carys showed me your reply. I knew this was the closest place in Connecticut." The vein in Seamus's left temple throbs as he speaks.

He's thinking what we all are. We're all livid someone endangered our wives. We're worried about our parents, but it's obvious they know what they're doing. This isn't their first rodeo. And it's not like the women my generation's married are shrinking violets, but none of them have lived through this. Not even the ones who come from mob families. Not even Carrie after what happened at the lumberyard. I understand now how Dillan, Finn, Sean, and Seamus felt when their wives were in danger while they dated.

I think how I feel now is another reason I didn't admit my feelings to myself. The rage coursing through me that someone attacked the woman I love threatens to consume me. It threatens to make me do something irrational and emotional. If I'd admitted how hard I fell for Carrie when it was happening, I would have done something rash, like bursting into Bartlomiej's house and killing him just for breathing in the same hemisphere as her. It would have likely gotten Carrie killed. Fuck. I nearly did that day on the trail.

"*Suas ann. Ar chlé.*" Up there. To the left.

Sean points to an SUV that's swerving. It could be someone on their phone. Or it could be someone we shot. We switched to

Irish because we never want anyone to know our signals. But we also do it because it comes as naturally as English. We frequently switch back and forth during conversations. Hell, half of us could speak Irish and the other half English during the same conversation. It happens.

I glance in the rearview mirror. No one's behind me, and the radar detector—illegal, but who gives a shite—hasn't alerted us to any speed traps. I speed up until I pull even with the car.

"Is that—"

"Motherfucker."

I don't let Sean finish before I cut in with my expletive and a stream of them in my head.

"Who is that?" Finn wouldn't know, but it'll piss him off when he finds out.

"Someone I'll kill with my bare hands for betraying Carrie."

This goes beyond what happened earlier today. This just got personal in a way this piece of shite can't possibly understand until I put a bullet between their eyes. All bets are off.

"Brace."

I glance in the rearview mirror again, then over at Sean to make sure they're all holding on with seatbelts fastened. I plow our SUV into the one carrying my target. It's sturdy, but it isn't the tank we make ours. Its reinforced frame won't stand up to ours. We have tires that roll even when punctured. We have plating on the chassis to protect us from IEDs. The windows and doors are bulletproof. There are small windows slots in the trunk that someone might think are for extra ventilation. They're so we can slide gun muzzles through them. The entire thing is a giant roll cage. We've all been in rollovers, and we've all gotten out dazed but in one piece.

All Four Families go to the same custom shop for our vehicles. It's Switzerland. The owner tries to time it, so we never run into each other. But if we do, it's neutral ground. We're on our best manners because no family can afford to be banned. It would be a death sentence. We couldn't defend ourselves from the very thing I'm doing right now. The only way to tell the different families' vehicles apart are the hubcaps which are unique like a family crest. It's handy when meetings don't work out.

I swerve harder to the left and push the SUV toward the shoulder. There's a steep drop on the other side of the guardrail. If they don't backdown and stop, I'll push them over the edge. I guarantee they won't survive the fall. If they aren't thrown from the vehicle, or impaled by something, the inevitable firebomb will kill them. That would *not* be a satisfying conclusion, but it would be unalterable.

"Get the quarter panel again. It's about to puncture the tire." Sean points to what I just spotted.

The sound of metal crunching metal makes the hair on my arm stand up. Dillan winds down his window and points his rifle at the people in the backseat. I can't see what's happening because I have to watch where we're going, or it'll be us flying over the rail.

"Ease off. I'm taking the rear tire."

I listen to Dillan and pull away enough to avoid the car when it spins out. It stops with the rear bumper against the guardrail, and the hood pointing toward the road. I box it in. They can try to push our SUV, but they're more likely to push themselves backwards over the edge. I made sure I have room to open my door, with the front tire even with their bumper. We flood out of the sides and back. Rifles pointing at the vehicle. I go to the front passenger side and pull the handle. I knew it'd be locked, but on the off chance...

I spin my rifle I grabbed on my way out of our vehicle and ram the stock into the window. Seamus comes to help me. The tempered glass holds for a while, but not forever. The moment we hear it start to give, I turn my rifle around, and Seamus steps out of the way. I shift my weight back and point the weapon at the dashboard. I fire, and the window shatters. I pivot and put the barrel to my new nemesis's forehead.

"Get the fuck out of the car on your own, or I'll drag you by your motherfucking hair." I think my parents'll forgive my language this time.

"Do you realize what you're doing?"

That gets a laugh from all of us.

"I'd listen to my brother. He's not known to be as patient as I am."

Sean's standing next to me now, his rifle pointed at the driver. None of them have reached for a weapon. They're going to die, but at least they aren't rushing us.

"Open the door and get out on your own, Angela."

She doesn't comply. Go figure. With my gun still to her forehead, I reach in and unlock the door. She goes for my hand, thinking she can pull my pinky back and distract me. She's not as fast as I am. I pull my hand back, adjust my target, and put a bullet through her right hand and into her thigh. She howls.

"Get out on your own, and you won't look like Swiss cheese. Make me say it again, and I'll torture you for the pure pleasure of listening to you beg. Then I'll find your family and do the same thing to them. Do you have kids?"

I'd never go after children. No one in my family would, and they'd never let me. But the fuck she needs to know that.

"Okay. I'll get out."

The other guys have already gotten the other passengers out. Angela struggles but gets her belt off. I move out of her way enough for her to get out of the car.

"Kneel."

As she does, I put the barrel to the back of her head and shove.

"My patience is gone. Too bad for you. Explain."

She remains silent. I put a bullet through the back of her left calf.

"Normally, I don't hurt women. Normally, I'd defend a woman. But you—you lost any chance for mercy. Finding you in this car means you wanted Carys dead."

"I'm good as dead, so what does it matter how I go?"

"You stupid bitch." I shift to bend over, so my face is in front of hers. "You have no idea the invitation you just gave me. You want to play in the big kids sandbox, now you're about to find out what it means to pick on a bully who doesn't back down. Goliath's going to win this one."

The rifle muzzle presses against her carotid.

"Finn, what'd they say?" My brother's Polish isn't fluent, but it's pretty fucking close.

"They're not feeling so chatty."

"Maybe a little truth serum will do the trick."

Dillan holds up three bottles of shitty Polish vodka. He must have found them when he popped the trunk. He hands me a bottle after unscrewing the top. He gives one to Finn, and the last one to Cormac.

Finn asks another question, but the guy stays quiet. He turns toward Angela.

"I'll ask you the same thing. Who owns the contract?"

He means now that Bartlomiej and Jacek are dead, who's keeping the mercenary contract to kill Carrie active.

Angela doesn't answer. I'm forcing my temper to remain in check, or I'll kill her before I find out what I need to know. I nod to Sean, who puts his pistol to her forehead as I grab a handful of hair and yank as hard as I can. It snaps her neck back and her mouth open as she howls in pain. I pour the vodka down her throat, not stopping as she chokes and splutters.

"You came near my wife. Now you pay."

I pour down her throat until I know she's on the edge of drowning because I don't relent long enough for her to breathe. She can't inhale through her nose while she's gasping, and every gasp just lets more vodka down her throat. The angle ensures plenty is going down her windpipe. I pause.

"Ready to talk?"

"Fuck—"

"I have a wife for that, remember? You targeted her. You're going to tell me who sent you. When I run out of vodka, I'll switch back to bullets. Who?"

"Someone who doesn't like you."

"You're going to have to narrow that down. We'll be here for days if I have to guess. Who?"

"Someone who thinks you're bad for business."

Something's off. I don't know what, but intuition's screaming it.

"Is the person you're working for the same person who's keeping the hit on?"

She goes quiet. She just glares at me.

"Two different people. Good to know."

I watch her as my mind leapfrogs from one thought to another, skipping some and doubling back to others.

"Someone paid you to infiltrate the Poles for their personal gain."

I see the surprise in her eyes, even though the rest of her expression remains neutral.

"Whoever this is wants something from the Poles, and they wouldn't mind punishing me or maybe my entire family while they're at it."

She controls her reaction this time. I pull her head back farther and pour more liquid down her throat. I let her go and let her cough.

"Let me guess, getting paid by one syndicate was good, but getting paid by two was great. You told Jacek about Carys. You're why he attacked her the first time. You're why Bartlomiej signed off on the hit, and Jacek ordered it. Did they know you were selling secrets to someone else?"

I look over her head at the men who were with her. They're taking punches to the head and torso, but none to the face. Not yet. We want to read their reactions. The guy closest to her doesn't hide his surprise like she does. He mutters something in Polish.

Finn exhales a derisive huff. "Seems she was fucking Jacek."

"Really now? Interesting considering what you wanted me to believe this morning. Jacek was a sick and deranged fuck. Was it just for the info or did you enjoy it? Did you get off on the torture? Oh yeah, we all know how he liked to torture the women whether or not they wanted it. He said 'was fucking' not fucked—as in ongoing. It wasn't a one off."

"Jacek's dead, so he can't tell you, and I won't."

"Oo. A little too much vitriol there. You had feelings for him. Does whoever sent you in there know you were getting off on company time?"

"It's not a job when you love the work." I want to smack that sneer off her face. "They don't give a fuck."

"You either blame Carys for Jacek's death, or you wish she'd died with them. It got personal when that happened. It wasn't about a job anymore."

"So smart."

"I graduated summa cum laude, so yeah, so smart. What made you turn on Carys before the plane crash?"

"You. Jacek told me about the lumberyard. Carys being with you was going to ruin it all. It did. They didn't get what they wanted, so they blew up Bartlomiej and Jacek."

"I've got the why and part of the who. Now I want to know all of it."

"Fuck off." She tries to spit at me, but I pour vodka over her face, making sure to get some in her eyes.

"Shane, look at this." Sean holds out his phone to me.

Seamus frisked her while I poured the first round. I saw him hand the phone, badge, and wallet to Sean while he emptied her gun's clip. I don't know when he got the rubber gloves from the back of the vehicle. He kicked the bullets around and tossed the gun over the rail after he made her hold it one more time. If we need to, we'll put a bullet through her head and let her drop over the cliff. Anyone finds her, and it'll look like suicide. I kept her focused on my interrogation, so I doubt she noticed what her hands touched.

Now, I'm looking at an ancestry website. Her driver's license gave Sean her name and birthdate. From there, he probably got her birth certificate and social security number.

"Which one?" I turn the phone for her to see.

The first real flash of fear registers.

"Not that close to your family after all?"

"Nothing you do can be worse than them."

"You keep inviting me to make your death more and more painful. They didn't send you in because they trusted you to do them a solid. Someone in your immediate family owes money to these distant relatives. Didn't you know lending and borrowing make for bad blood in families?"

"It wasn't about money."

I hand the phone back to Sean and put my gun back to the artery in her neck. "Keep sharing, and I'll be merciful. Force me to wait for my brother to discover this shite, and I'll make you pay for every minute you waste.

"No need." Finn puts a bullet through the guy's head who spilled the beans. "Her brother made a pass at the wrong woman."

I look at Angela, then back at Finn. "Is he dead already?"

She nods.

"You were restitution."

She nods again.

"What can you tell me to convince me not to turn you over to them?"

Her eyes widen to the point they might truly fall out. Or it would make it easy for me to pluck them out. It freaks people the fuck out when they see their own eyeball staring back at them.

"Krzysztof."

"Their uncle? He took over the contract?"

"Yeah. He doesn't care who caused the plane crash. He wants revenge because Bartlomiej loved Carys, and she betrayed him."

"You make it sound like you believe she actually did that."

"She did. She didn't have to make him fall for her. She didn't have to make him a little bitch. I told Krzysztof she's the one who shot Jacek. That sealed her fate."

"And put you in his good graces. Shite load of good it did you. You know he'd turn on you now that Jacek isn't there to protect you. If you think I'm a sick fuck, you don't know the half of it. You know he's been shot like eight times, right? Shanked at least half a dozen times in prison and knifed who the fuck knows how many times in street fights. The man will live forever. Certainly long enough to torture you, but he won't let you come like Jacek did. Who do you think taught Jacek?"

"None of that matters now."

"Mmm. Maybe it does. Maybe I'll trade you to him for Carys's life."

"He won't stop wanting her dead until she is."

"Okay. Then maybe I'll go back to my original suggestion. I wouldn't mind that family owing me a favor."

"Go ahead. They won't hurt me. I'm a woman, and even they have limits."

"She really believes that, doesn't she? She's really convinced herself of that in the last couple minutes, hasn't she?" Finn walks over to her and peers down. "You're the stupid bitch my brother called you. You were terrified of them a moment ago."

Dillan puts a bullet in the guy's chest he was guarding when Cormac went to get the gloves. He wanders over like he doesn't have a care in the world.

"She was just smart enough to get herself fucked, but not the kind she liked from Jacek. Sweetheart, the moment you got involved with a hit on a syndicate woman, you marked yourself the same as a mercenary. There's no immunity for that. It doesn't matter if the woman you went after is one of ours, not one of theirs." Dillan's patronizing tone pisses her off—which he can tell—so he laughs at her.

Seamus must be bored because he joins the conversation, too. "I'm hangry. I skipped breakfast because you forced me out of bed to deal with this shite when my bride was telling me the most fascinating story. She's a very vivid storyteller. I haven't had lunch because of the shite you caused. You're about to find out what happens to a guy who usually eats forty-five-hundred calories a day misses two meals." He juts his chin toward Cormac. "My brother doesn't have a wife, but you disturbed his morning plans, too. He missed both meals just like me. He eats even more than I do. I'd get on with it, if I were you."

"Tell you what. Tell me which woman, and I'll end it all now."

I shrug and hold out my hand with the bottle still in it as if to say, "so what'll it be?"

"Maria."

It takes a moment, then we're all laughing so hard, we sound like a pack of hyenas. I struggle to speak.

"Your brother was one dumb motherfucker. The most untouchable woman in all of New York. That's who he even looked at."

Maria Mancinelli is no princess. But she's a Mafia daughter, niece, sister, and wife. Maria's uncle is the don. Her father's their *consigliere.* Her oldest brother is the underboss. Her second oldest brother is the *capo dei capi*—basically the highest ranking general and third in line to inherit. Her husband's that brother's best friend and one of the senior most *capos.* His father is her father's best friend, and the guy's mother is her mother's best friend.

But it's more than that. Maria is like Colleen was. A woman with a kind heart and a wicked sense of humor and likely the least jaded person in her family despite being right smack in the middle of it. She loathes any syndicate man who isn't her family, but she'd give us the coat off her back if we deserved help. She's so untouchable, insulting her caused that melee that nearly got all of us killed in high school. When men kidnapped her, all the families worked to get her back before they could sex traffic her.

"I hope his death was ex—cru—tiat—ing—ly slow." I draw out each syllable.

"It was. I warned him."

"Seems nobody warned you."

I pull out my phone and unlock it.

"What the fuck do you want, you piece of shit?"

"*Ciao, cazzo d'Orro.*" It basically translates to Golden Prick or a guy a rich woman marries because she wants that dick.

"Shane, I'm busy. What the fuck do you want?"

"It's not what I want, Matteo. It's who I have who you might want."

"It's your wedding day, and you'd rather be on the phone telling me stupid riddles."

It doesn't shock me the other families know. It's the lesser syndicates knowing, like the Poles that isn't a joyous surprise.

"Remember Gianni Campenelli?"

"What about him?" Matteo's ready to hedge his bets.

"His sister just tried to kill my wife. She's still breathing. For now. I know you haven't given Maria that yacht you just bought for her birthday. Give it to my wife as a wedding present, and you can have Angela."

"You're trading her for a boat?"

"Save your indignation for the devil. It's a yacht."

A super yacht worth several million. It happens to be the one I was eyeing, and the twat knew it.

"I'm not giving you Maria's present."

"Fine. I'll kill Angela and dump her somewhere inconvenient for you."

"You're the meticulous one. You leave nothing that could be a loose end, like a body."

"Call it a gift that got lost in transit. I'll make it work."

"And what am I supposed to do with her? If she was stupid enough to get caught, then why would I want her?"

"Trade her to Krzysztof for whatever pissed you off enough to kill Bartlomiej and Jacek."

He doesn't answer.

"You have a lot to make up to me, Matteo. I'm giving you a chance to just owe me a favor. You had Angela target my woman to fuck up her investigation, so you could get to the Nowakowskis. She put Carys in Jacek's crosshairs, so she'd be out of the way of whatever you wanted, and I know you fucking know it. That's the same as you putting a hit on my wife."

"Not so great being on the receiving end, is it?"

"You motherfucking shite stained cum dumpster. We fucking helped you get Maria back, and we made sure she got her vengeance."

"That doesn't make up for—"

"The fuck it doesn't. You did this because of me and a bet we made when we were twenty. It's not my fault your dad found out.

You've waited this fucking long to get back at me, and like a little bitch who's been sulking, you knew I was too much for you, so you went after my woman. You better fucking hide behind Maria because if I get hold of you, I will finally do what I've been threatening since we were thirteen, and you broke Sean's brand-new phone and got me blamed for it. You petty, whiny little bitch. I will take it *all* from you."

I thrust my hand out, and Sean gives me his phone. I fire off texts in the minute Matteo's silent.

"You don't scare me any more than you did when we were twenty. I may have lost the bet that cost me that Ferrari, but you're the one who broke his arm crashing it just to beat me across the finish line."

I don't pay attention as he rambles. It buys me a few more minutes. I interject here and there to keep him going until I'm ready.

"I hope Maria's at work." I know she is. "Because it'll be awfully sad if she's at home." I know he's not there either.

"What the fuck did—"

I hear an alarm go off in the background. It's handy having your family live in the same neighborhood as your enemies. It means you have guards around to run errands.

"Shane!"

"Not my fault your guards don't know how to look up."

Sean's house is the closest, and he just got a very expensive drone that does more than take photos. Matteo doesn't have many windows left.

He goes silent, and I'm certain he's scrambling to figure out what I've unleashed. I hear a phone notification ping in the background.

"You will—"

"What? Hmm? What now, Matteo?" I'm patronizing as fuck.

"What the fuck did you do to my Bronx project?"

"You should lock up your demolition supplies better."

We have people at the station working some low-level Cartel guys over. Matteo's an architect, and he has a venture capitalist breathing down his neck to finish a project that fell behind. Now it fell apart.

Great coincidence it was a block from the abandoned train station where we handle our most unsavory tasks. I send one more text. The line remains quiet except for the sound of his fingers on his keyboard. Then he erupts.

"I'm the petty bitch? You *mi fa cagare*!" It means you make me shite. He basically called me despicable.

"If I can't have it, then neither can you."

"You had someone blow up the fucking yacht, *faccia de cazzo*!" Testicle face.

"Yup. I was going to steal it today anyway, so my guys were there already." I had. It wasn't until I waited for Carrie to come out of the restroom that I thought to give it to her.

"Enough! Kill Angela or do whatever the fuck you want. I don't give a shit. I don't have time to deal with her today. But don't go near Maria. I'm serious, Shane. Things are different now. If she was untouchable before, you have no idea what my family will do if you upset her even for a second."

That makes me stop. "Is she pregnant?"

"Yeah, and high risk, so stay the fuck away."

The call's on speaker. We all hear the catch in Matteo's voice. I look around at the guys. They all nod.

"Do you need anything? I know she knows Ally already, but should Finn tell her to talk to Maria?"

My sister-in-law's a neonatologist, not an OBGYN, but they're also friends. Ally's pregnant too.

"No, but thank you."

"Should our moms send over food?"

Matteo chuckles, the tone a hundred-and-eighty degrees from what it was a moment ago. "No. Our moms have already made enough to keep us fed till the second coming."

"So, she's not in any immediate danger?"

"No. She needs to take it easy, though."

"Then I guess Carmine'll have to make up for it."

"You sick fucker."

"I like your wife. I don't like any of the rest of you. Killing you will stress her out. She loves her cousin, but he's not you or her brothers. He also works closest to you. If I fuck him over, then I fuck you over without messing up a hair on your fucked-up looking head."

"What do you want, then?"

"Well, the yacht's not an option. We'll take the high-rise project you just got in Brooklyn. The incoming shipment from Jamaica. And I'd like that house Carmine just got Serafina on Corsica. That can be Carys's wedding present."

"You—"

"Decide or I blow up more shite, Matteo. I have bodies to dump. Either we make them disappear or make you do it. I want to get back to my wife."

"I'll do you one better."

"I doubt it."

"I found Enrique's new lab."

I glance around the group again. If Matteo's telling the truth, we could make billions between the product we take and what Enrique's competitors would pay for us to shut it down.

"Let's be clear. This doesn't make us good, Matteo. It makes me not blow anything else up. I won't forgive or forget what you did. We've never liked each other, but I was never the shite stirrer. You went after my woman before you could know who she would become, but you could have called it off. You didn't. Fuck me over on this deal, and you're going to explain a lot more to Salvatore than selling a lab.

"Fine."

"Fine." There's a long pause before I do what I know my mom would expect. "Sláinte to you and Maria. Pass all of our best wishes to her. We wish her a healthy and safe pregnancy and delivery."

"Thank you."

"For your baby—" I look at the guys. We know what the right thing to do is, even if it might kill us. They speak with me. "May God grant you always a sunbeam to warm you, a moonbeam to charm you, a sheltering angel, so nothing can harm you. Laughter to cheer you, faithful friends near you. And whenever you pray, Heaven to hear you."

"Th—th—*grazie*." Thank you. They switch between English and Italian like we do English and Irish.

"Last chance for Angela."

"Do what you want with her."

Chapter Twenty-Six

Carrie

I want to pace.

Mom and Ally already had the bullet removed, and Uncle Tate knocked out with pain meds by the time the rest of us got to Aunt Siobhan and Uncle Tate's house—I'm already thinking of them that way. I always claimed my mom was a bit of a prepper with the souped-up first aid kit in her car and the doctor's satchel that weighs like ten pounds. Now I understand why. We walked in the house, and she had a miniature surgical theatre set up in the dining room.

We've been here for three hours, and no one's heard from the guys. We've eaten and watched a movie. We've taken turns sitting with Aunt Siobhan since she won't leave Uncle Tate's side. My heart aches for her. Her husband's unconscious after being shot, and she doesn't know if her son's okay.

I understand any sons Shane and I might have are so far down the line of succession I'll never know—not truly—how she feels knowing her son's responsible for an organization with thousands of people who depend upon him. I don't yet understand what Aunt Saoirse and Mam—Breda—it doesn't feel right to call her

Mom in font of mine—experience as mothers either, but I understand how we all feel as wives.

Nothing I've done up to this point in my life prepared me for this. I'm holding my shit together, but only because I don't want anyone to think me weak or to draw attention to myself. I found out Ally's pregnant, too. The two top men in the organization have pregnant wives, and they're possibly dead to protect me. Guilt chokes me every time I think that.

Mam—even easier to think than I imagined—guessed my thoughts an hour ago and did her best to reassure me I'm wrong. But I'm not. I—

"Where's my wife?"

I don't know whose voice is whose because all five blend.

"Where's my mom?" Cormac.

The man's funnier than you'd guess. I discovered that at Shane's place while we waited to go to Sean's house.

Fortunately, Aunt Siobhan and Uncle Tate's house has a massive foyer. Probably for moments like this. Husbands lift their wives off their feet, and wives cling to their men. Their parents give us space, but I can only imagine how badly they want to hug their sons.

"Daddy." I exhale the word as he holds me so tightly I struggle to say more. "Greet your parents. Then come back to me. I don't want to rush."

"No. Kiss, Wife."

I obey the command, and it's like air's finally pumped back into my lungs. When we pull apart, he nods to my cocked eyebrow. He puts me down, and I step out of the way. Ally and Nikki must think the same thing as me. We move aside as Mam and Da engulf their sons.

She's sandwiched in the middle as her arms somehow wrap around Sean and Finn with Shane in the middle. Da's head is above all the others. The sons rest theirs on her shoulders or head. He lays his hand on Shane's head. I watched it shake as he put it there.

This never gets easier.

That's daunting and heartbreaking.

I watch Aunt Siobhan hug Dillan before she and Mair lead him to the dining room to see Uncle Tate. Aunt Saoirse and Uncle Kieran hug Cormac and Seamus as Tiernan comes to stand beside me. I like Ally, Nikki, and Mair tremendously already. But I feel drawn to Tiernan, and I hope we grow closer. I wish that with all the girls, but she and I just seem to have clicked.

The husbands and wives drift together after parents and sons reunite. The parents head into the living room, but before I understand what's happening, Shane and I are following the other couples upstairs. I glance over my shoulder and watch Cormac come out of the kitchen with the vat of potato salad Aunt Saoirse made. He lifts his fork in a "cheers" to me.

"I hope you get a stomachache, greedy guts."

I don't know how Shane knew.

"The man is a bottomless pit. I'm certain the shite's vegan, so no one'll take it from him."

"It is. How'd you know?"

"He's the cleanest eater. He read some article about processed foods when we were kids. He refuses to touch fast food. It's a good thing Uncle Kieran likes to bake because he had to make all Cor's birthday cakes. Spoiled rotten."

I glance back again as Cormac swallows an insanely heaping forkful, then winks and grins at me. I laugh, but everyone else is soon forgotten as Shane kicks the bedroom door shut behind him. We're pulling each other's clothes off, leaving a trail of them to the bed. We stop when I bump into it. Something catches his eye because he looks around my shoulder, then at me. I giggle.

"The girls made sure I had an impromptu bachelorette party in the courthouse restroom." I came up here earlier and spread out the gifts.

He picks up the dildo, shock radiating from him.

"Ally."

I whisper the name since she's his sister-in-law. No. Scratch that. Sister. No qualifiers in this family.

"I don't know if I'm supposed to thank her."

"Don't worry. I already did. I have some thoughts about that and a few other things here, too."

"Oh?"

I reach behind me and feel around for the ball gag. I hold it up.

"Tiernan said she didn't know it would come in handy so soon, but she suggested I might want to wear this tonight." I waggle my eyebrows at him.

"She did?"

He's completely stunned, but he finally shakes it off. Then he looks like a kid in a toy store—an adult toy store. He holds various items up. He even shakes a few in their packaging. His eyes light up at the two pairs of handcuffs. Apparently, Nikki didn't know Mair had picked out a pair, so I wound up with two.

"Stay here. Shh."

He grabs his pants and pulls them on as he hops to the door. He opens the door a crack, then sticks his head into the hallway. He disappears, but he's back two minutes later with a broom. I furrow my brow as he locks the door behind him. He kicks off his pants and rips into the dildo's packaging. Then the nipple clamps. He looks around, finding what he wants. He snatches the lube and shakes it. But then he freezes.

"Is this what you want, Carrie?"

"Of course. Why else would I put this out?"

"You want this for you, not just for me, right?"

"I want it for both of us."

"Oh, *cailín*. The hours I've had to daydream about handcuffing you to my bed. Such sweet dreams."

"Um, there's something for you too."

"Isn't this all for me?" He shoots me a lopsided grin.

"Well—uh—the girls said—they didn't assume anything—more like they thought it might be kinda fun—um. Shit."

I hold out a package I don't think he noticed. That or he purposely ignored it.

"A rooster?"

He splutters as he looks between me and the cock ring that fits over at least part of a guy's dick.

"It's ribbed."

"I see that."

He points to the package.

XXL.

"Who picked this out?"

"I believe that was a collective effort."

I peek down at his cock, then the toy named for that part of his anatomy.

"I don't think it's going to be big enough. I don't want you to totally lose circulation."

"Hmm."

Shane leads an assault on my neck, licking, nipping, kissing along it until I'm grasping his biceps to keep my balance. When I turn my head, he honors my silent request. His lips meet mine, and if ever the Big Bad Wolf were going to gobble up Little Red Riding Hood, it would be now. I'm growing lightheaded because I can't suck in enough air. My fingers bite into his arms now. It must register with him because he pulls away.

"Where do we start, *cailín*?"

"I want you to pick, Daddy." Partly because I don't want control right now, and partly because I can't think straight.

After what happened today, some wouldn't understand how I could relinquish more control since it was pure madness earlier. Someone like me would normally have a death grip on any control I could clench. But this is an interlude with my husband. The man I trust above any and everyone else. I want to let go of my fear and know I'm safe now. I want him to have control after a situation where everyone he loves most was in danger. I can't imagine how he felt.

I know my need's intensity, wanting to protect him and my parents and caring about my new friends and family. But I don't know the others the way he does. They aren't as significant to me *yet*. A situation like that is every man in this family's worst nightmare. I want Shane to know my trust hasn't wavered.

"My sweet *cailín*, that's like telling me everything in Santa's workshop is for me. We may never leave here if I get to choose. Turn around."

I obey and cross my wrists at my lower back. It surprises me when he pulls them apart.

"No, little one. You're not my sub. You're letting me take command, but I don't want this to be about what only I'll give and you must accept. I want you to know you can touch me however and whenever you want. I need you to."

I turn my head to look over my shoulder at him. I understand something I didn't before this moment.

His control isn't his strength. At least, not entirely. It's as much his vulnerability as it is his strength. Or rather, he's letting me see how vulnerable he feels even when he has control and dominates me. He leads us, but he needs to know I follow because I want this, not because I automatically relent to have this dynamic. That I'm not giving in to please him but agreeing to it as his equal.

"Daddy, you may have unleashed a Stage Five Clinger because I'll never let go if that invitation stands."

He kisses the back of my shoulder, then busses a quick kiss on my lips.

"I love you, *cailín*."

"I love you, Daddy."

I place my hands on the bed in front of me and lean forward. I watch him rip the tag off the paddle before he grabs the fuzzy handcuffs. He trails the artificial feathers up my left arm and over my shoulder before drawing them down my back, alongside my spine. The feel is ticklish and erotic. When he gets to my lower back, he sweeps them over the top of my ass. He pulls my ass cheeks apart and glides his cock along the length of the division. His fingers bite into my flesh as he tosses the handcuffs back onto the bed. It's enough to make me come onto my toes.

"What's your safe word, *cailín*?"

"*Digon*, Daddy."

I think about his attempted Welsh, and it warms me down to

my toes. I should have recognized his feelings then. I should have accepted mine. Right now, that doesn't matter because we're together.

His left hand presses between my shoulder blades, guiding me to lie on the mattress. He takes my arms and draws them over my head. He cuffs them, tugging them apart to test the cuffs. I watch him pull the key out, and when he moves, I assume he's putting it on the bedside table. He wraps his hands around my waist, dragging his thumbs up each side of my spine as he raises them until he slides them under my body and cups my tits. He massages them before tugging on my nipples. Pinching and twisting until I shift my weight from foot to foot. He lets go.

His long arms reach past me and snag the ball gag and blindfold.

"If you get too loud, then I'll gag you. But for now, I want to hear my name. I want to hear you beg Daddy for each orgasm I give you. And you will beg, little one. They belong to me—just like you do—and I decide when I'll give them to you." He drapes his body over mine, interlocking our fingers, his voice quieter. "You know I belong to you just as much, right?"

"Yes, Daddy. That's more precious to me than I can describe."

"I've never wanted this with anyone else, and I'll never want it with someone else. It's only ever been you, Carrie. Only you."

"God, I love you."

"I love you too, baby."

He reaches between us and taps his dick on my ass three times. Then he stands and slides the blindfold over my eyes.

"This spanking is for our pleasure. It's not a punishment. I know you could have argued with me today, and I know you have the training to handle a situation like that. But thank you for not insisting. I wouldn't have concentrated on anything but you if you'd stayed. That would have endangered all of us. Thank you for understanding that."

I can only sense when he picks up the paddle, but I don't know when he'll start.

Mother trucker!

Apparently, he's starting now. I stomp my foot as I squeeze my eyes shut behind the mask and clench my jaw.

"Ten spanks, Carrie. Nothing more. I won't go until I'm tired."

Thank God because that wouldn't be until next week. I suck in lungfuls of air through my nose, struggling not to scream. He's spanked me before, but not with a paddle, only his hand. Sweat drips beneath the mask and would burn my eyes if they were open. I don't realize how tightly I grip the comforter until my fingers cramp. He's in no rush, so the fire in my ass has time to burn.

Fuck. That was only six. I'm barely more than halfway. Does he think he's playing tennis with my ass?

When he lands the paddle across my horizontal crack, I turn my head into the bedding to smother my scream.

"Carrie?"

"I'm—I'm okay, Daddy."

"Don't lie to me, or this spanking will have a different purpose. If it's too much, say so. If I harm you—Just don't let me harm you."

"I know, Daddy."

I can take more, even though the pain's more than I imagined. I just need to get used to it. When the tenth one comes, he nails my horizontal crack and the meaty part of my ass. Except it feels like all the padding I usually think I have disappeared. I doubt I'll sit comfortably for a week.

"Carrie, talk to me. Are you all right?"

"Yes, Daddy. Give me a moment, then do whatever you want next."

He hesitates, and I hear the uncertainty in his voice. "If you say so."

His hand caresses my ass. Before I met him, I never imagined a man like him could be so considerate. He has been since the night we met. He nudges my legs apart, then he's kissing the welts and blowing cool air on them. He tips my hips back to him and licks my cunt.

Fucking relief. I moan and want to reach back to press his head closer, but I can't with my wrists cuffed. He licks and sucks my clit until I'm restless. I open my mouth to ask if I may come, but the words never come out. It's a scream instead. Not enough to wake the dead or even disturb anyone else, but it's my reaction to the clit clamp.

He stands and helps me straighten. My nipples are tight and hard, so he easily clamps those too. He turns us, so I know we're facing the mirror over the dresser. He brings my arms up and loops them over his neck before he removes the blindfold. To get my arms over his head, I must stretch. It pulls my belly taut and pushes my tits out.

I marvel at our appearance together as his hands roam my body. He's possessive, touching me however he wants, his hold on me keeping me close because he can. Everything about how we stand and how his hands glide over me screams *mine*. Nothing will stop him from having what he wants. I certainly won't try to because this is the most arousing experience of my life. I've never felt more desirable than I do right now.

"I crave you, Carrie. I will never get enough of you. I will never tire of the feel of you because it's you."

He dips his head and kisses my cheek. Then he lifts me and lays me on the bed. He unlocks the handcuffs and moves my arms around, rubbing them to get the circulation back into them. He's slow—watching me like a hawk—as he brings my arms back up over my head. He leans forward and kisses the bare skin above my pussy. I just got waxed a couple days ago. I'm glad I did.

He flicks the clamp with his tongue, making it vibrate. It sends a shot of need through me that makes my pussy clench. Fuck. I need to get off. I watch as he attaches a set of handcuffs to each ankle before pushing my legs as far apart as I can. The pressure on my ass as it shifts on the comforter steals my breath. I squeeze my eyes shut and breathe through it. He grabs the broom and slides it through the empty manacle on each set. It's an improvised spreader to keep my legs apart.

He rips open the dildo package and inspects it. He looks around and spots the foaming toy cleaner that came in the same package as the lube. He's in no hurry as he goes to the bathroom and washes the toy. I love watching him walking away, but it's even better when he's walking back. He's impossibly hard, and I have an overwhelming desire to suck him off. I want to feel the weight of his cock on my tongue. I open my mouth, turning my head toward him as he approaches.

He cups my head with his right hand as his left angles his dick into my mouth. He presses my head forward as he rocks his hips. The pressure is light on my head, just a reminder. But I want more than that. I let go of the headboard I'd grasped and wrap my hands around his chiseled ass. I push, wanting his dick deeper. He draws back and thrusts hard, making me choke, but I don't ease the insistence I show as my hands tighten around his taut ass.

"I'm going to come down your throat just so I can last through all the things I'm still going to do. It's the only way I'll have some restraint, or I'll fuck you to get off rather than spoil my wife. You are too fucking tempting, little one."

I suck harder, trying to relax enough to swallow him. I've only managed that with a guy once or twice. It'll take some practice since Shane has way more to offer than any guy in my past. I watch him grab the headboard to prop himself up as his other hand holds my head in place. He thrusts hard one more time, forcing me to fight my gag reflex. Then I taste him. I choke on his cum, and he pulls out, helping me sit up.

"Thank you, Daddy."

"I think I'm supposed to be saying thank you, *cailín*."

"Thank you for letting me have a moment of control and changing your plans. Thank you for letting me do something for you. You could have put my pleasure first and refused me. You could have put your desire for control first and refused me. I needed this."

He cups my face and brings ours close together. "I will always give you what you need. I love you. I'll endeavor to give you everything you want, but that I can't promise."

"I know, Shane. I'm a simple girl. All I need is a roof over my head, some food to eat and clothes to wear, and your cock in my cunt every day." I grin.

I lie back against the pillow. He squeezes my right breast before swirling his tongue around the clamp. He tightens each, and I arch my back off the bed. Fuck me. Those fucking hurt. He watches, making sure I'm still all right. I nod. Without preamble, he thrusts three fingers into me. I know he sees how wet I am even though it's been several minutes since he touched me to arouse me. But sucking him off, and him holding my head in place was arousing as fuck.

He works my cunt until I'm sloppy, and the dildo slides in easily. My sister made an excellent choice. Ten inches for the win, even if it's still not as good as Shane. He works my pussy with it, drawing me closer to the edge. I want to squeeze my legs shut, trapping his hand and the dildo in place, so I can come. But the makeshift spreader doesn't allow it when he presses his elbow on it to keep it in place.

"Daddy, please. I need to come."

He pulls the dildo out and slaps my pussy.

"No."

We go around and around until I'm thrashing. My entire body burns with the need to get off. Well, my ass burns from the spanking, but the rest of me burns from needing to feel him inside me.

"Daddy, I need to come. I need to feel you inside me. Please, Shane."

He watches me for a moment before he nods.

"Roll over."

He helps me get on my hands and knees, then removes the ankle cuffs and puts the broom aside.

"We don't have any plugs to stretch you. Can you take it if we don't?"

"Yes."

He dribbles lube into my ass and over his cock. He's gentle as he eases into me, giving me a chance to adjust. But once he's inside me, he grabs the dildo. Fuck. He's going to DP me with it.

"Can you do this?"

"Yes." Eager much?

He slides the dildo into my cunt and holds it in place as his other hand removes the clamps from my nipples and clit. Then he's thrusting his dick and the dildo, and I'm hanging on for dear life. The sensations are building too fast. The blood rushing back into my nipples and clit, my sore ass that's too full of him, and my aching pussy. All of it makes me lightheaded. I close my eyes to breathe through it, but that only makes it worse. I need something to fix my attention on. I look at the pillow, but my arms shake. Dots dance around the edges of my vision. I wheeze as I draw in air.

"*Digon.*"

I fear he can't hear me, but everything immediately stops. He pulls the dildo from me, but he's so careful as he pulls out. Then I'm in his arms, and he's cradling me against him.

"Carrie, what's wrong? What hurts? What's wrong?"

He repeats himself, and I think he's going to panic.

"Daddy, it was too much. I got lightheaded. I liked all of it, but it was just more than I could take."

"I'm sorry, *mo ghrá*."

"What does that mean?"

"My love. I should have thought about everything that's happened over the past two days. You must be exhausted. I pushed you too hard."

"I wanted it. I didn't think about what happened, and how the strain might add up. I don't regret any of this. I don't want you to, either. I want all of it again, but maybe when I'm a little more rested."

His expression screams reluctance. He's doubting this dynamic. I struggle to sit up.

"Shane, I need us to be this way. You need it too. I'm not upset. I want nothing to change. Yesterday and today were *not* typical days. Don't measure our kink and how I handle it by these two days."

He holds me like the night he carried me out of the construction site. I don't fear falling as he moves us, so he can lean against the headboard, his legs stretched out. He grabs a pillow and tucks it under my ass, so his legs don't feel like planks under it.

"I should have gone easier on your arse. I underestimated my strength."

"But I know you were being careful. We're learning each other, Daddy. Another day, and it would probably be fine. I see how guilty you feel. Just hold me. I don't want you to look back on this part of our wedding day with the same shit memories as you will after what happened earlier today."

His expression shutters. It's like I just watched a mannequin replace my husband.

"Shane, what happened earlier?"

"I don't want to tell you right now. Not on our wedding day and not when you had to safe word. But if I don't, it'll piss you off that I kept it from you."

I don't like the angle I'm trying to see him from. I shift to straddle his legs, and he moves the pillow for me to sit on. I'd rather feel his legs touching me, but my ass hurts too much. He's being conscientious.

"It wasn't just about the Poles who came for us. It's who was with them."

"Was, as in, we're talking about something that already happened? Or was like they're no longer alive?"

He stares at me. He won't confess to the crime. Not because he doesn't trust me or wants distance between us. I believe some of it comes from training. I think most of it comes from not trusting I'm really safe from law enforcement or testifying. What I don't know, I can't repeat.

"Who was it, Daddy?"

He's scaring me, and he can tell. He pulls me against his chest and kisses my forehead while running his hand up and down my back. His other hand rests close enough for me to sense a hint of his touch on my ass but not actually on it to avoid hurting me.

"It was Angela, *cailín*. She was the one who sold you out to your bosses and to Jacek."

"Angela? That's—that's not possible. How? Why? I know you wouldn't lie to me about this, but that's virtually impossible to believe. That's so—that just makes her not the person I thought she was. Then again, I suppose she could say the same thing about me. I don't necessarily have a leg to stand on for that. Why? Why would she do that to me?"

My thoughts tumble out, some incomplete and others repeat.

"Apparently her brother was involved with the *Cosa Nostra*, and he made some bad choices about who he showed an interest in. He paid the price for that. They asked more of her family than just him for restitution. They sent her to infiltrate your investigation, and she wound up involved with Jacek."

"Involved? You mean as in fucking involved?"

"Yes. But it seems, at least for her part, she believed there was some genuine affection with him."

"That psychopath?"

"She loved him."

"That says more about her than anything else."

When he stares at me, it makes me realize he must think he's at least a little like Jacek. It makes me a hypocrite to love him and accept the things that he does when I can look down on Angela for the things she did.

"Shane, you are *nothing* like Jacek. You do what you do because that's your responsibility. You do what you do to protect the people you love. Jacek claimed he did the things he got up to for the sake of his people and for the sake of his family. And maybe that was some of it. But he *enjoyed* what he did. He was a sick, twisted fuck. You are not. You don't revel in it. You don't think it's a great pastime to torture people. He did. He got off on those things."

"I know. Angela basically admitted as much about her physical relationship and that she enjoyed some elements of torture."

"You discussed their sex life?"

"No, not in detail, but just enough to get a sense of their dynamic. And you're right, it isn't—or it wasn't—like ours. But I see much of myself in Jacek, or much of Jacek in me, I suppose."

"Maybe two sides of the same coin, but not the same. There's only one person who's a mirror image of you. And it sure as fuck was *not* Jacek Nowakowski. If Angela was involved with Jacek, was she the one to feed his doubt? Make him question me?"

"Yes. She was already telling him things about you that caused him to attack you the first time. I'm certain she figured out more about us, or at least sensed something changed in you and told Jacek about it. He would have dug deeper, especially once he saw us together at the lumberyard."

"But that was entirely coincidental."

"It was, but I'm certain now he followed us after we left there. He knew about us going to the warehouse together."

I reflect upon that and remain quiet for a moment as I absorb everything he's just told me. It's a lot to comprehend when I realize the betrayal I committed, the betrayal Angela committed, and wonder whether I can find any way to justify hers the same as I justified mine. But I really can't.

"You discovered she was working for the Italians and betrayed me to the Poles because of her feelings for Jacek or to pass information along to the Italians. I don't understand that part."

I know whatever Shane's about to explain will be complicated. I pray I can follow along.

"The Italians certainly knew what went on and what the repercussions were by sending Angela in once I entered the picture. They could have called it off, or they could have told her to leave you out of it. But they didn't. Even if they didn't explicitly tell her to target you, their silence was consent. I've made them aware I don't appreciate that."

"What does that mean, Shane? You made them aware? How?"

He looks at me again. His expression shutters once more, and I know these are questions he won't answer. I'm putting him in a shit position, asking and wanting him to. It's stuff he won't tell me because I'm not a man. I'm not a mobster. And because he loves me and wants to keep me safe. That's always been his goal. His motivation all along has been protecting me.

"Is it done?"

"*Cailín*, it's never done. It will never be done. This skirmish might be over, but the war hardly is. I've made sure the *Cosa*

Nostra understands I'm not okay with what they did. That you are off limits. We also found out Maria Mancinelli's pregnant, and it's high risk. She's friends with Ally since they're both doctors and knew each other from residency. Moving forward, we're going to have to consider what that means for our business deals that involve the *Cosa Nostra*. We've all known Maria since we were toddlers. None of us wants to endanger her by causing her more concern than we have to, but men's business is still men's business. I ensured her husband knows he can't hide behind her."

"Her husband?"

"Yes, it was Matteo. He was the one who orchestrated this because Angela's brother hit on Maria."

We fall silent again as I try to come to terms with all of this. I believe I understand it. Now I have to accept it.

"If you've retaliated, does that mean they're going to retaliate against your retaliation? Does it mean I've put you in more danger because you had to prove you won't back down?"

"No, you did none of this, Carrie. None of this was your fault. If it hadn't been you, it would have been something else. You're just the excuse they needed to feck with us. That was part of what made me so angry. There were many things they could have chosen instead of you. They still could've had Angela in there messing with Jacek without her feeding information about you to him."

"What does this mean going forward? I get what you said about Maria and her pregnancy, but what about me? Am I still one of their targets?"

"No. I believe Matteo understands how he feels about Maria is how I feel about you, and how he reacted is how I did. We're back to our homeostasis of a stalemate."

I can only nod to that, but there's more I want to know.

"We didn't say we love each other until after we got married today." We married today for convenience because I'd become inconvenient.

"I wish that were different, *cailín*."

I hold up my hand to calm him. "I know, and so do I. But

that's not what I'm getting at. We both love each other, and I know how I feel about you is why I ultimately asked you to marry me. And I think how you feel about me is why you ultimately said yes. If we didn't feel this way, then the need to protect each other wouldn't be so strong. Now that we're married, they shouldn't be able to make us testify against each other, but that doesn't mean they couldn't still put either of us on trial. It doesn't mean there aren't plenty of other people who could testify against us."

"That's true, but that protection goes beyond they can't compel us to testify against each other. There's a reason all of us walk free every day. Who wants to testify against my family? No one who hopes to live to be an octogenarian. While you weren't entirely off-limits to the Four Families—I hate saying that—but so much worse could have happened if you hadn't met me. I know a lot of what you went through was because of me. But our marriage gives you protection you wouldn't otherwise have from other syndicates. The lesser syndicates know better than to test us. They live at the largesse of the Four Families, so they can't afford to ruin any relationships they have or create trouble where there was none."

I open my mouth to disagree, but it's his turn to hold his hand up for me to wait.

"As for the other families, like it or not, for better or for worse, if a woman's accused of crimes and put on trial, they will step back and not help the government. While we might feed some information to the DAs in order to screw each other, overall, the code among all the families is to never help law enforcement and to never help the government. Even if it means missing an opportunity to knock rivals down a peg or two. As for other people providing evidence to hold against you, I'm concerned. But I'm not scared now that you're an O'Rourke."

"But that doesn't stop the government from pursuing me anyway or using me to leapfrog to get to you."

"I know, and I need you to trust I'll take care of that."

I bite my bottom lip. I know what he means by trust him to take care of it. I don't want to ask questions. I'm good with not knowing. But I wonder if life will allow me to remain in the dark. I can't guess the future, and I don't want to. Understanding what happened today and the weeks leading to our wedding day eases my fear. It makes me appreciate Shane even more.

I don't know how I became so lucky, but I won't take for granted the man who loves me. The rest of the world doesn't matter when we're like this. When I'm in his arms. Peace settles over me now that we've all lived to see another day. Cliché and maybe even trite, but so true. I gaze into my husband's eyes, and I've never meant anything more.

"I trust you implicitly, Daddy."

"Then let Daddy do wicked, wicked things to his bonnie bride."

"Mmm. I love the sound of that, and I love you."

"I love you too, *cailín*."

Epilogue

Shane

It's been a month since Carrie and I married, and it's been a shockingly quiet one, all things considered. The first week we were married, we faced the DEA trying to raid us in four different locations. Every time, they came up empty-handed.

Every time, we thumbed our noses at them. When their fifth attempt wound up with them in a shootout against some Armenians, we knew they were growing too frustrated to continue. This particular campaign wasn't worth it to them.

At some point, they'll regroup, and they'll come after us again, but it won't be to retaliate against Carrie. Three days after the wedding, she put in her formal notice effective immediately—not that it surprised anyone. They called her in for an exit interview and tried to question her about our relationship. They wanted details about our marriage, but she remained mute. Eventually, the guy in HR gave up on his line of questioning.

Then Phil Hammond called her into his office, where he and Director Spenser both laid into her and tried to guilt her into admitting I forced her to marry me. That she did it against her will, and they could protect her. When they realized that was to no avail, they changed course and started threatening her with charges against her all over again, saying she would be my downfall, and she'd be the reason I wound up in prison. And not just me, but my entire family.

She told me afterwards she remembered the conversation we had the day I told her about Angela. They could try, but no matter what, my family and I have the resources to ensure no one succeeds and gives enough evidence to make charges stick. She felt reassured they'd realize the grievous mistake they made by trying to go against my family.

We've just arrived home from our honeymoon, and her boxes are lining the living room of the new house we just bought next door to Bogdan Kutsenko. Unfortunately, an unaffiliated family swiped up the home we really wanted from under our noses.

By the time they realized who'd wanted the home, we'd already accepted we wouldn't get it, and paid cash for the only other house we liked. We just have the misfortune of living next door to that bag of shite. Christina and Carrie get along well enough so far that I'm not too worried if one of them goes over to the other person's house to borrow a cup of sugar. But they aren't in any hurry to become best friends either.

"Where do you think we should put this?"

She holds up the swing my sisters- and cousins-in-law bought for us as a welcome home gift. My brothers had no idea when I called and asked them if it was a joke. It shocked my cousins just as much as it did me. Then all the married guys were pissed those of us who were unmarried when they partnered off didn't think about such a thoughtful gift.

"I say we turn one of the spare bedrooms into a pleasure palace."

I waggle my eyebrows at her, and she giggles. That sound will always do things to me. It makes my balls ache, and I'm looking around for the drill and hammer. I'll get that thing hung in the next five minutes.

"Daddy, are you thinking about hanging this up right now?" Her teasing voice only makes me want her more.

"Where's the ladder, *cailín*?

"I believe Finn's on it right now as he changes those light bulbs for us downstairs. Do you really want to ask your brother for it?

I release a beleaguered sigh. "Maybe not right this minute."

She puts the box down and looks around at everything else. We went through her place in Pittsburgh for the few items that were hers not the government's and her actual apartment here in New York. We got rid of a lot of duplicate things, either keeping the ones I already had or getting rid of my stuff and bringing hers over. It'll be a pleasant blend of both of our households.

The easiest thing for us to agree upon is that on Wednesdays and Sundays, if I'm not called away for work, those are our guaranteed sex nights in. Not that we don't have sex every night, but those are nights things like the swing will come in handy. When I told the other guys I wouldn't be available those nights, they immediately wanted to know why.

When I wouldn't answer, the meaning became obvious. Now each married guy has his own two nights a week he insists he's unavailable. Poor Cormac gets stuck with all the worst shifts at our night clubs and strip clubs because of that. But he'll survive. And it wouldn't surprise me if we aren't changing the schedule once again soon. He seems to fancy himself a knight in shining armor, but he's being even more closed lip than I was.

She notices something outside the window and moves to look. I have a knee-jerk reaction to tell her to step away, but I know we're safe in our home. As twisted and fucked-up as it is that we all live in the same two neighborhoods, the Four Families treat our community as Switzerland. It's a no fire zone because of the wives and children, so she can look out the window all day if she wants. I only broke that cardinal rule because I knew Maria wasn't home and neither were any of their neighbors.

"Who's that?"

"You met Laura Kutsenko."

"I know her. I mean the dog. Who's that?"

"Sebastian. He's the only guy in the family I like. Him and Niko's swearing parrot, Sammy."

"Swearing parrot?"

"Yeah, Bogdan taught it to curse. Their mom washed Bogdan's and the bird's mouths out with soap." She looks at me in disbelief. "Maybe just Bogdan's."

She turns back to the window. "I want one."

"A cussing bird?"

"No, the dog. I want a Mastiff, too. He looks sweet."

I block her view, then take her hand and lead her toward our bedroom door. "He is. Like I said. He's the only guy in their family I like. He's the only one worth knowing. Let's have lunch. I'm starving."

We get to the foyer just as the doorbell chimes. Carrie's brow furrows.

"We have no more deliveries scheduled for today. Are any of the other guys coming over?"

The law that the guys call before they arrive is now etched in stone since only Cormac's a bachelor. She checks the spyhole and glances at me before she opens the door.

"Hi, Laura."

"Hello, Carys, Shane."

She scowls at me, her left eye narrowing. But she shifts her focus to Carrie and smiles. When she steps aside with Sebastian, Carrie's able to see what's in Maks's arms. Laura's arsehole husband has a tiny squirming puppy. Sebastian's son is a mini replica of the beast.

"D—Shane?" Carrie's cheeks burn as she realizes her near slip.

I glare at Maks, who rolls his eyes. Laura smiles knowingly, and Carrie looks even more mortified.

"I thought you might like someone to keep you company when I travel."

I glare at Maks again when I'm done explaining. This time I

not only get an eye roll, but I also get one of his classic glowers. It didn't affect me in high school, and it doesn't affect me now.

"A puppy?!" Carrie beams as she holds her arms out.

When Maks moves to hand the little guy over, he says something in Russian that makes Laura widen her eyes.

"Maks!" She speaks fluent Russian.

But we all laugh when we see the puddle on his shirt. I love the little beastie already. I knew I picked the smartest one in the litter.

"Thank you for bringing him over." I can be gracious—when I want to be.

"You're welcome." Laura nods to me before she looks at Carrie and holds out a folder to me. "I have all his lineage and vet records in here. Normally—" She giggles. "—he's paper trained."

Carrie glances up at me once she has the puppy in her arms. I swear the dog sighs before he closes his eyes.

"He's really for me, Shane?"

"Yes, *cailín*."

She strokes his head. When she gazes up at me, she grins. Then she glances at my dick and cocks an eyebrow before she looks down at her hand that continues to stroke the dog. She's definitely offering to stroke something else later. Laura's grin tells us she understood what we didn't say. I rest my hand on Carrie's lower back at the same time Maks does the same to Laura. If I didn't want to kill him every time I see him, we might be friends.

Once they're gone, I wrap my arms around Carrie with the puppy sandwiched between us.

"Any names spring to mind?"

"Dafydd." She gazes up at me. "Dafydd O'Rourke."

The perfect blend of Welsh and Irish—just like us.

Cormac O'Rourke is the last man standing—until Jocelyn Bracero bumps into him. Cormac is unprepared for the tenacious social worker to turn his life upside down and discover secrets better kept hidden in a world where kindness and mercy could be his downfall in *Mob Knight*.

Carrie can't wait to show Shane how thankful she is for their wiggly new addition to their family. Discover how they put that swing to use in this bonus epilogue when you subscribe to my newsletter.

Don't miss the next installment

How did I get so lucky?

She shouldn't have been there.

She shouldn't have tried to protect me.

Now I'll move Heaven and Earth to keep her safe.

I'll be her knight in shining armor.

Stand in my way, and you'll breathe your last.

Nothing will stop me from seeing that smile when she's in my arms.

There's more to life than pleasure, but I'll give her more than she dreamed.

She's my light after the darkest night.

Meet Cormac and Joey

Get a bonus epilogue

Enjoy this free bonus epilogue with a scene from *Mob Bride* and discover how Carrie thanks Shane for her new puppy.

Check out this extra sexy scene with Shane and Carrie when you subscribe to my newsletter. Get your copy here.

Thank you for reading Mob Bride

Sabine Barclay, a nom de plume also writing Historical Romance as Celeste Barclay, lives near the Southern California coast with her husband and sons. She loves her days at the beach soaking up way too much sun, a good Netflix binge, and a strong hot chai. Her heroines are independent women who can defend themselves but love their Alpha heroes who want nothing more than to protect their soulmates in her Mafia Romances. She's Gen Y/Oregon Trail and loves creating engrossing contemporary romances that will make your toes curl and your granny blush.

Subscribe to Sabine's bimonthly newsletter to receive exclusive insider perks.

www.sabinebarclay.com

Join the fun and get exclusive insider giveaways, sneak peeks, and new release announcements in

Sabine Barclay's Facebook Dubious Dames Group

Do you also enjoy steamy Historical Romance? Discover Sabine's books written as Celeste Barclay.

The O'Rourke Brotherhood

Mob Boss

BOOK ONE SNEAK PEEK

DILLAN

I hate meetings like this. I don't need to wear pants from some shitty off-the-rack suit that are too tight to *try* to make my dick look bigger. I'm secure in my cock size, and I don't need to show how big my balls are for people to know I run this part of the city. I loathe strip clubs too. I'm past the point where naked women make my jimmy do jumping jacks. I can appreciate a hot bod and gymnast level strength, but it does nothing for me. These douchebags? They're practically ready to come in those cheap arse pants. Why am I here? I keep asking myself that.

Seamus and Shane are doing just fine with these negotiations. I'm just here to look good. I'm the muscle today. Or rather my name and my position. Who the fuck thought— way, way back in the day —that giving the mob hierarchy nautical names was a good idea? Fucking Skipper. This isn't motherfucking Gilligan's Island. None of these numb nuts are the Professor, even if they think they're fucking Mr. Howell.

But who is that? If this is *Gilligan's Island*, then she's Mary Ann.

I glance at Seamus, but he's focused on the Albanian he's trying not to lose his shite at. Shane smirks at me when I dart my gaze to him. I cock an eyebrow as the waitress walks over. She's definitely not a dancer. She has too many clothes on. But you can barely call the pieces of thread she's wearing clothes. She's got on a bikini top that's barely more than pasties, and the skirt she's wearing would make my Catholic grandmother do somersaults in her grave.

It's the standard uniform for this place, but somehow it doesn't look right on her. Not because she doesn't have a banging body because she does. Not because she's a butter face— but-her-face — as in great bod, not so great face. She's beautiful in a super understated way. That's part of what makes her look out of place. She has next to no makeup on. I think those are even her real eyelashes. The natural beauty is drawing way too much attention.

"'Scuse me."

She tries to step around Zef Hoxha, the *kyre* of the Albanian mafia here in New York. When he reaches out to grab her wrist, I'm out of my seat with my hand around his. He never gets a chance to touch her because my hold is so tight he can't bend his fingers. I keep squeezing until it must feel like I'll snap the bones.

"No touching."

Zef drops his arm as much as my hold allows. I let go and stare at him before I tilt my head toward the waitress. I narrow my eyes, and he knows what I expect.

"I apologize, miss."

"That's all right, sir. Here's your drink."

She's polite as she hands him his glass. Unfortunately, to put down the rest, she has to bend forward, giving everyone a view of her glorious cleavage. Tits and arse are what sell here, and she has them in spades. I'm certain it's why my cousin hired her. If I sit down, everyone will know I'm just as guilty as these fuck nuts because she's made my dick do something that hasn't happened in a strip club since I was like twenty-three. I'm now thirty-three.

Mob Star
Mob Princess

Mob Bride

Mob Saint
Mob Bride
Mob Knight

Do you also enjoy steamy Historical Romance? Discover Sabine's books written as Celeste Barclay.

The Ivankov Brotherhood

Bratva Darling
BOOK ONE SNEAK PEEK

LAURA

As I sit across from the four Kutsenko brothers, I press my lips together to keep from drooling. No four men should be so strikingly handsome. Not all from the same family, anyway. I fight a valiant battle against letting my gaze drift toward the eldest, Maksim, whose ice-blue eyes bore into me. After years of negotiating billion-dollar investment contracts while facing countless ruthless businessmen, I've learned to keep my expression studiously blank. But it's a true struggle today. Instead, I focus my attention on the squirrelly lawyer sitting across the conference table. While he's disingenuous with each comment, he's a good negotiator. But I'm better. How cliché am I?

While I feel Maksim watching me, I focus on Dmitry Yakovitch as he continues to argue the merits of the venture capitalist company I represent, RK Capital Group, merging with Kutsenko Partners. What he means is the merits of Kutsenko Partners acquiring RK Capital Group, then stripping it and making it another money-laundering shell corporation. While most people in New York have little awareness of the Russian mafia, I do. The Kutsenko brothers' names appear on no titles or deeds anywhere in New York City, but it wasn't difficult to determine which shell companies likely belong to them. Their assumption that I'm unfamiliar with them is proving beneficial to me as they continue to whisper amongst themselves in Russian. I think they may even believe they're convincing me that they don't speak much English.

The senior partners of RK Capital Group know who I'm negotiating with, though they may not know I'm aware of these Russians' more nefarious operations. They've given me the go-ahead to agree to a merger with an eventual acquisition, but only for the right price. A price to the tune of twenty billion dollars. Considering an investment firm like Goldman Sachs is worth nearly one-hundred-and-twenty billion dollars, my clients' asking price appears reasonable.

"Mr. Yakovitch, I shall stop you now." I raise my left hand, pen caught between my index and middle fingers. When I have his attention, I lean back in my chair and casually twirl the pen over my index finger and thumb. "Fifty billion is my clients' asking price. You know that. Your clients know that. RK doesn't oppose the merger. What they oppose is the insulting offer you've made. It's nearly noon, and I'm hungry, Mr. Yakovitch. I have a delicious ham sandwich waiting for me. I even have three chocolate chip cookies waiting for me. If we aren't going to make any progress, I shall let you go, so I can move onto my eagerly anticipated lunch."

I cant my head just enough for me to appear as though my gaze rests solely on the opposing attorney's face, but I can see each Kutsenko brothers' reaction. My face battles yet again against showing my emotions as I fight not to smirk. Their muted but surprised expressions confirm what I already know.

"Please tell your clients to make a reasonable counteroffer, or I will conclude this meeting and enjoy my ham sandwich and cookies."

Dmitry glares at me before turning to Maksim and his three brothers. In rapid Russian, he doesn't interpret my suggestion. Oh no. There's no need for that. I can't catch every word because his voice is too low. But I catch something along the lines of "The bitch refuses to budge. What now? A fucking ham sandwich. More like a stick up her ass."

Maksim swivels his chair to look at his brothers. In Russian, he says, "Fifty billion is ridiculous. She's not so stupid or naïve not to know that. My guess is they'll settle for twenty billion. We offer fifteen."

"That's barely better than what we already offered," Aleksei, the second-oldest brother, argues. "She'll be eating the fucking sandwich and dipping her cookies in milk before we walk out the door. We need the buildings."

"We offer twenty, Maks," Bogdan, the youngest, insists.

As I watch the brothers discuss, their voices barely lowered, I pull my lunch sack from the black leather satchel by my feet and set it beside my laptop. It's a ridiculously pink floral bag with an embroidered monogram, the L and D overlapping. It's an empty prop, but they don't know that. I watch as five sets of eyes narrow. I offer a smile that would appear innocent in any setting other than this meeting. It's patronizing, and I know it.

Bratva Sweetheart
Bratva Treasure
Bratva Beauty
Bratva Angel
Bratva Jewel

Do you also enjoy steamy Historical Romance? Discover Sabine's books written as Celeste Barclay.

The Mancinelli Brotherhood

Mafia Heir
BOOK ONE SNEAK PEEK

LUCA

This asshole is pissing me off. We've been going around in circles for five minutes, and the longer we stand out here, the greater the likelihood someone will spot us. I have a sixth sense about these things. It's why I'm still alive at the ripe old age of thirty-one.

"Espinoza, enough already. Either sell to us or don't, but we set the price. Your tequila is good, but it isn't nectar from the gods."

I'm watching Carlos Espinoza, some lackey for the Mexican Culiacán Cartel, try to maneuver me into paying more than the agreed upon price. I know it's so he can skim off the top.

"It's as close as you're going to get. You've upped the order, so the price per case goes up."

My uncle, Salvatore Mancinelli, is the New York don. He negotiated this deal, and I warned him it was a bad idea. But what do I know as his underboss and heir? I'm not backing down.

"Haven't you ever heard of a bulk discount? The more I order the better the price should be. No one else around here is buying from you. You know we're your only choice in three out of five boroughs. You aren't going to the Bronx because you won't get more than pennies there. You aren't going to Queens because you don't want to run into the Colombians. You aren't going to Manhattan because then you face the bratva along with us. And what are you going to do in Staten Island? Sell to us anyway? We control Staten Island and Brooklyn when it comes to liquor stores, so take the money and go."

"Luca, there are plenty of liquor stores in Brooklyn that aren't owned by Italians. I'll go there."

We aren't friends. He's patronizing me by using my first name. Fuck him and the horse he rode in on. I have other solutions for this shit.

"And I'll just take what I want from them for free. That's not a half bad idea. The deal's over. Take your shit with the worm in it and go."

"Motherfucking racist. Not all tequila has a worm in it."

"You're selling Mezcal. It's known for the fucking worm. I wouldn't start calling me names, you *penche hijo de puta*."

Fucking son of a bitch.

He has twenty-five crates of stolen tequila that he's trying to offload because he knows he can't sell it at his own liquor store.

"What did you call me?"

Carlos takes what he thinks is a menacing step forward, and his two bodyguards do the same. Not smart. Neither of my two bodyguards nor I react, but the three men in each of my cars open their doors. They won't do more than that. It's just a reminder that the Culiacán can try, but the *Cosa Nostra* still run New York City.

"This is the third and final time I say this. Sell or leave."

Every head turns toward the liquor store's back door as it opens. A gorgeous blonde steps out, and I wish I had the time to appreciate her beauty, but she's about to die. Carlos and his men draw their guns and pivot toward her. My men pull their weapons too, but we keep them pointed at the Mexicans. The woman stands like a deer in the headlights for a second before ducking behind the industrial garbage dumpster like a frightened rabbit. Three shots hit the metal almost at the same moment. That's all it takes for my men and me. The two bodyguards standing with me aim for a guard each, and I set my sights on Carlos. We squeeze our triggers, and the men fall. Screeching tires tell me Carlos's driver takes off. I hear more gunshots as at least one soldier in my cars tries to shoot the escaping vehicle. Glass shatters, but the sedan keeps going. I hear more tires squeal as one of my SUVs takes off and chases the guy. I holster my gun and wave my men to do the same.

I inch forward toward the trash can, but I see the shadow shift. The woman bolts from the other side. She's still the frightened rabbit, but I'm the fox pursuing her. She's fast, I'll give her that. But she has to be at least a foot shorter than me. My legs are a lot longer and cover a lot more ground with each stride.

She weaves among the cars, most likely believing it's harder to hit a moving object. She isn't wrong, but I have no intention of shooting her. I push myself harder and pounce as she darts out and tries to cross the last stretch of parking lot to reach a better lit area near a bus stop. I lunge.

"Stop running, *piccolina*. I won't hurt you."

I wrap my arms around her and pull her back against my chest, but I'm quick to spin her around and put space between us as I grasp her arms. Of course, she fights me.

"If I wanted you dead, I would have shot at you, too."

"It doesn't mean you won't kill me after."

She's breathless as she continues to struggle. I almost let go to take a step back, insulted at what she implied. But I can't blame her. If I were a woman, I'd be terrified of the same thing.

"I'm not going to rape you. I'm going to talk to you."

"Talk? You are not a man who talks if you just killed a guy."

"To keep him and his men from killing you. I told you, if I wanted you dead, I would have shot at you too. And I wouldn't have missed."

She stops struggling against me, but her eyes continue to dart from one place to another, trying to find somewhere to flee. I know I can keep her in place with only one hand, so I release her left arm.

I still have a firm hold on her right one, but I haven't held it nearly as tightly as I could.

"I'm Luca. I know you figured out you interrupted something you shouldn't have. Did that man know who you are?"

"Yes."

"What about his driver? Would he know you?"

"Yes."

"Do you have a name?"

"Yes."

"*Piccolina,* we won't get very far if yes is all you can say. Are you willing to answer me with more than one word?"

"No."

I knew that was coming, and I grin. I can't help it. I wasn't wrong about her being gorgeous, but I doubt she wants to know that's what I think. At least, not if I want her to know I won't assault her.

"Fine. I have more than twenty questions I can ask that you can answer with one word. Do you work at the store?"

"Sometimes."

Ah, an improvement.

"Did Carlos know you were still working?"

"No."

"Do you have a car, or do you take the subway or bus?"

She raises her chin and remains silent. Smart but counterproductive.

"The subway or the bus will get you killed. You're too easy to find and follow. Do you have a car?"

"Yes."

"Can you stay with someone instead of going home?"

She refuses to answer.

"If that man knew you and you sometimes work in the store, then he knew where you live. If he found that out, so will someone in his cartel."

"I know. Let me go. The longer I stand here, the more likely someone is to come back for me."

"No one will touch you while I'm here."

"Arrogant. If he shot at me, he would have shot at you."

"And he would have died, anyway. What's your name?"

"Jane."

"Look, I know you won't get in one of my cars and let me drive you somewhere. In most cases, I would say that's a smart move. But you did nothing wrong tonight except for leave work at the wrong time. I know that, and you know that. But the Culiacán won't see it that way, *piccolina*."

She freezes for no more than five seconds before she trembles so much that I can see it. I don't know what drives me next, but it's the same instinct that's made me call her little girl three times. I pull her to my chest and tuck her head against it. I stroke her hair down to her shoulders, rubbing my hand up and down her back. This is the most inopportune moment to notice she isn't wearing a bra. I will my body not to react.

"What does that mean?"

Her voice is barely more than a whisper, but I know what she's asking.

"It means little girl."

"I should be insulted, but the way you say it..."

"It has nothing to do with your height. I know you're not a child."

God, do I know she's not. She feels amazing. Her tits are soft as they press against me, and I can see she has the most delectable ass. I'd love nothing more than to cup it and squeeze until she goes up on her toes and begs for me to wrap her legs around my waist and fuck her. For fuck's sake. Stop, you disgusting asshole. That is not what you need to be thinking about.

"Why didn't you shoot me? Whatever you were talking about, if it was with a Cartel member, then it wasn't completely legal. Carlos didn't want me alive to talk about seeing you together. Why are you letting me live?"

"I told you. You did nothing wrong but try to leave work. He should have checked the building before starting the meeting. That was on him. The only thing I take issue with is you leaving by yourself and walking into a dimly lit parking lot. I suspect you do that often, and that's too dangerous. Jane Doe, I don't hurt women."

Sabine Barclay

Mafia Sinner
Mafia Beauty
Mafia Angel
Mafia Redeemer
Mafia Star

Do you also enjoy steamy Historical Romance? Discover Sabine's books written as Celeste Barclay.

www.ingramcontent.com/pod-product-compliance
Lightning Source LLC
Chambersburg PA
CBHW020520110726
47899CB00004B/1178

* 9 7 8 1 6 4 8 3 9 7 4 7 9 *